The Determined World Predetermined

Book 1
Talphi and Krn'v'rnk Saga

The Determined World Predetermined

Book 1
Talphi and Krn'v'rnk Saga
t-ALL-f-eye & krin-vah-ring-k

Joel Dau

Talphi: t-ALL-f-eye
Krn'v'rnk: krin-vah-ring-k

Cover design by Joel Dau, Firefly Assisted

ISBN-13: 979-8-9921984-0-9
Digital ISBN: 978-8-9921984-1-6

joeldau.com

Table of Contents

Chapter 1

In the forests west of the Grand Plains was the village of Grubein. It was a collection of mostly log-built houses scattered through the trees with some man-made clearings and paths carved into the ground by human travel. There was only one established road for traveling beyond Grubein's borders. The population was only seventy since the Kingdom of Garrin had conscripted nearly every able-bodied man. The Kingdom was again trying to advance its claims across the Grand Plains through a show of force.

The overwhelming demand for men and increasing requirement for supplies made things difficult and drove their lives to misery, but the oldest members of the village remembered over two decades ago when raiders from the Tokkin lands would attack the village. The Kingdom claimed their distant goals were worth the hardship even though it was the villages furthest from the capital which bore the burden of manpower.

Beyond the memories of the living was the knowledge that there had been centuries of pushing and pulling between the Kingdom and the Tokkin. The Kingdom of Garrin was named for the western city that housed the throne. It was the first of its kind, and as the structure of its society spread, it became known simply as the Kingdom. There was a defined lineage and order built on the ideals of preserving life and pushing back against the chaos the first Tokkin created. At present, no one in the Kingdom was certain how the Tokkin lands were governed or what they had built east of the Grand Plains. What was known was that all Tokkin are physically different from normal humans.

The first Tokkins were born to human parents, and there are still occasional births without Tokkin parentage, but all Tokkin have Tokkin children. Their thoughts and feelings are human, but their bodies are advanced and distorted in some way. Some parts were shorter or longer, larger or smaller, and more exaggerated than most humans, but all shared gray skin hues.

The physical difference between the humans was noticeable enough to distinguish the two types and helped write the protective laws of the Kingdom based on appearance. But it wasn't just about the look of the Tokkin. This was about the actions of the Tokkin as they forced their will upon the land centuries ago. It was only thanks to the Sisters of Forn and their discovery of the relics that the world found order.

It was noon on a brisk spring day in Grubein. A soldier's horse draped with the Kingdom of Garrin's banner was tied up at the village center in front of the meeting hall. The meeting hall was the only building that the village owned as a community. It was built with planks, unlike many of the log cabins that hid in the trees around the town center. That's where the patient horse stayed waiting for its rider to return. This obvious location notified most of the village that troubling news had arrived.

Rachael's husband had been conscripted by the Kingdom of Garrin, along with nearly every other man in Grubein. They had moved to Grubein four years ago as newlyweds, and she had finally started to think of it as home just before he was drafted. She had believed that their tiny town could survive while her husband was away from her, but since he had been gone, the selfish and heavy demands of the Kingdom had drained their town and her hope.

She imagined that facing Tokkin raids could have produced the same results, but she only had the second-hand stories to carry that thought. Still, if her husband returned with the other men, they might recover, but the soldier that came to visit destroyed her last hope.

2

The Determined World

The soldier read off his parchment without locking eyes with her. He couldn't afford to express sympathy since he needed to inform this entire town of their loss. "It is the regret of the Kingdom of Garrin to inform you that..."

Rachael didn't let him finish telling her. Her gasp of breath blared out, "No!" She screamed at him to get out before he finished the official statement. She had heard a few other cries before he had visited her house, but her last hope was that he wouldn't visit her home.

Everything about the soldier's appearance burned and clung to her mind even when he was gone. Rachael could still smell the armor oils, see the dark figure standing in her doorway, and hear his callous voice speaking meaningless words. He was the face of the enemy and her pain.

She gripped her dull brown hair and pulled it down around her face to help hide herself from the world as she slumped to the floor. Rachael sat there, unable to perceive any reason or motivation to move. Her dark and tired eyes pulled away from the light while her hands followed her defined chin line, wishing to touch her husband's face one last time.

Less than an hour after slamming the door behind the soldier, there was another knocking. It was still light out, so she could see the familiar faces. Rachael opened the door, eager to share her distress. It was two of her closest friends, Meridith and Susan, and her husband, Anthony, who was the mayor of Grubein. "Oh, Meridith," she felt safe to let out everything to them. Rachael's typically understanding look was twisted with anguish and doubt. No words were needed for them to guess the worst about the soldier's visit. Meridith embraced her as they stood out in the cool fading light.

Meridith wore a long black dress for this solemn occasion in contrast to the rugged pants and tunic outfits most of the women had converted to in order to work the land without men. Her hazel hair was tied back, and she had removed the extra coloring she usually applied to her puffy cheeks. Anthony was a few inches shorter than Meridith and just as tall as his wife. He was stocky and wore tall hats and boots that added some height. Susan was petite and could hide behind Anthony completely if needed. Her round face was long today as grief pulled it down.

Meridith squeezed her tight. "Oh, my dear. I'm so sorry." She had seen him stopping at two other houses before coming to Rachael's. The soldier had over a dozen homes to visit. Every man conscripted from Grubein had died.

Susan looked apprehensive, but she joined the hug instead of waiting for her own separate embrace. She was the youngest and shortest of the group hug and might be mistaken for a girl if you didn't know she was only two years younger than Rachael.

Anthony stood apart from the hug. He was one of the only conscript-able men that had been exempt. "Do you want to go in and sit down, my dear?" In his opinion, it was rather inconsiderate of her not to invite them in. There were other houses that he would need to visit, but Susan had insisted and cried a lot about visiting Rachael first with Meridith. Since it was easier for his wife and Meridith to console, he obliged their first visit to Rachael's.

"Yes." Rachael squeaked after a moment. The two other women released her so she could lead the way to sit. She chose to sit on the bench along the table. It wasn't the most comfortable, but it was large enough for two, and Meridith sat next to her to hold her hand. Susan pulled up a wooden stool so she could be closer while Anthony took the padded chair at a safe distance.

"Let it out, dear." Meridith said as she moved to hug her again, but Rachael turned away and cried on her own for a few minutes. They continued to hold hands. Meridith was 18 years older than Rachael and had lost her husband 8 years back to illness. She had since become the village's matron. The wrinkles had come quickly for her after his death, and she looked weathered for a thirty-eight-year-old woman.

The Determined World

After a few moments of waiting, Anthony spoke. He needed to get things moving along. "He was a strong man. I'm sure he fought well, just like every other man that was lost today." He looked around at his wife and Meridith, letting them see him nod so that they could agree with him and move the visit along quickly.

Anthony's voice burned at the back of Rachael's eyes, changing sadness to anger and drawing her glare right to him. His tone, his words, and his mere presence shattered her sadness with distrust. "He was my husband, Anthony." She saw him sitting in the chair she was keeping maintained for her husband. "He's not just one of the men, can you understand that?"

Susan knew her husband meant well, and he had given her what she wanted, coming here first. "Rachael, we're-" she included her husband, circling everyone with a wave of her hand, "are so sorry for your loss. We've lost so much. I can't imagine what it's like for you, but this hurts everyone." She expressed everything she felt.

Rachael listened to Susan. It was so much better hearing her friend. They had all lost so much, but she had never talked much with Anthony and didn't trust his opinion. She hadn't considered that others had lost sons and husbands. It made her feel guilty that she was glad others were feeling her pain and that she wasn't alone.

Meridith would have never wished this loss on another woman. Now, she was surrounded by the pain once again, and she hoped they could find consolation in each other.

Anthony found Rachael's reaction more severe than other times he had visited widows of accidents. He hoped all of them wouldn't be like this and glanced at Susan to let her know he had been right, even if he had bent to her begging earlier.

Susan knew his superior look. She needed to show him that it wasn't a mistake to visit Rachael first. Rachael would listen to the good news, and it would help her. "You should know that the Kingdom of Garrin is going to establish a garrison nearby, and nothing else will be asked of our town."

Rachael was annoyed. "Oh?" The Kingdom had bled them of their men and only now considered protecting them. How could more soldiers bring back the dead? Why were they off fighting such a distant war?

Anthony was eager to expand on Susan's introduction of the good news. "Yes, finally we will have the Kingdom of Garrin's protection. They know they are responsible and will establish a real presence." Anthony was angry at the Kingdom, too, as he relayed this information. He thought back on all his letters and constantly ignored pleas. "I've worked so hard for this. It's about time they live up to their promise." It had finally cost him and the town too much.

"And all it took was my husband's life?" Rachael said condescendingly. Her loss meant nothing to Anthony. He spoke over her husband's death like it was necessary to get attention.

Anthony narrowed his eyes at the narrow-minded Rachael. She couldn't see past her front door.

Meridith closed her eyes and prayed for Anthony to hold back on his views. This wasn't about the pain of the town. She had been there herself and knew this moment was about Rachael's loss. Meridith had to speak first for the good of everyone. "Rachael, none of the men should have died. This is the worst thing that could have happened. We have all lost, and your husband's life wasn't worth paying for the Kingdom's protection."

Rachael burst out, "Who are we fighting? The Kingdom comes and takes what it wants and sends off my husband to die fighting an enemy I have never faced. What's the point? A garrison of soldiers. For what?" She rose from the bench and clenched the table.

Anthony replied calmly, "We used to hold those lands to the east, including the Grand Plains." It was the most basic knowledge and history. He knew that she knew it, but why would you need to come face to face with an enemy to know why you are fighting? "They continuously attack the land that is ours."

Rachael leaned forward and nearly stood up from the anger. "Oh yes, I've heard that before," she retorted, "but when have they attacked me? The only ones taking from me is the Kingdom of Garrin."

Susan begged, "Rachael, please!" She didn't like talking about such things and was glad Anthony didn't discuss them inside their home. "We're so sorry for Henry's death, but... but... please don't be angry." Susan looked around at everyone as she spoke, hoping they would all agree and stop yelling.

Rachael directed all her anger at Anthony. "I don't care about Garrin. I don't care about their garrison or their reasons for stripping my life away." It was so easy to blame him for not stopping the Kingdom's demands. "His death is meaningless. Don't use him to support your war."

Anthony stood up in defiance. "You don't understand. This is not my war. I didn't start this, but I do have to deal with all the problems that it causes. This war hurts all of us and not just you. I'm sorry that Henry died, but you're not the only one, and we're not the only village. Our neighbors suffer, and they need our help. The Kingdom of Garrin sees our suffering, and they know they cannot ignore the Tokkin anymore." It was infuriating. If she cared to understand, she would know that he was right. She's choosing to ignore what is right.

Rachael stood up. "We wouldn't need to be saved by the Kingdom if they didn't take everything we need to defend ourselves. My husband is dead for what? They have bled us dry." Rachael clenched her chest and made the motion to rip out her heart. "You can't feel this, Anthony. You'll never understand what they've taken."

"I understand, alright. Yes, I do. They have asked much, and we needed to sacrifice more than we wanted to. But you fail to see that we need to sacrifice that much to stop the Tokkin. I have seen their destruction for myself..." he shook his head that he shouldn't justify himself to her, "You're so sheltered and selfish for it."

Susan tried to pull Anthony's attention by moving from her seat to her husband's side. "Anthony!" She agreed with her husband, but she felt as angry and distraught as Rachael looked.

Anthony had had enough of this situation. "Enough." He still had his thankless job to visit the other widows. Susan grabbed his arm, but he wasn't going to listen to her for the remainder of the evening. She had used up her wish. "You're not worth the time. Susan, we're leaving. Meridith, we're moving on to the next home. So, stay or leave, it's your choice," he sneered.

Rachael had never wanted to strike out at someone like she did at this moment. He wasn't a wife and widow, alone with broken meaning and drenched in blame. She dug her nails into her hand and put all of it into her voice as it cracked into a fading scream, "Get out!"

Meridith hung her head solemnly. Her heart raced with the same pains as Rachael and she wanted to fix Anthony's insensitivity, "Rachael, I'm..."

Rachael wasn't going to listen anymore. "Just leave," she dismissed all of them.

Anthony led Susan out with her squeezing his arm. It was so awful that his wife was so concerned about Rachael and that Susan should be made so much more upset. It was completely insensitive of Rachael.

Meridith followed the couple out, praying that Anthony would now know not to involve himself in their grief. He was the man who didn't die and had agreed to the Kingdom's demands. Tonight, he was an enemy and needed to stay quiet.

Rachael stayed in her house for days like the other widows. When she went outside and met the remaining neighbors, they were only able to talk for a few words before emotions would get the better of them. There was no gossip and no joy in the little things. They had no stomach to speak of revenge on the Tokkin or discuss the Kingdom's plans. Only Anthony wanted to talk about such things, but he quickly realized that no one wanted to listen to what he thought was important.

The Kingdom of Garrin had established a garrison to their north within three months of the loss. At that time, there had been no raids from the Tokkin, but they still had to provide the Kingdom with the food and supplies leveraged years back for the war efforts. Once the garrison was established, Anthony met the commander before the patrols started.

The soldiers that patrolled started demanding supplies and alcohol besides what the Kingdom of Garrin took. Despite their insistence that they were fighting Tokkin a short distance away, the villagers of Grubein never saw a Tokkin raiding party. The gossip that had died down now returned when some of the widows found it easier to offer their bed instead of the food and drink demanded of them. The arrangements only increased the demands on villagers unwilling to make such deals.

After ten months, there was an overriding consensus that their village couldn't fulfill the demands. Requests through proper channels failed, and confrontation wouldn't work. Anthony corresponded with a cousin of his far to the west and learned that such demands were not required of towns further from the Grand Plains. Since they were so few, they could easily be absorbed by other villages or by one of the large cities. They kept what they needed and took what they could carry and left before the next patrol could arrive.

But Rachael was defiant. Their town was dead, and this was her grave to stay in alone. She didn't have to work too hard to stay hidden since the patrols didn't search thoroughly. The garrison gladly shrunk their patrol route to exclude the deserted Grubein. She imagined that life would get easier now that there were no more demands from others. A few hens, her established garden, and her years of living without a husband prepared her for this.

Chapter 2

In a large room of a castle, King Fredrick Antoin sat in council with Duke Cassinon Medrick and Lord Jacob Fuller. The room was draped with green banners and curtains to give them the most privacy. The table in the center of the room wasn't decorated but instead was covered with a large map. This room was set for a private discussion. It was midday, but they had all the torches lit in the absence of natural light. The chairs were up against the wall, as the table in the center with three chairs took precedence. The two vassals the King had chosen for this meeting controlled the largest holdings and could direct orders down the line for the quickest results.

King Antoin was in his forties, and his balding head was hidden by his crown. There were problems inherited from past Kings that wore on him and added many more wrinkles than a man his age should have. His full eyebrows were heavy with gloom, and his eyes were sunken in with stress. Still, his red and white robes, with layers of fine cloth, left little doubt about his importance. All the troubles had cut into any joy he hoped to find in the authority passed down to him.

Lord Fuller was older than the King, but he had learned to handle the weight of his nobility more gracefully and looked younger in expressions with his full head of hair. In contrast, his broad chin was free of hair and made a bold statement about his confidence. He didn't wear a headdress in celebration of his head hair and kept a trim amount of fine layers to display his healthy form.

The Determined World

Duke Medrick was the youngest and wore his title with audacious pride. His wide mouth was well practiced at displaying emotions he wanted others to see, but the large blank area of his forehead reminded others that there was always a hidden intent. He looked as if he was looking down on everything because he was. Even when he bowed to the King, it seemed like he was looking down on him. He dressed more like a King than a subject to a King.

They had just received the message from their scout. This was the castle at Garrin, the greatest and largest city of the Kingdom. It was the most protected city thanks to the distance from the Tokkin lands, but this also added to the difficulties of continued expansion. But now that distance didn't seem far enough to protect it from the Tokkin threat. All the expedition forces and first-response armies were destroyed. The Tokkin army could press toward Garrin itself without resistance. On a fast march across the remaining plains and through the western forest and mountains, the Tokkin could reach Garrin in 60 days. But that would be assuming the Tokkin army would need to stop for food or rest.

"Well then, it is hard to disagree with such information." Lord Fuller moved his hand along the line that the Tokkin army followed. "We cannot win this war with marginal responses anymore. It is imperative that we commit more than we think is necessary. The window needed to gather our forces into one will close soon."

Duke Medrick protested. "No. I refuse to lend my men to another slaughter. There is no proof that more men would yield any different result. Besides, there is only so much room on any battlefield." The young Duke glared at Fuller and held the fringes of his fine robe. He knew the Lord wanted more of his men. So far, he had been able to keep an adequate number of men in reserve for his own safety. Giving any more was not negotiable.

Fuller spoke with incredulity. "Limited room? In the King's army, how many of my men do you think are left? Your men would give us a full army.

Overcrowding is not the issue." That was putting it politely. Medrick had a habit of holding back support. Usually, he would talk about how he couldn't spare any men, but maybe if he ruled more wisely, he wouldn't need all the protection from his own people. Fuller knew such advice wouldn't fix the problem. You can't humble a greedy man.

Antoin agreed with Fuller, but it was better for this fight to stay between his vassals as he had enough problems. He would let them take out their frustrations on each other.

Medrick wouldn't be bated by Fuller. "We do not control where our engagements occur. Without the proper fielding, my cavalry would be utterly destroyed. I will continue to provide my services as always to the King." Medrick nodded at Antoin to acknowledge his importance.

Lord Fuller grinned. "Food, a few swords, maybe some mints to purchase mercenaries. Do you have enough mints in your treasury to buy a full army of mercenaries?" He didn't let Medrick reply before continuing, "Those small bits are not enough at this moment. The only thing of consequence is to have men filling the ranks. Your straw men won't do."

Medrick retorted. "Without my men making, forming, and supplying such things, the armies would wither and disband. Would you have a sword made by your wife, perhaps?" He had explained this so many times to Fuller that it could have been written down on parchment and held up each time Fuller complained.

"The Tokkin have their weapons made by the women." King Antoin said without looking at either man. The odd fact had come across his blank thoughts since the imagery of Fuller's wife working over a smelting furnace was amusing.

The Duke stopped his usual tirade to give the King his attention. "Pardon me, my King, what was that about the Tokkin women?"

The King spoke more specifically since he had no idea how to stop the coming invasion. He distracted them with a small insight that wasn't useful. "The women of the Tokkin produce many of the weapons their men use. We learned from the smugglers that the women have taken up many of the crafting and farming roles as the men fight."

Duke Medrick chortled. "Weapons by women, are they kitchen knives and thimbles?" He tried to imagine a woman swinging a hammer and hitting everything but the metal. "I am sure they cannot match the quality of my craftsmen."

"You should ask the few of your men who have seen battle Medrick," suggested Fuller, "they would attest to the quality of the Tokkin weapons. I have captured many of their weapons over the years and they put your clumsy broad swords to shame."

Medrick had no time to compare his work to the enemy. "We don't make weapons for girls. A poorly trained soldier is what makes a weapon clumsy." He was working with what little resources were available. "The metal we receive from you, Fuller, is only so strong."

Fuller knew that Medrick wasn't worthy of his title. "Typical. You are the master of shifting blame," he said with an exacerbated snort. Medrick's title was bought, and he had squandered any opportunity to make himself invaluable.

Antoin spoke in between them, "We can see that this could continue endlessly." The two vassals silenced themselves. "Before we discuss numbers, we must mention the request by the Sisters of Forn."

Fuller had found the Sister's future vision, scrying, useless as they often suggested the most obvious conclusions. "Did they have a useful vision?" He asked respectfully, regardless of his feelings. The Sisters of Forn were responsible for the creation of the Kingdom and would often interfere over the 300-year history when it suited them. The King respected them more than Fuller and always sought their advice.

The King nodded and began, "We asked them to focus on the Tokkin army and what was needed to defeat it. It took them considerable time, a grave sign, but thankfully, they have come to us with a solution." The Sisters always entertained his inquiries even if they asked for prices that he couldn't afford, but truly this was the first time in his life that they were helping without price.

Medrick was eager to jump on the opportunity. "Excellent. Now we can be certain what is needed to save the kingdom," he pandered to the King. He knew that Fuller would be made a fool by the witches' prediction. They would prove Fuller wrong. Medrick believed their predictions were proof that a strong will, like his, could forge certainty in the world, and the King was wise to listen to them. "How large is the Tokkin army?" He believed that his men would not be needed.

The King sighed, and both vassals strained to hear an answer. "They couldn't give us an account of the Tokkin force." He continued his foreboding speech. "They were disturbed by what they couldn't learn. Whatever leads this army is unique, and it has hidden the force's numbers and power."

Fuller was glad the witches didn't know for sure. "So we don't know." Vague reports from scouts and the uncertainty of the witches supported his belief. Even though these witches created the Kingdom, the nobles and relic wielders were the only ones truly able to defend it. "We'll have to fight with our knowledge and skill this time."

Medrick wasn't ready to admit anything to Fuller. He could see the King's disappointment and focused on him. "My King, did they not have any advice or direction?" Medrick needed to believe there was an answer.

Antoin wanted them to feel the worry he had had to bear these past weeks. "They swore they would not fail us in this task and continued searching for an answer that could guide us to victory."

Fuller tried to act interested. "What did they discover?" But the King was just playing for the sympathy that he was obligated to give.

Medrick hung in suspense. His jaw slightly dropped as he eagerly sat forward.

The King stared absent-mindedly at the table before them. "It is as grave as Lord Fuller suggests. The only way they saw a future for the Kingdom of Garrin was a full assault on the Tokkin army. We must each field all of our armies and every member of the Relic Wielder Order that we can reach in time. Anything less will lead to the end of our reign. There was no future for them to see without a full assault." He was disappointed in their answer since it had been less than certain and graver than he'd ever dreaded to hear.

Fuller coughed. They suggested just what he had concluded, and he earned the credit for suggesting it. That was his proof of the right to rule. He was already committed to such an action but was curious about the witches' answer. "Did they mention how many losses will be sustained?"

The King did know but didn't know what it meant for his life. "According to them, one-third will come out of the fog of war. They could give us no other advice on strategy. We must rely on ourselves for the battle plan." Antoin scratched his rough beard. It was the greatest weight he had ever endured.

Medrick was lost in desperation. "That would leave the land nearly defenseless." He could lose everything as the land would plunge into chaos without his loyal men as deterrents. Medrick believed the people under his rule were more difficult than the rest of the Kingdom. He needed a forceful hand, but he couldn't argue with the King just yet.

Antion had thought about Medrick's complaint. "Thankfully, the Tokkin army has seemed to absorb any force that might threaten our flanks. With an absolute defeat of the Tokkin army, we will see peace in our land and the unopposed expansion of our borders." He tried to imagine the best since there was no guarantee that he would be alive at the end of the battle, but as long as they fielded all the armies, victory could be assured.

Medrick asked calmly as he imagined the third that lived could be mostly his men. "That is certain? We will be victorious, and at the cost of two-thirds of our armies." Perhaps that was what was meant to happen. If he played it right, there would be no one left to lead but him.

The King continued, "The witches worry about their own safety as well. They believe that if we do not stop this army, they will be destroyed themselves." Antoin smiled. "They agree that their services will no longer come at a price if we act as they suggested." Antoin adored the idea of not having a price attached to his many requests.

Fuller pointed out the redundant opinion. "Excuse me, my King, but why would they do such a thing? We all agree on what needs to happen, and the Sisters of Forn, like every other witch I've heard of, enjoy demanding guileful prices of their service."

Medrick knew he would have held back his support if not for the witches' advice and the prospect of having their service free in the future. This was meant for him to hear. The Sisters of Forn were selective in who they scryed for, and they always wanted too much from him.

Antoin nodded in understanding. "You commit everything for me, Lord Fuller, but we would not have committed my personal guard or called on so many relic wielders." He looked over to Medrick, "And we have not heard you protest the vision of the witches, Duke Medrick. Do you agree to supply your whole army and personal guard?"

Medrick was eager to seize this opportunity. "Of course, my King." Whatever it took, he would come out of this triumphant.

This just made it worse. Fuller would have liked Medrick to protest since his agreement suggested some favorable outcome for him. "In that case, how can we trust them?" Fuller asked. "They'd say anything to save themselves. How do we know that their powers have not diminished to the point of desperation?"

King Antoin nodded, but it was the first time he had considered it. He didn't want to consider it since it would just add to the problem. "We trust them. They have never led us astray. The Kingdom has been in their hearts since guiding its creation. I don't believe they wish us harm."

Medrick nodded. "I agree with your judgment, my King. All my forces are at your disposal."

Fuller knew it was careless for Antoin to ignore the desperation of the witches. They already regularly scryed for the King with little protest. He didn't care for their offer, and the King's gain was marginal. Medrick was too agreeable now.

The King nodded, having put Fuller's suggestion out of his mind. "We shall gather twenty-four days from now on the plains of Pullingham. There is adequate room for our formations." The plains of Pullingham were an area west of the Grand Plains, surrounded by dense forest. Maybe it was cleared long ago, but the large treeless area, ten days' walk from the Grand Plains, would meet the requirements for a full army.

Medrick eyed the battle plans as Antoin pointed to the map. "What if they pass our force and head into the heart of the Kingdom?" He found the location adequate to expel his first complaint about the space for formations, but all of the battles up to that point had occurred in impromptu locations.

There was a certain amount of assumption given the Sisters of Forn's prediction. "They will not expose their rear." Antoin tried to sound certain. "This force is here to destroy us. They won't resist the chance to attack the King." There was hesitation in his voice since he was suggesting he was the bait. Putting his life in the hands of the witches was very different than trusting their judgment, but they were all that he had to believe in. "Gather your forces and meet there in twelve days." He stood, and his vassals stood, too. "You are dismissed." They bowed to the King.

Fuller and Medrick slowly gathered themselves to make sure the other was leaving and not staying any longer to speak with the King privately. Antoin sat back down and watched the two. He had other matters after they left and was eager for them to be gone. "You only have twelve days. We will see you again at that time, no sooner." Both men picked up the pace to leave before the other, with Medrick making it to the door first.

Tiffany, one of the seven Sisters of Forn, came in from a side door once the two were out of the room. As she entered the room, her hair seemed to defy movement. It framed the soft curves of her face and directed his eyes into hers. Her eyes were welcoming and peaceful, and her warm smile showed off her sparkling teeth. After drowning in her face, he followed her line downward along her slender exposed neck onto her low-cut dress. "Excellent. I will inform my Sisters of your decision, and we will gather at Garrin. We will be at the service of the King."

She was the warm welcome face he craved, but the dreadful moment clung to him. "Fuller is right." Tiffany's arrival pulled Fuller's suspicions to the forefront of his mind. "You're desperate, and we wonder now. What are you truly sacrificing if you are willing to give up your original customs?" Again, he thought of himself as the bait to lure the Tokkin army and wondered if they would commit the crime of sacrificing their King.

Tiffany bowed and calmed the King. "We are desperate to protect the Kingdom of Garrin, my King, but if you did not risk the field of battle today, then the army would crush all remaining defenses. This is the only way to save you from that defeat. We believed our offer of service was a necessary gesture." She said it with the greatest hopes and regrets that she could weave together.

Antoin looked away from her and stared at the floor. "We hear your words, Tiffany, but they are not as comforting as we wish." He stopped talking and got up out of his chair. All the beautiful clothes and perfume she wore seemed to hide the confidence he wanted to see in her today. He pulled away several of the curtains to let in the light, but when he looked at her again, the additional light shone with no reassurance. "We need reassurance that 'I' will live."

She needed to lie to keep him moving forward with the plan, but she wanted him vulnerable enough to be influenced, whatever the outcome was. Each Sister had guessed differently who would live. They had never needed to guess before, but the fog that blocked their scrying created that unknown. "The future favors you, my King, and we have committed ourselves to you." Personally, this was true. She wanted him to live, given their intimate encounters. She enjoyed him, and he enjoyed her regardless of his marriage and nobility.

Antoin was still worried no matter what she said. He moped back over to his chair and sat down. "That is all, you may go."

Tiffany smiled, having struck the right balance. "Perhaps I could offer you some additional comfort?"

"Tiffany," The King smiled, "Your voice is music to my ears, but I do worry about your manipulation of me at times."

She serenely smiled back. It was true. Witches had learned to manipulate life to extend its pleasure. They could keep up appearances through old age and control the cycles of birth thanks to centuries of experience. Like all witches, she had the skill to hide her age, which was actually 56. And she had prepared herself to become pregnant at this moment even though it was far past any normal woman's time.

"Your majesty," She bowed low to show her voluptuously pushed-up breasts. She kept eye contact with him as she did this. His attention didn't require any of her manipulation abilities. "Every time we're together, I feel the heat build in me, and if I can't feel your body, I end up spending hours afterward trying to catch my breath, calm the raging fire."

Antoin surveyed her and imagined his hands gliding over her skin. He knew her heat well and felt the worries being burned away. He was eager to relieve himself of the burden and drive out his fear. She made him feel like they were the only two people in the entire world. Antoin stood from the seat and released his cloak.

Tiffany surveyed Antoin's response and took her time with him. She wanted to savor the touch just in case it was the last time. The daughter she would have wouldn't be royalty. The Sisters like to have children with noble lovers to intertwine with the essence of the Kingdom. It wasn't about silly titles. It was about daughters who were part of the Kingdom. The Sisters of Forn had developed methods for guaranteeing the birth of daughters to carry on the legacy of their mothers.

King Antoin found his stress-free and youthful self with Tiffany. He didn't concern himself with Fuller or Medrick, even though his life depended on them. He put all his belief in Tiffany.

After Antoin was settled, Tiffany returned to her sisters, who had already gathered at Garrin to confirm with each other. The current Sisters of Forn all varied widely in age since they had all been through several lifetimes. The original seven Sisters all had a child by the methods pioneered by their mother. They each birthed a daughter when they chose to and would impart their memories and life to the thirteen-year-old girls through a process that let the experience and legacy of the sisterhood continue.

The current Sisters were Tiffany, Surbozza, Autumn, Charity, Clair, Celest, and Francesca. Their meeting spot was a few hours from the castle in a small grove of apple trees. Tiffany spoke first, "It's set. The King and his men are on their way. May certainty guide them." Tiffany had released some of her visual disguises and was shorter, and her hair was dragged down by gravity.

Surbozza replied, "Did you need to explain the uncertainty?" Her surreal silvery hair had a shine that persisted through the shade. The wrinkles on her face were deeper today with worry. The large earrings she loved to wear pulled her lobes long.

Tiffany shook her head. "I didn't need to feed their fear. They assumed the uncertainty on their own and only wanted reassurance from me."

Clair's matted hair kicked up and flared out wildly for dramatic effect. "And did you tell him you were the only one that thought he might live?" Her olive skin grew brighter with the devious stare. Clair enjoyed this horrific risk to the Kingdom and the Sisters more than any of them.

Autumn hit Clair on the back of the head, and Clair's hair went flat again. "What sort of woman would tell her lover that everyone thinks he's going to die?" Autumn's burning red hair draped over both sides of her shoulders. She was currently the third oldest, and she never hid the age in her face or body. Only her hair continued to capture its youth.

Celest and Francesca were both stunning blondes with tall frames and highly maintained visages. They were actually in their twenties and didn't need to hide their age. Their mothers had had the same lover and decided to put a little more effort into their daughters and help ensure that they looked like sisters and nearly like twins. They liked to finish each other's sentences.

Celest assured them. "It's all beside the point as long as they are victorious at the end of the day," and Francesca continued, "Our Kingdom is protected. It can take as many nobles as the Tokkin need to kill." Celest nodded in reply. "Those savages only know conflict."

Charity interrupted. "We should keep searching. Scrying may have revealed a favorable outcome, but what sort of Kingdom will exist after the battle? Order might take years to be realized." Charity's plain dress and simply braided hair helped her present humble questions, but it usually didn't sway her sisters to be less dependent on scrying to solve problems. Her long cheeks shortened as she gritted her teeth.

Having waited for her turn to speak, Tiffany replied, "They claim their ownership of the Kingdom, and the Relic Order will meet as gruesome a fate as the nobles. We need to worry about ourselves more than any institution at this point. We built it up once, we can do it again, as long as we live." Tiffany started to cry thinking about Antoin. He was probably going to die.

All of them took in Tiffany's tears. They had all experienced loss and knew what she was going through. It was these close Sisters against the chaotic forces of the world. The fog that blocked their scrying and followed the Tokkin army was an incarnation of a belief that would tear down their world. They didn't understand it. They didn't need to. It just had to be stopped.

Chapter 3

Miles away, Medrick was making his way back to his keep. Now that he didn't have the other two to contend with, his imagination was truly free to wander. He could see himself now on the hard-fought battleground. The King and Fuller would be dead, and their armies would be decimated. He would be the victor and the savior of the Kingdom, and his reward would be kingship. It was his future to seize and his reward.

All his daydream planning and perceived paths to the crown had been paved in so many assassinations that he would never escape the wrath of the other nobles. Those like Lord Fuller would remain loyal to the King, and the other bloodlines would attempt to assassinate him. He was not popular, but this battle could create his popularity and eliminate much of the opposition to him.

Medrick thought about the witches' offer to King Antoin for no-cost service. It was unfortunate that the witches always asked too much to scry for him in the past, even though he was eager to have them in his service. They wanted him to give up his power and authority as Duke. They had asked that he release a criminal who had poached on his land or that he care for a woman who they claimed he had made pregnant. It would all undermine him, and they never saw the simple benefits of aiding him.

It was a three-day hard ride back north and east to his keep. He spent the first day of the ride brooding about the path to his goal. There had to be a way to guarantee the King's and Fuller's deaths and save his life since this was the best chance he would ever have. But the Tokkin army couldn't be relied on like a normal army since they attacked without regard for traditional ranks and roles.

Late into the second day, they came to the Indeet River, which flowed quickly from the nearby mountain of Pebble. The name described the look of the mountain from a distance. The pebbles were actually giant boulders that looked like they had been dropped from the sky in a large pile. Dirt and sand had found their way between the boulders over time, but the piles of man-sized rocks created many holes and caves, which many thieves and robbers often used to hide in. The river was flowing too quickly today for them to cross downstream, so they had to go further up the slope even though it had the risk of ambush.

As they climbed up the mountain toward the crossing, Medrick's heart rate grew heavy, and he felt cold. It felt different from the other times he had traveled up a mountainside, but it could just be the stress he was already under. Before reaching the crossing, he had to stop. He hoped it was just the altitude and not a failure of his heart and body.

Medrick looked around at the rocky terrain. There were hundreds of places to hide from his view, and he had the feeling they were all being watched. He looked to his three guards. "Check around us. Make sure we are not being watched."

They obeyed the paranoid request and started slipping in and out of view as they searched behind and around the rocks that surrounded them. It was at that moment when all three were out of sight that he saw it.

Medrick couldn't see anything recognizable, but he looked directly at it. It was a space between the rocks that was like looking at suspicion in physical form. He listened to the feeling and stood to catch the spy. His guards weren't near that boulder, so it was up to him. Medrick drew his sword and picked up a torch in his off-hand and lit it. He would need it to see through the shadows around every corner.

Medrick stepped toward the edge of the feeling. It wasn't a feeling of dread or a foreboding of death that he had come to expect from past experiences. It was more of an irritation that he was being watched. Rock after rock, he followed the strength of the feeling. Not for a moment did he question how far he had gone or whether the pursuit was worth it.

The trail led him to a small opening between some rocks. It looked like any other opening, but he knew that it was the one he was looking for. He moved the torch across the gap, blurring the lines of light and dark. Medrick crouched as he entered a cave without an immediate end. As he followed it to the back, it continued to twist, drop, and snake through the earth. He stayed crouched the whole time and began to sacrifice his clothing to get through the narrowest spaces. At the splits, he always took the one that seemed darkest and dank. It made some sense that a spy would pick the darkest corners.

At last, he found a chamber dozens of feet tall and wide where it was easy to stand. From the torchlight, he saw it was marked with many stalactites and person-sized, perfectly round boulders. No matter where he moved, a person could hide and move between the available shadows. If he hadn't been looking for his suspicion, he might have noticed the evenly spaced pattern of the boulders. Each stalactite's length was just a few inches longer or shorter than its neighbor, creating peaks and valleys consistently along the ceiling.

His heart was still chilled, but it was steady and certain. The fatigue he had felt as they climbed the mountain was gone. Even with the stale air, he was breathing easier. He couldn't see the spy. "Show yourself," Medrick called out.

But his voice didn't carry very far. It was muffled by the barriers surrounding him, and as he looked, he thought that the light was making it harder to search by creating too many shadows. Suddenly, Medrick decided to agree with the urge and put out the torch. He thrust it into the wet muck and stood still.

Medrick's mind snapped to his troubles. His plans for seizing the opportunity during the coming battle were useless. All the suspicion that had led him into this cave was gone, and oddly, there was no fear of the darkness. He spoke out and poured out his feelings, "I need to know. I need confidence and certainty. My will is strong, and I need a way forward. I need to see a way forward."

He reached a hand forward and found a rock that he could press it against. Medrick needed to explain himself. How could he convince the rest of the Kingdom that they should follow him? "I know there is a reason all things happen." The words steadied him. "It's more than belief, it's certainty."

His hand guided itself away from the rock he had touched, and he started to slowly turn on the spot as he spoke to the cavern, "I don't just deserve to rule, I am certain to rule. The kingdom needs to be shown the true path, and I'm the only one who can make it happen. Sure, the Sisters of Forn might have been responsible for the Kingdom's birth, but only I can set the path further." He felt like he had someone's attention. Opinions, beliefs, and lesser visions of the meaning of life slowed to watch him.

Medrick continued his speech as he heard something like a whisper from an enraptured audience. "The Tokkins are the perfect enemy for my Kingdom come. They are the rallying cry that motivates and binds each human to our common belief. Loyalty is built by such threats. And their existence is truly the result of wicked influences in our world. I will be the champion of our Kingdom. I am the only one that guarantees a future where we are the reason and the cause for a pure and good life." Medrick felt pride and felt a surge of confidence. He felt stronger. This is what it must feel like for relic wielders. Was this place a relic?

Medrick summoned whatever force he believed was watching him. "Come to my certainty. The future of the Kingdom is in my will." There was a lurch from all sides of his body. A sound spilled out into the cavern. It came from not one point, but Medrick spoke with the sound, "Krn'v'rnk." What was it? A name, an idea, a belief? It didn't matter. He accepted it into his body.

Medrick felt it like it had always been part of him. He just needed the courage to stop listening to foolish doubts and start following his righteous intent. And this was the truth, that there was a reason, a purpose, for all events, and he was the one that could make everyone believe. Until everyone saw it his way, the ultimate truth would evade all humanity.

Medrick had a revived view of the world, and his confidence was never stronger than now. More so now because he could see more. There was no light in this cavern, but he knew where everything was as if it were full daylight. He looked at his own hands. He wasn't a wicked Tokkin now, but something like relic power pulsed in him. It was knowledge to manipulate the world around him in ways that would make relic wielders jealous.

The torch was no longer needed, and his new sight could make out all the detail the flickering torchlight had missed. He would never need his path illuminated again, and he wondered how he could have ever doubted his special purpose.

He did have to shelter his eyes as he exited the cave. His new sense of the world was still fresh, and everything was much busier than inside the cave. Medrick climbed down and around the boulders leading back to his horse.

The hulking guard, Brian Fortrane, yelled as he spotted his Duke. "Duke Medrick. Are you alright? We thought you might have been taken." Brian had exceedingly short hair and a square jaw with a neck as thick as his head.

"I am fine, Fortrane." He slowed his pace as Brian hurried towards him, slipping on the rocks as he approached Medrick.

Brian yelled for the other guard. "Kane, I have found him." He knelt at the Duke's feet, regretting his failure and prepared for punishment. "I am sorry I didn't find you sooner. Forgive me."

Kane Amber came around some boulders and approached much more gracefully than Brian. Kane kept his hair under his expansive hat collection. His narrow eyes quickly marked the surroundings. "Duke Medrick. Forgive our response. We feared that you might have been kidnapped. Is there a bandit we need to chase?"

The two guards were from noble families in Medrick's domain. They had been given the duty of his personal guards as a favor to their families. It was a safer duty than any other posts, and they were kept in high regard among other nobles. Now, the two knelt to him and expected a punishment which would have been his response at one time, but now he saw the advantage to their obedience. He just had never seen the right way to use it.

"Where is Guard Triel?" Medrick looked around but already knew the answer when he asked himself. Triel had ridden onward to return with help for a search. Medrick had a habit of demanding answers from vassals but now realized that he had all the answers to those mundane questions.

"He rode back to bring reinforcements," Kane replied.

Medrick knew that punishment could be replaced with a chance to repay him for their failure. It was good that Triel was not here since he now understood, thanks to the cave's experience, that he would maintain his loyalty to the King if tested. It was certain. "Kane, Brian," he disregarded their last names to show his confidence, "I have a duty for the both of you." He knew they would not refuse. "You will remain my personal guards if you agree."

They were eager to escape punishment and replied together. "We will, my Duke."

Medrick explained without fear of their reactions. "I will be assigning both of you as commanders in our coming battle. You will obey only my commands even if the King should try to give you orders. You will ignore all other orders on the battlefield except mine." He looked at each of them so

28

they could show their agreement.

Both Kane and Brian were experienced nobility, and Medrick's ambition was known to them, but this suggestion was surprising. They could both easily imagine the King attempting to direct Medrick's forces personally, given all of Medrick's battle hesitation over the years. In this request, he was asking for treason.

Their silence may have been disturbing to Medrick hours ago, but he knew they would agree.

"My Duke," Kane replied, "You know we seek to serve you, but what if the King were to send us commands?"

Medrick clarified their duty without concern. "You ignore the King's orders. As a reward for your obedience, you will be granted use of relics, and you will be allowed to keep your noble titles and land." The relics that granted similar strengths to the Tokkin were restricted to the Relic Order. Medrick asserted that he would be King after the battle by offering them the use of the relics without typical restrictions.

To use a relic with permission from the King meant that you could not own land or title. Relic wielders were paid and housed by the King and nobility. They were enforcers of the law that would go where the King and nobles needed. Relic wielders could create destructive force, bend or peer into a person's mind, or construct buildings without tools, all depending on their inclinations. The Sisters of Forn had been responsible for gathering some of the first relics and placing them with strong-willed and appropriately determined people. Since that time, there had been rogue relic wielders, but that's another reason the Relic Order existed.

Relics were found in many shapes and sizes. They could be pearl-sized or as large as a human head. They always had an improbable shape to them, like a perfect sphere or a hollow disk. They looked man-made, but no one had ever crafted one. The size didn't determine the strength they gave, but if they were broken, the power would diminish as the privileged knew.

Relics had always been in the world just like every other rock, but the direct connection to holding one and forcing your will into the world was thanks to the insight of the witches. They had done personal research into the differences between Tokkin and others. Humans like to have keepsakes, and some individuals already had relics before they were categorized and defined through methods explored by the Sisters of Forn. Their understanding helped to remove the chaos and determine a safer future.

The Duke had just put Kane and Brian's heads to the guillotine. Refuse and face a punishment of dismissal and stripping of rights by Medrick. Or accept and face the punishment of execution for betraying the King. The reward Medrick promised would make them more powerful than any other. They looked at Medrick with astonishment, but what they felt and saw coming from him was pure confidence. It radiated like a warm fire, and it made them sure that Antoin would die and Medrick would live and reward them.

Kane spoke first. He was convinced by the Duke's confidence in the outcome of the battle. If everything went according to Medrick's plan, he would be in the perfect spot. If the plan failed, the disaster would be tied to his death on or off a battlefield. "I will agree to the duty. I am your loyal servant." He would agree now and follow Medrick as long as the risks were understood and he felt the certainty of his Duke, the future King.

Brian was amazed by it all. Never had he imagined that he would be in such a circle of confidence. It was thrilling and terrifying. He was excited that he had a chance to show Medrick that he was his most loyal vassal. Brian nodded vigorously, "I agree to the duty, Sire, my Master."

"Of course," Medrick replied. "We will head back to the castle to prepare now. I don't believe that either of you will break my confidence. If either of you is asked about missing me, you will explain that you found a bandit attempting to abduct me. You killed him and threw his body in the river." The men lowered their heads and nodded in understanding. "Retrieve the horses, We have a war to prepare for."

Chapter 4

The flats of Pullingham were a cleared area that might have been ideal for farming if water were more plentiful. The tall grass served as a home for all sorts of small critters. It was quite the sight to see them scatter as the area was invaded by the King and his men. The full army had gathered on the field, trampling the grasses to give themselves a clear view up to the forest's edge.

There were six thousand men spread out and standing apart by their noble banners. Lord Fuller had supplied the bulk of footmen and archers. Medrick supplied his equipment, light cavalry, and a sizable number of lowly trained footmen.

The King followed the tradition of giving his vassals permission to train only certain types of soldiers. This was so that no one could make a fully ranked army to challenge the King, and it had been very successful for centuries. Unfortunately, Antoin's armies had lost many skilled soldiers, and he was left with the lightly armored skirmishers and knights, who were the least experienced. Despite all the losses, Antoin had more men on the field than Medrick or Fuller.

The rare sight on the battlefield was the relic wielders. Having a handful wasn't uncommon in large campaigns, and their skills made them worth a dozen men each. There were over a hundred relic wielders in the Relic Order, and this was the bulk of them. There were eighty-two of the most powerful men in the Kingdom of Garrin, wearing their dazzling battle cloaks and serious expressions. Typically, they wore modest clothes to secretly perform their daily duties, but battles meant they should be seen to create intimidation. Antoin now thought of them as the key to winning since he would never have fielded them without such desperation and promise of victory by the Sisters of Forn.

King Antoin and his vassals convened on the raised rampart that they had constructed to give them a higher view of the flat expanse. The rampart was a few dozen feet in elevation and was only wide enough for twenty or so men.

Fuller was nervous about their location now that he was there in person. He had expected more variations in the terrain with a few strategic positions, but they had nowhere to back into or defend themselves in a retreat. They could be attacked from any direction. Fuller voiced his concerns. "We are exposed from all sides, my King." He would have called it a death trap if not for the witches scrying that the King put his faith in. "We need to find this army and engage so that we may pull them into a trap here." He suggested the best strategy available to them.

Antoin disagreed with the proposal. "We do not need to employ such a risky strategy. We do not want our men to split up." He reassured himself since he shared the same wrenching feeling as Fuller. "I will not allow our men to be pulled into the forest. We need this clearing to be effective." Antoin had never faced a Tokkin army and was only guessing since all the most experienced soldiers had died at the hands of the Tokkin's most effective campaign. "I sent out scouts before you arrived. I gave them information about our location, expecting they might be captured and interrogated. They will be certain of our location, and they will come to us just as they have faced every other force before now." Antoin nodded and seemed to smile, "One of the scouts did return and reported just a thousand Tokkin to our southeast."

Medrick rolled over the numbers that he hadn't known up to that point. "A thousand?" His belief had been un-wavered despite not knowing that fact, but now he needed to reassure the King since Tokkin forces were known to fight greater than 5 to 1 ratio. "The witches were right that it'll be a hard battle, but we can be certain of our victory now that we are in the moment." He moved around the King so he could see the confidence on his face.

Fuller's suspicions of Medrick were unending, but this new way Medrick spoke was disturbing. It showed none of the typical greed or self-concern. "They are all Tokkin, and I can't recall a time when a force this large has attacked at once. Their numbers might count for more than simple addition." Fuller tested his doubt against Medrick.

The King spoke up before Medrick responded. "They have never faced an army like this before. Our numbers count for more than addition too, Fuller." It was not typical that the King needed to quell Fuller and take stock in Medrick's encouragement, but perhaps the stress of the moment was bringing out true colors. He pointed to the map as he spoke. "We have the only elevated point on the field and can direct movements no matter their attack. It will compel them to take this rampart." Again, he feared for his life. It was too much, and he wished that he could be comforted again by Tiffany, however, she and the other Sisters of Forn were not combatants and were far away from this battlefield.

Even though the plan was simple, Antoin kept going over it, hoping that each pass would ease the situation. Fuller looked out across the field. Hopefully, it helped their soldiers to see them planning and preparing. "We should move to our position and set ranks. Regrettably, we do not know when they'll attack."

Medrick knew it would be soon as he could feel the fog approaching. It clouded visions of the future and created the uncertainty the witches had seen. The difference was that he knew that he would survive after the plunge into chaos. That is the piece the witches had been uncertain about, and he could feel with new determination. "Given their time of attacks and the distance they've covered, we can be certain it'll be today." He wasn't going to give them his hourly prediction, so he remained slightly vague. "I think they'll attack when we are prepared as if to destroy our defenses at their greatest strength."

Fuller doubted this analysis since it was the first time it had been discussed. "That is quite the assumption, Medrick. Why would they attack us at our greatest defense?"

Medrick cast off the doubt with an easy answer, "All of the reports of our defeats have shown that our men were in full defensive positions. There are no signs of night attacks or underhanded opportunities."

Fuller quickly replied, "It doesn't mean they are bound to follow that method."

Medrick smirked since he had easily eroded Fuller's confidence. "Give our formations two hours, and then we can plan for waiting. It will raise the men's morale." He knew only the King's confidence was important. Antoin needed to be the target for the Tokkin.

Antoin smiled approvingly. "We agree with you, Duke Medrick. This battle is about the decisiveness of our actions. Confidence is the correct course. Return to your positions on the field and prepare your men." Medrick's certainty pushed away Antoin's need for the Sisters of Forn's guidance. It was refreshing, and he drank the resolve of Medrick's offer. "Prepare for a southern attack. I will have the scouts positioned and reporting back regularly from the other directions."

The two bowed and took the orders to give to their men. Medrick returned to Kane and Brian, who were in command of the spear men and Medrick's long swords. "You two will position yourself according to these orders," he handed the King's orders to them, which gave more than simple field positioning, "You will follow the orders I gave to you previously after that point." They understood that they would begin betraying the King once the battle was underway.

Fuller passed the order to his commanders with an additional message.

Even if he didn't want to put any faith in the witches, he couldn't ignore their one-third prediction. The message was, "Have faith in the brother next to you and protect him before you would shed your life for the King." It was the closest to treason that he had ever come, but this whole battle was carried on the promises of witches and misplaced faith in Medrick's actual support. If it cost the King his life, Fuller could accept that.

Chapter 5

Eight months ago, the Council of Nine members of the Tokkin gathered to attempt yet again to organize an offensive against the Kingdom. The Council members were sometimes elders, accomplished warriors, or friends of existing council members. There were many reasons a Council member was accepted, but all the members were acknowledged as leaders. Tal'Abrac was a thorn in this authority, and he could sway thousands to question the Council if they should act on blind faith according to Tal'Abrac. They avoided such actions to spare themselves the grief of Tal'Abrac's disruptions. It was difficult for them to ask for his help in the face of his annoyance, nevertheless, they called on him.

Tal'Abrac was a massive man who stood seven feet tall. His grey skin seemed to reflect blue in the right light and looked rough from thick hair. The iris of his eyes was so dark that the pupils were hard to distinguish.

Unlike any other Tokkin, Tal'Abrac had a tail, which made him the furthest Tokkin from human anyone knew of. The thick, long tail seemed to work as an additional sense. It peered with its point in different directions as if aware of its surroundings. The description of rarely seen dragons suggested a tail not unlike his, which Tal'Abrac had used to suggest some additional importance to his existence. However, Tokkin that share aspects of other animals had no special kinship to those animals, they were just physical differences.

The private council room was a circular chamber beneath the council's amphitheater. They matched in layout, but the upper level could seat over 10000, and the center ring was over two hundred feet in diameter rather than a twenty-foot round table in this below chamber. Each member sat at the circular table with open space between them all. Tal'Abrac stood at the guest location on the outer circumference. Each member wore varying-colored robes with hoods to shroud their appearance and differences, with only their hands completely exposed. Their hands gave away additional identifiers of rings and tattoos.

Councilman One spoke formally as he read from the parchment. "Tal'Abrac, The Council of Nine has called you here to assign you as leader of our newest force aimed at striking the capital city of Garrin. Many others were considered for command, but you are our choice. The honor of this great task is yours." He wore a white robe, and there was a ring on four of his left fingers. None of the Councilmen looked directly at Tal'Abrac. They had frozen themselves in mid-motion, prepared for the response they guessed he would have.

Tal'Abrac was illuminated by the dozens of torches lit around the outer wall. "I doubt I am your first choice. You have many other qualified and experienced commanders." Tal'Abrac replied with a shrug. The building of an army was not news to him since they had been responding to a demand by the people for action. The Kingdom of Garrin's had been pressing across the Grand Plains and were fortifying their captured positions.

It was obvious they were waiting for an argument from him. "I would like to know why you would choose me." Tal'Abrac spoke to the room at large but looked only at Councilman One. They didn't respond immediately because he hadn't acted offensively enough. "You must be waiting for me to say what the witches foretold, that I would reject the offer," he finished off with a mocking tone of shock and covered his mouth with his hand in pretend amazement. He hoped mocking the impossibility of scrying his actions would get them talking. Simply put, he couldn't be scryed for because he didn't care to know the future. More complexly, his disbelief prevented his actions from being known outside of the moment he was in.

Councilman Three wanted him to accept, "We are not joking with you Tal'Abrac," but there had been too much friction in the Council over the appointment to rehash their discussion. "This is a serious appointment, and we need an answer." His chin led out from the cover of his light gray robes. The thorny tattoo pattern wrapped around his right hand. It was a marking from the raider gang he used to belong to in his youth.

Councilman Five laughed. "I knew you wouldn't be honored by the position. A loyal Tokkin would jump at the opportunity to lead our force." He was one of the 'friend' appointments to the Council and took the position seriously. He chose a white robe to match the pure ideals he held for the Tokkin. The rings on his thumbs tapped together when he would clasp his hands. They were the Council and needed obedience to prosper. He was eager for Tal'Abrac to refuse so that they could get on with other plans.

"You, Councilman Five, never see anyone as honorable as yourself. I doubt that if I had accepted immediately, you would see me as honorable. Most likely, you would see a usurper grasping for power." Tal'Abrac wasn't afraid to point out Five's hypocrisies, but it did derail conversations into arguments that only produced malice.

Councilman Five yelled at him, "You have done nothing to earn the respect and honor of the Council. This is the most important task we could trust to anyone, but you're just too selfish to see it." It was so clear that Tal'Abrac was saying this just to incite him. It wasn't stupidity that made Tal'Abrac an enemy, it was his intent.

Tal'Abrac retorted, "I don't want your approval or honor." He was done with his long-standing argument with Councilman Five this evening. It was clear that Five didn't want to appoint him as the commander. That made the choice more disturbing. Only desperate faith would make them act against their prejudice. "You still have not explained."

Councilman Five continued his tirade, "You divide us with your arrogant speeches. We must stand united against the Kingdom of Garrin, and you promote dissension. Are you so blind to the needs and suffering around you?" He slammed his hand on the stone tabletop and bared his teeth as he snarled at Tal'Abrac.

Councilman Two was too tired to listen to much more of this. He didn't like it any more than Five, but he believed in the witches scrying for a successful strike into the Kingdom. He kept his tattooed hands hidden underneath his dark gray robe for the most part. His position in the Council was about the future, not his past actions. "It's your influence that we want, Tal'Abrac. You could unite the force if you were leading it. There would be a chance for it to succeed." The alternatives to Tal'Abrac would undermine the Council's power.

Tal'Abrac looked at Councilman Two and guessed that it was true. More would join if he were to lead it, but they had promised an attack on Garrin. It was months of travel within the Kingdom, meaning certain defeat through attrition, and that was something he could never promote. "This force is doomed to fail. I can't imagine that the scrying of witches has suggested anything else. Do you really think that because I cannot be scried for that the outcome would be any different?"

Councilman Two shook his head no. "The men that have joined are loyal and strong, and with your influence, even more will see the hope and eagerly join. If you were to command the army, then it would grow beyond any vision the witches have had. It could do whatever is needed to survive."

Councilman Eight interrupted Two's wishful prayer. This wasn't about tempting him into command. He had the ability, and he owed it to the Tokkin. "You are more than capable, Tal'Abrac. We must each serve how we are best fitted, and you are the best fit for this battle. I have no doubt that you could see to the army's victory." Eight's black robes were foreboding, but he was practical. His bare left hand met his single-ringed and tattooed right hand in a high triangle with his elbows on the table.

Councilman Two didn't believe Tal'Abrac saw himself as part of the Tokkin. He interrupted Eight to define the difference, "You are one of our brothers, Tal'Abrac. Even if we disagree, I would personally join you in defense of our land."

Councilman Five didn't share the sentiment and would never fight with Tal'Abrac. "It has nothing to do with that. You divide us, and the witches have seen that our army will fail because of it. It doesn't matter which commander we appoint. You have divided us so deeply that we are already defeated."

Councilman Nine spoke solemnly and without addressing Tal'Abrac. "His powers are greater than any other commander we could appoint, Five." His deep blue robes were motionless as he addressed the Council. "The fact is that regardless of any feelings we have, he is the best chance our army has to succeed, regardless of any witch's scrying." Both of his hands were at rest on the table. The right one had two rings on the center finger and a leaf pattern of tattoos leading out onto the tops of his fingers.

Tal'Abrac had never thought the Council could be so divided and reach an agreement, though all of them were reluctant. It was incredibly curious to see such a result, and since he had no love for their request, he felt safe challenging their order to learn what would happen if he refused. "So, if I refuse, what will happen? Would the army go anyway, or would it be dissolved?"

Councilman One took the opening and tried desperately to keep from falling into the argument that led them to this. "The army would be given a different objective that is within another commander's ability."

Councilman Five couldn't help bringing up the division of Tal'Abrac.

"And it would undermine the Council's power again, and since you are so committed to destroying centuries of growing stability, that should be your choice."

Tal'Abrac wasn't trying to destroy the Council's authority, but it shouldn't be absolute like Five would prefer. Councilman Five would never see his authority as needing to be anything less than absolute and certain. "This is a desperate plan that you committed to, but I am not so desperate to lead it."

"Traitor." Councilman Eight huffed. "You fail to see the importance of this army. The victory isn't as important as the hope, and that hope can't be fostered when defeat is certain. You have a chance to bring hope to the people in the face of their desperation."

It was the best twist of the words that Tal'Abrac had heard, and it rang out the real reason he was chosen. They wanted hope, and none of their normal sources could fulfill that hope. It led back to their desperation, but that was his opportunity. The Council was waiting for him to answer. So many people give up their own reasoning to rely on a higher power. That's what gave the scrying of the witches reason and purpose. That dependency on purpose should never be given so blindly or a person distorts the opportunity of the moment. Desperation. He tried to teach independence from certainty, grand reason, or whatever higher intent they might claim. This was an opportunity to show them what he means.

Tal'Abrac finally spoke up and intentionally paused after speaking, "I don't like your goal."

Councilman One spoke for all of them. "The goal is the whole point of this army."

Tal'Abrac spoke louder, "And so the point is a destination that does not consider what will be gained and what will change in the end. You really want this to end the conflict that has continued for generations. Right?"

"Yes." The whole Council confirmed with some sound or gesture.

"Well then," Tal'Abrac continued, "The goal of this army will be an end to the conflict on my terms and without the vengeful acts of pillaging their land to raze their capital."

Councilman Eight shook his head in disappointment. "You gave us hope for a moment there, Tal'Abrac. That act will give our people hope. The Kingdom of Garrin has been the source of our problems, and the city must be razed." He hadn't imagined Tal'Abrac so blind to the needs of the people.

Tal'Abrac continued to paint his imagination for them, "I imagine our city on fire. It would be a symbol of hope for the Kingdom of Garrin, but it would be a symbol of desperation and anger for the Tokkin. It would end nothing. You see it, don't you? I want to end that." Tal'Abrac spoke simply, addressing each of them as he turned on the spot.

They could see his point, but it didn't change what each of them wanted individually. They were committed to their own beliefs.

Councilman Four used a red robe to mark him as the most accomplished warrior. He never joined a raiding gang but was known for his authorized assaults against the Kingdom. He had no tattoos on his hand but marked each index finger with a ring. He didn't need to argue his belief, but Tal'Abrac spoke about a wishful idea while the strong attack on Garrin was a real plan. "Your goal is a wish of women and children. I have fought them, and I can tell you that there is no negotiation or peace to be found."

Tal'Abrac nodded, "I agree. They are as stubborn as each of you. I will not negotiate or offer surrender. Nor will I raid villages, attack women and children, or take revenge for past defeats. I will destroy their forts and armies. I will take the lives of their commanders and King. And when I have done this, I will return."

Councilman One could easily accept those terms. "That is all we ask."

"I disagree." Tal'Abrac needed them to see. "You want to take all the pain they have caused and visit it upon them. It's all equal. In some sense, it might be better if the same were to happen to us, that we would have no chance to rebuild and to not retaliate because frankly, I don't trust any of you to relent after victory. Which makes me the perfect commander for this army."

Councilman Eight hissed at Tal'Abrac, "You have not shared the pain, Tal'Abrac, so it is easy for you to dismiss it." He pointed to the separation that he perceived as Tal'Abrac's reason for not seeking revenge. Tal'Abrac lived off his notoriety and didn't have land or family to protect. "If you had lost loved ones, then you would know the real pain they cause."

Tal'Abrac pushed onward. "Regardless." He knew they would be deaf to the explanation because it was just like Eight said. It was personal for them. "I will lead under my goals. It might take traveling to Garrin to achieve this, but I have a feeling that my assault will cause a different result than your witches foresaw."

Councilman Five wanted his last words for the evening heard before anyone accepted Tal'Abrac's conditions, "And what happens when they rebuild from such a weak attack?"

Tal'Abrac understood the fear. They wanted to follow history and do what they understood, but that would always have the same result. "This is a cycle I'm breaking, Five. They will gravitate to it just like you, so I am sure they will rebuild. But we will not start anew by doing the same thing that has always been done."

Councilman One was ready to take what was offered. "The Council accepts the terms of your command." This might produce a different result, and even though he didn't know what the consequences might be, it was worth trying. "If any member doesn't concur, say so now." It took six members objecting to overturn One's decision.

Councilman Five and Eight raised their hands to show their continued disappointment in Tal'Abrac. Both of them knew that there weren't enough votes to overturn One, but they just wanted their dissent seen. Tal'Abrac's appointment passed. And he did just what he said he would. He had gathered raiders into his army and directed their entire focus to his goal. Their numbers tripled from when he first took command, and they had done what he said they would. The army of the Kingdom of Garrin had come to him far before they would have ever reached Garrin.

Now, Tal'Abrac watched the formation from a treetop over a mile away and sighed, "Untypical size." Even though he had volunteered to lead this army against the Kingdom, he had his doubts about its success. Sure, they had won each fight easily, but the goal of crippling the Kingdom wouldn't solve the real problem. They were separate and didn't share a common threat. The Tokkin had become the Kingdom's threat, and they were theirs, but he had come this far, and eliminating the Kingdom's military would bring years of peace to the Tokkin. Maybe escalation could turn to decline.

The gaudy cloaks of the relic wielders caught his eye. He had killed one prior to this battle, and they had shown enough talent to be a threat above the number of men on the field. The Kingdom of Garrin was positioned right where the scout's information had said. It was a direct challenge and a suggestion that they understood the nature of his assault against their military. The timing and location of this army were concerning, though. He had expected a gathered defense deeper in the Kingdom and not as close to his intended path. Either it was expert planning or scrying by a witch that aided them.

Tal'Abrac jumped down from the tall tree to reach the ground quickly. A few of the fresh leaves were pulled from their branches as he fell past them. Kimmy, a Tokkin scout, was waiting on the forest floor to keep watch below the canopy. He jumped back as Tal'Abrac landed suddenly. The scout was only three feet tall with a series of shallow humps protruding from his spine. His gray skin tone was whiter than most. He wore simple leather clothes and looked more like an entertainer than a fighter.

Tal'Abrac smiled and read the shock on Kimmy's face. "I take it you weren't looking up." He patted him on the head. "They are in the open and make no attempt to hide. They are ready for us to attack."

"Is that a problem?" Kimmy chuckled and looked up proudly at Tal'Abrac. Tal'Abrac had led them into every battle without hesitation, no matter the attacks or the defenses the Kingdom forces used. They weren't hiding from them, which meant he had won a bet among the other men that the next battle wouldn't be an attempted ambush by the Kingdom.

Tal'Abrac stood up straight, looking around for any dangers Kimmy may have missed on the ground. He didn't believe Kimmy's attention was acute enough. He spoke to Kimmy again, "They have guessed the obvious path of our army and have stuck themselves in our way. The Kingdom's forces were facing south in his direction. He could attack from a slight eastern or western position, but moving more would surely get them spotted. Run back and tell the forces to meet me in the southwest. Make sure they move quickly and without being seen."

Kimmy giggled and ran off.

There was no need to alarm Kimmy about his suspicions over the witches scrying. When he had taken command, he knew that the Kingdom of Garrin would fall into a desperate path. He had defied their defense, and in desperation, people typically fell back on their beliefs. Tokkin people were no different than the people of Garrin in that way. Even the Council of Nine fell to their beliefs when planning attacks against the Kingdom of Garrin.

Witches had scryed for the Council, and they couldn't gain an advantage on each other. The Sisters of Forn had always helped the Kingdom, and the remaining witches weren't as organized. The only thing that changed the calculation was his leadership of the army. Tal'Abrac's disbelief fogged the certainties of scrying by witches. They couldn't make out the results surrounding his actions until after the moment had passed. It was those who believed in a purpose to the world that gave them this power, and there were so many of those people on this battlefield.

Tal'Abrac met his force on the southwest side of the clearing, far enough away from the tree line to be unseen. They were dressed with the light armor pieces they had owned prior to joining. Only the leather pads and chain mail pieces of the raider gangs that had joined them matched each other, but the army was still without formal ranks. It was necessary in part because each individual believed they could be a hero and small group strategies had always worked for them. Tal'Abrac knew this and led the armies' striking pattern to match their experience.

Grill, the witch observer, was waiting for him and was irritated as usual. She wasn't a Sister of Forn. There were dozens of known witches in the world, but the Sisters were the only covenant. Each had the tenacity to charge for their services, and each was without any Tokkin markers despite their gifts. The witches kept their ancient history and separated paths to themselves. Grill had been appointed by the Council of Nine to aid Tal'Abrac and provide scrying if he needed it, but he didn't listen to her any prior time.

Grill forcefully suggested, "Tal'Abrac, you must not attack. They are prepared for you and are fresh. Waiting till night or delaying till tomorrow would be the most advantageous." She was a mature woman in her early fifties and had hidden her appearance to her thirties when they first set out. She had since dropped the pretense because all her charms and persuasion weren't effective on Tal'Abrac. Her black hair now showed long streaks of silver, but her skin had kept its slightly palm-gray tone. Given that witches could more easily adjust their appearance, their skin could match their neighboring culture. This technique was one of their social tricks, and it didn't have the drawbacks Tokkin and relic wielders experienced when trying to alter their bodies.

Tal'Abrac continued to march on by her. "Why would I start to follow your advice now? I appreciate your honest assessments, but all your suggestions follow the Council's will." He continued to move to the front of his army as Grill pressed her point.

Grill followed. "It's wonderful that you like my assessments, but your success in spite of my advice has been luck. You would do well to listen to my experience, which outstrips even your own. As soon as I saw this army, I scryed for more detail, and I found that they are taking the advice of the Sisters of Forn." She had her reasons for despising the Sisters, but that had nothing to do with her advice. "You need to listen to my advice."

This was the first time Grill had mentioned the Sisters of Forn. Tal'Abrac knew who they were, and their involvement was on his mind. It meant Garrin believed this was the final battle and that they had fallen to the desperation he tried to create. Scrying wasn't a vague action, though. Scrying and learning of the Sisters meant she had to scry while guessing their involvement. "You scryed for the Sisters of Forn? How long have you been waiting for their involvement so you could push your objective? Is this one of your plans?"

Grill resented his assumption of her. She had the Tokkin lands' interest at heart. "I have no plans, just a desire to see you succeed, but since you haven't been listening to me, I've been spending more time looking beyond each battle. I've been trying to get some insight into the effectiveness of your plan. You're far too defensive and suspicious of me." She waved away his accusation over the craftiness that she aspired to. "I can't imagine how much effort they put into scrying to direct this response. This is the King's full army, just as you wanted."

Tal'Abrac didn't hear anything new. "I understand that already. They have put everything they could muster on the field, but that's not your point, is it?" Grill's assessment didn't worry him or change anything. Tal'Abrac had guessed correctly that it would come to this, but this was a risky battle, and he needed to know if he was missing something.

The Determined World

She clenched her teeth. Grill spent most of her time in their travels performing the Council's real request. They wanted a way to scry about or around Tal'Abrac's actions. They, too, didn't appreciate the fog he cast during typical scrying attempts to predict the future. She had had some unusual success and had an assumption. "The point is that you are walking into a trap. They must have foreseen a favorable outcome. In desperation, any action that would let them foresee pass the battle would be seen as favorable."

"Explain that to me." Tal'Abrac stopped. Some of the men that were gathering around him, ready for his command, circled the two of them to listen. This wasn't the best place to discuss the problem since he had spent a great deal of energy convincing the men that they needed to shed their beliefs in determined outcomes and the tools of scrying. They become a more effective fighting force when they stop imagining a defined outcome or absolute purpose and start believing in the consequences of the assumptions.

"Of course." Grill got his real attention for the first time. "An example. I cannot foresee how you will perform in battle, and I cannot foresee your opponent's action because they engage you. But I can foresee them dead on the ground when you leave the field! There are limits to the time and area of your influence, and this battle may have a result where your influence has ended, and the Kingdom has won. Whenever you interact with someone, I could successfully scry for your fogging of that period. It's the difference between not seeing anything and knowing that my sight is being blocked."

He considered it for a moment. It was a clever twist that he had not heard before. It was an adaptation by the witches he would admire if he didn't loathe their desperation to scry. "That's quite dangerous." It was dangerous for his men to hear and dangerous for him to consider or believe in. "But that doesn't change what I plan to do. Such a scrying would be a guess at a half-truth designed to promote the result. If I were to be swayed by this game of scryed outcomes, then I might change and become more determinable. You are promoting an idea designed to feed their own lies. Scrying will work for those who believe in it, so any future they see doesn't include me, regardless of the outcome." He moved away from her as the men gathered to his position.

Grill knew there was nothing else to say to him. She headed out of the hustle of warriors to find a spot where she could observe the battle safely. It was her hope that Tal'Abrac was right about her fear. She didn't want to see them defeated since he had done so much to inspire the men. They learned from his example and found a new discipline to guide their actions. Instead of assuming roles and certainty, they had learned to use the opportunity of chaos. But they were new followers of Tal'Abrac's methods, and fear could easily drive them to their old beliefs. She hoped they would survive.

Tal'Abrac's army had gathered at his request without being spotted. None of them needed to be told the importance of attacking all at once. They kept a watch for any shift of the Kingdom of Garrin forces or of any sign that they were discovered. Tal'Abrac watched the flat lands as he prepared himself for the moment of battle. The bulk of men stood back a hundred feet in the forest as Kimmy stood a few paces back watching Tal'Abrac at the forest's edge.

Kimmy couldn't stand waiting. He looked up at Tal'Abrac and piped into the silence, "Tal'Abrac. Are you ready to address the men?" The battle could begin once Tal'Abrac addressed the men. This was their chance to change the course of the Tokkin people, and he was only a few feet from its director.

Tal'Abrac looked down on Kimmy, "Soon, though it would be easier if they just remembered my speeches and ingrained them. It would save time." He had taken the time to instruct his men before each battle and wouldn't skip it even though he had suggested so.

Kimmy's eyes sparkled with the purpose Tal'Abrac's guidance gave them. "We do remember, but it's great to hear it from your voice. When you say it, it sends a chill down my spine."

The enthrallment of his followers spurred Tal'Abrac to speak about his vision. There was a grand thrill in being heard and knowing they wanted to listen to what he said. This was his greatest following, and he tried his hardest not to get too self-absorbed, but he loved it. Tal'Abrac smiled and reassured him, "Perhaps something slightly different this time then."

Kimmy nodded. Everything Tal'Abrac said was wonderful to him.

Tal'Abrac spoke to Kimmy again before speaking at large. "This time, it is different. They want the promise of glory against the King's army. Today will test their resolve in chaos. Before the battle is done, many of them will fall back to their old beliefs and pray for some divine purpose." His army of Tokkin men was scattered among the trees. They waited for his word. They needed that last bit of strength to be confident and ready. Even though hundreds could not see him through the trees, they all knew where he was and looked to him.

When he spoke, the pitch was soul-stirring and reverberated in their bodies as his aura penetrated the cover and trees. Most Tokkin and relic wielders could create auras in a radius around themselves that expressed their emotion or thoughts. Their skill and understanding of what they felt limited the size and intensity. Some Tokkin could never do anything as insightful as creating an aura, while some could exclusively channel their ability into this sort of connection to the people around them. This aura let him call to them all without yelling or speaking out loud.

"This day is a day of results. We have worked toward this for many months and wanted a conclusion so badly that it would seem that this is our self-made purpose." He felt many of their hearts leap with joy, but he had baited the introduction to crush that belief. "But you know as I have told you that it was not certain. It was not written down or scryed by a witch. It was decided in our hearts, in our minds, and through our involvement in the moment. That is how we have come to this point. Do not call upon the world to write down our names or to see to victory. Our names and our victory only exist because we know the impact of our actions. We have taken responsibility upon ourselves and shouldered our own vision free of wishful desires to have this world defined for us. THEY," He directed their attention out onto the Kingdom army, "have become lost and cling to the shattered illusions. When we crush their desperate grasp on their destined purpose, they will be powerless. DO NOT SETTLE YOURSELF TO EMOTION AND FEAR OF THE UNKNOWN. NOW, SEE YOUR ACTIONS, COMMIT YOURSELF TO KNOWING THIS MOMENT, THIS CHANCE TO CHANGE THIS WORLD, AND END THIS FEARFUL CYCLE. DEATH TO THEIR VERSION OF THIS WORLD, LIFE TO OUR FUTURE. ATTACK."

The men yelled back with a battle cry, perhaps loud enough for the Kingdom's army to hear.

Tal'Abrac hoped that their battle cry was felt by the Kingdom of Garrin's army. Fear would serve this battle well. The Tokkin poured out of the forest all at once and onto the field of battle.

Chapter 6

The Kingdom's relic wielders felt the aura Tal'Abrac was generating and alerted the King, but there was little time between their feeling and when the Tokkin army emerged from the forest. All the divisions heard the battle cry and looked in the direction of the Tokkin army. There was little time to react as the Tokkin were closing the distance fast, and they would have to depend on their current formation.

The King had only moments to react hastily. "Hold the lines. The relic wielders must have a stationary front to engage. Order Medrick to start a flank to the east." The flag bearers on the ramparts signaled Fuller and Medrick. They ordered Medrick's cavalry to circle around the east. Fuller's footmen were ordered to guard the relic wielders in the initial surge time.

The order fit with Medrick's plan, and he relayed it to Kane, who led the light horse mounted men to the eastern field to take up a position. Immediately, the cavalry traveled east to prepare a flanking attack. He kept Brian close by with the remainder of the men under his command.

Fuller's footmen steadied themselves between the horde and the relic wielders. They were able to position themselves in a locked formation but had little support in the current formation. The push from the Tokkin would likely break the ranks in moments. Fuller would have his men weaken the middle of their formation as the Tokkin struck against the King's orders in the hope of protecting his men and getting the full army engaged to surround the Tokkin quickly.

Fuller's archers moved toward the northwest to gain an angle of fire since the front would start to cave quickly. They would fire as soon as they were in position and might hit Medrick's cavalry or some of the footmen when the King initiated the flanking attacks. It was easier not to think about betraying the King now that the moment to protect his own interests had come.

Antoin continued in ordering his heavy cavalry to the west ahead of Fuller's archers. He didn't object to Fuller's archers' moving northwest, but he could see the weakness in the center now that the threat charged at him. He cried out, "Skirmishers to the front. Slow their advance." There was little time for the skirmishers to do a proper job and slow the Tokkin.

The relic wielders began their long-range attacks. They leaped into the air over a dozen feet to gain a higher arc and pushed out with their destructive will. Destructive assaults from relic wielders and Tokkin alike manifested as everything violent they could conceive. The loud cracking wood, the thundering of lightning, the roar of the heat of fire, the crashing of waves against a puny boat, and the unstoppable crash of rock falling down a mountain all combined to their expressions of destruction. The rapid volley rained down on the fast-approaching army, meaning they would have to fight hand to hand sooner than desired.

The ranged attacks struck the Tokkin, and several died before they could respond, but after the first hits, the most experienced Tokkin started leaping up and throwing their own destructive blasts into the relic wielders' attacks. It allowed the Tokkin to push in faster. They couldn't win a ranged battle with archers, but they could use bodies as shields, and broken ranks are ineffective. They clashed with footmen's shields and pushed into the protection of friendly fire against the relic wielders.

Antoin never imagined anything like this rush. All the positioning and formations he could use were useless. In horror, he ordered, "Attack. Everyone attack from their position." The volleys from the relic wielders had slowed the Tokkin enough to let Antoin's skirmishers position themselves to throw at least one of the light javelins, but there wasn't time to create a line of heavier infantry. The battle was on top of him, and he didn't see himself in the third of the army foreseen to survive. His army looked like men fighting a bear with their empty hands. They didn't have the tools to win this fight.

Tal'Abrac's battle cry was heard and felt as he leaped into the mixing of footmen and skirmishers as he pushed ahead of his men toward the rampart. The rest of the Tokkin didn't follow him and were instead focusing on shredding the closest resistance. This was the longest fighting they had done, and their lack of strategic formation started to show.

The relic wielders had moved to engage where the other soldiers still stood their ground. They stopped some of the push as they matched the Tokkin in enhanced strength and speed. The hand-to-hand combat didn't require weapons since a jab or strike with a fist could create piercing hate that cuts and breaks bone. The defense slowed the Tokkin, and the arrows started to fall from Fuller's men as the heavy cavalry continued south to flank from the rear.

The lurch forward by Tal'Abrac was not followed by his army, and he stood apart from them. The pocket of Tokkin inside the human army was taking the brunt of the arrows. Tal'Abrac knew the casualties would be high, though he could see the sharp decline in Kingdom forces. Killing the King would help rout this army, and archers only had so many arrows.

Fuller and Antoin noticed that Medrick's army had ignored the order for an all-out attack and was still stationary, but there was no time to force Medrick's hand. They were all going to be overwhelmed soon.

Medrick looked at Brian. "Now, fall back with your men. We don't want any of our men in the way." Brian nodded and ordered the men to follow. Medrick dismounted and took a few paces forward, leaving his horse behind him.

Tal'Abrac was surrounded by the Kingdom's forces, who kept their distance and guarded themselves. There was no challenge to his supremacy, and he was able to dispatch the soldiers that got in his way. The rest of his army fought the bulk of footmen, archers, and knights, leaving him to reach the King and their ramparts first. They were surrounded, but they were winning easily. He laughed, thinking about Grill's warning.

Antoin looked at Medrick's forces one more time. It was intentional. "Traitor!" Antoin screamed to his guards, but no one could act on his word. He drew his sword and ordered his twenty personal guards with a yell, "Kill the Tokkin!" He pointed his blade at Tal'Abrac and hoped to take at least one Tokkin to the grave with him today.

Fuller saw the tide of the war and made up his mind. They needed to retreat and rout, but he saw the King in a position that could still be reached. He didn't have the heart of Medrick and knew he could do something to save the King. "Save the King." He ordered his personal guards to follow him as they rode to the rampart.

Tal'Abrac roared out, "Death!" A shockwave that looked like a mirage bending light around him followed his roar, throwing bodies into the air in a great display. Smoke rolled off him, and heat seared off the hairs on his skin. Tal'Abrac felt the limitations of his body to channel such power, but it didn't matter now since he had broken the final lines of the Kingdom's soldiers.

Medrick spoke to himself, "What a triumph. All of them are so close to each other." The relic wielders were overwhelmed, but what remained of their numbers outside of this battle would be needed later, and they would certainly come to serve him.

Medrick was now far enough away from his guards and army to act. This was his future now, and the understanding he had been given in the cave manifested in this moment. There was more to existence beyond what could be seen by their senses. Through his belief, he could reach out and hold those elements for moments, allowing him to play upon the rules of existence. He could erase these squabbling armies from this location for a time. A time they couldn't survive in.

He focused and began to channel his thoughts and unwavering belief to open a tear to a pocket of space that once existed before humans. No one on the battlefield had ever experienced such a space, and they would have no defense against his turning it into a weapon. He directed the blinding tear toward the King and the Tokkin. It expanded as he pushed it down upon the battle. The devouring air screamed with pain, and the earth quaked with fear. Every man that stood in its way would be pulled to it. The fighting ended at that moment.

The few remaining men of the Kingdom of Garrin's army scrambled to flee, but they stumbled over each other. Tal'Abrac's tail pulled as if to point toward the expanding pocket before he saw it himself. The edge of the space quickly surrounded them, and he had one moment to react. He pushed away from the source to the only exit that was rapidly closing. The exertion pushed beyond his body's limits as it burned his skin and yanked his bones and flesh, throwing him to safety. Others tried too, but the exhaustion from battle slowed them, and they were doomed to be entombed.

Chapter 7

The King and his men were gone, along with his most loyal vassal Lord Fuller. There was neither a Tokkin nor a Kingdom of Garrin man left where Medrick's pocket had devoured. The scar in the land was thousands of feet wide and a hundred feet deep. The soldiers of Medrick looked upon a horrific fate, glad that they had lived but terrified for their future. The fog created by Tal'Abrac had lifted on the battlefield, and Medrick grinned. One-third of the Kingdom of Garrin's forces had survived the battle.

No Tokkin knew what they were attacked with and had been consumed. But Tal'Abrac had reflex enough to save his life. He had thrown himself from the field into the forest along with his broken presence and the scrying fog that surrounded him.

Tal'Abrac limped to his feet, not aware of his senses. His sight and hearing were numb. The pain from the retreat was joined by the pain of crashing into branches and trees. His bones wailed in pain, but nothing had broken the flesh from the inside. The force he used to escape had protected him enough to live. He grabbed the closest tree for support and breathed in slowly to collect himself. When he tried to squeeze the tree with all his force, he could only pull the bark off. He had never felt so defeated and diminished.

There was no time to dwell on it, though. He slowly opened his eyes and blinked several times at the abundance of light in this small clearing. He was surrounded by the deep shade of the forest. This was not a natural clearing. The ground was dug up, and a path of trees had been broken. His fall had made this impression. He let out a groan and let himself collapse against the tree to regain some strength.

Tal'Abrac regained his thoughts as he rested. He recounted the emotions as he established control. He had seen so many manifestations and manipulations of Tokkin and relic wielder abilities, but that attack wasn't like anything he had ever encountered. Grill had been right about their defeat after all, but how could her scrying have missed something like that? He really must have been fogging up her vision. Grill was most likely already gone. He couldn't depend on her to help him now. He needed to escape the Kingdom of Garrin on his own.

Tal'Abrac started to make his way south and east since all that remained of the Kingdom of Garrin's army had been in the north in the clearing. It would keep him in the territory of the Kingdom of Garrin for the time being, so he used what strength he had to move subtly and cover his tracks.

He stuck to the darkest parts of the forest and managed to travel for two days, chancing wild game and sticking to shadows thanks to the continuous forest, but he was running out of endurance. Even the little time to clean himself and his battle-worn clothes in a stream felt like time wasted.

His wounds were not healing properly without him focusing on them. The deep gashes were still bleeding because he was moving continuously. He needed to rest and stay still, but he was operating under the assumption that he would be hunted and followed. He couldn't shake Grill's words and fears, and that made him paranoid that he might be traceable. With luck, he could find a place to focus on the wounds without needing to stay aware of his surroundings.

Tal'Abrac moved out of the dense forest and came across a crude road. It was washed out and overgrown, but it was apparent enough to only be a few years into decay. Going back into the forest meant hoping he could find a place to hide from feral animals to heal. The road meant man-made shelter, and the decay suggested people had left this area. An overwhelming wave of hungry desperation and dehydrated empathy made the dangerous option the choice. The road led north to south, so he followed it south, knowing that if he were seen on the road, it could mean his capture and death.

The road led to a village after half a day. A broken signpost read Grubein. Tal'Abrac had disposed of all attempts to hide and only focused on forward motion as death circled him. He had accepted his unwise action caused by desperation. He could live or die with the consequences. It was becoming dusk as he entered the small herd of buildings.

Everything was abandoned, and this lifted his spirits. Shrubs and the wild were retaking this land. It was so far gone that the roofs had fallen in on most of the buildings. There were plenty of hiding spots he could use to sleep and recover. Tal'Abrac moved to a house on the edge of the main cluster. He found a deep corner with the most protection inside the house and channeled himself into a sleep that could heal his wounds.

It was nearly a ghost town at this point, and all the homes and buildings in the center of town were empty, but Rachael still lived in Grubein. She had come into the town center to salvage some planks to repair her house. It was too much work to make her own building materials as well as everything else, so she felt justified taking from other people's abandoned homes.

"What would I do if it weren't for the generosity of Grubein?" Rachael chuckled to herself as she ripped a plank off from the still-protected underside of a house. She had taken up talking out loud to herself because it was the right thing to do for a 'crazy lady'. They called her crazy when she refused to leave. Such insults from the former townsfolk had kept her going for quite some time, but her loneliness was surpassing her defiance.

Rachael had a lonely routine that kept her busy. Clothes needed to be washed and mended, and the fallen branches needed to be gathered for heating and cooking. She went out to check the critter traps around her plantings. Her gardens and berry patches were the perfect lure for trapping. The tiny amounts of fur and skins were enough to keep her patched clothes from coming apart.

The routine gave her something to do, but it had become pointless. It wasn't courageous to stay anymore, and she had trouble building the courage to leave. The resentment toward her neighbors reminded her that she didn't like the prospect of new neighbors, even if she was lonely. She had trapped herself in this place. It was a prison, and she needed something to set her free. She feared it would be her fate to die here alone if she kept waiting for the world to deliver her an opportunity.

The planks she was carrying were thicker and heavier than she thought they'd be. She needed to get home before dark, so making multiple trips wasn't preferable. They fumbled from her hands, and they dropped as she pulled them. Stooping to gather them caused her eye to catch something gray that reflected blue in the nearest house. She had been this way thousands of times. It was not a normal color in any of the houses.

Marsh hounds' skin could blend with their environment, but every color around here was earth tones and never reflected blue. She left the planks and watched through the cracks in the house. Her breathing was steady and with a purpose as she took step after step up into the abandoned home. The walk to the side room was slow and heart-pounding. It was a wildly dramatic feeling, and she almost ran away, but there was a need in her that embodied her hope and fear. Everything will change now. She had seen hopeful nothings before, but this was real.

"Keep going," Rachael whispered under her breath. The gray-blue spot grew larger and more defined as she peered into the room. It was true, all true. She focused on the slow breathing form. It was a Tokkin. Her feelings snapped to fear, bypassing years of how she thought she should react to an encounter. "How can this be?" She clasped her hand to her mouth to make sure she wouldn't scream from the shock.

In the presence of another person, a Tokkin, she lost her planned dialog. She gazed, looked, and studied his balled-up peaceful form. After a few moments, she could point out his head, arms, and legs. It was good that he was asleep so that she could stare. There were some large cuts across his body. A fear that she decided was respect kept her from waking him. He was hurt, and the realization gave her the resolve to invent new plans for this encounter. Rachael walked back to her house, leaving the planks, and prepared a peace offering. A meal. It felt good to imagine the peace offering that he would wake up to.

As she prepared the meal, she fit all the pieces in her mind. Rachael made up a new story for herself without thinking. Her feelings made a new purpose for her staying in Grubein, a sacred reason she had suffered. She was here to find this wounded Tokkin and care for him. Rachael felt the fear of the unknown Tokkin, but this was the moment she needed to change everything that had gone terribly wrong in the world.

Rachael returned with the meal, even though it had turned dark. She had a torch and weapon with her this time to protect herself on the noble mission. He was still asleep to her relief. There was no plan if he were awake. It all revolved around her peace offering being accepted first. She placed the meal clearly in front of him so that he would see it when he woke up. The meal was on a plate with an elegant lid she had found left behind at the Mayor's home.

Rachael returned home to wait. He would wake up to a good meal and realize that there was a friendly person nearby. He might expect a Tokkin, but her gesture would prove her good intentions. She put a candle in the windows of each side of the house to signal her location. He would sleep through the night, but she wanted to be ready just in case he came looking in the dark. Besides, there was no way she could get to sleep now, and waiting in the dark was creepy.

By morning, she started to worry that his wounds were too severe and that he was dying, not resting. She would need to do more for him if that were the case, but if that was happening, then she had already failed. "I should have done more. Is it too late?" Rachael stood up and milled around her house, pondering the answer. Her pacing convinced her that she needed to do more, but as she looked out into the still dark morning, she could see the marsh hounds scavenging nearby.

The hounds are only two feet long, but they hunt in a pack. When they are confronted, their hair stands on end and mimics whatever's directly behind them, making the hound harder to see. She had seen them attack a rabbit before, surrounding it and catching it by surprise no matter which way it turned. She could fight a few since biting was their only attack, but they could overwhelm her.

Rachael rocked herself back and forth. It was even worse now. They must have heard and smelled her activity last night. "I should have done something. I'm such a coward. I should have protected him and stayed by his side." It was worse to think that she had contributed to his possible death. It was too much all at once, and she let herself cry. She had killed her only hope.

Tal'Abrac's eyes were open with the first cracks of light through the hole-filled walls. He saw a marsh hound nudging the protection of a covered plate with its nose. They were primarily scavengers, and cooked food was enough to attract and confuse their habits. His deep wounds had healed with the night's rest. He stayed still as he watched the hound. The plate was new to the room, and he could smell something cooked just like the hound.

The hound was adventurous for being so close to him since most animals smelled him as a threat, but this was miles away from those forests. Tal'Abrac reached out without its notice and grabbed the hound's neck. He snapped it without so much as a yelp from its mouth. He let it drop to the side and uncovered the meal without caution. It was some seasoned meat, boiled grains, and early spring lettuce. The free meal's origin only concerned him for a moment before hunger ruled. It was enough for now and sparked the thought and curiosity of the provider. The scars weren't complete yet, but he was healed enough to move and search the houses.

Another three marsh hounds had appeared at the doorway into the room and stared at him. They blended into the floor, but he could mark their eyes following him. They started to circle around toward the marsh hound's corpse as they kept their eyes on him. Tal'Abrac stood up, and the hounds scampered, digging their nails into the wood. Several other hounds broke from the perimeter of the house in mutual fear.

As he exited the house, he looked for recent tracks leading away. He could have been dead right now, considering he had slept through the delivery of the meal. The meal was probably an invitation from a cautious person, or he'd drop dead from poison in a few moments. Until that happened, he planned to thank them before moving on. He thought back to his desperation on the road and how lucky it was that his worst fears hadn't come true.

Tal'Abrac found the most recent set of tracks. There were many tracks now that he was looking for them, but they were all from the same-sized person. He followed them to a small house with foliage growing close to the sides, giving it cover. All the other houses that were nearby had been stripped and were overgrown. There was a candle in the windows on each side of the house.

As he approached, he heard crying. It was a woman crying, so he stopped and listened for a moment. It was the sort of weeping that he had heard at funerals and during tragedies. He didn't share whatever sadness she faced and dreaded trying to sympathize with her. Despite that, he still wanted to thank this woman since she earned his gratitude. He finished his approach and knocked on the door.

The crying subsided into a curious silence. There was no audible movement, so he knocked again. The silence persisted.

Rachael was petrified. The moment was upon her, and she couldn't move. She had already cried for his death, and now the knocking suggested otherwise. But she wasn't sure, and there was the faint possibility that it was someone else. There hadn't been a visitor in two years. All the wonderful and horrible possibilities raced through her mind. She couldn't move herself through the worry.

Tal'Abrac could only speculate why she didn't answer. Fear was always the number one reason, especially in matters of the Tokkin. Time could be wasted if he spent too much time guessing. He was prepared for any possibility and spoke loud enough to be heard anywhere in the house, "I know you left me the meal. Thank you. I did eat it, and I am glad you had the kindness to take pity on me." As he spoke, he paired his words with a grateful aura that could reach anyone in the house.

He may have continued to talk, but upon hearing his soothing voice, she ignored the rest of his words as she crossed the room to the door. Rachael was drawn to the speaker and wanted to be closer to the peace his words gave her. She opened the door and gave a startled pullback as she saw his chest before she saw his face. He was taller than her door.

She gave a startled yelp, breaking his speech, "I'm sorry." She responded to her startled reaction. "I mean, I'm not frightened," she looked down and away, "You're tall." The words were muddled, and her thoughts were scattered. She breathed in and looked into his face. Despite his gray skin, his face was handsome with a soft expression, strong cheeks, and a gentle smile. It relieved her fear. "Thank you... for thanking me." She blushed furiously like she was fourteen again. Rachael kept looking down at his body and noticed his tail for the first time. It was fascinating.

She suddenly realized she hadn't planned on such feelings. They were supposed to meet, and she would be an ambassador to bridge an honest and fair understanding. Instead, she was flush with fears and curiosities. He was doing much better with his side of her plan.

Tal'Abrac waited and smiled a bit, gathering amusement from the awkward reaction. This wasn't as dreadful as he had guessed it would be since she wasn't weeping anymore and not crying out in fear. He was content to let her drift around in thought.

"Come in," Rachael blurted out. "Please," she calmed her words further, "come in. I can't have a guest out on the steps." She stepped aside, and he walked in, hunching over to clear the top of the door. There was relief in his civil manners. It already proved she was right. She watched him slowly gaze around. The wounds were still visible on his body, and she moved unconsciously over to him as his back was turned. She wanted to care for the wounds and him. He turned to her just as she came within three feet of him. Rachael said, startled, "You're hurt." She recognized what she had unwittingly done by moving so close. "How can I help?"

Tal'Abrac smiled, "I can heal myself. These wounds have stopped bleeding. So all I need is rest and some food."

Rachael took a step back and looked at her storage spaces. "Yes," she said with some excitement. Those were things she could provide. "I can help you, of course. I have some more food. It's not much, but it'll last till I gather some more." She started to one of the food lockers. This was the clearest action she had taken in a while, and it now helped relieve the pressure. It felt like purpose, and she missed the feeling. "Please sit or lay down wherever you'd like."

Tal'Abrac took her at her words and moved to the third room. It was the bedroom. He hadn't had a bed in months, though he would have to curl up to fit on the length of the bed. It looked harder than the beds he was used to, but it was the only maintained bed he had seen in weeks. He pondered the situation. Here was a beautiful recluse, a vacant town, and the chance to regain the strength to make a stealthy journey east. The floorboards creaked as the woman returned to the main room. Her steps were quiet as she moved to the bedroom. He heard her pause outside the door.

Her apprehension was clear by the sound of it. Tal'Abrac knew she hadn't intended for him to stray beyond the main room. "This is the first meeting you've had with a Tokkin, I take it." He ignored the infraction into her bedroom as he came back out into the main room. She stepped back to give him space. "My name is Tal'Abrac, so that you know. It was rude of me not to announce it when you greeted me at the door, and it was rude of me to enter your bedroom."

The comment snapped her into action. He was absolutely right about the actions being rude, but she wasn't angry at him. She was still afraid and feared the reinforced stories of Tokkin raiders. She set down the plate on the table. "My name is Rachael."

Tal'Abrac explained himself. "I haven't seen a bed in a while, though that isn't an excuse for entering the room."

"Oh." Rachael's voice quivered slightly, and she did her best to think of him as just a typical person that she had no attraction to, but she felt herself melting into longing each time he spoke. "Please, eat."

It could still be poisonous, but Tal'Abrac made the thought as remote as possible. He knelt at the table rather than sitting on a chair and risk breaking it. The same consideration was given to any house that he visited.

Rachael had made herself a plate, too, and brought it to the table to eat with Tal'Abrac. It was silent but not bad, like the silence she lived with every day. This silence made her want to fill it with conversation. The silence before had made her want to hide herself away.

Her feelings for her husband and the dealings with the townsfolk were building as she sat across from Tal'Abrac. Everything bubbled up so quickly, and she wanted to tell him about all she had done waiting for this moment.

This moment was so far from what she had envisioned the day before. She bent forward and rested her chin on her hands so that he could see her desire to talk. She needed his permission to veer off her newly formed ambassador plan.

Tal'Abrac glanced at her anxious face. It was clear she wanted to say something since he had seen the look dozens of times before. He had never bothered to guess that women in both regions would have similar signals, but it would save time if he assumed the expressions matched. "Can you tell me about this town and why there is no one else here?"

It was a complete relief to hear him ask for the words she burned to say. Tears of relief rolled down her cheeks. The frustration of it all had built up for so long. She wanted to recount all her anger toward the villagers. "They're gone. They left after the Kingdom of Garrin refused to protect us. It wasn't raids from Tokkin; the Kingdom just demanded too much. No one could survive without giving more than they had to give... some women soiled the memory of their dead conscripted husbands, but I refused to do that, so I hid." She got it all out, but not nearly with the detail and emotion she had planned to convey.

Tal'Abrac asked calmly, "You were able to hide from the garrison forces?" Her words were pent-up and rushed, but he could hear remorse as she tried to explain anger and frustration at the same time. He wondered if the idea of her leaving with the other neighbors would have been preferable.

She didn't want to recount too much about that depriving time when she had to hide in little corners and dark spaces as soldiers took what they could from her house and gardens. This was about building a bridge that everyone else had given up on. They had failed, and she was proving them wrong. Rachael started fidgeting, unaware of what Tal'Abrac could see. Remembering the answer to his question hurt too much, so she didn't answer him. She wanted to bring the conversation back on course.

The Determined World

Tal'Abrac thought he may have asked a question that reminded her of a more severe trauma. He asked something less personal. "How long have the others been gone for?"

"Oh." Rachael wasn't sure if the question was right for her plan, but she could answer. "Two years?" She wasn't sure of dates, and even the few seasons made her skeptical of her own memory. "The Garrison stopped coming shortly after the town was vacated."

Tal'Abrac could see her loneliness. It seemed that she was desperate to meet a Tokkin to fulfill some sort of personal proof. "And you stayed here the whole time?" He kept his assumptions to himself.

Rachael was excited that he was following her imagination now. "Yes!" This was more on course, and it brought her mind to the point. "Everyone said it would be dangerous and that Tokkin would attack, but I, I... don't think the Tokkin are any worse than the Kingdom. And the fighting just keeps going on and on. I wanted to stay here and stop supporting their pointless war. And now that you're here, we can finally begin to put things right." She stated her mission out loud. Hope began to fill her heart. He was listening and considering her idea.

Tal'Abrac agreed with the concept since he too saw the cycle as she did, but she was sheltered, living by herself, and had unknowingly been sheltered from the real threat of Tokkin raiders that his army had pulled into its ranks. He wished he could be an ambassador of the Tokkin if she could speak for the Kingdom, but they weren't those people, and the Kingdom of Garrin had just delivered a near-death blow to the Tokkin. The question was how much of her dream he should kill. "We are just two people, and we do not represent each side of this old and cyclical conflict."

Rachael was eager to attack this point that she knew would be coming. "It just starts with two people talking and spreads from there. I might be the first to try, but it's worth the chance for peace. We can come to an understanding."

She realized he hadn't agreed to anything, so she needed to sell the idea to him first. It might be radical, so it would take a while. "Why should we keep fighting? Does anyone really remember the reason it all started? The pain I've felt isn't deserved by anyone. There should be peace, or the pain will only grow. Don't you think?"

Tal'Abrac was thinking about the safety of the village while she spoke. He was still in the Kingdom of Garrin, but the chance of a routine patrol was remote. There was no reason anyone should be looking for him here. The devastation at the battle was an alibi for his death. Her pause queued his response. He needed her help, but she was going to keep this goal of hers since she had put two years of isolation into it. "There have been merchants that travel between both areas at times, trying to promote peace and understanding as you suggest, and it has limited success, but something has always happened to break each peace. Tokkin raiders exist, and they would attack the Kingdom on their own to capture new lands or prove the power of their youth. Or the Kingdom of Garrin might have internal conflicts and blame the Tokkin, sparking another war. Neither wins, and neither is destroyed, and the scars remain. I agree with you, and that is the problem. I already tried my hand at resolving the problem, but some pain is a part of living. Fighting will always continue."

Rachael protested his placation. "Then you need to try harder." This was going to work, and Tal'Abrac needed to follow her idea. "My husband did not die just because it's always been that way. We can stop it!"

Tal'Abrac attacked her position, "Did he die defending a Kingdom village or attacking the Tokkin lands?" She had mentioned conscription before, which meant he was unwilling but still fought. Rachael could have made her stand on this issue at that time, but she waited till she had lost something personal to her.

She stared at him. The facts she assumed about her husband's death had seemed so clear in her mind, but thinking about it made her realize how little she knew. It was an assumption that he had died defending some useless piece of land far away. The Tokkin had killed her husband, but the Kingdom of Garrin had put him there. She had believed her husband was blameless, but she couldn't answer Tal'Abrac's question. There had to have been a convincing answer at some point, she thought.

Tal'Abrac's effort had stopped the tirade, and there was no reason to hurt her. "I'm sorry. You don't need to answer. You have given this a lot of thought, but there are things you don't know about the Tokkin and the conflict. I can offer to explain what many of the Tokkin feel and think. I also know a great deal about the Kingdom's actions far beyond this region if you would like to know." He could see she was just naive with her half-formed conclusion. This offer would give him time to heal as there was more than enough to explain. She seemed like she wanted to know more than was comfortable.

Everything was moving around Rachael, and she felt dizzy. "Do you know where my husband died?"

That's not what Tal'Abrac meant. "No, I was not fighting two years ago. I can't know that." Maybe she wasn't as curious about the truth, and she was just driven by an obsession to prove her pain.

Rachael just stared at the table. "It all needs to stop."

Tal'Abrac apologized for his lack of knowledge even if he had no reason to be sorry. "I'm sorry," he said anyway. All he was interested in now was cultivating enough time to rest. She hadn't asked about how he got his wounds, so she really didn't care about his reasons for being there. He just needed to keep her generous, and having an open ear would help with that.

She had expected him to say more. In the long silence, he did not lecture or scold her beliefs. He only sympathized with her and offered what he could. The moment sank in, and she felt like crying for her husband again. She was able to let go of her composure in Tal'Abrac's company. It was safe to cry, safe to sob, safe to say, "I miss him so much. Why did he die?" She couldn't understand why so much had been taken from her, and she couldn't accept the reasons others propped up.

Tal'Abrac moved around to her side while she cried. He knew he didn't want to trust her, but she seemed desperate enough to trust him. She may not react kindly to him, and touching her may cause a negative reaction, but it would build the trust she wanted to form. He moved closer and relaxed his posture to soften his image.

Rachael saw him moving toward her, coming close enough to touch her easily. He didn't attack but put his arm on her shoulder gently. The touch was perfect, and she wanted to be held. She closed her eyes and stood up from her chair to hug him. Her moment of fear was that he would push her away, but he didn't. He put his other arm around her, and she found his warmth and real touch blissful. Tal'Abrac wasn't her enemy. She held him tight.

Every feeling, every memory, and every random thing that flooded her mind, she spoke as soon as it materialized. He was cushioning all the pain as she recounted the years. She stared at nothing as she spoke partly into his chest and slightly muffled.

Tal'Abrac listened and breathed steadily. He was right about her need for contact, and this was a price easily paid. After all the fighting, it was easier to listen to her simpler troubles. There wasn't joy in the pain of another, but there was relief in sharing. She had been too hard on herself all these years. It was a course of some tragic events mixed with anger and a refusal to give in to letting go. Self-pity was an endless bottle that accompanied sorrow. There was no reason to suggest a failure on her part. He spoke after a particularly long pause with several sighs made by Rachael, "You were a wonderful wife to him. I'm sorry for your loss." There were no judgments to be cast even if he would have done things differently. She was just herself.

The Determined World

There was a small whimper from Rachael, followed by a cough. "Not according to the mayor. He said my husband left me because I wasn't a good wife." She had earned herself some structured thought after her outpouring. She had run dry for now.

Tal'Abrac understood the misguided ways authorities react to suffering. "You know that's nonsense. The mayor wasn't your husband, and he does not speak for anything but his own delusions. I can tell that you're devoted. Any time I've seen such devotion, I know that separation hurts the couple tremendously."

He was right. It was foolish to have listened to the mayor, but she couldn't ignore it. The words still hurt, but she listened to the words of a stranger. They were the only words that seemed to counteract the mayor. Rachael closed her eyes. She felt pacified and tired. "Mmm," was her only response. He was still warm.

The sound was telling, and Tal'Abrac replied. "You need to rest." It was still morning, but so much had happened in the last few hours. He began to release, but she held him tighter.

"No. Don't leave... Just stay here."

Tal'Abrac gently started to pull away from her. "You need rest."

Rachael pleaded, "Don't leave me."

Tal'Abrac shifted backward, releasing her with a force she couldn't match and held her at a distance while she looked up with regret. "I still need to heal more, and I would feel safer doing it here. So, I will not leave, but you need your rest, too." Tal'Abrac moved to a spot near the bedroom door. "I'll stay right here. I will be asleep for a while." He didn't wait for her to accept his action and put himself into a cycle of healing that would keep him asleep all day and night till the next morning.

Rachael watched him and felt guilty that he was using the floor. She laid down on her bed and tried to rest, but her thoughts wouldn't let her because

Tal'Abrac wasn't close enough anymore. She tried to sleep for two hours but eventually gave up and went out to gather what she could with the remainder of the day. He was in the same place when she returned. Exhaustion finally took hold, and she was able to sleep, taking comfort in his presence even if she wasn't in his arms.

Chapter 8

Rachael awoke the next day with a startle. The panics of yesterday returned before the comforts. She quickly got out of bed and checked for Tal'Abrac to recapture the moment. He was awake on the spot and looked up to the sound of her movement.

Tal'Abrac asked, "Are you alright?"

She found relief quickly and was overjoyed that he was there. Rachael let herself relax and fell back into her room since she wasn't fully dressed. The indecency consideration brought up a giggle, "Yes. I just didn't know if you would still be there." She was glad he was still there since it was proof that all her pain was part of a plan. He was meant to find her.

Tal'Abrac rolled up to stand and looked away from the door. "Good. How can I help around here? I need some more recovery time before I can go, but I shouldn't be your burden." He stretched and felt his recovery. Nothing was in fighting condition, but he could do chores.

Rachael's heart fluttered. "Oh." He planned to leave her eventually, but that was arbitrary, and she would like it if he spent more time with her. "It may be best." She started the sentence before thinking what would be best. She resorted to what she knew. "We should just go through my routine. I usually get an earlier start than this. Though, with your help, we should finish it all."

Tal'Abrac agreed. "Very well." He moved to the front of the main room while she continued to get ready.

Rachael thought about putting on fresh clothes, but she knew she had two more days in her current dress, according to her routine. Thinking about clothes was more distracting now. She wanted to impress him, and she couldn't help but think about what his opinion might be. His powerful, mostly exposed body parts were more distracting now as she remembered his warmth and embrace.

The routine was routine, but she had more fun doing it than she could ever remember. She giggled when she was splashed by her misfooting at the stream. Tal'Abrac had a pleasant humor about routine. Mostly, he talked about other humorous accidents he and others had in daily chores. She found it pleasantly distracting even if the distraction cost them the time they were supposed to be making up.

The food they gathered was enough for two people. She resolved to do more in the future days and not to be so relaxed about the food trapping. It was a matter of an hour before the night was fully on, and the marsh hounds would come out.

They prepared the food they had gathered that day. Rachael brought out the wine she had salvaged from the village. She only had five bottles, but this was the moment she had saved them for. It was the best she had eaten and drunk in the years since her husband died. Their conversation slid back to the more serious from the easy daytime chat. She continued to describe her life and husband to Tal'Abrac. She had gained a great deal of composure. After this day, her past seemed more distant than ever before.

Tal'Abrac felt comfortable asking her serious questions now that she had begun volunteering more painful details. "Do you plan to stay here after I leave?" He asked after she had mentioned her thoughts on setting up more traps for them.

Rachael hadn't expected the question, and it was contrary to her feelings that day. She had planned to do more with him now that he had arrived, and she enjoyed his company. There was no plan for exactly what was happening, but she wanted to hold on to the rejuvenating feelings. He was still planning on leaving, of course. When he left, there would be no point in continuing to live here, and she could return to civilization with proof that there could be an end to the fighting. She reflected with her own question to him. "How long do you plan on staying here?"

Tal'Abrac knew that kindness was what Rachael needed, and he was willing as long as it would keep him safe, but the emotional hole in her was filling with his kindness as if it were love. It could still work to his advantage, though he had to consider her reaction when he pulled away. Still, at this point, honesty would earn him the credit needed to stay in her good grace while delaying love: "I foresee three nights. By that time, I'll have enough strength to return through any resistance."

Rachael wanted to help him. "Resistance?" He didn't need to leave. The local garrison didn't patrol here anymore, and she knew of few villages to the east. "The local garrison won't stop you. They never come out this way anymore. You can stay as long as you want." Maybe the best way to fulfill her plan was to live with the Tokkin or build a home to welcome Tokkin into the Kingdom. She didn't want to be here alone, and there was nowhere else she wanted to be, but she knew that she couldn't be alone anymore.

They hadn't talked about how he came to be there. Tal'Abrac had offered the story, but she had never asked him to recount it. Knowing why he was there was an important thing to think about, but she was just feeling. The truth would help to render her 'Tokkin and Human Peace Plan' moot while keeping her as a temporary ally. He popped her bubble. "You should know that this war is over. The army of Tokkin I led was destroyed in a battle with the Kingdom of Garrin. It was a catastrophe. It was only by chance that I survived, but I believe they will know I am alive." He now remembered Grills mentioning the inverted way the witches could scry. "I must leave as soon as I can."

Rachael looked pale. "Leave? Over?" The words were contradictory to the day they had spent together. There was no urgency or paranoia on Tal'Abrac's part all day. Could there be such a grand backdrop to all this? It wasn't real to her. She felt teased by the events, and this information added to the poor hand life had dealt her for the last few years.

He nodded.

Rachael couldn't let it be true. "But," She wouldn't, couldn't, and didn't consider how or why. She only thought, "Won't," and felt like she was sinking from lack of air. She leaped for the only breath of life available. She needed to be with him. He had come to her, and this was important. "I don't care what you've been through. Since I helped you, you've proven that there aren't any real barriers between us." Her surge forward and breathlessness caused her to pant. She added, "You asked me when I'd leave. I'll leave with you when you leave." She was suddenly excited by what she was saying.

Tal'Abrac wasn't in love with her. He wasn't sure she was in love with him, but her leap to leave with him suggested the chance that she was acting on passion, or at the least, it exemplified her naivety. He mentioned simply, "I'm going back deep into my land. There's no telling how far the Kingdom of Garrin will be able to push into Tokkin lands now." He looked thoughtfully at her, and she could follow him by her own choice, but he wanted her to know what was in store. "I can't stop you from following, but you'd be among strangers, and you would feel their disdain. The hatred on both sides is equally vile."

She replied automatically, "That's fine." Rachael wouldn't deny the chance even if he had said she would certainly die. She only wanted this option.

Tal'Abrac knew she would find a new misery by following him, and she wasn't following wisdom or reason. She would end up heartbroken, but that was a problem a few days from now, and he still had a use for her. "It's your choice. I won't be able to protect you." He imagined her trying to replace her husband with him. It would be up to him to keep her only as close as he needed and leave her before entering Tokkin lands for her own safety. Using her imbalanced attraction to him any longer would be abusive, in his opinion. He liked it when people followed him for a reason, not for desperation.

Rachael experienced a little flutter of relief, and she returned to normal breath. The events fit together reasonably. "It's meant to be. You coming to this place and me being the only living soul. I just knew it was meant to be." She gazed at him loosely, but she was caught off guard by his serious look.

Her dreamy interpretation of her desperation made Tal'Abrac want to groan with disgust. Of course, she believed in existential meaning, but that she should associate him with an unbelievable belief was regrettable. He turned his back as he walked to the other side of the room and then slowly turned back as he calmed his reaction. Tal'Abrac was at war with people who put their belief in such orchestrated events, and Rachael had attached it to her daily life and his arrival.

He assumed she believed the world revolved around her without consideration. Every moment he spent with her would strengthen her belief. Tal'Abrac looked at the door. Leaving would put a stop to this, and it made staying that much harder. He needed rest, but witches or scrying and Grill's consideration about the clashing effect of him against Rachael's belief could draw attention.

Rachael jumped out of her seat as he looked at the door. "Don't go. I'm sorry, you don't have to take me with you, please." She guessed why he would act like this. It's what she said. She didn't know why he would leave unless he was afraid of what others might think of him. Rachael would say anything to keep him here. "Please," she begged.

Tal'Abrac didn't make any movement to leave, but he didn't know if it was worth his effort to explain her mistake. Her framing of events was a mistake, and her belief was entrenched and powerful. She trembled as she watched him. He wouldn't stay three days, but leaving now was still too dangerous. Another day and night would greatly increase his chances of success.

If Grill was right, then Rachael's belief could lead to the Kingdom of Garrin locating him. But if she could release her belief, then they would have nothing to reference once he left. Belief can change with the practice of a willing person, but it takes longer than a day. Still, it might help her realize her feelings and begin acting with thought. "I will not leave now, but there is something you must come to understand. Truly understand. Don't just nod your head and say what you think I want to hear."

The dazed Rachael replied hopefully. He was giving her a chance. "What?" She would do anything. He would tell her what she needed to do to stay with him.

Tal'Abrac began an earnest explanation. "It is not part of some grand plan that we have met. I see that our meeting is by chance. I think that each moment we live in is a chance to make new decisions that aren't part of a plan determined for us. Your belief is a suggestion that all the cruelty that existed up to this moment has a purpose."

Rachael firmly believed there was a meaning to her suffering. "My pain wasn't for nothing. I know that our meeting is meant to be because I have endured the course," she began to argue. It was gorgeous to feel the reward after hard times.

Tal'Abrac disregarded balancing his reaction since this was a threat to him. It was not just an idea. "I don't doubt you feel fulfilled after such hardship, but there are consequences to any belief. They bind us to see events in one way, and the way that you view the world is a threat to me." He hesitated to add the scrying theory to her understanding since it might add to the belief rather than diminish his clashing perspective with her belief.

Rachael was getting angry. She didn't know why her belief should matter to him. "What's the consequence?" She didn't know if there was more to relics and Tokkin that would put her in danger, but she was ready to face whatever needed to be done.

Tal'Abrac explained the logic as he saw it. "From what I've seen in this world, our beliefs mold and shape this world. The whole reason Tokkin exists perhaps may be because of what or how people believe. Some people are born with the ability to make their will felt in the world more than others, and those strong wills make strong beliefs. I've seen the evidence that believing in a set future makes a set future. Witches, you know of witches?" Rachael nodded yes to him as he continued, "They can scry into the future and see events, watching people that will accept their inability to accept anything else."

Rachael could accept that, and she could share his fear if he told her what she needed to do. "So, you are concerned with witches?"

Tal'Abrac smiled, "I don't fear them. Though, I do fear what it means. To have someone else determine your life. And just like believing that everything happens for a reason, my views that our moment-to-moment actions are all that determines the future has left me immune to scrying."

Rachael was amazed by this power. "Really?" If true, he must be the most powerful Tokkin to determine his own future. "Your belief must be so powerful to overcome such odds."

Tal'Abrac's shoulders sank. "No, Rachael. Belief is personal. This is the power we have over ourselves. Your own belief gives you away. The witches can scry for you. The Sisters of Forn work for the Kingdom, and the Kingdom wants to kill me. They will find me through you."

She tried to pick up on the step in reasoning but couldn't believe it. "Because I believe in a future of peace between the Kingdom and the Tokkin?" She frowned and felt defensive. If she was such a threat to him, why would he stay? What could she possibly do to change what she believed was right in her heart? "So, why are you still here? I'm just going to get you killed.

Right?"

He sighed, "I'm here because I want to live, and your compassion has kept me alive. The risk might not occur, and today, I have seen you in the moment taking every chance to make a connection between us and improve this world. You are so capable of being mindful in the moment, and you don't need the approval of a grand plan."

Rachael felt his appreciation, and he made her believe in herself. "So," she cleared her throat as the compliment swelled in her chest. "Be present in the moment and don't assume I'm part of a plan?"

It might not be needed, it might not matter, but Tal'Abrac felt like she was listening for the first time and that he was having a conversation with a follower. "There is so much that we can take for granted. Assuming a path is made for you, defining a feeling as good or evil, or choosing to believe the Kingdom and Tokkin can never be at peace, which you have challenged. You've already proved the power of your belief; keep going, and don't stop till you breathe your last breath."

She moved over to his side of the room and got within hand's reach of him. Rachael wanted to show him that she was indeed willing to challenge her assumptions. She could go further and challenge more if he could teach her. Not even her good husband had made her feel so powerful in her own body. "I can do that. Would you teach me more if I leave with you?"

Tal'Abrac reached out and placed his open hand on her chest below her neck. She didn't shy away, and he could feel her increasing heartbeat and rising breath. "You have everything you need inside you, but yes, yes I will take you with me." Coming across the room was her bridging the distance, and his reaching out was the connection he knew she needed.

Rachael was getting hot, and she decided to take more of his advice and stop judging her lust as evil. She took hold of his hand and kept it on her chest. "Sleep with me tonight."

The Determined World

There was the risk of being exposed to the scrying trick, but if she came with him, there would be no time after he left her that a witch could exploit. They still might not even be looking for him. She wanted him, and his fear of her had rapidly diminished over the day. It had been weeks since he last had companionship. The physical touch quickly pushed thoughts about her vulnerable state out of his mind. He brought up his other hand to her shoulder, and she pulled herself in close.

Rachael's face nuzzled against his chest. His daily scent was soothing to her. It was so comforting to be this close and relaxed. She gave a soft purr. "Mmm."

The softness and the purr were perfect to Tal'Abrac, and he closed his eyes. He enjoyed the feel of her pulling herself close. They both were melting into each other's needs. He moved his hands slowly on her back, massaging her tired defense.

Rachael relaxed in him. Her mouth relaxed as her lips softly parted. Her breath slid over and out as it then bounced off his chest. The warm embrace became blissful as they stayed close.

Tal'Abrac's hands searched for more of her reliance as the heat rose. His hands slowly moved down and up and past any version of a simple comforting embrace.

Rachael's hands moved and responded in kind. It felt so good to want someone and to have him so close. There was no doubt. She couldn't imagine anything better at the moment.

Tal'Abrac breathed over her forehead as he kissed it. "Rachael." He moved his hand low and lifted her slightly.

"Yes. Tal'Abrac, yes." Rachael was breathing deeply, and her body tingled with heat. She felt his size and strength and kissed his chest. "Yes." She whispered and looked up as he looked down.

He lifted her to his kiss. It was her first kiss in years, and it felt new and clumsy. Her feet didn't touch the ground, and she was soon being carried. They carried on with their kisses. She gripped over his broad shoulders and passed her fingers under the hair and across the skin. It was rougher and more traveled like a hard day's work. He gracefully laid her down on the bed.

Tal'Abrac was careful with his actions since she had been alone for so long. He fulfilled her passion and paced their encounter of trust with each thrust. It was about being close rather than finishing. The depth of the encounter and her release into him made him long to bring her back with him to the Tokkin lands. Tal'Abrac found more meaning in the moment than he had expected to find. It could have been just lust, but it was an intensity he hadn't thought to find in a small, deserted village on the border of the Kingdom.

Rachael softly woke up the next day with the memories of yesterday in her thoughts. She looked over at Tal'Abrac. He looked like he was asleep, but she didn't know how deeply. Waking up next to him filled her with promise. She smiled and hoped that breakfast would impress him. As she moved to stand, she felt a wave of fatigue that came from a night of love. The night was fresh in her thoughts as she put on the dress she had thrown on the floor last night. Gingerly, she moved around the house, gathering everything needed for the tasks. The memory of him lying next to her kept her content.

She moved slowly to the vegetable patch behind the house and considered his requirements for staying close to him. She was supposed to abandon grand meaning and claim her motivation as reason enough. It would be like abandoning an old friend after a stranger told you they were a villain. It still felt in this moment that their meeting was meant to be and had always been in her future, even if she had originally stayed on her own to be alone and depressed. It felt good to think of it as justification for all her sorrow. This was rewarding and the best thing, given all the pain she endured.

The painful strength of her husband's death jabbed at this idea. She felt it when she uprooted the first vegetable. What were she and her husband now?

The Determined World

What were their years against the moments of comfort in Tal'Abrac's arms? A sudden tear rolled down her cheek, and she swept it aside. The hole where her husband had been was still there. It hurt, but she felt the new piece of Tal'Abrac, and it felt good. She gritted her teeth and pulled another. She shed another tear that she wiped away with a dirty hand.

Rachael moved on to the hen house, which was located halfway between the village and her house. It rarely produced eggs, probably because its heavy fencing was often tested and harassed by the marsh hounds, which stressed the hens. She wondered if this would be her last trip to the hen house. She didn't dare to leave here until she met Tal'Abrac.

Questions plagued her over the history of staying, staying till death, and abandoning the little life she had as she moved forward. She didn't want to question herself so much. The last years happened because her husband died, and now, she was giving up on her years of devotion to that life. It wasn't devotion now. Looking back now made it feel like insanity, but she felt like she was betraying him, nonetheless. She needed her simple belief back. Rachael wanted to think it was purposeful again, to know what was right or wrong, and to stop challenging herself as Tal'Abrac had suggested.

The weight of her confusion was not happy or blissful. She was asking herself why Tal'Abrac's words brought her such doubt while the memory of his body brought her such comfort. Rachael asked the hens as she entered the house, "Why can't I stop feeling so confused?"

Sudden surprise pushed away the dreary thoughts. Three eggs. Never had there been so many. She smiled out loud and laughed. Her belief was confirmed, and it provided her with such a bounty. She knew Tal'Abrac was weary of her belief, but she couldn't see the purpose of caution in the face of its wonderful existence. This was meant to happen, and she refused to question it. Rachael whispered out loud to the three eggs, "I will keep it to myself. He doesn't need to know how good my belief is for him. It'll be our little secret." She tickled the eggs with her finger.

Rachael stooped out of the hen house and into the fenced area for the hens. Her sudden breath was sharp and shocked as she found a dozen men with swords and spears surrounding the hen house. She released the breath and continued in sharp, panicked intakes.

The one on the horse commanded, "What is your name, and what are you doing here?" He wore a captain's hat, but you could see his gray hair sticking out the brim and behind his head. His reddish nose and bushy eyebrows made his expression fatherly and stern. He didn't slouch on his horse, even though they had been traveling for hours. All the garrison men wore tired blue uniforms that hadn't been updated since she had seen them last. His eyes were focused on Rachael, and his intense stare drew out the wrinkles over his face.

She didn't answer. Overwhelming betrayal came down on her like a guillotine, cutting her capacity to talk. Her fear for Tal'Abrac and her coddling belief twisted her eyes, and she felt faint. She connected her irrational fears to reality. It couldn't be that her most recent thoughts and feelings brought them here, but they were here, and she blamed herself without question.

The commander asked again, "What is your name?" He waited and tried to break through her petrified gaze. "Who are you... Dear?" He pretended he was talking to a child. He kept his gaze steady and focused on receiving an answer.

She squeaked out, "Rachael," and she heard herself like she was a little girl caught in mischief. Rachael felt small and timid under the gaze of so many eyes. The longer they looked at her, the more she thought they knew. She remembered her last days and found herself believing they knew everything. It was wrong. Her transgression was Tal'Abrac, and she had betrayed him. There was nothing worse that could happen.

The commander had a small measure of patience, "And what are you doing here?" he said slowly. He knew that he might have to repeat every question for her to hear.

Rachael limited her answer so that they might overlook her treachery. "I live here." She said quietly.

He chuckled. "Live here? How long have you been here? This village had been abandoned years ago, and my troops had stopped patrolling down this way. It's not safe here."

Rachael wanted to apologize, but not to them. "This is where I've lived for the last six years." She felt sorry for being here for the last two years. If she hadn't, she wouldn't have betrayed Tal'Abrac. Her tears welled up and made her eyes misty. This fate was cruel, and she only had herself to blame.

The commander retorted, "Impossible. This village has been vacant for over two years. We wouldn't have stopped protecting it otherwise. How long have you been here?" This woman was too dainty to be protecting herself, and he would never have ordered the removal of his patrols if he knew there was someone still living here.

This was what she needed to hear. It reminded Rachael of the distasteful attitude years ago and all the reasons she hated the Kingdom of Garrin. "Protection? Your garrison patrols were just as bad, no, worse than the raids that never happened. You bled Grubein dry with ridiculous demands and constant harassment from your soldiers." She spat on the ground to demonstrate her disgust. A part of her wanted them to cut her down. She would die staying true to herself, in sacrifice for her mistakes.

The commander pointed at her. "Seize her, Everitt." He didn't have the tolerance for disrespect. "Take her back to the garrison so I can question her later."

Everitt stepped in close to take hold of Rachael. He looked like all the other soldiers except for his stupidly huge grin. It was a rare privilege to escort such a woman. He would have hours alone with her and could take his time getting back.

Rachael's stomach turned, and she stepped back and dropped her basket, breaking the eggs inside. She knew what he had in mind, and she had to fight back now. She screamed, "No, stay away from me. You won't take me anywhere. Stay back!" Rachael pulled away from Everitt, but he was quick enough to jump the fence to grab her arm. She pulled back with all her might. "No." While she couldn't break free, she continued to make an unavoidable scene.

Everitt whispered to her as he got her into a bear hug. "Come along, precious."

The commander looked down and locked eyes with her. It was easy to see how terrified she was, and it would have been easier if she had just answered him in the first place without disrespecting his command and honor.

Rachael pleaded with the commander. "Please." Her breath was escaping as Everitt squeezed. "Don't do this to me."

The commander knew all about the complaints that Rachael had echoed, and she might have stayed hidden, but he was in command. He knew the type of man Everitt was, and choosing him had made the desired effect. "Everitt, halt." The soldier stopped with disdain in his posture. "I need to ask her some more questions. So, if you answer, you won't have to go with Everitt." He gave it a moment for his words to reach her reasoning. "I know you won't run. Everitt, let her go." This would demonstrate his authority, and she wouldn't disrespect him again. Everitt reluctantly let her go.

Rachael sobbed, but knew that answers and this man kept her from Everitt. She needed this commander to take his men away. Then she would leave Grubein forever. Her voice was still wispy from being out of breath. "Thank you, sir," she needed to earn his favor. She was trapped in the hen house, and this was the only way out.

"You can call me Commander Arprot. Why are you here?"

Rachael pulled back as far as she could in the fenced area. "This is my home and was my husband's. I've lived here for years." She didn't elaborate beyond answering his question. She looked at Arprot intently, ignoring the others.

He already knew this had become a widows' village. Her story cleared up the first question. "I find it hard to believe that you've been here for the last two years, though you have a hen house and all." There was a level of maintenance that he observed now. "Since you've been here for a while, what have you seen in the last four days?"

Rachael didn't answer immediately. She looked away from him and looked around for anything else to look at. "I haven't seen anything." She breathed in deep as she tried to plan the defense of her questions.

She appeared to be more insane than a normal woman for living out in this region without protection, but Arprot had seen enough people lie to know she wasn't truthful about having seen nothing. "Rachael. You will stay with my horse and my squire as we search your village. Come with us now to the village square." He led her to the dilapidated center of town so that she would be surrounded by their search. It would also let him gauge her reaction to the buildings they were searching in.

Once they reached the village square, Arprot dismounted and handed the horse off to his squire. The young man didn't look battle-hardened or mischievous and seemed more terrified at the prospect of guarding both the horse and a beautiful woman. "Look after them both, Porsche." Arprot gave him a confident pat on the shoulder.

Porsche said with as much confidence as he could muster, "Yes, sir." His cheeks were rosy from embarrassment. But the steady gaze of his brown eyes was serious and responsible.

Arprot kept watch on Rachael, but she didn't have a strong reaction or avoidance to any building that they moved to search.

Rachael caught Everitt looking on in disgust at Porsche's lack of manhood. Everitt knew the squire wouldn't take advantage of his duty. He whispered to the other soldiers who shared his sentiment and spent most of their search taking looks at Rachael.

Rachael could accept this for now. She stayed close to the horse and provided what distraction she could. It would be ideal if she could warn Tal'Abrac, but this is all she could do to make up for her shortcomings now. It was a lot to assume a witch had found Tal'Abrac through scrying, but it was the only reason she could imagine they'd come back to the town. Was it her fault for not believing as Tal'Abrac had suggested? She turned herself over and over in her mind as she stared out at nothing, holding a respectful pose.

After an unknown time, she barely heard Arprot speak out, partly to her. "Alright. Let's move on. We need to keep moving. Madame, we'll be leaving you now, and I want you to consider leaving this place and heading back into the heart of the Kingdom. It's not safe for you here." He was sincere, and he'd rather Rachael not be a victim. They had found nothing in the buildings or at her house, and their orders required searching too large an area to dwell long here. Arprot thought about the chaos that had occurred at the battle to the north and how the thirty men he had spared for the King's hasty request hadn't survived the battle. The dozen men he had left at the fort weren't enough for this search.

Rachael caught a glance of Everitt, and her mind ran in circles of joy, but she tried to show no signs. They hadn't found him, and she could leave with Tal'Abrac now that he was safe. Her determination had pulled her through. She felt safe now, but Arprot wanted to see an obedient woman, so she replied, "Yes, you're right."

Her transition from a vitriol defender to a compliant follower was hard to believe, but she wasn't in a panic as if she had seen a Tokkin warrior. Arprot guessed her insanity was to blame for the mood swing. "Madame," He had to explain, "we are looking for Tokkin that may have headed this way. The worms are on the run from their defeat. They could end up here." He saw her unchanging expression. It was too odd.

Rachael played ignorant. "Was it a raiding party?" She wanted him to leave, but the more he engaged her, the less likely that seemed. He was fixated on her, and she wouldn't be able to keep up a facade forever.

Arprot chuckled, "No. It was an army greater than anyone they have ever attacked with, but we were victorious." He scarcely believed the magnitude and the success, but only Duke Medrick's men had survived. Still, it was a relief to say it out loud despite the casualties and loss of the King. This was the first person outside the garrison he had told, but she was also the first person they had seen. "The raids, the war, it's all over. Any remaining Tokkin in the Kingdom are being hunted down by the Duke. Sadly, the King gave his life." He added solemnly, but now was not the time to linger.

Rachael reacted. "Oh no," she replied in response to the truth about the Tokkin army and the demolishing of any peace just like Tal'Abrac had said. Her reaction fitted with the news of the King's death, but she didn't think about that. Her eyes got watery with the confirmation, and she wiped them away.

Arprot's wife had cried also at the news. It was good news, but these two seemed to reflect on the lives lost and not the outcome. He believed the raids would stop and all that remained was the Tokkin that escaped the battle. He elaborated on his role, "So you see, we have our task of routing out any remaining Tokkin."

As Arprot finished his speech, another man rode up. "Commander Arprot, are you already done with the search?" The man was in a red cloak as opposed to the blue of the soldiers already here. It was the color of Medrick's coat of arms.

Arprot bowed and replied, "Director Amber, we have finished with the search." He had met Kane Amber when he arrived at their garrison and told him about the battle and their search effort. Kane had been given the Director title to signify his command position in the temporary rule of the Duke in the face of the King's death. He took his orders directly from Medrick.

Kane ordered Arprot. "Well, if you didn't find anything, we must search this village again." He got close to Arprot and talked in a whisper. "The Duke sent a message that the Sister of Forn is certain he is here." The Duke had sent the message, but it was a lie that it came from the Sisters. Medrick could scry himself now, and the Sisters of Forn were far away in the heart of the Kingdom, but their name was a helpful utensil.

Arprot didn't want to go on the word of a witch, but Kane was his commander. "Do you know where he is?"

Kane dismounted. "No, just that he is in the village. No specifics, just that you will find him here." He had prepared himself and the relic Medrick had allowed him to use. Medrick had assured him that the Tokkin would be wounded and the scant amount of relic understanding he had would be enough for a fight. His trust in Medrick was rattled by the successful betrayal of the King, but that's why it was best to be at Medrick's side and not in his way.

Arprot yelled to his annoyed men. "Alright, men. You're going to do it again, and this time, I want four men per house. We're going to find one of those Tokkin here. Move out." The organized men stopped pretending to care and now actually looked afraid.

Kane slowly moved between the groups to guarantee the search. He had his relic in hand, but he still had his doubts. He could hold something or someone in place with his thoughts channeled through the relic, but his limited use of the relic paled in comparison to the Tokkin power he had witnessed. Only the image of Medrick rising and destroying the horde gave him faith. He had been chosen by Medrick and was certain to succeed with such a powerful leader.

Rachael squeezed a strap on the horse's harness next to Porsche and did nothing. Each of her attempts to think was blotted by remorse. They had been tracking him with scrying. It had been so close to working out in her favor. They would've left, and then she could leave, and she would be forgiven by Tal'Abrac. It felt like her fault. She could have done more than protect herself from rape. She could have lied and told them he had come through and had moved on. This was her fault.

Tal'Abrac had awoken in time to hear the soldier's coming. His strength was enough to stay hidden from them since they didn't seem too concerned with searching for him. He was able to produce an aura to help them to ignore their duty. This aura was a departure from his usual attention-getting one. Manipulating feelings of complacency and the desire not to be troubled was easier in many aspects. He had followed them into the center of Grubein but stayed out of sound range. Rachael was there, and she looked distraught but unharmed at a distance. Waiting where he was would be the best thing.

Before they could leave, he watched a man ride up on a horse. It was easy to tell the rider was a relic wielder. If he had more of his strength back, he would have heard what the rider and commander had said, but it wasn't necessary. Tal'Abrac watched the soldiers begin a second search as a result. This time, they were really looking for him, and his distracting aura would not be enough. They wanted trouble.

He needed to react quickly, but he thought about his concern for belief and scrying that plagued his thoughts the night before. They were acting like they had been given reliable information about his presence there. He blamed himself for not acting on the judgment to leave even sooner. Rachael had distracted his sense of paranoia.

Tal'Abrac had wasted a chance to run and needed to try to take them on his terms. Waiting would just make the problem worse now that they were aware. He would make something of the situation, and maybe he would escape it after enough bloodshed. The commander had stayed with his horse, squire, and Rachael in the village center as the men searched, with Kane supervising and directing.

Tal'Abrac closed his eyes to summon what strength he had, then came out from hiding. He ran toward the horse and three people. He would take down the commander first and use the horse to escape.

Arprot's back was turned, but Porsche caught sight of Tal'Abrac and let out a piercing scream. The commander spun in time to draw up his sword. Arprot cried out as his sword was knocked away from his desperate grasp. He fell to the ground, and the horse reeled up. The horse pulled away from the fight, dragging Porsche, whose hand still gripped the reins. Tal'Abrac tried to grab the horse's reins, but he wasn't fast enough. Rachael seized up and watched Tal'Abrac's sudden arrival.

The men came running to their commander's aid, but they were too far to stop him. Tal'Abrac brought down his other hand and stopped inches away from Arprot's face. He hadn't stopped himself, but not putting all his strength into the attack was a mistake.

Kane had gained a view of the fight and used his relic to bind the movements of Tal'Abrac. It was the only technique he knew with confidence, and it pushed him to his limits immediately. If he had had more training, it would have been easy, but his near-virgin standing with his relic was taking its toll. The power began to burn and send shocks of pain through his arms from inexperience.

The soldiers had come in within ten feet of Tal'Abrac, but none of them attacked, horrified by the scene and the looming threat over the Commander. They had never seen anything like this and didn't know what they could do. Kane couldn't talk through the struggle, and he was losing to the pain every moment.

Tal'Abrac roared and pulled up his hand that had been stopped so he could bring it down again. Kane had not completely bound him but had only blocked some of Tal'Abrac's movement. He would break through the weak barrier with brute force.

Arprot looked to his sides and his stationary men. "Kill him. Kill him with your weapons damn it."

Rachael was pushed aside as the soldiers all flooded in to thrust their swords. She fell to the ground and cried out, "No," but her fall muffled the words, and no one was listening to her.

Weapons that normally could have been deflected when he was healthy sunk into his torso, legs, and arms. Tal'Abrac shuddered to resist the sinking blades, but the twist of death came for him. He fought for his last breath. "Death!" he yelled loud enough to startle some of them to let go of the entrenched blades. Pride and the final dregs of power chilled his spine and set his hair on end. The power released in all directions, knocking them all down and slamming Arprot into the ground by an inch. Every soldier, Kane, and Rachael was pushed and held themselves with the pain of the shock wave that echoed from Tal'Abrac. His body then slumped down on top of Arprot.

Each soldier was slow to rise. They had to roll Tal'Abrac off Arprot and help him since his ribs were cracked. He could barely breathe but had survived the blast. Rachael curled herself to the ground. The pain, the sorrow, the pointless suffering that was her unwitting belief consumed her. She wanted to be free, but she trapped herself in her own mind. She started rocking herself and holding tight until the pain and breathlessness caused her to black out.

Arprot was being held up by two of the soldiers as Porsche negotiated the shaken horse back to his commander. He looked down on Rachael's unhinged form. "Take her back to the garrison." He said it to no one in particular, so a soldier moved forward to obey, and he snapped to awareness, "No," Arprot corrected himself, "Porsche, take my horse and ride back with her. When you are there, you are to bring her to my wife and let her care for her until I return. Is that understood?"

Porsche whispered, "Sir, you're hurt, though."

Arprot knew Rachael wasn't as strong as she needed to be to live out here anymore. "Don't argue, boy. Do it." She needed to be cared for. He knew his wife would agree.

Porsche nodded and resolved to fulfill the order without fail. He brushed the dirt off his wounds from being dragged by the horse. The men placed her on the horse, and Porsche brought her back to the garrison ahead of the soldiers.

Chapter 9

Rachael blinked at the draped window and listened to the conversation outside her room. She couldn't remember arriving here, and her consciousness was faint. It wasn't clear if she had willfully ignored the world around her or if she had been damaged in some way. She had heard things and seen things happening around her, and it had all been useless. As the memories returned, she found hope that if she lay here long enough, despair would finish her life.

A familiar man's voice spoke just outside the room she was in. "She has not moved or left the bed for three weeks now."

Rachael had heard the voice before, but she listened to what he said this time. The three weeks was the first mention of time she recognized. She should have been dead after three weeks of waiting for an end, but a tiny spark of caring about herself had returned. Where was she that she would not be dead by now?

Rachael had been numb to everything outside of her broken life, but she remembered seeing two women in her room. They came in to feed her. The young, homely, and ragged one would change out the chamber pot. The older, pristine, and proper one would talk to her and always open the curtains to the blinding light. She didn't care to remember anything the women had said at those moments.

Part of what she now thought about was the voice of a man asking questions and wanting to overhear the conversation.

The man asked, "So you think she was raped?"

The woman's voice returned in a lowering tone, "You'd need a surgeon or even a witch to know for sure. I hadn't thought to check weeks ago, but there's been no sign on her garments that she isn't pregnant. Abey said she has seen no signs either."

He paid no attention to the woman's hushed tone and spoke loud enough for Rachael to overhear. "So she could have been raped. And she's... she's not right anymore, Margeret. Her time out there, or that attack, broke her. We'll have to contact a witch and see if there is anything to be done."

Margeret raised her voice to a whispered shout, "No, Thomas. You know how I feel about them. A witch would make things worse. They always ask the most absurd prices."

He replied, "I know, I know. But our surgeon is horrible; I can attest to that firsthand. Regardless, it's been weeks, and I didn't take her in so I could care for a cripple. She's a burden, and this just can't continue."

She agreed, "Yes. I'm tired of her lack of effort. A person can only take so much, but I was hoping she would have listened to me and found her way back to sanity. I thought having lived in the wilderness all those years would have made her stronger than this."

He spoke again, but Rachael could hear him moving away. "Whether or not that's true, it doesn't matter now. I have to get back to my duties." The continuing voice of Thomas was unimportant now.

Rachael thought about their conversation. They were right about the timing and the chance that she could be pregnant. She tried to add up when she had bled last and when she had made love with Tal'Abrac. The image of Everitt came back to mind and being raped while she was comatose wasn't outside of chance either. The painful memory of Tal'Abrac's death cry came back to her exhausted reality.

Had she been raped while in this room or found love with Tal'Abrac? Had she been damaged in some way? She held her stomach to think and connect, but only the memory of the clenching pain returned. She had fallen to the ground and felt the pain that damaged her. Pregnancy from Tal'Abrac seemed preferable since it would give her a chance to honor him. She had lost her love, but this would be her hope.

The wish was soft and fearful. Rachael had found a reason to get up: a child. It was not useless or pointless like anything else she had been through in all these weeks. She could not stay in this bed to wait for death. She moved her hand to feel her heart beating for the first time since it shattered. It was there, and she held it there to feel its wonderful beat.

Rachael pulled the tucked-in sheets and moved to get up. Her limbs were not in collusion with her heart and mind. These limbs needed to be woken up. A new type of pain pierced her, but she didn't cry out. Her eyes watered as she worked. These were tears of struggle, and her determination felt good. The physical pain and her hope blotched out her suffering and sorrow. She was alive again.

The green walls swam and shook with each push toward mobility. She set the goal of pulling back the curtains herself. It may have been a lofty goal, but it was the one she chose. Her first attempts to stand were wobbly, and building her confidence required all her attention.

Rachael reached the window before anyone came into the room. The thought of someone coming in and coddling her back to bed was pathetic. She had to get this done before anyone saw her. It would be very satisfying to see herself in front of the window looking out at the unknown outside. The mystery of it would surely be a letdown, but the excitement in the unknown was real.

She pulled back the curtain and revealed a sunlit courtyard. The dirt courtyard was more of a square as she looked at the surrounding buildings. Looking down and around, she found that this two-story house was separated from the plain wood buildings. Soldiers came and went. This must be the garrison, but this house was set apart from the main buildings.

Rachael pulled her eyes away from the activity outside and examined the green-walled room. There were two colors of green striped through the hanging sheets. The side of the room she had come from had the nicest bed she had ever slept in. The wooden posts and headboard had been carved with an elegant pattern. The rest of the room was furnished in the same style and expense.

She imagined the extravagance of the rest of the house if this was the room she was kept in. She would take in the rest as she searched for her caretakers. The familiar male voice must have been Commander Arprot. This was his house, and Margeret must be his wife. Her mind had regained momentum with her movement. She thought of the conversation she had overheard and acknowledged their burdened sentiment.

Rachael made her way to the door by waddling and keeping her legs mostly straight. Her knees weren't ready yet. True walking required more balance than she could afford at the moment. The door opened without a sound, and she looked for the correct direction. Luckily, she heard two women's voices and saw the staircase at the end of the hallway. The hallway had a few paintings, and wallpaper had been afforded for these walls, too. She marveled at the embroidered staircase as if she had never seen stairs before. She took generous utility of the railing as she climbed down.

Rachael paid less attention to her surroundings as she approached the voices. Her anticipation for their reaction was distracting. More attention needed to go into her movements as she had to brace herself against the wall. She passed into the rear of the house if the front had been facing the courtyard she had just looked onto. She pushed open the door and entered part way, staying in the doorway into the kitchen. Margeret and Abey stared at her and stopped their conversation. "Hello." Rachael held her breath after the greeting. They were taken by surprise.

Abey remained shocked, but Margeret replied, "Hello, dear." She beamed at the wonderful sight of Rachael. It relieved her so much that Rachael wasn't in bed. She imagined the well-placed conversation between her and her husband had had its effect. "Your name is Rachael. Correct?" Margeret was in her forties with blond hair pulled back into a bun. She had a deep crease down the center of her forehead and shapely eyebrows.

Rachael replied, "Yes." Her face was flushed from the attention and the effort of moving. She needed to express herself. "Thank you for," she pieced together her gratitude, "three weeks of what must have been a pain for you." She smiled, though a large smile hurt a bit.

Abey smiled with Margeret as they received the truth. "Welcome back, dear," Margeret said as she put down her cooking and came over to hug Rachael and bring her into the room to sit down. Abey carried extra weight and had her tan hair tied up much like Margeret's. She took a bite of the food she was preparing before coming over to greet Rachael. Her cheeks bumbled as she chewed the food quickly.

Rachael saw how pristine Margeret's clothes were and recoiled. "Oh no, I'm filthy." But she was hugged by her regardless.

Margeret replied as she hugged Rachael. "We can easily fix that. You just need a proper bath." She let go of Rachael and took her over to a chair. "Abey will draw up a bath while you have a seat." Abey left to start preparing the bath water. "You can sit here while I continue to cook."

Rachael needed to make clear that she would repay them for their care as Abey was out of the room drawing the bath. "Mrs. Arprot..."

"You can call me Margeret, dear."

"Margeret, thank you. I can only imagine how much of a burden I've been. I will repay you." Rachael lowered her head to show her submission to any labor that could repay the debt. She wasn't afraid of hard work, and she preferred to put her hands to work since she knew it could bring her peace of mind.

Margeret didn't act surprised or delighted by her answer. She had expected it, and she was glad Rachael was now meeting her expectations. "Of course." She patted Rachael's hand to accept the invitation for repayment.

After her bath, Rachael helped as much as she could with the cooking. They cooked many of the midday and evening meal items for the garrison in addition to an appointed male chef who fixed breakfast and the bulk of meals for the soldiers. As the evening drew in, the tentative conversation over the decor died out in anticipation of Commander Arprot's return.

Rachael followed Abey's instructions to set a proper table. Abey instructed Rachael to put her plate setting in the kitchen but told Rachael to ask about her own place setting. Kitchen or dining room.

Rachael asked, "Margeret, where should I set my place?"

Margeret chuckled to herself. "You can set your place on the other side of Commander Arprot. We will be discussing your offer to repay our hospitality." It was darling that Rachael should ask. The girl truly was lost and looking for direction.

Rachael wanted to show them the respect they had earned. "I should address him as Commander Arprot?" She didn't blame the Commander for what happened to Tal'Abrac since she already had herself to blame. The Commander had brought her to his home and protected her when she fell. Now the Commander was her best chance to recover her strength. If she was pregnant, she would need even more assistance, and she planned to work for that too.

Margeret confirmed Rachael's assumption. "Yes. He will let you know if he wishes to be called something else. Oh, and you needn't compliment the furnishings." She had grown tired of talking about such mundane things. "Those were all my choices, and some he wasn't in favor of adding."

Rachael worried that all her questions had worn out Margeret.

The Determined World

Margeret continued, "You probably won't have to offer any questions. My husband is direct and will ask you enough to fill an entire evening." She finished, lazily guessing her husband's questions would drown out a pleasant meal.

Rachael thought this would be the case and was willing to answer. The commander deserved answers, but she was afraid of the questions surrounding Tal'Abrac. She didn't want to lie, but full disclosure could cost her the safety he was providing. It was still unclear to her if she was pregnant, and discovering the father before the birth would not be easy.

The three women were in the kitchen off the dining room when Thomas entered the house. He spent his lunches with the men but always dined in the evening at home. Abey excused herself to attend to the Commander's boots and jacket.

Margeret wanted to show her husband that she was right about Rachael. Rachael had recovered, and she could gloat through her presence. Acting naturally would make her point. "Take a seat, dear. I don't need a surprise party in the entryway." Rachael sat as Margeret went to her husband and ushered him in. She didn't tell her husband that Rachael had come to her senses. This would be a nice, quiet way of proving him incorrect.

Arprot entered the room in front of his wife and saw Rachael sitting there. An inquisitive look spread across his face. He didn't know at first if she was being propped up with sticks or if she had made a recovery since their conversation that morning. "Good evening, Rachael."

"Good evening, Commander," Rachael replied.

Arprot smiled and continued on his path to his chair. "Ah, good. You are actually aware. I was wondering if my wife had dragged you down here and propped you up for effect." He moved to sit at the head of the table, and Margeret moved to the other side, facing Rachael.

Rachael agreed and was prepared for any jabs at her. She didn't expect sensitivity. "Yes, I am here under my own power." Rachael wanted to jump right into the depths of her repayment, "and I heard the conversation. You're right. I have been a burden, and I'm going to correct that now."

He showed no emotion to her reply since he was still thinking about how his wife had been correct. Rachael was aware enough to understand their planted conversation. Arprot replied, "I see. Is that all it took? Overhearing that conversation? I would have tried it two weeks ago if I had known." He would have tried it sooner if Margeret had bet him sooner.

Rachael didn't find any praise in her commitment to him. He had been focused on the debt she had accumulated and not on the repayment. "Thank you for helping me. I don't know what would have become of me." She wanted him to acknowledge the good nature of what he had done. It hurt her to be thought of as a burden without him recognizing her humility.

After the quickest of glances at his wife, he replied, "You're welcome. I'm sure you've thanked my wife." He realized Rachael was back to being a normal person seeking approval. She would need to build up his approval more before he came out and said it. "But now, Abey," he called. Abey brought the first course, and they began to eat. When Abey brought the second course, the Commander had formed the most obvious of questions. "So, do you agree with our conversation? You too think you may be pregnant?" He didn't care anymore why she was in the village by herself. He was concerned about what he had brought into his house.

Rachael had her answer ready. "There is a chance that I am pregnant since it has been three weeks without certainty. I can't be certain if something is wrong."

Arprot sat back and pointed around and gestured with some pain from his cracked ribs, "There was a time before I came out here that I needed delicate conversation, but this is the frontier of our land. So, answer me directly. Were you with a man or did that Tokkin rape you?" He stared Rachael down, and

The Determined World

Margeret tried to stay unresponsive, but she cringed at every blunt word.

Rachael replied with a version of the truth. "No. There was no man and I wasn't raped. I do remember the Tokkin attacking you and me and that horrible wave that pushed us all. The pain was so bad I've started wondering if it damaged me." She looked into his eyes as convincingly as she could. It was true but didn't contain her feelings. With the facts of the situation, he might draw his conclusion in her defense.

The Tokkin's attack was questionable. He had experienced the pain too, and it had broken bones. She had reacted so sharply to his soldiers claiming their abuses that he wouldn't guess she'd be casual about the rape by a now-dead Tokkin. She could still be false or true. For now, she was not dangerous to him. "Yes. There was damage to everything around him, and maybe these last three weeks were caused by that Tokkin's attack. I will have to keep my ribs wrapped for weeks more. And it may take weeks more to know your condition."

Rachael quietly affirmed, "Yes." She had successfully quelled the risk.

Margeret felt it was the right time to focus on the positives. "Rachael has asked to repay our care through her labor and service to us. I," she paused so she would have his full attention, "have agreed that she should repay us, Thomas."

He chortled. Looking at his wife reminded him of a chess match. He loved her perseverance even in her assumption. "Very well." He needed to clarify that he could say no if he wanted to. It just so happened that he wanted to get paid back and that he had the latitude to get what he wanted. "Though, if the war were still on, it would be a definite no, but the current situation allows for it."

Rachael asked out of turn, "What is the current situation?" but she had been unaware of the surrounding world for so long. The social mistake didn't occur to her until they both looked at her with raised eyebrows. It was almost like they had practiced synchronization.

Thomas cleared his throat and explained why he would let her stay. "You need to wait to speak in turn, Rachael, if you would like to repay us through service," but he needed to correct her disrespect before he began. "For us, the border garrison forces have been given a huge influx of supplies so that we can secure the territories that we protect. I am receiving forty men to replace those lost in the battle, so there will be plenty to do around here, and we have room for you."

She apologized for her interruption, seeing that she was not supposed to be their equal. "I'm sorry. Thank you for the explanation." It was taking every ounce of her concentration to keep track of her new position. She didn't believe she was a rude savage, but she knew she was in the presence of company like her former mayor. Arprot must believe respect comes with his position and not through his actions.

Thomas nodded. "I'm sure you'll learn." He left his comments at that and continued to eat.

After the pronounced silence, she decided it was her turn to speak. The Commander had explained himself, but he didn't explain why the circumstance existed. "Commander, if I may ask, what has happened in the greater Kingdom of Garrin beyond the garrison?"

He studied Rachael's question. She knew nothing of the recent weeks and the past years. It could turn into a very long explanation, but he felt that he had her full attention. "Duke Medrick is staged to become King. Since the end of the war, he has been organizing the remaining forces. Without his support and direction, we could have fallen into months or years of chaos." Thomas wasn't thrilled about the Duke's rise to power, but he did admire the stability the Duke had enforced.

Rachael thought that with the stability and the influx of supplies, they were planning to continue fighting eastward. "So the Kingdom of Garrin plans to attack the Tokkin lands?"

The Commander was pleasantly surprised by her questions. They weren't knowledgeable, but they were relevant. This question followed the subject he was interested in, while his wife mastered questions designed to change the subject. "That would be the wishful thinking of some, but the situation is more fragile than I stated. There are several nobles besides the Duke taking advantage of the situation. All of them want to be King and with the death of King Antoin's sons the right of kingship becomes political."

Rachael gawked at the death of the sons. She knew that King had two sons, but they would only be fourteen and six at this point. "What!?" She couldn't imagine a reason the boys should have met an untimely death.

Thomas nodded, knowing the suspicions, but it was not his place to throw around conspiracies. "Yes, there was a fire hours before the battle even took place. I imagine the King didn't receive word of it in time, seeing how far he was from the capital. With no direct heir to the throne, I feared that the Kingdom of Garrin would be ripping itself apart, but the Duke has managed to keep the remaining soldiers of the Kingdom of Garrin under his command."

Thomas continued. "With everyone declaring their right to the throne, he is the only noble acting like he is a King, maintaining peace and asking for time to resolve the disputes. It's the best thing that could happen in the worst situation." He didn't see how the Duke could maintain control while he was so hated by most other nobles. He might not have taken orders from the Duke himself, but he continued to receive reasonable orders and supplies from Medrick.

Rachael assumed that the Duke probably killed the King's boys. "So, the Duke is in charge?" It was easy for her to be suspicious of the man and his improbable luck.

Thomas understood the incredulity but carried on in his best interests.

"His orders are the ones I am following. Five other nobles have tried sending me orders about moving my garrison to their keeps, but the Duke is the only one sending supplies with the orders to protect the land we have. Personally, I agree with his desire to secure and maintain the land we control, don't you agree?" He asked for her agreement because he didn't need to share her suspicion.

"Oh." Rachael couldn't un-imagine two children being murdered. She couldn't appreciate the Duke's actions as the Commander did with the Duke's guilt in suspicion. She wanted to ask who killed the boys, but Thomas had already drawn away from the topic once. It was pointless to ask with so many nobles to suspect. Arprot had an opinion and wasn't looking to have it changed.

Thomas brought up the events relevant to her. "This is why the situation allows a second servant. The funds are available, though your service will extend beyond the house and into the rest of the garrison."

Rachael accepted a range of services matching his description when she accepted the idea of repaying them. She would have the Commander's protection, but she would be at the service of the garrison. "Yes, that's fine."

Margeret clapped in agreement. "I'm glad you can repay your debt, dear." She smiled at her husband. She was glad to see the conversation easily turned back to a subject she felt comfortable with. She could influence her husband toward kindness, but it was limited in the aggravating moments. "I don't think the timing could have been any better."

Her comment stirred and reminded Rachael. She thought of her own belief at that moment and questioned Margeret's assertion. There felt like an obligation to do what Tal'Abrac had asked and doubt the assumption. She instead pulled herself to the opportunity of the moment. "Yes. So many other disasters could have happened." She didn't mention all the good things that could have happened as well. "But I like our arrangement, and I will not forget why I am here." She wanted to move forward without forgetting herself, and she needed to believe she, too, could create the future in the present moment just like Tal'Abrac suggested.

It was a whimsical comment, but the Commander didn't disagree. "You'll be less likely to repeat yourself then, good." He didn't have any other praise for the thought. It was the responsibility of each person to learn from their past.

She nodded as she closed her eyes in respect and bowed her head. "Thank you, Commander."

The question about her pregnancy was answered after another two months. Rachael knew before it could be seen. She felt strains that she had never felt before that were identified from other women she had known in the past. Out of respect, she told her host that she was pregnant. She wanted to believe that Tal'Abrac was the father.

Thomas did not push her to confirm or deny the possibility. The attack in Grubein had set his mind that Rachael had been manipulated by the Tokkin, but she was a victim. There were measures he would take, but for now, he was far too busy receiving envoys from nobles and attempting to keep stability at an expanded range as the Duke had requested.

As Arprot had promised, her chores extended beyond the house. The wooden walls and barricades were her borders. Her proximity to the soldiers was a nuisance. Her service to the Commander kept the fabricated stories to backroom fantasies and away from any physical assaults.

The cat-calling soldiers would flirt with her and claim to have access to the local wench. She got to overhear all sorts of tales about her promiscuity. Fresh stories about Rachael's mystery had replaced older, tired ones about Abey's role as a fantasy harlot. After four weeks of service, every man claimed to have had an encounter with her.

Her own fabricated story for the future sprung from their fantasies. When she started showing her pregnancy, the stories of wild sex dwindled as each man distanced themselves from fatherhood. It was too late for any of them to deny what they said, so they stopped embellishing. Rachael could easily claim any of them as the father when she left this place. She needed a plausible story six months from now. The story would be useless here if the child was Tokkin. Non-Tokkin can have a Tokkin child, but the truth of Grubein would draw a hostile conclusion.

Each day, Rachael would wake up and focus on Tal'Abrac's words. It was hard, just as she had predicted. She had trouble changing her beliefs. She could say it to herself, but practicing it required constant attention to her assumptions. It wasn't easy to doubt her first reactions, but the reward meant that she felt more in control of her life. Rachael felt more prepared for uncertainty than ever before. That made any looming consequences that much easier to bear.

On one occasion, Abey had been scolded for forgetting clothes out on the line during a sudden rain shower. In Abey's defense, Rachael claimed that she saw the clothes and could have brought them in before they had gotten too wet. She apologized for the incident in the face of Abey's mistake even though her feelings were telling her to hide and let Abey take the fall. Thomas claimed it was Abey's responsibility, but Rachael explained, "I'm not sure I believe in sole responsibility, Commander. I could have done something." He didn't argue the point and spared Abey's punishment while telling Rachael she could clean up Abey's mess.

Rachael believed that this was what Tal'Abrac meant. She paid more attention to her role in everything and every decision and didn't jump to her first feeling or reaction. It was a new way to feel when everything seemed beyond her control. Abey seemed to appreciate the shared responsibility even if the Commander saw it as a failure of organization. But it wasn't about opposing the Commander's vision or saving Abey from punishment. It was about what she wanted to believe. Tal'Abrac had believed it so fervently that she knew it should be passed on to his child. She was honoring him by doing this.

Rachael remained true to her post and continued working until four weeks before she expected to give birth. Thomas gathered Rachael and Margeret to inform them of his decision. He had put aside his curiosities about Rachael's child since he decided he would send her away before the birth. They sat in the comfortable parlor that evening as Thomas prepared to give Rachael her new assignment. Rachael was glad to be off her feet for the rest of the day.

Thomas arranged the two in front of him so he wouldn't have to look from side to side. "Each of you knows that King Medrick has begun reorganizing the Kingdom of Garrin after his coronation. For the last month, he has been removing my personnel and adding replacements. Subordinate Commander Phillips is an example of one of those arrivals. I've been informed that those moves were just the first in the King's vision. It appears that my work as the Commander of this garrison has not gone unnoticed. I'm being promoted to the Commander of Willbington."

"Willbington!" Margeret was shocked with glee, "That's fantastic." Willbington was a short distance from Garrin. Many Willbington garrison Commanders had been promoted to Garrin, the Kingdom's stronghold. "I'm glad that all the orders you took these past months are to be rewarded. I mean, what if he hadn't become King?" She was so relieved that she forgot her own rule about commenting on Kingdom politics.

Thomas smiled. "We'll most likely run into many of those nobles at my new post, Margeret. We do not have control of such politics, but an organized and prudent commander is always desirable." He downplayed all the second-guessing he had done and the stress he had felt. Rachael didn't know the difference, but Margeret had noticed her husband's pains. "I have done most of what the Duke, now King, asked. It was the wisest thing to do, and we have earned this reward, Margeret."

Margeret fidgeted with excitement. "Yes." She had become relieved when Medrick became King and now could smile for the road her husband had traveled. She relaxed in her chair and dreamed about the reward. They deserved it.

Rachael was slightly concerned. "Congratulations." Her participation or role was not addressed. She was going to be affected by this news and began to wonder how she was going to be treated. She couldn't imagine staying at the garrison without the Commander and his wife. "That's wonderful news. Then I guess you won't be needing a pregnant garrison servant?" She grinned slightly over her absurd description.

Thomas said with a nod. "Yes." It was easy to address sensitive subjects with Rachael since she volunteered them before she was asked. "You've kept a good pace with the work despite your pregnancy, but we will have no need for you in Willbington. Your time has repaid any debt you had to us."

Rachael nodded graciously. "Thank you." She accepted his judgment and agreed that enough time had passed. There had been some fear that he could never believe that she had repaid his kindness since he didn't forget her mistakes easily. Thankfully, his good news put him in good spirits. It would be a relief to her not to be a servant for him anymore.

Thomas turned his attention to Rachael's stomach, which his wife was looking at in sadness. "I understand you have rebuffed the idea of a witch to scry for the birthday?"

Rachael nodded. "Yes." She didn't feel a need to explain. She needed to be done with the witches' domain. Let them look if they wanted, but she wouldn't draw attention to herself by seeking them out.

Thomas continued. "We move in one week and will be traveling for four more." His wife was still watching Rachael. None of their children had ever made it to birth, and he knew his wife would love to see Rachael's baby being born. The miscarriages had broken his wife's spirit for children, but she had steadily become more anxious to act as a Nana. Thomas addressed Rachael but watched his wife closely, "While you are welcome to come, we may be on the road when you have your baby."

Rachael was shocked, and Margeret gasped at her husband. Margeret had not expected this from him. He had expressed his belief to her that the baby would be Tokkin. Despite that, she wanted to see the birth of the child, but such an offer in the face of a Tokkin birth could ruin his career. "Thomas, are you certain?"

Thomas didn't want Rachael to come and needed to be clear now. He loved his wife, but he couldn't let there be anything left uncertain. "Rachael, if the child is Tokkin, there will be no protecting you, and I will protect my family if I am questioned. You will be in the heart of the Kingdom of Garrin, and it will end badly."

Rachael sighed in acceptance, knowing that she could never accept his offer. "Yes, I know." His accusation was her hope, and she didn't want to hide her belief. "You must protect your family and position. I won't come with you."

Margeret didn't know Rachael was that comfortable with the likelihood that her child would be Tokkin. "Rachael." She wanted her to rage against the Tokkin and offer an alternate story, but she had to accept Rachael's resignation of the facts. She couldn't help but feel tricked by Rachael's acceptance. The culmination of all her charitable thoughts to this point made her feel used. "Do you want it to be a Tokkin child?" There could be no other reason Rachael wouldn't want to travel with them.

Rachael had felt loved by them despite what they may think of a Tokkin child. "Margeret, I love you both so much, and this birth is something I worry about too. If I had spent all my time worrying about the chance, it would have destroyed me." Her resolve was unchanged by Margeret's horrified look. She didn't destroy Margeret's hope, but she was close. "I can't be certain. Tokkin or normal, I must be cautious and protect myself and you." It was odd. At that moment, she felt like telling them the truth, but she doubted that first impulse and allowed them to keep their assumptions. Was this a moment where she should set them straight, or was that her old beliefs talking?

Margeret protested to her husband. "Thomas, we can't just leave her here. We have to help her." Her husband's nod to Rachael and Rachael's peaceful acceptance of a dangerous birth was too callous for her desire.

Thomas stated, "We aren't leaving her here." Margeret sat on the edge of her seat, poised to stand and fight. Rachael watched him in curiosity. He had planned for this. "I wouldn't leave you here for a garrison surgeon. The best option is for her to head to one of the asylums. We will be providing transportation for her. She won't be alone for the birth." He directed his words to his wife. He believed Rachael would accept it. "I know they will take in a woman who does not have a husband. It's common enough."

Margeret looked at Rachael to check on her approval. "Is that all right, dear?" It meant compassion for Rachael, even though it tore at her own desire for children. Asylums all had their creeds and routines that could look crazy if judged hastily, but they provided refuge for those who were lost or needed to be out of the public. They either took mints, the precious metal currency, as payment or labor if the individual was down on their luck.

Rachael approved of the idea. "That's more than I would have asked of you. Thank you, Commander." It was easy to humble herself given the situation, but he could have offered more. This entire ordeal could have been much worse than it had been. She had gotten what she needed to live, and her time serving the Commander had given her a story to recount when people asked about the father.

Margeret wasn't satisfied by the distancing of her husband's offer. He should do more. "We can do more, Thomas. Is there anything else you need, my dear? Perhaps some mints?"

Margeret's offer of the currency didn't impress Thomas. He eyed Rachael's response. "She doesn't need any additional mints, Margeret. The cost of the asylum will be paid, and that will meet any need she has." Arprot talked down his wife's desire to share his future payments from the Kingdom.

Margeret watched Rachael's face. She realized what she could personally do. "I know, you should have a letter of reference. You served us loyally these last months. A letter of reference will help you if you ever choose to serve again. You can get a much better position with one, especially one from the wife of a Willbington Commander." She rambled off the brilliance of her sudden idea. Thomas liked the idea since it kept their distance from whatever might happen to Rachael going forward.

Rachael hadn't considered working after the birth since she believed she would have a Tokkin child, and she would have to flee the Kingdom of Garrin. "That would be wonderful." It might come in useful if the baby wasn't Tokkin. The resolution suited the Arprots, and Margeret made a letter of reference for Rachael. So, it was settled that she would travel to the asylum to continue her pregnancy.

Chapter 10

Rachael traveled to the asylum before Thomas and Margeret moved. She was close enough to term that waiting for their departure could mean birth in transit. Traveling at her stage was more dangerous each day she waited. She wanted a safe birth, and an asylum would be more understanding of a Tokkin baby this close to the border.

Asylums offered sanctuary to individuals who wanted or needed to pull away from normal society. They were sponsored by nobles through the use of land and the mints that arrivals donated. Most of them were closer to the border since most people didn't want to associate with the oddities. It meant they were built like forts to protect against raids but had no soldiers guarding them. It wasn't uncommon for nobles and common folk of the Kingdom to think of them as prisons run by insane prisoners.

The asylum she was heading to did not look upon witches kindly. Asylums posted their beliefs and creeds for all who were interested. They expressed their attempt to understand the world through hard work, eating only meat, extending the definition of family, or attempting to write phrases over and over to make them true. Each had its own obsessions that extended in new directions. Everything outside the asylum already had its definition of the world, and the asylums wished to find a path outside that system.

Rachael was glad to avoid witches. She favored Margeret's opinion that witches profited from what should be a woman's sacred duty as a wife and mother. The witches were responsible for the death of Tal'Abrac, in her opinion. She felt less responsible for his death today, but she still saw the enemy in her old beliefs. They guided the blade, but she had been their beacon.

The carriage ride was three days to the asylum and passed uncomfortably and sickly. The roads were not well maintained, and there was no real way to relax. She had little faith in the carriage driver's ability as she imagined him intentionally hitting every hole and bump. He must have been trying for speed since he required extra for the risk of her pregnancy but denied any responsibility if something should go wrong.

The asylum was the Sisterhood of Quiet Dawn. They were all women, and they welcomed her as they do for all wayward pregnancies, but they had rules that needed to be followed. They were allowed to ask any question they wanted, and everyone inside the walls was obligated to answer, even if it were a lie. All the formal Sisters were very inquisitive, and they enjoyed rooting out lies from the occasional arrivals. The mints donated on behalf of Rachael earned her a nicer room, but it did not excuse her from the inquisition.

Her nicer room included a personal stove heater with a modest amount of wood. The room had stone walls and was not as drafty as the wood and adobe ones they could have assigned her. This room was as big as her bedroom in Grubein, and it reminded her of Tal'Abrac. It certainly wasn't as nice as the Arprot's guest room, but that room had felt gaudy at times. This room would be her home for the next few weeks as she prepared for birth, so it was fitting that it reminded her of him.

She answered the Sisters' initial questions with a suggested tale of a garrison soldier using her without giving them his name. She kept details to a minimum so that she wouldn't have to remember a complex lie. They continuously asked for details as if to interrogate the truth from her. Rachael hadn't imagined an asylum to contain so much gossip. They called it being enlightened and aware of the nature of the world. Rachael didn't want the gossip of a Tokkin child, nor did she want the anxiety that all this created.

"Good morning, Rachael." Sister Clare entered the room with one knock on the door. The Sisterhood of Quiet Dawn didn't view privacy as a privilege, in addition to their constant questions. The one knock was given as a warning of a swinging door. Rachael couldn't get a handle on the custom, given the months of continuous respect required by the Arprots at the garrison. It always startled her to the Sisters' advantage.

"Good morning, Clare," Rachael said softly, hoping to deflate Clare. It had been suggested by one of the other Sisters that she have a name prepared at birth. She had been worrying about the right name for some time. Tal'Abrac was a Tokkin name, and she wanted to give her child the right name. She asked Clare as she brought in a few logs for Rachael's stove. "Sister Clare, do you know how other people choose names?"

Clare dropped the logs and was blindingly eager as she swooped over to Rachael's side. Clare was a bit older than Rachael, and her shorter hair was a near match for Rachael's hair color. Her nose was dainty, and her small mouth was always slightly open, showing off her two larger front teeth. The work dress she wore was tan and tired, but she wore an exciting headdress of plum feathers and black lace. The asylum rules didn't include a dress code, so Clare liked to don exaggerated hairstyles and wore eye-catching hats.

She was thrilled to answer the question but restrained her response. "Well... I know some wait till the moment of birth and let the moment decide for them. And still, others choose based on relatives' names. If it were a boy, you could name him after his father." Like her Sisters, she didn't believe Rachael was truthful about the father. They loved watching her ruffling for answers. "What was the father's name?"

Rachael maintained anonymity for the father while reassuring them the child did not have multiple fathers. She knew she had set up Clare's leading question, but it would have been nice to have a supportive conversation rather than an interrogation. "Clare, the father will have nothing to do with his child." The truth was twisted around his death. "I'm not sure naming my baby after him would be easy for me." She had no idea what name would be appropriate or if a common Kingdom name would be best regardless of his Tokkin nature. She tried to smile to show she wasn't offended by the suggestion.

Clare sighed, appreciating the smile. "I suppose." Many women would yell at them for their belief in questions and answers within the first week of their arrival. The yelling hurt despite their good intentions. This asylum was the Sisters' home, and the members weren't trying to hurt. They were building a community without lies. Still, community ideals are mixed with personal feelings. It was hard to separate anger at the rules from anger at the person living by the rules. "He should come any day now."

"He? What makes you say that?" They had never discussed gender, and it couldn't be certain without the help of a witch.

The Sisters each took to guessing the gender of each woman's baby. They all had their telling signs to determine gender. Some of them guessed correctly more often than others, but none of them were foolproof. Most of the Sisters were betting on Rachael having a boy. "I think it'll be a boy. I've seen you sleep on your left side most of the time. It's a sure sign that you are having a boy."

Rachael adored the superstitions. "Is that so? Any signs that it should be a girl?"

Clare grinned, knowing her guess was in good company. "Not in my book. Only Sisters Irma and Helen are guessing it will be a girl." She added to her insight. "You should be careful if you choose to name at birth. Many have accidentally chosen the name of the father. You wouldn't like that secret to get out, would you?"

Rachael smiled, but she was done playing to Clare's intrigue. Tal'Abrac would be difficult to say by accident. She didn't have a name planned, but naming him after birth seemed right. She wanted to see his face to know who he was. A name now would be like passing judgment on the unborn.

Clare was right about the arrival of the boy. The birth did come within two days of her conversation with Clare. Rachael was brought to the Sister's birthing room. It was near the center of their compound and was protected from the elements. It was a pool of water that they heated to ease the pain of birth. Their great experience was reassuring, and it benefited from decades of successful births. All the births were easier once they started using the pool. Their success was necessary with all of the husbandless women they had to care for, thanks to the devastation of wars.

Rachael had already been given an introduction to the pool and had removed her clothes. Sister Erin said firmly, "Rachael, the pool is ready. Stand and come into the pool." She was in the hip depth part of the pool and knew the right temperature. Erin had a motherly tone and gentle green eyes that pushed away Rachael's tension.

Rachael was breathing with her contractions and sitting on a broad, cushioned bench as she waited for the Sisters. "Stand up? Can't I just stay right here?" She wasn't interested in moving anymore. The contractions told her she had moved enough.

Sister Erin reassured her. "The heated water helps with the pain, and squatting will be easier in the water. It will be better, trust us. Sisters Clare and Jillian will help support you into the pool." The two moved in to help her up as Erin continued to instruct.

"Is there anything we could do to help?" Bridget asked. Bridget was 4 months pregnant and was obsessed with holding her stomach all the time. She was with two other expecting mothers who were guests of the asylum. They were new arrivals to the asylum and were all eager to see the actual method of the Sisters. Most women arrived with more time till the birth than Rachael.

She had cut in line in some sense.

Erin instructed the three. "You can make sure we keep the heater warm. The baby doesn't like the cold air, and neither do we." Though most of these things were already taken care of, she liked to have everyone feel helpful. Tending the fire was not very intensive, but it was important.

Rachael was glad most of the Sisters were there. The various oddities of her situation and coherence to her story had already made her the most attractive topic. With everyone here, the rumors would be recountings instead. "Alright." She put her weight on the two as she stood up. Getting off the bench wasn't happiness. She ground her teeth with disapproval.

Erin encouraged her forward, "Into the water, Rachael. You can use the ledge to sit for a moment, but you will be able to come to a squat for pushing more easily."

The sisters guided her in. The water was perfect, and while the pain persisted, she felt more at home. The anxiety from the unknown wasn't important right now. It was all easier in the water, and the Sisters didn't need to help as much. Some of the feelings fell into place, and she felt prepared. She was giving birth regardless of the consequences.

"Good?" Erin asked, knowing that the water and position would start some movement.

Rachael let out a puff of tension and closed her eyes. It wasn't possible to think about anything else, and the Sister's words were more like noise. "Yes."

Erin took Rachael's hand to feel her pulse and negotiate the birth. "Now, feel the contractions. Those are your windows and your chance. Listen to your body, and it will tell you when to push. We were all made to do this, and you are more than capable."

As she listened, Rachael's body warmed to tighten, and she used the time to push down with her pelvis. Sister Erin was right, and she found the rhythm of birth as they echoed instructions in her movements. The Sisters supported and encouraged her forward. There was pain, and there was blood, but this moment wasn't like other past events involving those two things. It was an epiphany of hope, not an accident or violent encounter.

"The head is out, Rachael," Erin reported. "Now the shoulders, a big push when it comes. You can do it."

Rachael thought about the head of a Tokkin child, and a small panic said stop, but she felt the contraction and pushed to clear the obstacle. "Ahhhh," Rachael cleared the shoulders and finished the birth. Sister Erin moved quickly to bring the baby gently out and up. They cleaned what the water had not rinsed off and removed the umbilical cord. The baby cried, and the cloth cradled the child in Sister Erin's arms.

Erin spoke softly as she brought the boy over to his mother, "It's a boy, Rachael."

Rachael sat back on the ledge. The expecting mothers and Sisters stole a peek as he passed into his mother's arms. She held him and cried. He looked perfect and normal without any sign of a Tokkin parent. Her curious confusion showed as she checked the portions under the cloth. It was overwhelming joy, but her tears stung with confusion.

"He's perfect," Erin said reassuringly. She wondered if she saw disappointment in Rachael's reaction.

Clare said suggestively, "You were expecting a girl, perhaps?" She, too, had picked up the same disappointment they were all witnessing.

"No," Rachael whimpered and coughed. She didn't know what it meant. Had she been raped in her sleep after leaving Grubein or was this some sort of trick? She knew it was her son, but she couldn't express the twisted joy and loss. Rachael closed her eyes for a moment, and when she opened them, she saw her child. "I just... love him so much." She finished in a whisper.

Bridget asked, "Do you have a name?" She was holding a bundle of branches that weren't needed.

"Tal..." she wanted to call on Tal'Abrac to make him the father in the face of her confusion. Before she continued the second part of his name, she realized her position. She had a notable pause and passed her thumb across his cheek. "ph'i. Talphi." She didn't know if it meant anything in some Tokkin language or if it just sounded right, but she knew it meant her son.

Erin asked, "Talphi? Not a usual name." The name didn't sound like any of the dialects in the region. It wasn't the wildest name she had ever heard, though, but it wasn't normal.

Clare giggled, "I told you that you should have asked for naming help, Rachael. Now you have a baby named Talphi." She threw a blanket over Rachael, covering her head.

Rachael didn't talk anymore. She focused on Talphi and watched his face and little pulls and movements. His normal look was a blessing in terms of rumors and reactions from the Sisters and mothers. It was a curse to her imagination. She imagined the chances of unknowingly being raped while she was in Commander Arprot's home.

Rachael continuously felt Talphi in her arms and fought the confusion. It would be better to believe this was Tal'Abrac's son. Rachael closed her eyes to rest and did as she had been instructed by Tal'Abrac. She doubted her confusion and committed to this moment. She would be a mother, and this child would know what it means to cast disbelief upon a defined future.

Chapter 11

Rachael spent a few more months at the asylum before setting out. Talphi was healthy, and he wasn't Tokkin, so there was no need to stay there or to head into the Tokkin lands. She had promised herself she would head out there, but their survival could be more easily managed in the Kingdom.

The Sisters of the Quiet Dawn had knowledge of and access to many noble families for donation purposes. Rachael used those contacts and sent out offers of service as a housemaid and childcare provider. It wasn't uncommon for women with a child to serve noble families, raising children of the same age. The maternal instincts were recognized, but this servant role was highly protected. The referral from Margeret did the trick and brought the trust of the noble stratification.

The Monten family took up Rachael's offer since Mrs. Monten had given birth to a few children already and found that she needed more assistance in caring for them. They lived in Jamin. It was a well-maintained town in the southeast of the Kingdom in a large valley of the hilly terrain east of the Green Mountains. Jamin was nearly three weeks travel to the west of the Grand Plains.

Jamin was not a defensive location and had built itself as a place of commerce. It was ten blocks of closely built shops and homes with a loose sprawl surrounding the center. Only the best rains were able to wash away the smell of curbside waste. It was large enough that the residents wanted to be called a city, but they could not shake the definition of a town. They did not have a proper wall as the Kingdom of Garrin demanded in exchange for City declarations. Most of the buildings were wooden and two stories with a few taller stone buildings. The best streets were cobblestone.

Rachael raised Talphi and the Monten children for years as the town prospered despite fear of a collapse due to the death of King Antoin and Lord Fuller, who was Lord of this region. Medrick's continued control and actions upset the nobility, but they maintained stability in the lives of the common folk rather than seek a civil war.

Talphi followed his mother closely as she led him from the meat section of the market. He didn't like to hold her hand. It was warmer than he liked, and it made his hand sweaty. He was seven years old, and Jamin had been his hometown for as long as he could remember. His tame hair had trouble deciding which color it was. It liked to be blondish in the sun and brown in the winter. His slightly narrow eyes were brown, but if looked at closely, it seemed like the brown was painted over a green base. His nose, ears, and mouth were bigger than normal, but he was cute enough for seven. When he smiled, he never showed his teeth.

Rachael had finished her shopping for the Monten family and was headed back through the back paths. There were raised walkways built on the main street, but she found the dirt ones faster, even if they smelled more. Talphi had the privilege of seeing the world on his mother's trips through the town, while the Monten children had the privilege of staying home during his mother's routine shopping trips.

Talphi quietly observed his surroundings as they turned from the walkway to the street level and a thinner road. He looked back and around as they walked. He had already looked in the direction that they were heading enough times. Suddenly, he spoke, "I know where we are." Talphi could speak well for his age, but he rarely exercised the ability. His pointed statements were his new favorite use of words. It was a good reason to talk.

Rachael had been using one of her shortcuts and looked down at him. "Really?" She was curious how much he knew. "Where would I go if I wanted to go back to the house?"

He looked forward away from his mother and pointed, "Forward, then," he made a right gesture with his hand, "Turn at the shoe place. Then we go till the road with the bell and then that way."

She beamed down, "That's right. You do know where we are." It gave her great pride to think of her son as observant. It was a trait she knew was necessary for being critical of what one believes.

He glanced up to see her looking down but looked away from her when he knew that she understood what he had said. Talphi continued to gather his surroundings as he followed her to the clothing section of town. He knew they were heading there without her saying so, but there was no reason to talk about it.

Rachael never intentionally let Talphi out of her sight and would have held his hand if she could. As well as he could follow her, he always seemed to find his own path. Each time she lost him, he found her again without believing that he was lost. He had merely been without his mother.

She occasionally checked the linens that were for sale even though it wasn't a routine request. The quality varied too much from week to week to wait until cloth for new sheets and clothing were needed. She stopped to check a cloth bolt for defects. Rachael ran her hands over the fabric, feeling its strength and consistency. Her mind flipped back to Talphi quickly as it often does in town. She looked to her sides, and he wasn't there. She looked a little further at the people around her and noticed most of the men staring at the other side of the courtyard. Rachael looked too, hoping their line of sight would lead to Talphi.

All the men were gawking at one thing. The women attempted to go about their business, too, but they would glance and glare in Madame Scully's direction. She was in the very front windows of a shop, removing her layers of garments as if she were in a rear changing room or her bedroom. Despite the stares and scoffs, no one made any attempt to shut the doors. Men stared, and women made all sorts of noise to raise awareness of the inappropriate nature.

Madame Scully was like a city geisha, but this was just a town, and there were very few impressive meetings of nobles, just men who liked the idea of seeming important. She had no husband, no labor, and lived beyond the means of every other woman in town. She was good at what she did, and this was one of her advertising schemes. The last woman who tried to stop her advertisement became part of the show when the madame tore her clothes in reprisal. The fight just drew more attention.

Men watched breathlessly and remained still enough for Rachael to quickly peer between the frozen forms. She regrettably saw a few curious boys rubbing themselves and panicked to push the human obstacles out of her way. She caught Talphi by the shoulder as soon as she saw a piece of his clothes. He was looking in Scully's direction, and she had to set him straight. "Come along." She led him away, disappointed in herself. She had been so careful about things like this. "It's times like these," she murmured under exasperated breaths, "I wish you would stay close to me."

Rachael finished thinking after they had gotten far enough away. In the time it took to reach a safe distance, she thought of what would help him understand. He was too young to be thinking about women like that. It was a horrible example of what a woman should be. She needed Talphi to look for a decent woman when he grew up. "Talphi," she knelt to his level. "You were staring at that woman?"

Talphi turned red and didn't look at his mother. "Yes." He felt ashamed that his mother was talking to him about it. He wanted to see more, but her tone suggested he was doing something wrong. He didn't think looking was wrong but couldn't grasp the feelings.

"I don't want you wandering off and blindly following what catches your attention. You are very observant, and she was a pretty woman, so there is no shame in seeing that beauty. But you were staring, and you completely wandered away from my side. I must know where you are, so you must be aware of where I am and then stay close while we are in town. Do you understand?"

Talphi nodded but kept his eyes averted from Rachael's face. "Yes?" He understood the logistics of staying close and being distracted, but he was more embarrassed by the powerful urge to stare. It was an uncomfortable feeling that his mother had caught him in that moment.

She continued to express her dissatisfaction with Madame Scully, "That woman was trying to get people to stare. Don't be lured in by her seduction." This was part of being a good man. She hoped he would remember this and wouldn't dwell on Madame Scully.

He said with limited understanding, "Alright." Talphi knew she wanted him to stay close, but the staring at Madame Scully was confusing. He looked around freely at the girl-free world, and his red face faded as his mother led the way back to the house.

There were four Monten children that Rachael helped care for. Mrs. Monten did a lot of the caretaking herself but would accompany Sir Monten to events in other towns or cities, and she needed Rachael for those times. Mrs. Monten's first two children died from illness before she employed Rachael. She blamed her absences without a proper caretaker for the deaths. Rachael and she kept to the boundaries of their classes in the presence of observers, but Mrs. Monten was only a few years older than her, and they were mothers raising children together. She depended on Rachael, who did not disappoint her expectations.

Their manor was reminiscent of other wealthy houses in this region. It was three times the size of other homes and was surrounded firstly by a four-foot-high stone wall. A grove of trees between the house and wall protected it from wind and prying eyes. The wooden siding was slightly meek and unimpressive, but the inside was over-decorated and even gaudier than the Arprot's home in the garrison. Rachael returned from the errand with Mrs. Monten waiting anxiously with a carriage outside.

Mrs. Monten began speaking when Rachael was within twenty feet, "Thank goodness you're back." She was in one of her black event dresses. It was fitted and boastful of her figure. Her eyes were a gorgeous green and were alluring even when she was upset. Her thinner lips were defined and moved exactly with each word. "Sir Monten has again requested me to come to an event at Baron Fuller's, and I didn't want to leave the children alone."

Rachael nodded. "Of course, Mam. When can I expect your return?"

Mrs. Monten started to enter the carriage. "Late. If I understand, an emissary from the Kingdom of Garrin is here. Most likely, he will politely berate us for a lack of support for the eastern expansions, but with all other concerns, it seems foolish... I'm rambling and will be late. Either way, my husband needs me at his side." She settled herself in the carriage. "The children are in the back. Tell them I'll see them in the morning."

Rachael bowed. "Of course, Mam." The carriage pulled away, and she looked down to Talphi, who watched the wheels pull the carriage away. "Would you like to play with the others while I help prepare dinner?"

Talphi said absently, "Yeah." He didn't know what he wanted to do and was open to suggestions. He still thought about the Madame and had been thinking about Aria, Mrs. Monten's daughter, too. He compared the feelings and decided they might be the same. He should be careful not to be lured.

Rachael grinned through his distracted attention. "Alright. I'll be in the kitchen." She watched him head off to the back of the house before going inside.

Talphi found the other children in the back of the house near their favorite tree. The two boys were climbing as the girls were playing with some dolls in the shade.

The two boys, Matt and Eric, were older than him by four and two years, respectively. They each had well-trimmed brown hair. Matt's chubby cheeks were pinched each day by his mother. His heavily cute face was nearly matched by his brother, but Eric didn't pick up weight like his brother even though he ate as much. Their ears were smaller than normal, and Talphi had caught his mother saying it was the reason they missed what they were told so often. Both of them promised to have broad shoulders like their father.

The girls, Aria and Brianna, were one year older and one year younger than him. Aria was her mother at age eight. Instead of a dirty blonde, she was a pure blonde, and her eyes were hazel green. She kept her long hair up in a ponytail most of the time, and Talphi loved to watch her neck as the hair bobbed past. Brianna had inherited her mother's thinner lips, but she took up her father's bushier brown hair and solid brown eyes. She kept it short and didn't play with her hair as her sister did.

Talphi couldn't help but stare at Aria to see if it was the same as looking at the Madame. Looks aside, it wasn't the same. She wasn't trying to get his attention, even if he wanted her to have it.

Eric was on one of the tree branches four feet off the ground. He jumped for a tiny growth of a higher branch and missed. "Damn, I can't reach it." The growth on the bottom of the branch was only 4 inches long and had one leaf on it. He had braced for his fall in anticipation of missing.

Matt laughed and then jumped from the same spot and missed. "Ouch," he yelled from a hard hit. He had been higher than Eric when he fell but was just as unsuccessful.

Aria and Brianna looked over. "You're going to get hurt," they said together in their mother's words and with her tone.

"You're trying to grab that?" Talphi pointed at the tiny twig at the bottom of the eight-foot-high branch.

Matt confirmed and encouraged Talphi. "Yeah, give it a try." He had climbed trees with Talphi and would like another challenger. He had gotten the closest so far, and Eric was no real challenge.

Talphi agreed, "Alright." His thoughts about Aria were distracted by the challenge, and he was eager to prove himself to the boys.

Aria and Brianna gave their attention to the competition. "Talphi, you'll get hurt," Brianna said. She moved to the bottom of the trunk and clenched the side of the tree. Aria watched silently, bored with their competition.

Talphi moved himself up to where Matt had tried from. He took a moment of silence and then leaped. He didn't expect to miss like Eric and grabbed the branch, clenching it tight without sliding off.

Matt and Eric cheered, "Wow." They didn't care that it wasn't them. They knew it could be done and would do it themselves next.

But the cheer was followed by a gasp from the four. The tiny twig was not meant to hold a person and broke from the branch under his weight. Talphi slammed to the ground, and the boys stood stunned. Aria jumped up, and Brianna stumbled down to her knees weakened by shock.

Talphi rolled over, grabbing his elbow, then sat up, kneeling. His eyes began to tear up in pain. The sudden crunch had knocked the wind out of him, and he struggled to pull it together. He didn't want to cry in front of Aria.

Eric asked, "Are you alright?" Brianna crawled a few steps toward Talphi on all fours.

Talphi looked over at the girls and breathed back the tears. He couldn't speak and didn't want to at the moment. He let go of his elbow and stretched open the hand of that arm. A twig was in it.

Talphi felt mocked when he looked up at the tree and the branch that forfeited a piece of itself. He looked at himself and took account of his body's pain. Something broken would have hurt more. Dirt covered him and had impacted itself into his skin. He stood up without the others' help and ignored their rapid questions. Talphi focused on controlling the pain and moving back to the house and its water buckets on the side to clean off his mess.

The four children were terrified as he moved away and kept their distance. Matt mustered to ask another question, "Did you break your arm? Or anything?" It wasn't clear what would happen to them if Talphi was hurt. Would they be punished, and would Rachael hate them? This was uncharted territory. Talphi had always fallen when a parent was nearby, and they were never to be blamed.

Talphi called out once he was far enough away from them, "I just need to clean up." He kept a hold of the twig he had torn from the tree for and didn't let go of it yet.

Talphi went around the side of the house and opened a water bucket. He took off some clothes and washed the dirt off his skin. He scrubbed out the skin burns with tears forcing their way from his eyes. Talphi stared at the damage once it was cleared out of the dirt. Focusing on it and breathing calmly released the pain, and the cuts seemed shallower the longer he watched them. The surrounding world seemed to disappear as he stared at the damage. When he snapped back to attention, the pain was light enough, and the bleeding had stopped. He dusted off his clothes and put them back on to cover up his damaged skin.

Talphi returned to the Monten children without informing his mother. The play afterward was seriously muted by each of the kids' preoccupation with the chance that Talphi would have told their parents what happened. Talphi went back to climbing a different tree while Matt and Eric played catch with their ball to distance themselves from the trees. Aria occupied her own attention with her dolls, and Brianna watched Talphi when she wasn't watching her sister play.

Their odd silence carried into the next morning but went unnoticed by Mrs. Monten. She was occupied by what they had learned from the emissary. After barely touching the breakfast for twenty minutes, she snapped to attention. "Children, finish your breakfast; we have a busy day." They were just about ready to be excused from the table, so telling them to finish was pointless. "Rachael, I need to speak with you in the parlor." The children would wait here.

"Yes, Ma'am." Rachael nodded and took off her apron to hang it by the doorway.

They went into the parlor, and Mrs. Monten closed the door behind them. "I'll cut to it quickly. The dinner was less of a dinner and more of a meeting. We find ourselves in a bind and have little choice in responses. The King has seized a large amount from us, including this house."

Rachael acted shocked but wasn't surprised. "Dear... why?" She had heard about the seizure of many noble houses and land since coming to Jamin. She thought there was a chance the King's agenda would work its way to the Monten family, but they aren't very influential with only a handful of personal guards and small holdings. The seizures over the last years had all been done through legal tracks available to the King, though stories of subversive tactics framing or sabotaging nobles existed. There was rarely violence during these repossessions, and the results created new communities governed by appointed commoners under the direct authority of the King rather than under the traditional noble structure. King Medrick was arranging a new system for the management of his land, steadily and without setbacks.

Mrs. Monten appreciated Rachael's shock. "I'm guessing the King sees my husband as a threat, even though he swore allegiance the day the King was crowned." She saw the continued question on Rachael's face. "You know we are cousins to the Fullers? His campaign of giving charters to commoners and creating governors and mayors has been most pointedly targeted at those related to the Fullers. And of course, every attempt to stop him has just given him more reason to enforce his Re-Appropriation Law."

Rachael saw the benefits of what the King was doing, though she personally liked the Montens and cared what happened to them. "Is there any way to perhaps gain one of those new positions from the King and keep what's yours?" Jamin received news from all over the Kingdom, and one of the first places this had occurred was Saven, a town a week's travel to the north and west. They had prospered and grown in unique ways without local noble ownership. Craftsmen had established themselves, and children were educated through community efforts. Still, the Montens were good people, and there was no reason they too couldn't be part of that change.

She understood what Rachael was asking, especially given the hours-long conversation about just that yesterday, but she knew the noble system had existed successfully for hundreds of years, and she felt there was no reason to change it. None of them could accept it. "That would be giving up, no, the right course is to seek our Fuller cousins and join them in resisting this ruthless law. The King's law still matches the purview of his rights, but he will overstep that someday, and we must be ready to unite against him. We will regroup and recover what he has taken through the laws, but for now, we must think about our children's welfare."

Rachael knew what it was to have the world crash around you. "I'm sorry." She could tell Mrs. Monten to stop dwelling on the past and see the opportunity of the moment, but that sounded like hostile words in her mind. Mrs. Monten was putting her children first, and arguing wouldn't change her belief; it would just damage their friendship.

Mrs. Monten smiled as she played with Rachael's apology. "Thank you, but it's not your fault this is all happening." Rachael's pity didn't occur to her. Reminiscing made her realize how nice it was to have another mother she could depend on all these years. "It's been so wonderful to have you with us,

The Determined World

Rachael. Those were hard years before I found you, and I don't want to lose your company, but these will be trying times, and we can't afford another carriage to move you with us. Our cousins have full homes and not enough room for you and your son... and the children are getting old enough for me to manage on my own." She spilled out all the reasoning to press back the desire to bring Rachael with them.

Rachael smiled softly. She wasn't a pet that needed to be taken to the new home. She was a parent herself and knew the limited extension of her relationship with the Montens. "I understand. I have enjoyed my time in your service." She had enjoyed the children, but the uncertainty of future support returned. Again, she focused on the moment the same way she had after Talphi's birth. Don't focus on the worrying future and familiar past; focus on the possibilities.

Mrs. Monten took a breath and began her final instructions. "Good. Sir Monten will be taking the boys with him today, and I need to get Aria new dresses since it might be a while after leaving here that I'll feel safe to spend mints on such things. Then we will be leaving tomorrow when our wagons and carriages arrive. We have arranged to move as much as we can before the Ginru Force comes. They are going to take whatever they want and use it to prop up the mayor they put in charge." Mrs. Monten became flush, mentioning the Ginru force, and stopped abruptly and closed her eyes to take in a deep breath.

The Ginru Force was the name of the King's re-appropriation enforcers. They handled the transfer of the land and protection of the new mayors and governors assigned by the King's unknown reasoning. Some of the appointees were noble, but many were common and unheard of, but all of them turned out to be successful in their positions. The Ginru Force were also the ones responsible for the subversive techniques and putting down the seldom violent transfers of land and duty.

Rachael gave her a moment to take a breath. "How can I help?"

Mrs. Monten was drawn back to action by Rachael's willingness and opened her eyes. "You will need to watch over Brianna for the day. Aria's dresses will go quicker if I don't have to handle Brianna's pleading for a brand new one also. Brianna's just going to have to take Aria's older dresses for now." Aria was a very careful girl, and she outgrew them before they were worn. Brianna played rougher while following Talphi and the boys. Her dresses barely lasted till she outgrew them.

Rachael nodded. "Of course, Mam. I will help prepare what I can for transport. I'll focus on the children's wardrobe and see to it that the ragged items stay behind."

Mrs. Monten would miss Rachael's ability to pick up the slack. "Great, thank you, Rachael." Rachael bowed to Mrs. Monten as she left for the dining room to organize the children.

Rachael stayed a moment to think. She thought about telling Talphi immediately, but it broke her heart to see him cry in her mind since she herself felt tearful. She reasoned putting it off so that the other children could be told the news by their parents instead of secondhand through her son. Talphi was going to be playing with Brianna all day, and he'd surely mention the move within that time. Brianna loudly protested being left behind, but she quieted right down when it was explained that Talphi would be at the house too.

Once Mrs. Monten left with Aria, Rachael directed Talphi and Brianna to play in the glass room. It was an extension off the back of the house made for the children. The Montens were lucky enough to afford large glass windows along the sides of the sunward-facing room. The panels were all different opaque colors, and the effect was splendid as the refraction changed throughout the day, adding playful moods in different corners of the room. Even though the sun was out today, the colorful room didn't dispel the foreboding of activity in the house.

The Determined World

When Mrs. Monten got back from the town, she pulled Brianna out of the room to give her the news and begin their packing. Rachael was a short distance behind her and decided that now was the best time to tell Talphi their plans. "Talphi," she said in a gently pained voice.

He folded his arms, realizing the moment of explanation had arrived. Everyone was acting strangely, and he knew there was something wrong. "The Montens have to move, and I can't continue to work for them. Tomorrow, we will be heading to Saven." She had decided while she worked that day. All the news from Saven was that it was willingly accepting more common families excited by the chance to prosper. Rachael wasn't interested in being a home servant anymore, so this forced relocation was a chance to use her talents with equals.

Talphi prompted with some confusion, "Why?" The news had a sting to it, and he kept his arms folded, but there had to be a reason.

She explained softly as she looked for the hurt in his eyes. "They need to move to be closer to their family." It wasn't necessary to give the detailed background that Mrs. Monten had relayed. The simple truth was enough. Someday, Jamin may end up like the prosperous Saven, but the coming chaos wouldn't be safe.

The small sting of hurt was joined by twigs of anger. That wasn't reason enough to leave them. "Why aren't we going with them?" He demanded. Talphi mostly liked the Monten children, but missing Aria was more on his mind. He wanted to be close to her even if she ignored him most of the time.

Rachael couldn't save him from the pain of their move. It was the first time she had ever moved with a child, and she wished she could keep him with the Monten children. She had spent all her life in one town when she was a child and could only guess what he was feeling. It had to be different than all her departures as an adult. "I know it hurts, but we have to part and go our separate ways. I wish I could stay with them too."

Talphi yelled as he interrupted, "No." She was just talking about the separation, and he was past that. He wanted the real reason. They had been talking in whispers, and he could sense something more. She had to be hiding it because he was young. Grownups talk in private and never include children. If he were older, she would tell him the truth. "Tell me what is happening. Why are they moving?"

She needed to soothe him. "Baby." He was so innocent and wasn't ready to learn about that world.

Talphi pushed back again. "Tell me the truth. I want it." His voice reverberated throughout the glass room. He wanted the truth so badly that he needed it. It wouldn't change the pain, but it would give it a face.

Rachael looked down at him with wonder. She had planned to spare him the whole truth because it might add fear and more confusion. Nothing she explained to him would change what they needed to do. He looked and waited, and she worked against her desire to protect him. This moment was about more than what she wanted for him, but now that he pressed her, she thought about the belief in this feeling. He might not understand, but was fueling ignorance the same as protecting innocence? "Alright. They are leaving because the King has taken this house and their land. He has sent a group of men, the Ginru Force, to take this place forcibly if needed. They must move to protect themselves, and we aren't going with them because it's too dangerous to follow them." It was partly because of the danger but mostly because it would be a dead end. The more she had thought about it, the more the King's pattern of actions mattered.

Talphi cried a few tears when she told him. It was an incredible struggle to get the truth. The King, Ginru Force, and Fullers were all things he had overheard and were talked about by many sources, so he understood the roles. The King was forcing the Monten family, and even if he couldn't understand everything at the moment, he managed to form a question and ask calmly.

"And why are we going to Saven?"

Rachael watched the calming effect of giving him the answer. "They are a community of common folk like us. They will welcome us, and I can continue to help raise children there. It's a town without a noble lord that won't be targeted by the King." Saven was the first, and Jamin is now the most recent of the town charters. This won't be the last of the King's charters as the numbers had been increasing each year, and Rachael saw no reason it would end. "We should be safe there, and I'll be able to provide for us."

Talphi sat down in exhaustion. "Right. You'll be watching more children." She was always taking care of other children besides him for as long as he could remember. The Monten children had been under his mother's care and attention. He didn't receive her undivided care. It made him jealous even though he didn't feel he needed more of her attention.

Rachael felt that she had compromised herself by telling Talphi all of this. But he seemed calmer despite peeling back a layer of innocence. Her jewel of a child hadn't lost his preciousness even as the color in his face changed. She asked without as much sympathy. "Are you alright, Talphi?"

He answered shortly, "I'm fine." Being alone and quiet felt preferable.

Rachael held out her hand. "Then, I need to continue packing. You will help." It wasn't a request; it was an order. The work wouldn't be exhausting, but she knew that the physical work could help distract his feelings and organize his thoughts. It always had for her.

He didn't take her hand but did come to her side as if he were holding her hand. They packed what they could and didn't talk anymore about the move. Both families were docile as the day came to an end. Their departure was so sudden, and there was too much work to spend any time dwelling on what was being lost.

Rachael talked Talphi into waking up early the next morning. "Talphi, time to get up. We must get the last of the Monten's belongings on the carriages so they can leave."

He rolled over in his small bed in their personal quarters, which were cramped from the two beds. The small room limited their possessions for the best. His and his mother's bed had been separated by a makeshift curtain partition. She put it up so that there would be some sense of privacy. It wasn't her plan to share a bedroom with her son. A new home in Saven would hopefully have space for a better partition.

The sun wouldn't be up for two hours. Rachael and Talphi ate in silence and started to move belongings in a quiet organization. Mrs. Monten was the only Monten to wake up with the servants and helpers they had hired. She had decided to give her daughters the time to be children in their home. Talphi was helping the adults, and he felt better for being treated like an adult.

Even though the activities were different today, there was still a structured efficiency like all other days. They finished loading the wagons and carriages before the sun was up. The Monten girls were hurried through their breakfast as Rachael gathered up their travel packs.

Rachael was worried about the Montens gathering with the Fullers. It felt like a trap. Was following the Fullers simply naive? What was the right thing to defend? "Be safe," she told Mrs. Monten and hugged her even though the contact would be frowned upon by the other helpers.

Mrs. Monten was taken aback by the gesture. She had an initial impulse to scold Rachael, but she needed the hug, so she hugged her back. "Thank you, thank you." There was more than the threat to her family. She feared that this move could wear on her and that her children's health would suffer. She couldn't take losing another child.

Brianna ran over and hugged Talphi since their mothers were hugging. Talphi stood shocked, and Mrs. Monten laughed seeing her daughter mimic her. He didn't know what to do. Touching or hugging someone wasn't what he wanted to do at that moment. Before he thought of what he could do,

Brianna quickly pulled her tear-ridden and red face away, ran past her sister, and hid in the carriage.

Rachael echoed Mrs Monten's joy for the connection of their families, "How nice." It was a good goodbye. "Goodbye, Mrs. Monten, goodbye girls." Aria made a small nod and tried to pull Brianna out of the carriage to demonstrate manners.

The carriages pulled away within a few minutes. Mrs. Monten started pushing them to hurry. The Ginru Force would be arriving today, and they needed to put as much distance between them and the house as they could. This property would soon be re-purposed for the guards establishing the charter and mayoral rule. Rachael and Talphi left as soon as the carriages were out of sight. The house continued to be salvaged by the servants who were left behind.

"Well," Rachael looked down at Talphi and gave a reassuring smile, "Are you ready, dear?"

"As much as I will be," he said wittingly and without looking at her. The direction the carriages went still occupied his mind. It was impossible to be certain what was down that road they traveled. All that he knew was that it was a point of separation and divergence. He paid attention to the point in time.

His words felt like something her son would say, though it was the first time he said it. She coughed but smiled at his sudden spurt of adult retort. "Yes, smart."

He looked up at her, not really understanding why it was a smart answer. They gathered up the packs on their backs and the side packs with daily essentials. Their route brought them into town first.

It was an hour's hike to the town. When they arrived, the Ginru Force was already in Jamin proper. The town responded like news of an approaching storm had come in. The windows were closed, and very few people had ventured out to carry on normal business. Still, a few were eager to interact with them since more people could mean more business.

Talphi watched the horses and a small group of well-equipped soldiers. They dressed in crisp blue, and all wore left-shoulder plate pieces with ring mail shirts. Some carried shields and swords, while other soldiers had torso-length poles with metal cones at one end. They slowed as they passed by a larger collection of adventurous townsfolk talking with some savvy soldiers. One soldier was explaining the new weapon. The new weapons were great recruitment tools the Ginru Force used to establish the new local guard.

The soldier spoke loud enough for everyone to hear, "Well, I'll be honest, this is only a Ginru Force weapon, but that doesn't mean that the same ones won't be available in a few years from now for the local forces. Establishing order and keeping the land safe is the King's top priority after all."

One of the men in the crowd begged, "Please, your description sounds amazing, but can you show it to us?" He was already eager to join the new guard they were establishing, given all the promises and benefits he would receive.

The soldier looked over to his captain. They had established a good crowd, and this might draw more supporters. He called out, "Captain, can I give them a demonstration?"

The captain feigned annoyance at their presentation. "You make sure your target is secure, and no one gets hurt, or it'll be your head, soldier."

The soldier replied eagerly, "Yes, sir." They already had a spot set up a few feet away, backed against a stone wall and clear of accidents. Rachael had stopped out of curiosity and to prove her feelings about the coming changes to Jamin.

The soldier loaded the gun and prepared the firing pin. His fellows made sure the area was clear and that everyone had a chance to see it. The moment of recruitment had arrived. The gun fired with a bang, hitting the target and shredding the hanging canvas against the stone wall. The sound startled everyone to a jump, and a few fell to the ground.

Rachael's heart exploded in high-speed beats, and she grabbed Talphi's hand to lead him as fast as they could out of the town. She didn't want them to recruit her son. There were enough awe-struck boys fascinated by the Ginru Force to make her concerned for Talphi's future.

The two were used to traveling to town and back with packs filled with food or other necessities for the Montens. Today, they walked through the town with those packs containing their clothes and side packs containing most of the food they would need over the days traveling to Saven.

They made it out of town and were on the northern road. Rachael sighed her first relief just as a woman called to them. "You there, are you moving? It looks as if you are moving." Their packs stuffed with clothes had given them away to the caller. Rachael respected the call and turned to see who from the town was calling her. The woman wasn't a Jamin resident. It must be someone who had come with the Ginru Force. The woman was too old to be walking so briskly and wore clothes too fine to be a commoner.

Talphi replied, in the absence of fearing the question from a stranger, "Yes, we are moving."

The woman had her hooded cloak back, showing off her bright red hair. The red hair was full and bounced just as youthfully as Aria's. Her face was old and wrinkling but warmly kind. The staff was not required for walking, and she didn't put any weight on it as she moved. She smiled at the boy who answered for his mother. "Where are you moving to?" she asked.

Her appearance made his mouth feel relaxed, and her voice was sweet. He didn't trust the feeling since it was so dissimilar to other strangers he had met. The comfortable feeling was out of place, it was a lie. "I don't know," he said without doubt as he ignored the answer and prepared to defeat the lie he felt coming from her.

The witch watched his confidence. Given the aura of relaxation she projected, she assumed he must not know. He was certain about his uncertain answer. Children might lie easily and absentmindedly, but he had looked her in the eye and should be well under her influence.

Rachael spoke up finally after resisting the urge to tell the truth, "We are moving to Dandrine." It might be a mistake to lie, but the comfort she felt from this woman was in stark contrast to the fear of the Ginru Force that drove her at this moment. This woman might be part of the Ginru or some traveler looking to take advantage of them. She nodded in Talphi's direction and looked down, hoping he wouldn't protest, but he didn't look back at her. He was scowling at the witch and her intrusion.

The witch started to move closer to them now that they were standing still. "Oh, Danbrine is a nice place. Oh dear, my manners, I'm Autumn. I'm a Sister of Forn. What are your names?" Autumn didn't have anything else important to do than chat with the locals for gossip. The King's men in the Ginru Force never needed her help, even though the Sisters of Forn were indentured to the service. The Sisters of Forn struggled to keep their good reputation with communities because of this deal and the disruptions of the King's actions. She needed to present herself as a Sister of Forn and aid as many people as they could to combat the trajectory.

"I'm Rachael, and this is my son Talphi." Rachael struggled to create a polite way of excusing them from the conversation. She knew she shouldn't have lied to a witch and would have to tell as much truth as possible to not get caught. The worst would be if this witch was aware of her service to the Montens. Rachael stood on the moment, afraid that her old beliefs had intercepted her again. What decisions would protect them and set them free?

"Mmm," Autumn observed, "Talphi and his mother Rachael." The son's name was not common in the Kingdom of Garrin. He was definitely more interesting than the mother and the Monten seizure. "That is an interesting name, Talphi. Who are you named after?" She wanted the staunch boy to entertain her. With a little effort, she increased her relaxed aura. The aura loosened the tongues of most people.

Rachael looked to her son, who looked only to the witch. It was hard for her to swallow without answering as her jaw relaxed. She couldn't contain such an easy answer and started to speak, "He was...", but Talphi spoke up.

His jaw was tight, and his eyes narrowed. "It's just a name. I wasn't named after anyone." Talphi failed to stop what this witch was doing, and he didn't understand his answer, though he had thought about it from time to time. Her effect was infuriating, and even though he was losing, he liked resisting.

His mother's loose tongue was covered by her confusion. Was it just a sound, or had she named her son after Tal'Abrac? In truth, it was just made up at the moment of his birth. Either way, she didn't want to mention Tal'Abrac. This situation was out of her control, but if she focused, she could keep her thoughts inside her head.

Autumn was just as confused as Rachael. Names are sometimes built off meaning, but not usually in the Kingdom of Garrin. His mother did not look like a foreigner, and it sounded like a foreign name. It shared some familiarity with the sounds of Tokkin names. "Is it a Tokkin name? How odd. Did your father name you?"

"No," Talphi replied before his mother could think. "My mother named me." His teeth ground into each other as he stopped talking. Clenching his jaw stopped him from speaking. He wasn't a chatty boy, and this foreign compulsion to share was distasteful.

Autumn addressed Rachael. "Are you familiar with Tokkin names? Or maybe someone suggested the name?" This boy may have a keen future if he was given a name from a Tokkin. Perhaps there is more to these two than a move to a new town.

Rachael replied, "No." She was ready to excuse them from the company of this witch. They didn't need a reason not to stand about talking with Autumn. Standing still with a pack on your back is much harder than moving with it. "We..."

Autumn continued before giving Rachael a chance since she knew Rachael was telling the truth. "Interesting." She looked down at Talphi and got too close to him. "I've never heard a name like yours in the Kingdom before. Do you know how to sign your name? Maybe you can write it on the dirt."

He was done sharing. "No." His mother hadn't taught him to write his name, though he had doodled and invented a sign to signify himself when the Monten children wrote their names in the dirt.

Autumn was very interested and eager to learn it. "I see." The name could have been accidental, and asking them anything else might be pointless. Going to the source would be the best way to learn what she wanted. "Would you mind if I gave you a scrying Talphi? I may be able to learn the sign for your name."

For the first time since the witch appeared, Talphi looked to his mother for an answer. He didn't know enough about this witch to know what scrying meant.

Rachael wanted to scream no and pull her son away, but they were too close to the Ginru Force. "We really must be underway. These packs aren't getting lighter." She held her panic back with logic.

Autumn assumed the resistance was all because of the Ginru Force association. "Well, put them down for a moment. It'll be a short reading, and there's no charge." She needed to combat this and show these people they could trust her. They reluctantly complied as she explained, "The wonder of scrying this sort of thing is that the sign will just spring into mind when your name is spoken. I'll just be looking into your yesterday." Autumn waited till they were at rest with their packs on the ground.

Rachael hoped it would be quick and not raise suspicion about her past.

The Determined World

But now she thought about all of yesterday and the Montens. She hoped her and Talphi's familiarity with them wouldn't cause them problems.

Autumn moved her staff along the ground and made a circle. Her eyes closed, but she was looking at the circle. The words Autumn spoke were not audible, but her lips moved precisely. "Hmm." There was a short pause, and she spoke without sound again. Talphi was muddled in the scry, and she couldn't make out a proper sign for his name. It appears he was right about himself and that the name was just a sound.

She was already scrying for the boy, and she was still curious, so she kept going. His future was fogged, but that wasn't uncommon for children and only concerning when scrying adults, so she looked into his past. With a few seconds more, she stopped and laughed. "My oh my." She stopped scrying prematurely and beamed down at Talphi as she reflected on Talphi's hug with Brianna.

"What?" Rachael asked with genuine worry. She was ready for the worst, that they would be taken prisoner or that the scrying would wind up harming the Monten's escape.

"Oh..." Autumn drew out. There was no reason for Rachael to worry. "It's nothing bad. Your son made a real impression on the young girl, Brianna. Maybe you'll marry her someday. Oh, is she one of Monten's children?" Marriage might not be possible in that case, but the classes were shifting. The possibility ran into conflicting thoughts, but it was of no real consequence, and all this would explain Rachael's departure from Jamin.

Talphi looked at her, distraught and with building anger. He liked Aria. Why would she tell him that Brianna liked him? Autumn had just cut into him with disdain for his daydream.

Rachael's fear for the Monten connection was real. "Oh. Yes," she replied, preparing for something worse.

Autumn smiled at the reaction and got to work. "Don't worry about the

Montens. They aren't going to be harmed. You don't need to fear me." She looked back to Talphi and smiled as she squatted down to his eye level. "That young lady won't forget you, Talphi. When we're so young, we happen to remember only a few events, and I have a feeling she'll never forget you."

Talphi asked in anger, "Why?" This witch was too close to him. She needed to move away. Why couldn't Aria remember him? Brianna was younger and not as mature as her sister. He wouldn't forget this.

Autumn didn't need to explain what Talphi would learn as he matured. "We just... well, you'll understand when you're older." She turned to Rachael and sighed as if to communicate without words. Mothers understand these things about growing up.

Rachael did find some reassurance about the Montens, but her association with the Kingdom, the Ginru Force, and everything that happened to Tal'Abrac held firm to distrust. "Did you see his sign?" She took slow breaths, focusing intensely on appearing innocent with her pointed question.

"Oh." Autumn seemed shocked that Rachael didn't pursue Talphi's relationship with Brianna. "I suppose I was distracted, and it appears there is no set sign for your son's name. It's the first time it's been used, so whatever you or he comes up with will be the sign of his name."

Rachael nodded. "I see. I guess that's what happens when you name a child at the moment of birth... See anything else?" She recognized that Autumn had gone beyond her declared intent, but keeping her as a friend would be better than attacking her for the trespass.

"Well," Autumn considered, "The future of most children can be foggy and vague at best. They have developed much of their personality by this age, but there are still so many formidable years ahead. Scrying the future is best on people who are more set in their ways."

Rachael replied delightedly, "Oh! I didn't know that." She thought a child would be more vulnerable to scrying since they act so much on feelings. But seeing another deflection of scrying made her see the connection. It's that future of change and possibility. She must continue to mindfully connect with the world and be as uncertain as a child's future.

Autumn was glad that Rachael was finding ease around her. "Yes, but when he's done growing up and has some firm beliefs, his future will become clear through scrying." She knew it all and was happy to share her insight with Rachael.

If scrying meant more of being told his desire for Aria was not returned and instead, Brianna liked him then he didn't want scrying to be right. "I don't want your scrying." He couldn't stop growing older, but he could reject firm beliefs if that meant he could reject scrying.

"What?" Autumn put her free hand on her hip. "Why would you say a thing like that? Scrying is an amazing and reassuring thing." She calmly soothed her voice and let her relaxing aura fall so he could feel the weight of the world. She wanted him to react naturally.

Talphi thought about himself learning about the rejection of Aria's attention, but it seemed just as horrible for anyone else to be told such things. "What if I don't like what it is?" He had been told enough times by adults that he would be like someone or would feel some way when he was older. He despised it each time and didn't want to be how others said he should be. Even the grand and favorable suggestions couldn't match his feelings.

Autumn sneered at the concept of liking the order of the world. "Like?" Some people wouldn't like to know their future, but they need to have one to fit into the world. "This is about your purpose, and you could spend your whole life searching for it. You wouldn't like knowing you have a purpose? It's a good feeling to know you have a place in the world. To be part of something bigger than you. It's part of growing up, and you should be eager to find it." She had the experience of several lifetimes, but imparting it to a seven-year-old would probably fail. He was too young to understand, but he would certainly obey his instincts.

Talphi pouted, "I don't want you telling me anything else." His mind was clear. She was wrong.

Autumn laughed at her conversation with Talphi. He was clearly smarter than most children, but he didn't have real experience. "I don't expect you to understand yet. You may never understand, but you will grow up and find a place to settle yourself. Trust me, boy."

Talphi didn't respond after she called him boy. Rachael had found the conversation reviving. Autumn's description of adulthood seemed so uninspired and stale. Talphi's childish pushback was fresh and captured a resistance she wanted to embody. Rachael smiled at Autumn, who returned the smile, both for different reasons.

Autumn was satisfied even without finding a sign for Talphi's name. "Well, you should be getting on your way. I've held you up for long enough. Safe journey, Rachael and Talphi," she smirked at the boy. This conversation was great fun and would go well with mending opinions of the Sister of Forn when Rachael speaks about it with others.

Rachael replied, "Safe journey." They elevated their packs, and she took Talphi's hand and led him away. He tried to pull away from her, but her grip was too firm at the moment. Talphi turned to glare at the witch since she was the reason his mother was holding his hand.

When they were out of sight, Rachael did let go of his hand, and they were able to walk faster. "I don't like her," Talphi said after an hour. "She's wrong."

Rachael replied, "Witches live a long time and have a great deal of experience, but she sees what she wants. I like your decision not to believe everything she said. Keep challenging those firm beliefs she spoke of." Talphi looked up eagerly at his mother. Rachael smiled at her son and added, "She thinks everyone should believe the same things. If you want to challenge your belief all through your life, you do it."

The Determined World

Talphi looked forward down the path and agreed, "Good." It was good that his mother saw it his way. It was nice to think he had some ideas that adults didn't have, but it still bothered him that she was marking him as a fool. "Why would she say that if you don't agree with her?"

Rachael didn't need to answer that she once wanted what the witch was promoting since that would be too personal. "She likes to know everyone's business. She would be upset if she couldn't see someone's future. It's just who she is." There wasn't a need to speculate anymore.

Talphi needed to clarify where they were moving to. "You told her we were moving to Dandrine."

Rachael acknowledged the lie, "We are moving to Saven. I needed to lie to her because she came with the Ginru Force, and they're the ones forcing us away." She stopped walking and felt like she needed to see his eyes. He stopped and looked up at her. "Autumn wasn't as bad as I thought she might be, but I couldn't be sure of her intent. I won't be lying to anyone else about where we're going. Now, come along, we have days of travel."

It was like his mother had just christened him into his first adult conversation. The memory burned into his thoughts just like those little moments Autumn had mentioned. Even at his young age, he would remember this into adulthood.

Chapter 12

Rachael's arrival and willingness to teach were greeted well by the Mayor of Saven. Her first-hand experience with survival training on the frontier was just as useful as her time as a caretaker for the Montens. Under this new system, encouraged by the King's charters, any person that has a child was expected to help educate all the town's children. Not all the teachers were as effective as Rachael, and some were seen as glorified caretakers, but those that did educate had their housing and most basic needs met by the actions of the other residents.

Talphi was under Rachael's tutelage from time to time, but other teachers were giving him lessons and knowledge, too. His mother would watch over him like her son when she was teaching. The other children waited till they were out of her sight before committing any pranks on him. He focused his friendship efforts on another boy, Arron, whose father taught trapping once a week out in the hills. They both received similar treatment from the others.

Talphi sat with Arron on the stone wall as they talked about the mud fight show. Talphi was twelve years old now, and it was springtime. "And Corin threw that mud ball that hit Miss Wilcoot. I was hoping a stone was in there, but I suppose the simple fact she was covered by mud is an improvement."

Arron laughed with him. His jet-black hair framed his grinning face. The few freckles seemed to become brighter the more he laughed. "I thought my side was going to split when she threw her pouch, and it caught Darrel in the back of the head, launching him onto the mud. Splauuush. They couldn't have planned anything like that accident." He clenched his side as he laughed. "Too much."

Talphi's thoughts turned to the consequences. "That was great. Do you think Darrel and Corin will have to pay the Wilcoots for the *not* actually 'ruined' dress?" He thought vocally. It was a spectacle to watch, but the Wilcoots were notorious for acting more important than other townsfolks and vocalizing their discontent.

Arron groaned with the thought, "I hope not. The two of them don't make much from their shows as it is. But it's just mud. It should wash out." He bounced his feet against the wall to listen to the scraping sound of feet hitting rock.

Talphi knew how clean Miss Lauren Wilcoot liked to be. "I don't think they care." Thinking about her made him burn. He hated how superior she acted, but he felt hot when she was close and hated himself for lusting for someone he knew was cruel. It was easy to insult her and hard to think about her without wanting to touch her. Movement is the only cure for the thoughts. "I should head home."

Arron asked before Talphi left, "Did you want to do something tomorrow?" He expected a yes answer. They always fit in some time to play, but he knew Talphi's mother liked to spring projects on him that Talphi forgot she mentioned.

Talphi would make the time to play. "Of course, though my mom may need me in the morning. She keeps thinking the chores will take me all day. I think that she's surprised I finish by noon each time." There wasn't anything he couldn't do effectively if he wanted to. He jumped down off the wall and laughed at his speed in doing the chores.

Arron's parents never taxed him too much. "Right, then I'll sleep in late." They were second-generation town folk and didn't have the same constant drive to survive. "You can come over to my house once you're done. I still don't understand why she makes you do all that." Arron shook his head at Talphi's continuous stream of chores.

Talphi wasn't happy about spending all the time doing chores, but it wasn't hard. "They just need to be done. Till tomorrow."

Arron held up a hand to Talphi's exit. "Bye."

Talphi's circle of friendship didn't extend past Arron. Everyone else was an acquaintance, or they were people he needed to learn how to interact with. The more children he was surrounded by, the more separated he felt. And the more people he was surrounded by, the less he would talk. He thought the children who needed more attention talked the loudest and loved to hear themselves speak.

Talphi tried to keep himself unnoticeable since they didn't care about him. Arron cared, but as much as Talphi trusted Arron, he never talked about how tormented he was by Lauren Wilcoot's existence. He thought about this as he walked through the lightly populated eastern part of town. The act of walking wasn't enough action to drown out all the thoughts. She knew how to flirt already, and it was unnerving to watch her flirt with other people. He wanted her interest but knew it was a tormenting daydream, a lie. Talphi told himself he didn't need to talk to Arron about it and couldn't disgrace himself by admitting the torment.

Rachael was waiting for him today. Talphi would arrive at an empty house on days when she was kept late by teaching duties. Her multiple talents had shown through, and she had positioned herself as the most active teacher. On the days he arrived at an empty house, he would either make a small fire in the fireplace or climb in the trees around the house. His fall from the tree years back hadn't discouraged him from climbing. "Hello, Talphi." Rachael asked as he walked inside, "How was Arron today?"

The house was huge, with four rooms. It was a perk of her hard work. There were two bedrooms, a large living area, and a storage room as large as their bedrooms. There was only one house within sight of theirs. A mix of young trees and beefier ones surrounded their house and provided cover from the wind. They were only a ten-minute walk to the center of town. They didn't own the land, and they didn't have enough space to farm, but Rachael had planted a robust garden behind their house.

"He was good," Talphi answered simply. "We saw a mud show by Darrel and Corin today." He volunteered the information as he wandered into the house.

Rachael took the opportunity to talk about his day. "Oh. Did they have a big crowd?" She finished what she was doing and turned to him.

He smiled, "yes," thinking of Lauren getting hit, but blushed thinking about her pulling the dress to display the mud, but inadvertently pulling it too high and giving him a near-peak from behind. "It was entertaining." He replied plainly in an attempt to remove emotion and hide any sign his cheeks would give off.

"Good." She moved on to the next chore and asked, "Would you bring in two logs for the fire, Talphi?"

"No," Talphi replied as he moved to the door and proceeded to bring in the logs.

Rachael sighed. This pattern began two years back. He would say no and still do the task. She knew children rebelled in different ways and at different times, so she accepted verbal defiance as long as he actually did what she asked. It didn't require further evaluation in her eyes.

It was a few days later when Talphi had another vivid dream. He had been having dreams that he could remember and stayed with him into the day. It had been going on for months, and he wondered if there was any deeper meaning. As fictitious as the dreams were, the emotions were stronger than any he ever contended with while awake.

The man opens his stride
His every muscle flexes with strain
He is a competitor
This is the greatest race
They all run the path
And the judge stands at the finish line.
But the child plays with blocks
He doesn't understand his actions
The stacks make something
But he is just a baby
The world is an endless space around him
And all he sees are the blocks to stack.
Each competitor races forward
The line is always just ahead
The judge is on a pedestal
He watches the line.
The baby laughs at the falling blocks
They spelled nothing before being knocked down
He makes some noises to talk
But they are just noises and sounds.
They run with no path beneath their feet
They, too, are in that vast space.
The baby's sounds carry onto the path
He is insignificant.
They fall forward to the finish line
But this race is insignificant.

Talphi woke up in a cold sweat. He was breathing hard as if he had just run a mile. Tears started to fill his eyes and flow freely. It was a dream. It was pointless, but he felt the meaning. He couldn't forget it. It had to mean something if it hurt so badly, and he had to find its importance.

If he focused on it, he wouldn't forget it. The dream was made into a memory, and the real emotions of a fictional world were true. He didn't try to stop crying. He wanted to feel it- that this world is nothing. It is small. He is small. He is like a baby, and the race is for nothing but death. He is a runner, but it's meaningless.

He clenched himself in this crisis. It was the future. Everyone's future. He had dreamed of the end, and he would never forget the scope of his life since it would end like everything else. Curling into a ball and holding himself was warm. Why hadn't anyone told him this? Were there others who realized this? There had to be, but what do you do? He couldn't figure it out throughout one night and fell back to sleep, but he remembered the dream.

After the following free day, Talphi and Rachael returned to their sessions. Talphi was headed to a woodworking session, and Rachael was teaching the younger children their letters for reading and writing. She had taught children Talphi's age less and less over the years as he had gotten older, and other adults agreed to teach the older children. Her precious time with Talphi shrank against her desire. Rachael knew it would happen in time, but it wasn't any easier as she felt Talphi's personality was more certainly a piece of Tal'Abrac. Her son was introspective and intuitively saw things as she imagined Tal'Abrac would.

Rachael prepared to leave for the day. "I'll be home when you get home this evening," she said as she hugged him. He didn't hug back, but that didn't stop her. He wasn't comfortable with the hugs, but she was happy even though he didn't hug back.

He pulled away as soon as she released him. "Alright." It was embarrassing to be hugged around other people, but he mostly avoided them because his mother had the body of a woman, and he shouldn't think about her as he thought of Lauren and the other girls and women.

Teacher Surrivan was instructing them in wood treatment. It was at his home in the north of town. He had a field next to his two-room house to practice his sessions. There were three-foot-high practice buildings spotted around, with a collection of benches in the middle.

It was a subject important for both the boys and girls and they were in a combined class. Most everything was expected of both girls and boys. There were only a few tasks that were being taught that one or the other shouldn't know. Survival could be forced on anyone.

The wood treatment was part of each student's housing construction training. But the task was boring because once the treatments were mixed, they had to wait two hours for it to soak the wood properly. The students just sat and waited as Surrivan wasn't creative enough to have something to fill the time today. He appeared preoccupied with some designs he had been working on.

The group of ten weren't all friends with each other, so the group at large never talked among itself. The largest group of five friends that were talking were the only ones doing so, and they only addressed each other. Their small circle was loosely surrounded by those who weren't talking. Arron wasn't there today, or Talphi would have ignored the others. He stayed quiet and only listened as they discussed a dance lesson.

Ralph laughed. "Yes, and Teacher Morgan tripped over his own feet. I can't believe our teacher is such an idiot."

Nicholus added, "They aren't small enough to be feet... they're the size of wine barrels." He set up the joke for one of his friends.

Lauren took the bait. "No." It was so fun to laugh this hard at the adults. "He drank the wine barrels. You could smell him from 30 feet away. That's why he was falling." They all laughed joyously.

Even Talphi and the other listeners smiled. It was absolutely true about

The Determined World

Morgan's habits. Talphi was watching the ground and did more than a smile with a chortle short of fully laughing. There was a particular silence that took hold after the laughter that caused him to look up from the ground. He saw Lauren looking at him, quite interested, as the four boys in the center continued their conversation. He blushed and quickly looked back down at the ground. That look was too sharp and focused on him. She was looking right at him, and he felt in trouble for acknowledging his eavesdropping.

Lauren spoke again, interrupting the boys' thread. "I remember that dance well. Do you remember when you and I danced, Talphi?" A creative thought had come over her, and Talphi was there to be its target. It would be a lot of fun to play with Talphi, he was blushing already. She knew what that meant.

It was a lie. Talphi couldn't stand the dance training, and since sessions weren't mandatory, he skipped them. The dances were terrible thanks to the touching and formality. "No, I haven't been to a dance." He looked up for a moment to see them. All of the center five were now looking at him eagerly and expectantly. The attention was oppressive, and he tried to return to the sedated state from minutes ago.

Ralph wanted to see this. "Sure, I remember when you two danced." It was like a cat playing with a mouse. This was just play, and he enjoyed watching Lauren play.

Lauren stood up from the inner circle. "You remember what happened?" She said it without question or mistake. The story was perfectly formed in her mind, and she just needed to lead him down the path.

The looks and attention burned Talphi, so he didn't answer. He begged himself to become hidden, but he wasn't in control of them. Their attention could not be changed or diverted with anything he could do.

Nicholus wanted to be part of this game. "Well. I remember seeing you two leave, right?" He wanted to bat around the prey also.

Lauren agreed, "Yes." She had moved over to Talphi and was standing in

159

the space next to him on the bench.

She was closer than he wanted her. His embarrassment was attention, disdain, and attraction. "I've never been to a dance." It was the only thing that made sense to say. Her waist was in view next to him. He channeled his vision into a tunnel as much as possible to forget her proximity.

Lauren was drawn to the moment. It gave her control. "You were so good at dancing... the way you touched me. We went behind the bakehouse, and you started to kiss me." She brushed her hand across his face and down his burning cheek.

Ralph was aroused by the direction of her story and added, "You were behind there for an hour, it seemed." He said excitedly, like he wanted to be touched. It made him want to touch himself, but he restricted himself to keeping both hands on his thighs and moving slowly.

Lauren sat next to him on the bench, close enough for her hip to press up against his. "It felt so good." She whispered into Talphi's ear but loud enough for her quiet audience. "We took off our clothes, and I kissed you all over." Her hand wandered down to his thigh and rubbed inward toward his crotch. She gripped control and explored the power of her position.

Talphi couldn't watch. He stared forward, hating. Hating. Why? The suggestions and the touching had given him an erection, and he wasn't in control of anything she wanted. Stop. It won't stop. He screamed into his head as his teeth were clenched tight.

Lauren whispered lust into his ear. Touching him and rubbing him put the control in her hands. She blew into his ear when she finished each part of her description to cool his burning face. Her audience gave their undivided attention. No more improvisation was volunteered by the captivated few.

A voice came from a short distance through the tunneled senses. "Everyone, lunch is ready. The treatments will be ready when we get back." It was Surrivan calling to them from many yards away.

Upon the command, Talphi stood up and followed the tunnel as the voice had suggested. Why didn't he stop her? Why did she do that to him? She just took something from him. Was she able to because she could see his weakness? Was he an obvious target and easy plaything?

His focused eyes caught the shape of a brier plant as he sped away. It was uninviting, sharp, and protected. Animals stayed away from it, and the plant was less likely to be eaten. He had to be like that plant. Hard, causing pain when he was attacked. He must be undesirable... untouchable... strong, be the plant no one will want. This would be his training. Self-loathing and resolve consumed him.

The memory of his dream returned to him as he ate. Talphi saw himself as a runner again, but he had stopped on the path of empty space. He wasn't stupid enough for it. Stopping gave him strength as he stood apart. The child stopped stacking the blocks. Talphi breathed heavily as goosebumps waved over his skin and up his spine. It was the same thing that occasionally occurred when he listened to some music. But this didn't have the same uncomfortable foreboding of rejection. This was empowering. This was his strength and not inspired by a muse. He focused on it and felt it again and again. "I can do this. I can crush this pathetic lie," he whispered to himself. The man at the race exploded into a raging fire, consuming the race. The baby pushed down the blocks and stood. He had asked himself if he was the first to dream and realize whatever this was. Was he the first to react like this? He questioned his realization. But no one around him acted as if they understood. They all ate and clucked about meaningless things.

For hours each day, Talphi tunneled his mind toward the image of defense. He would guard himself against everyone around him who wasn't important. There was no point in interacting with them since they wanted to hurt him and sharpen their claws on his weakness. Focusing on what he could control and doing the work was better than dwelling on his failure. He could work till it hurt, and the pain of his struggle was his reward. His pain was preferable to feeling worthless.

When it turned to night, he continued to work on his thoughts. He was alone, and the darkness could lead to loneliness, but he needed to strengthen himself. The night wasn't going anywhere and the feeling of being alone was a fact. Talphi fought back the loneliness by sitting in his bed and listening to the silence. It didn't speak to him as he had hoped, but it had a lovely sound. By taking in the silence and taking in the absence of life, he came across a solution. He could embrace his split from the world.

Talphi cried as he focused on the feeling of permanent separation from this community, but his skin tightened, and his hair stood on end. A wave like a chill carried down his spine again, and he breathed in with it. It was like euphoria and like a promised hidden power. He was alone and sad, but by accepting the empty space, he could be more. He wouldn't turn a blind eye to the painful truths.

The days that passed were indistinguishable as he repeated his mantras and focused his energy on the only thing that seemed to matter anymore, his sanity. Talphi thought of the plant again as the hurt continued, and he became resistant like it. He was still thinking of the plant when Chris bumped into him without apologizing. Chris was his age and wasn't accepted by the inner circle Talphi despised, but he was no friend.

Talphi cut back verbally since Chris made no sign of apology. "Hey, watch it, prick."

Chris replied loud enough for everyone nearby to hear, "What did you call me?" He wasn't going to let someone talk to him that way. There was no way he would back down from a reason to bust someone's head. He was known for starting fights. The boys and girls nearby stopped and watched Chris do his routine.

Talphi didn't back down. "I called you a prick for walking into me." He had no fear of Chris's girth or reputation at this moment. He was slightly taller than Chris, but that didn't matter; only the need to finally hurt his offenders mattered.

Chris pushed Talphi backward with both hands. He expected Talphi to fall or curse him as he fell into submission. Maybe he'd have to punch Talphi a few times to keep Talphi on the ground. Everyone needed to be reminded that no one could push him around.

Talphi was ready to release his rage and so glad he was pushed. It gave him reason to do damage because he should be untouchable, and Chris had touched him. Talphi stepped into Chris quickly after regaining his balance. His teeth were clenched. "Die," was his only thought. His fingers wrapped around Chris's neck, and he squeezed through the fat and closed off the breath and blood. He lifted him into the side of a house a few feet away, pressing him against the wall with one hand, and looked into the horror and shock that pulsed in Chris's eyes.

Chris fought back and tried to reach or push, but Talphi had length, and Chris's feet were off the ground. He was fading from lack of air as the seconds ticked by. His hands pulled at Talphi's arm, but there was nothing he could do, and there was no end to his breathlessness. His eyes peaked, bulged, and begged for life. There was only fear in Chris at this moment.

It was horrifying to Talphi. He was taking life, and this is what it looked like. Nothing about Chris's expression fueled his need to crush him to death. He pulled away from the moment. It was disarming to see the feeble and meek begging for life. What sort of monster was he making of himself? Glad to finally unleash his power but horrified at the pain he was causing.

The breath for Chris meant relief from terror. One breath back into life and he knew he had to strike back, so he lunged forward. He simply applied his mass into a bear hug that didn't and couldn't hurt Talphi. Going after Talphi's neck would have been a way to kill Talphi, but he wasn't trying to kill. Chris needed to be menacing when he wasn't home.

Talphi didn't have to disarm Chris from him as two teachers had arrived to separate the two. Chris still struggled to attack, but Talphi stood passive and was lost in his display of power. He knew his anger caused this, but his demonstration of violence was foreign. A rush of pressure had joined his effort. A moment of feelings, understanding, and body had collided with a belief. His emotions were worn out while his body felt awake.

As the teachers led them away in the opposite direction, the teacher started to question Talphi. "What were you fighting for?"

Talphi gave the short version. "He bumped into me and didn't apologize. I called him a prick. He pushed me, and I fought back."

The teacher added to the problem. "You could have hurt other students too. Did you think about that?" The teacher had pulled Talphi away from the other students as he reprimanded and thought up a punishment for him.

Talphi replied, "No." He was still ashamed of himself though this question seemed foolish. He had answered the first question honestly, and the teacher seemed to want more remorse than his honest answer.

The teacher wanted to see shame, but he wasn't getting it from Talphi. "Well, why not?" He asked, without needing an answer. "You will come back here after your lessons for the next week, and we will assign you your tasks for your punishment."

Talphi said in agreement, "Alright." He felt like he needed to be punished, but he didn't care what or who he had hurt. He had thought he was gaining control of himself, but this whole encounter made him realize he was failing. It didn't matter how strong he had felt because this outburst was a weakness. This punishment was well deserved, and he accepted it.

At the end of each day, he stayed for the punishment, but the structured discipline he expected crumbled like a sandcastle. The tasks were easy. His mother made no effort to increase the punishment, which should have been obviously easy in her view. He didn't learn what he thought his punishment would make him feel.

Talphi learned a different lesson than what they probably wanted him to learn. He imagined that they wanted him to feel guilty, which he did, but not because of the punishment and their harsh words. The guilt was already there and was his own. Maybe it was meant to give him time to think, but he already thought all the time. If that was the reason for punishment, then he didn't need anyone to punish him. He already punished himself.

That was the truth; that was the lesson he taught himself. He was the judge of himself. No authority needed to tell him what was right and wrong. It was clear through all the consequences and reactions. It seemed so obvious, and it made him proud to accept responsibility for his actions. He would have to battle his wild emotions on his own.

Rachael did confront Talphi when she learned about the punishment. She didn't want to believe the fast-moving rumors that he had attacked another child unprovoked, believing that would undermine everything she saw in her son. "Talphi, I don't know why you and that other boy fought. I know things haven't been easy, and I'm not home when you get there." It was an explanation she had been working on. Perhaps it was partly her fault that he lashed out.

Talphi hadn't thought that his mother had any role in what he did except to act as another one of the teachers. How could she and their home have anything to do with what happened? "What? My fight had nothing to do with that. He... was annoying me, and I fought him. It was wrong." He wanted to show the proper amount of self-disapproval.

Rachael was glad to hear him say it was wrong, but she needed to make sure it wasn't her. "I know, but sometimes, if people are upset over something else, they will lash out against those they normally wouldn't. They might attack someone else in frustration." She looked for his eyes to connect with hers. He needed to address what was wrong, even if it was her.

He could remember the anger he felt leading up to the attack, but he didn't want to feel it at the moment, so he blocked his thoughts. He sidestepped the block and focused on the problem he knew. "He's always picking on people. I was having a bad day and fought back. I'm sorry."

Rachael watched him deflect again and added, "It's alright to be upset, but you shouldn't fight people. Someone could have gotten really hurt." It was important that he did not attack people. She had never had to say it out loud to him, and it felt cumbersome. She couldn't explain all the intricacies of struggle and fighting back in one conversation, so she began with simple rhetoric. Fighting someone because they were annoying is not acceptable.

Talphi shared his experience: "I know. I almost did." He remembered Chris's terror-driven eyes nearly popping out of his head.

She looked for clarification. "What do you mean?" She knew he understood that people can get hurt in a fight, but it sounded like he worried about more.

Talphi held his head low. "His eyes. I could see him... it was wrong." Thinking of the eyes made his eyes water. The eye contact he had with Chris was the most he had with anyone. "It was like I could have killed him, and I was watching him die. It's the only thing that stopped me. When he pushed me, I felt certain that I wanted to kill him. Every part of me wanted it, and when I grabbed him, he was like a doll. Easy to throw against that wall." He was afraid of himself as the anger returned, and he squeezed the door frame. It creaked in distress, but Talphi didn't hear it as he tunneled into the moment with his thoughts.

Rachael's eyes widened as she watched the wood under his hand start to buckle. She always wanted Tal'Abrac to be his father, but she had never really thought about the chance of Talphi having Tokkin powers because he didn't share a Tokkin appearance. The arrival and age of such displays in Tokkin society were completely unknown. She needed to move to action quickly and find some way to prepare Talphi for whatever he was truly going through. "Well, I know that in such moments, people can push past limits. And growing up causes many changes in our bodies. But-" she paused. The possibility of Tokkin powers influencing him was her conclusion. "This is something your father would have known more about."

Talphi interjected, "This isn't normal." He said it more as a statement than a question.

It wasn't normal, but how could she help her son without needing a Tokkin? "No. It's nothing like that. Even though I am a teacher, there are feelings I don't know about as a boy grows up. I am a girl, after all." She smiled to relieve some tension and delay the truth; however, she figured on presenting it. Talphi looked up momentarily to smile back at her observation. Rachael couldn't ignore this, but she'd need help.

Rachael continued, "Don't worry about a thing. I know some men I could ask. The strength a man has is good, Talphi. It's nothing to be feared, but knowing when and how to use it may be something a man would be best to teach you. I wish your father were here." She didn't mean to say the last part, but she longed for it so much that she needed to say it out loud.

Talphi didn't react for minutes. It would be safer if this was just a man's strength and not an abnormality. It didn't change the feeling that he was abnormal. He was a threat to others, and he was the only one who could keep himself at bay.

They settled to address the problem in the morning, and Rachael could only think of one man who had the resources to help Talphi if he was displaying Tokkin abilities. The Mayor of Saven, Mark Hilbin, could help secure passage for them or assistance to Talphi. There was no way she could keep this secret, so it was either trusting him or leaving the Kingdom, and she had a life here that she wanted to stay in. Her choice was bolstered by the good friendship she had formed with the mayor, which he occasionally intimated could be closer. Exile was the usual course for Tokkin births in the Kingdom, but King Medrick had kept the execution laws on the book, so she needed guidance from someone with more familiarity with the current situation.

Mark had been appointed the first Mayor of Saven and had remained in that position under the King's continued approval. He had successfully bridged the divide between the King's vision for stability and negotiating that change with the townsfolk. He wasn't just a pawn of the King like a Ginru Force soldier. He had a vision. Mark had accepted Rachael into Saven and given her a life she hadn't imagined. She trusted him to find the best path forward for her and Talphi.

The next day, Rachael went to the mayoral office, a building at the highest point of the town. It was built by the community to serve as an office and gathering hall. They had overbuilt it so that it could weather the worst conditions like the great halls in the colder north. It was tall enough for a second story, but it had an open ceiling to expose the highly sloped roof. The office could seat hundreds of people on benches facing the table at the head of the hall.

When she needed to talk to Mark in the past, she had always come when she knew others would be seeking his advice. This time was different. She needed to be alone with him, so she used her knowledge that he came hours before opening the doors. "Good morning, Mayor Hilbin."

Mark was sitting behind the table with stacks of papers. He was tall when he stood, and his brown hair framed his face down to his shoulders. His blue eyes locked on her, and his welcoming lips widened to a smile. "Hello, Rachael. You're here early; that's not typical of you." This was the first time she had come to see him outside of hours.

Mark was married and incredibly handsome. He had occupied too many of her dreams over the years, but she had remained respectful of his wife by keeping their interactions public. This was one of the reasons she had always come when there were others. Even though she needed to be alone with him, she still felt guilty for being there. "It's not typical, but this isn't a typical need." She nodded her head in appreciation for the departure from tradition. It felt critical that she set the tone or risk his refusal.

Mark sat forward eagerly. "Please! I would be happy to help." Whatever she needs is surely in his capacity. She was well worth it. "This will be the first time you've come to see me while I'm alone. Have a seat." Mark pointed to the chair across his desk and close to him. This rare moment alone with Rachael was not going to be squandered. He wanted her as close as possible.

Rachael wanted to be honorable, but she knew their attraction to each other would be helpful. "Thank you." She came up to the desk and sat facing him. "I guess I'll be direct with the issue."

He wished she wouldn't hurry. It would be better if she had come without any issue, but he knew it must be serious for her to break all patterns. "Please."

Rachael crossed her legs and stared at the desk for a moment to prepare a quick set of points. "My son was in a fight a few days back."

Mark had heard about the fight and had hoped her problem would be serious. "And you thought the punishment ill-fitting?" What a letdown. He had expected something a little more dangerous or something he could play the hero to, such as dangerous creatures near her house or harassing men he could protect her from.

Rachael thought the punishment was fine. "Oh, no, no. It's not that. You see, when I asked my son about it, he said that he felt like he was afraid of his reaction." She sounded silly and over concerned, "Boys will be boys and fight, but he was frightened by the attack. He wasn't hurt, and the other boy was on the receiving end. He was frightened by his loss of control, and it could have been a lot worse." Rachael fumbled her hands in her lap.

Mark liked to see Rachael struggle to explain since he wanted to ease her struggle. "Oh... I see." He knew about Rachael's son, and this concern sounded more like something his wife would come to him with when their children acted out. "The boy never knew his father, did he?"

Rachael confirmed, "No, he didn't." Mark was a father of four, and his insight might apply before her concerns about the Tokkin power Talphi might have. She needed to ease Mark into the discovery. She would have to play the old role, like when she was pregnant and feigned ignorance. That way would help Mark find it in his heart to protect Talphi from exile.

Mark nodded in understanding. "And you have no other man to talk with him, do you?" This was not a role for a mayor, but he was eager to be her knight, and this was better than the examples he had thought up.

Rachael leaned forward. "That would be wonderful, but it's more than that." She paused before continuing. She wouldn't have come to Mark if it were as simple as a father figure. The Tokkin concern didn't need a Tokkin father, but the right story could plant the seed. "I worry there is more to his strength than just a boy growing up."

He doubted her suggestion, but he was curious. This was her first child, and she was missing a husband for the boy. "Why do you think that?" It would be easy to set this straight.

Rachael replied, "Well, his father is what concerns me." She stopped again so that he would ask for more information.

Mark was insightful, and his mind raced ahead. He knew where she had come from before Saven, but before Jamin, he only knew she was in the east. Talphi was a normal-looking child, so the father subject she danced around seemed very unlikely to Mark. But the thought did appear. "Who was his father, Rachael?" She didn't answer him and looked away and off to the east. "You think your son is Tokkin, don't you?" She looked up, and he knew he had the right thought.

She replied with a nervous laugh, "Ridiculous, right?" But uncertainty was her game to play. "No one knows what causes it, and every parent holds their breath till birth, but the things Talphi said about the fight concerned me. I might be thinking bad things, but how can I be certain?"

Mark started to investigate. "You're certain his father wasn't a Tokkin?"

Rachael had arranged a story over the years and was prepared to share the fabrication. "His father was just a deserter. When they caught up to him, they..." It was the evolution of her lie. It was more acceptable than not knowing the father, and it was closer to the truth. "They killed him when they found him. Maybe he was a relic wielder, or maybe there's more to it. I don't know what to think." Rachael only knew she feared for Talphi. Things might get a lot worse for him.

Mark brushed the concern to the side. "Well, he doesn't look it, for starters." He thought of another reason without dismissing her concerns quite yet. He took the relic lead she suggested. "Relics can do Tokkin-like things, too, and I've heard of people finding new relics before. Perhaps he has some odd stone that he keeps as a charm?"

Rachael liked the excuse, "Not that I know of," but it wasn't feasible. It showed that Mark wasn't rushing to judgment. He was more likely to help her.

"Wait," Mark held up his hand to himself and looked down, "I'm getting ahead of myself." He needed to know firsthand. "I need to hear your son's feelings for myself, and I'll put his strength to the test. Maybe he was just overcome." He chuckled, falling into her fear so easily. "One thing at a time, no hasty conclusions."

She released her breath. "You'll help? Oh, thank you, thank you so much." She leaned forward far enough to take one of his hands on the desk. "I've been so lucky to always find people who help me when I've needed them the most."

Mark perked up. "Oh?" He wasn't the first?

Rachael beamed. She truly was grateful. "Yes, Commander Arprot helped me when I needed it, and the Montens were a wonderful family that took me in. And now you." She let go of his hands and put her hands to her heart. It felt good for her heart to beat with relief.

He watched her hands and drew parallels from her past. "Well. I've heard of Commander Arprot and the stability he's brought as the garrison commander of Willbington. And I heard the Montens were kind nobles and good people. So, from what I can see," he included himself, "you have a talent for finding good people. You work hard, you are caring." He looked at her hands buried in her breast and continued up to her soft face. "You are beautiful. Naturally, you should find help when you need it."

Rachael blushed profusely and felt the heat she tried to avoid around Mark. It mixed with her longing to release this new pressure about Talphi. Her voice trembled in reply, "Great, thank you." She looked too long into his eyes in silence before speaking. "So, what did you have in mind for Talphi?" Her fear was subdued by his strength.

Mark stood up, walked around the desk, and put his hand on Rachael's shoulder. He moved his hand down her arm. She released her hand from her chest and took his hand with both of her hands. Rachael kept from turning to him completely and being overcome by his presence. He spoke, "This evening at dusk. We can meet at the eastern town marker. There is enough privacy out there. I will speak with him, and we will run a test."

She looked up into his face. "Then?" His touch ignited her feelings, and she enjoyed losing her thoughts so close to him.

Mark squeezed her hand. "Then? We will know what to do. I am here for you no matter what." He kissed her hands, holding his. This service to her would bring them closer, and he was relatively sure now that this would be easily resolved.

Rachael was slow to respond. She just blinked into his eyes. It was so enthralling to listen to Mark since he was just what she wanted, and he knew what he was doing. She would let him lead her. "Great." She had been a single parent for so long that she embraced the chance to follow Mark's lead. She stood up, releasing his hand, and pressed her lips onto his. He didn't stop her and pressed in, pulling her closer.

They released themselves from each other, acknowledging where they were and who could see them. It was momentary guilt, but the blossoming trust between them made it feel right. The close trust they had built over the years had yearned for this moment.

Rachael nodded and stepped back to excuse herself. "Till this evening."

Mark smiled and nodded, "Till then."

Rachael was excited to see Mark again, even if she remained nervous about her son's fate. She told Talphi that they were going to test his strength and prove there was nothing to fear about himself. The truth was uncertain, but her belief in Mark gave her strength. When they met in the evening, Mark led them out to a small clearing where a thick rope lay on the ground. He pointed for Rachael to sit off to one side. "Talphi, could you remove anything in your pockets and take off your shirt?" Mark wanted to see if there were any markings and how his body and skin responded while they tested. Though his knowledge was limited, he knew that proof of Tokkin influence might be subtle, and he didn't want any possible relics in Talphi's possession.

Talphi looked at his mother blankly. He wondered if he had made a terrible mistake by opening up to her about the fight. It was just a shirt, but he was still removing clothes.

Rachael reassured him, "It's alright, Talphi. You can do as Mark asks." But she hadn't explained her concern over his possible Tokkin abilities. Nor had she talked to him about relics. She had said that they were testing his strength as a man.

Thankfully, Mark helped the cause with an excuse. He removed his shirt, too. "We don't want them to snag on anything. And during a tug of war, we don't want to possibly fall on something in a pocket."

Talphi removed his shirt and went to clear out his pocket, but there was nothing in them. Mark was rather certain he didn't have a relic and moved to the other side of the rope. "Alright, Talphi, we're going to perform a little test. Very simple." He took up the end of the rope. "I want you to hold onto that side of the rope without wrapping it around your hands or waist. I will be holding the other end. When I'm ready and give you the word, I want you to pull your hardest. Pull the rope from my hands or pull me to the ground if you can."

Talphi laughed. It didn't seem likely. He had played the game before, and his mother could have done this test without Mark's help. "That's it?"

Rachael captured Talphi's attention. "Yes, Talphi. You told me about what you felt fighting that boy, and both Mark and I know what it's like to grow up. There is confusion and mistakes, but there are sometimes questions that need to be answered. So, we test the best we can. This test will help prove that there is nothing wrong with what you felt. Mark is here to help us."

Talphi picked up his end of the rope. He waited for Mark's order as Mark worked the rope into position along his arm, around his back, and bent up into his other arm. Talphi knew what to do since it was a common enough game. It was unfair to match him against an adult, but the test and his mother's explanation fit the situation. Once Mark was in position, he announced, "Begin Talphi."

Talphi brought the rope up and pulled it taut. He didn't try to jerk it away. With the rope taut, he moved the rope into position like Mark and began to pull. And pull. He was straining but couldn't budge Mark. Mark looked reassuringly at Rachael. She was wondering if she had made a good and disappointing mistake, but Talphi didn't see either of them; he was pulling hard enough that it hurt.

The line went relaxed as Mark spoke, "Talphi." He needed to be sure before they stopped this test. "When you attacked that other boy, you were angry?"

Talphi said panting, "Yes." A foolish question; of course he was.

Mark pushed for Talphi to show him what his anger added. "I want to see that anger. I want you to get that angry right now. Show me the strength, you won't hurt me." He watched Talphi's eyes widen as he begged for the rage. "We have to see it."

Talphi was frightened by the rage, "I can't." He didn't want to use it.

"You can. This time, I give you permission." Mark held the momentarily relaxed line and waited for Talphi to pull again. "Put yourself in that moment again."

This sounded like a horrible idea to Rachael. She didn't want Talphi to relive the moment. But it would be a relief if Talphi couldn't pull Mark. This moment could change her life all over again. If Talphi couldn't pull Mark, it would be another reason to doubt Tal'Abrac was the father, but if he did pull the line, it could be proof.

Talphi didn't speak again but pulled the rope tight and began to exert himself. When he was ready, he thought about and relived the moment. The memory of Chris taunting him made it so easy to tap into the anger. He clenched his teeth and pulled with the memory. His thoughts brushed the memory of Lauren in an attempt to find the reason for his rage and fury burst from him, crystallizing his feelings, thoughts, and body into one voice, one belief. There was no question of strength, size, or means. He needed to pull this rope to end the struggle. "Die!"

Mark was shocked, and he couldn't dig into the clumpy earth hard enough to keep from moving. He leaned back as Talphi pulled him forward. Talphi repositioned his left hand and pulled again with the same force, yelling. "Come on." He reached over with his right arm and pulled again. There was a visible lash of purple light that leaped from his reaching arm and cut the grass and earth with malice and contempt. "Is this what you wanted?" There were no panicked eyes of Chris this time to stop him. Instead, he felt the tears of self-anguish pour down his face. He stopped as he answered his own question. It hurt, and this is not what he wanted. Talphi dropped the rope and dropped to his knees.

Rachael cried, too, and stood up to relieve her son's pain. Mark had let go of the rope and motioned for her to stop closing in on her son. "Wait," he said to her. He quickly moved near to Talphi, looking for any blemish that looked Tokkin in nature. There was nothing he could see. Talphi fell into a category he didn't know could occur. Not Tokkin or relic wielder. Only witches have powers without Tokkin features. Was Rachael a witch? She wouldn't hide that. "Rachael, are you a witch?"

She was shocked but replied immediately, "No. If I were a witch, I would have never come to you." It hurt her to hear him say it, but she needed him to be on her side. "I don't know what to do. I need your help."

Mark wanted to help her, and he had promised her he would help, but the course of actions he had played with in such a scenario was costly and dramatic. Talphi couldn't simply stay with her here. Mark wanted to keep Rachael near him, so Talphi had to go away without his mother. Mark turned to Talphi. "Talphi, stop crying." Talphi obeyed after a few more sobs and looked forward into nothingness. Mark had a resource in mind, and he thought back to the King's guidelines. "You are strong, and you will make a fine relic wielder."

Talphi hadn't expected that answer. He thought he was abnormal and that he might be a monster, but he knew what relic wielders were, and that wasn't bad. "How do you know that?" Still, he didn't look at his mother or Mark since he was ashamed of himself. He didn't want their attention. His mind was clear enough to remember the attention his encounter with Lauren had created, and he felt powerless. Talphi started to cry again, begging himself for control.

Mark forged his lie. "Relic wielders have a certain aptitude that you have just displayed." Rachael had never heard this but listened to Mark continue. "With a relic, you will be able to put your strength to work. It used to be that relics were tightly controlled by the Relic Order, but like all things, the King has improved on the system. He's acknowledged that new relics can be found, and those that find them are given entry to train for the Order."

Rachael was skeptical, but this would mean that she could be secure in the Kingdom, and Talphi could be accepted regardless of the truth about his father. This would help him find a place in the world and might save him from the struggle. "You have a new relic, Mark?" she asked. The possibility and rarity suddenly weighed on the cost of this course.

Mark locked eyes with Rachael. There was no malice, but the heavy stare conveyed the price and would test the bond they shared. Rachael breathed deeply, and tears formed in her eyes. She would see her son down this path.

Mark looked at both of them. "I know how to get one. There are channels for such things, and the King's laws now welcome previously unknown relics into their ranks. But Talphi, I hope you realize the debt you will owe. To this town and the King's service for your training."

Talphi took this seriously. This was an answer and a chance to prove he could control himself. If a relic is what he needed, then he would do what it takes to be granted one. "I understand." He looked at each of them, and he could see something else in their faces. There was a sharpness left over from the experience of releasing his anger. They cared about him, but they had a secret. He saw more adults keeping something from a child. There was no point asking them, he'd have to figure this out on his own.

Chapter 13

Tiffany rested in her chair, waiting for her daughter. The green armchair had extra padding because it was under constant use. The room was a chamber in the King's castle. It was spacious, with two large windows, and had two rooms for their organization. They were allowed to decorate it however they wanted. The chamber was supposed to be a place for the King to come for the guidance of the Sisters of Forn as per their agreement, but he did not need them as advisers. Instead, he used them as figures of legitimacy.

It was her day to be on duty for King Medrick. He had never come to visit, so this was the most solitary assignment. The other Sisters were dispatched to watch over the King's servants like the Ginru Force. However, they could see it as a way to keep them occupied and separate from each other. Their actions and advice to Antoin had done what they wanted. They were alive, the Kingdom was spared chaos, and except for the nobles that opposed Medrick, people were happier. The price of the victory was knowing they could not oppose the King without driving internal war into their beloved Kingdom.

Tiffany was close to death. There had been a cost to keeping her figure so youthful for extended periods for her lover, King Antoin. He had known her age, but her outer appearance was always to his liking. That degree of manipulation of her own body had cost her decades of extended life. Her face now wore deep wrinkles, and her silvery hair was wearing thin and wiry. She had the strength to keep herself mobile when needed and not much more. Thankfully, she had her daughter. Jasmine was nearly fifteen and the love child of King Antoin. Many of the Sisters of Forn believed he was going to die in the battle, but Tiffany had hoped he would live.

Her daughter entered without knocking. Jasmine's light summer dress was stylish for her age, and the fabric was of a higher quality, requiring more care and maintenance. She had abandoned the innocent look to accentuate her intelligence. Two thin braids of brown hair framed the sides of her face. Her bright brown eyes could easily draw a favorable response. The fashions she had chosen matched the calming expressions. She had mastered her inviting elegance at a younger age than most girls.

Tiffany scolded her for bad manners, "Jasmine, you are in the King's castle. You must always knock before entering a room. This is not our home." This was technically their home and haven inside the walls, but there was still no excuse.

Jasmine cleared her throat and agreed with her mother in gesture, but not in words. "I know, but I knew you were the only one in here. If there was someone else in here, I would have knocked and displayed proper manners."

Trained witches could feel the space around them. Everyone gives off signs of their presence. Sometimes it's breath or heat or slight sounds. That training wasn't a good reason. "That's no excuse. Create the habit or be undone when you are distracted."

Jasmine restrained from rolling her eyes. "Yes, Superior." She addressed her mother as all daughters of the Sisters addressed any of the seven Mothers. "May I be seated?" she asked politely. It was in her best interests to behave with manners. It makes one more approachable.

Tiffany continued without more disciplining. "Yes, this may take a while." She pointed to the free seat across from her. As soon as Jasmine was seated, she started. "I'm sure you know this is called the Seeing Room. The Sisters of Forn set it up for the King to have the services of the Sisters on hand at all times."

Jasmine nodded and sat properly with neatly crossed legs and a straight back. She wanted to be perfect in pose since anything worth doing was worth doing well, even if she ignored the rules from time to time.

Tiffany asked, "Do you know how many times the King has used our service in the castle?" She watched Jasmine holding her posture. If she didn't know her daughter well, she might think Jasmine was holding such posture to mock her earlier scolding.

Jasmine guessed, "None?" She wasn't sure if there was a time when the King had visited since it had been a running joke since her birth. "Did he visit just recently?"

Tiffany confirmed the answer. "No, he has not visited recently. He has not used our talent for scrying since the fog vanished." The Sisters had taken to calling the Tokkin army that was defeated 'the fog'. She sat forward and pulled her voice in. "We are here night and day, and yet he ignores us nearly completely."

Jasmine knew this, so without anything new, it must not be a serious conversation. "Well, that seems foolish." She relaxed her posture slightly, but Tiffany coughed, and Jasmine corrected herself in the chair. Jasmine had mistakenly thought of the conversation as a casual comment and not a lesson Tiffany was about to give.

Tiffany explained, "You'd think it makes him a fool, but it does not. He has disproven that assumption at least eight times, but I imagine there have been more occurrences we are not aware of. There should have been eight large and successful rebellions since Medrick became King."

Jasmine hadn't heard that before. "There have been no rebellions. There haven't even been minor, weak, or failed revolts, only talk of rebelling."

Tiffany ignored the rude interruption with her own excitement. "That's because all of them were crushed before forming. He is seeing them on the horizon without the help of a witch. With pinpoint accuracy, he cuts them off without any witch's help."

The Determined World

This was twice the news to Jasmine. She hadn't heard through any Superior that there were supposed to have been eight rebellions and that there was a chance someone who was not a witch could have such foresight or could scry for the future. "He couldn't have! There must be another witch helping him." The King couldn't be a witch himself. For starters, he was a male. Tiffany shook her head no to repel the assumption. "Then some Tokkin person or a dragon, perhaps."

Tiffany almost laughed. "You stretch for an explanation, my dear. I doubt the King would have such a Tokkin person in his presence, and I've never heard of a dragon taking up scrying. If anything, dragons have the opposite belief in the ordered future since they can't be scryed for." She smiled, seeing Jasmine's thoughtful glance. It was nice to see the spark of interest still alive in her eyes. Jasmine usually extinguished those sparks quickly with mastery. "We do have an idea as to what we are dealing with." Tiffany was lower in her seat and spoke with an excited hush.

Jasmine suddenly spied around the room. "Are we safe to talk here?"

Tiffany carried on. "Oh, yes. I believe so. Knowing what I am about to tell you won't change his response to us." If Medrick could predict and stop the rebellions, letting her daughter know what the Sisters of Forn knew wouldn't change anything.

Jasmine sat at attention on a knife's edge. "Alright, if you say so." Her heart hadn't pounded with this much excited curiosity in years.

Tiffany gave Jasmine the knowledge her Sisters kept secret. "We have scryed on our own regarding the Kingdom of Garrin and the King. It is how we saw the missed rebellions. But we have been scrying for the path of King Medrick since the war ended. He himself is void and protected. It's the sort of protection that we may bestow on someone to block scrying."

This similar protection to a witch supported Jasmine's first assumption. "So other witches are helping him?"

Tiffany grinned when she said, "No. We know about nearly every other witch outside of our covenant, Jasmine. It is no witch, it is him now." It was like telling a horror story around a campfire. She enjoyed animating Jasmine too much.

Jasmine was pale from the loss of breath. "He is a Tokkin?"

Tiffany didn't think that was accurate, but it was closer to the truth. "I suppose someone could be transformed into Tokkin, but that would change so much of what makes a person themselves. No, he is still himself, but somehow his belief and ability have been enhanced. The world is full of pieces we don't understand. One of those pieces was relics, but we came to understand those in time. Another piece was at Pebble Mountain. That piece is no longer there, and we traced Medrick's course before the battle, traveling past that location." She raised her eyebrows to imply that the piece was now attached to Medrick.

Jasmine asked breathlessly. "What was it?"

Tiffany delved deeper into the story. "If you were to scry him, you would not be able to see anything. It's not like the fog that the Tokkin brought, shrouding everything it approaches. Instead, it is a force of belief that makes every event around it even clearer to scrying, but its own actions aren't observable. It's like the manifestation in the belief of a center that all events revolve around. Maybe that's how the battle was decided."

Jasmine searched with her eyes around them, but asked, "Did you know what would happen after the battle?"

Tiffany shook her head no. "No, that was the remaining twist that could not be seen beforehand. Even looking back hasn't produced complete clarity."

Jasmine scoffed, "So you didn't try to learn about this 'piece of the world' at Pebble Mountain? You let it happen without interference." This seemed like an obvious threat that they had known about for quite some time. They had put their faith in the unknown to escape uncertainty.

The Determined World

Tiffany hadn't imagined Jasmine's anger. "Why would we? We had the Kingdom to worry about; that is our piece of the world. Without doing what we did, the Kingdom would fall into the fog, plunged into chaos. It was a choice between an end to our way of life or allowing our world to continue under new leadership." Scrying was a cornerstone of the witches' power. Jasmine's accusation was too accurate, though.

Jasmine's face stayed tight as she tried to play out her mother's choice in her own mind, but there was something worrisome about her reaction. "Why are you telling me this? I don't understand the choice. Wouldn't I learn all this when you pass the memory on to me?"

Tiffany let her sadness show through because of the real reason she asked Jasmine to come there. "We are approaching that point, Jasmine, but." She breathed to calm herself. "I question the choice to aid the King and Medrick more and more every day. The reasons I came to the same conclusion as my Sisters have plagued me." She was saddened enough by the confusion to cry slightly. "Seeing him work, I don't know what we've done. I think I did what was in my heart and what was right. But I think I should have asked the same question you asked just now. I didn't. We so quickly embraced this chance without question. Why?" Tiffany reflected on what may have led her astray.

Jasmine sat as far forward as she could. "What do you mean, Mom?" This was not a casual conversation or a lesson like she had thought. This was a real problem.

Tiffany let her head fall back slowly against the back of the chair. She looked up at the ceiling. "Recently, I've started to feel as if I was led astray by my memories. You are young and have become incredibly capable. But you don't have countless memories of scrying for the truth. You can easily challenge the customs and traditions that I inherited from the past memories of my Mothers. You are right to question our decision."

Tiffany paused for a minute before continuing and let her heavy head fall into her hand. "Maybe it's because Antoin died, and that caused me to question our continued life. I've gotten old and have so many regrets." Jasmine didn't reply to Tiffany's words. "I question, without the memories, would I have let the fog continue? Letting it go would have changed everything I've ever known. It's easier to change when you are young. These memories from my Mothers made me old when I was young, and I don't want you to suffer the same aging."

Jasmine was concerned about what her mother was sharing, "Do you not want to pass on your memories to me?" She was not angry if that was her intent. The revelation of her mother would explain why Tiffany was revealing what she would learn from the transfer of memories. Tiffany's regret was her concern.

Tiffany looked up at her daughter. "No, you deserve them because they are your birthright. It is the reason we each give birth to one daughter. You have been raised to handle them, but when I think how young I was when I was given the memories, it makes me think that you are too young."

Jasmine scoffed at her mother as if it was a simple concern of age. She was well beyond the talents of her age.

"Jasmine," Tiffany said sternly. "You are as talented as any witch, but if I were to wait, then maybe the memories would be simple memories, and they would not influence you as much. I want you to be you. I don't remember clearly, but I wonder if when I received the memories, I became the memories and was no longer myself. All the memories feel so real and so personal. They are not a reference, they are me."

Jasmine struggled to recognize her mother's suggestion. "But wasn't this age, my age, the age chosen? Why change it now if this is the right age? All witches transfer their memories at this age." The problem was obvious to Jasmine. Tiffany intended to delay.

Tiffany continued her regrettable confession. "You are technically able, and it was the age we chose long ago. It's an impressionable age where the memories of the past would be the most understandable and influential. Not much thought has ever been given to what our daughters have wanted because they become Sisters of Forn before they know what they want." They took advantage of the nature of maternity and the trust of their daughters. It wasn't till this lifetime and the last few years that Tiffany had begun to see the abuse.

"Wait." It took a moment for Jasmine to gather the selfishness of the Mothers, the Sisters of Forn. "But I still want the memories."

Jasmine trusted the feelings that Tiffany questioned. Tiffany asked Jasmine to question more: "I would ask myself why I want them. Do you covet them, or have we taught you that they are your birthright? I always saw them as a birthright, but now that seems like a ploy. Never has so much been in question, and never have I questioned myself as much about these certain things." She closed her eyes to slow the spinning thoughts.

Jasmine wondered how far this crisis of faith had spread. "And do your Sisters feel the same?"

Tiffany sighed. "We haven't spoken about it. They may feel the same, or they may not, but I don't dare bring up my concerns."

Jasmine saw the weight of the confession. It was the role of the Sisters to support each other. Secrets were not healthy. "So, speak with them."

"No," Tiffany replied bluntly.

Jasmine saw an obstinance she hadn't expected from her mother. "Why not?" All the confusion and doubt were pushed aside by these being her mother's secrets. Her mother's doubts were just questions, but refusing to talk about it was a lie. The doubts were of concern to all of them and their way of life. Keeping that secret would be a failure.

Tiffany saw this as an individual burden and not a referendum on their way of life. "Because this is between me and my thoughts and my memories. This crossroads is as deep as when our sisterhood broke upon the creation of the Kingdom of Garrin. It cannot be negotiated with a consensus. It must be decided separately for each one of us." She would never reveal this doubt to her Sisters. Tiffany had her own plan to change it. Any other way would violently rip the Sisters of Forn apart again.

Jasmine relented. "Alright, fine. I know I don't fully understand, but what do you want me to do? Or not do. You do have a plan, right?" She was at the end of her suspense. Tiffany had dragged her along with the goalless reason long enough.

Tiffany locked eyes with Jasmine and revealed herself. "We are going to hold off on the transfer as long as we can. I want you to be yourself before you are a Sister."

Jasmine sat back and closed her eyes to imagine the result of holding off. "What do you want me to do till then? You've had me prepare my whole life for the moment that you are now delaying."

Tiffany beamed, "I need you to do whatever you want, my dear." She imagined that if she were told this when she was fourteen, she would be awestruck and giddy with ideas. But she was too far from fourteen to guess the feeling.

After moments of blank expression, Jasmine replied in anger. "What am I supposed to do? You can't open the door wide to a lifelong caged bird and expect it to know where to fly. I haven't a clue beyond what you've wanted, and now you want me to happily follow interests that I wasn't allowed to have?"

Tiffany shined the figurative apple she was offering to Jasmine. "You need to engage the world outside these walls. Travel, meet people, follow your fancy." It was a beautiful gift, and Jasmine was only seeing a burden. Life was wasted in youth.

Jasmine picked apart the offer so her mother could see the absurdity. "Good, sweet Mother... that could take ages. I'm sure you know people search for their entire life and never find what they want; that's just a fact. So, you give me the smallest window and, and... what if when the day finally comes I refuse to take the memories?" This was not a wonderful gift like her mother was pressing.

Tiffany welcomed Jasmine's thoughts. "Then that would be your choice and yours alone. It's just like my choice to do this without my Sisters' help. I will be proud of you either way." It would be terrifying and brave of Jasmine to do that to her. She would cry, but she would understand. Tiffany had put enough thought into this, so nothing Jasmine said was a surprise.

"What?" Jasmine looked at her calm mother. "Oh." She looked at her mother looking at her. She could see that Tiffany had thought this through. The anger seemed childish and too young, given her mother's calm. She wasn't ready for this.

Tiffany smiled and began to talk in a soothing and certain voice. She told the tale that Jasmine was quite familiar with but with a new insight. "Recently, I've thought about the Grand Mother, Pamela. No one has her memories, but I've thought about what she must have gone through. Born a Tokkin, she must have been feared. At that time, the Tokkin warlords conquered lands, enslaved, killed off threats, and tried to breed offspring. She must have been so desperate to find a way out."

Jasmine watched the lips of her mother as she told the story. She had heard it several times, but this time sounded more important.

Tiffany continued. "Imagine dedicating your entire life to escaping. Having to commit such violence to do so only to find that your own freedom doesn't change the world. She saw firsthand the savagery of the Tokkin warlords. Instead of resigning herself to that world, she wanted to break the cycle that had controlled her life." Jasmine listened intently to Tiffany. All other tellings had been so hopeful, while this time, it sounded desperate.

"She spent decades experimenting, learning, and trying to figure out the pieces of the world no one was looking at. Scrying helped her escape and avoid further bloodshed. It helped her find a path forward. She devoted herself to the belief that there was a way to save the world, and she was part of it."

Jasmine replied, "A noble cause."

Tiffany shrugged, "But was it? Think of what she did at that moment. She did what she had been forced to do up to that point. She had more children. Only this time, she found a way to suppress the Tokkin features of her children. Giving birth to gifted children for the fight as she saw it. She made twelve of us the benevolent witches, the Sisters of Forn, that would save the world. People trusted us."

"That's because you didn't pillage and murder." Jasmine thought it was odd that she was the one defending the Grand Mother.

Tiffany did not relent on her new perspective. "Aye, we unified, but how much of it was because we didn't share the Tokkin features? No, that's not the problem; that's just how people are. What I'm really getting to is that our mother used us. We existed for her purpose, and her daughters have continued down that path. I think that may have been one of the reasons the other sisters left, though they complained mostly about the Tokkin being systematically targeted."

Jasmine tightened up. "When you put it that way." She did feel used. "You bred me to take up your position." She could see Tiffany crying. They loved each other, and this realization was an unfortunate wedge. Neither of them wanted it, but ignoring it wouldn't help them move past it.

Tiffany nodded, "I think so, but now I see a chance to change the mistakes we've made. I will give you my memories if you want them. And I believe that acknowledging this will let you define the experience. Time being separate from me will help define what you want."

Jasmine got up and moved over to kneel next to her mom. "How much time do I have? Have you scryed for it?" She was low enough to look up to her.

Tiffany was going to do everything she could to extend her life. "I'll call for you when it's time. I'd rather you not count down the days, don't worry." She patted Jasmine's hands and brought one up to feel it against the side of her face.

Jasmine didn't like the answer. "I'm going to worry even if you don't tell me."

Tiffany remained seated and read her daughter's intent. "It would be my wish that you would involve yourself with your own life for now. Leave this old lady behind."

Jasmine stood up. "But what am I to do? It's like letting a broken horse loose for one day." It was crazy to refer to herself as a broken horse, but she added some funny animations that distracted from the sadness. "It doesn't know what to do, and I don't know what I'm supposed to do. What is the best thing for me to discover in such a short time?"

Tiffany laughed at her horse grazing gestures. "You're right, you're right. It can take years or even a lifetime to learn what to do, and it's not like you can scry for such a question. It is a daunting task, but you have some options." Tiffany pointed to the comfortable seat Jasmine had occupied a few minutes ago.

Jasmine sat back down in the chair and returned to her proper position. "I still can't believe you're suggesting this if it's so daunting. I don't know if I have a day, a week, or three hours. Is this what you expected when you planned this all?"

Tiffany formulated some options. "Enough, Jasmine. Things this important never go as we imagine it, but I yield to your point. I'll give you some directions. What you do will be up to you, but let me put you where you could learn something unique." She paused to make sure Jasmine was done protesting. "You can go to the King's vocational institution." It was Tiffany's only idea, and she envied it. She would have liked to go to the school herself and see Medrick's advancements in education. It would be exciting and informative. She then quickly generated another suggestion that she might have followed herself, "You could travel out to the Tokkin lands and meet our sisters that abandoned the Kingdom." Tiffany added a pause since she couldn't generate a third option. She hadn't planned to supply suggestions.

Jasmine laughed and didn't wait for any suggestions past the two Tiffany gave. "The school set up by the King?" With everything they had talked about, more education seemed absurd. The institution existed to further the King's goals, just like the purpose the Superiors prescribed for their daughters. "I need the King's education?"

"Well," Tiffany saw the point, "you wouldn't be going there for what they teach, and we already serve the Kingdom in our own way. But this is what is happening in the Kingdom. Hundreds and maybe thousands of people are getting training to build for the King. I understand the tools and methods are completely new." It was the epicenter of change in the Kingdom. "Also, the Relic Order is training their new wielders alongside the workers. Given the Order's previous restrictive nature, this coordination is amazing." Despite her feelings toward Medrick, she appreciated his newest push to advance the lives of so many.

Jasmine asked, "All I've heard is how upset the nobles are, and training more commoners is even more reason for them to be concerned. I didn't know that the Relic Order was involved like this." Jasmine hadn't heard much about the Relic Order. So many of them were lost that they had fallen mostly delinquent in the role of containing new relics that were discovered.

Tiffany knew everyone bent to King Medrick now. "Well, the Order is always at the service of the King. They are grateful for the King's position, recognizing the need to rebuild and reshape their role." She laughed. "Maybe they got tired of being thugs and wanted to build something." Tiffany elaborated. "It's easy to entice people into service with a promise of good work, a healthy life, and relief from restriction. Relics are found from time to time, and it's easier to welcome those in possession of the relic than to seize them and handpick the wielders."

Jasmine agreed. "You just have to change the training to making roads and building houses."

Tiffany was eager to reveal the possibilities. "Precisely. Think of all the people you will meet there that would never before travel or take on roles of leadership." She could see that Jasmine wasn't grasping the wonder of the unknown. She needed a more formal reason and purpose. Along the way, Jasmine would hopefully be led astray by her curiosity. "Maybe you even befriend future servants of the King. Gain favor and friendship with those leaders."

Jasmine perked up. "Like a spy?" She was comfortable seeing a defined task.

Tiffany replied slyly, "Like a wise witch." She was happy the idea was capturing Jasmine's interest.

Jasmine became nervous and giddy as she imagined herself talking with suspicious people. "And they won't be suspicious of my role there? The witch that just happens to be there observing and prodding?" It was the craziest and most amazing assignment her mother had ever suggested.

Tiffany smiled back at the nerves. "They will know you are a witch, but you could always entertain the methods they use, commoner or relic wielder alike. You will be just as fascinating as you'd like."

Jasmine smiled. She knew her mother was massaging her ego. "Yes, yes. I could. I think I understand now." She laughed. "Wow, I did not expect this." The feeling was what she imagined her mother wanted her to feel from the first suggestion of delaying the memories.

Tiffany defined the situation and gave a warning. "The Sisters are bound to the King's service, and we go where he tells us, but you are not. You won't be stopped from observing or participating as long as it serves the King. I'm serious about this, you must not defy the King, because the moment you do, he will put an end to the interference." As Tiffany spoke, Jasmine stopped laughing and nodded in understanding. "I've seen it happen. So just let his plan unfold, and you can do whatever pleases you."

Jasmine nodded. "I understand." It was daunting to think that she could be a threat to the King and foreboding that he would know if she were about to. "This school is in New Evenwright, correct?"

Tiffany added, "Yes, though don't call it a school. It's not for children. It's for young and older adults who want to be trained. It's his Institute of Vocation and Service."

Tiffany continued to tell her what she needed to know about the Institute and how to get there. Jasmine knew she wanted to meet the new generation of relic wielders more than she cared about the tools and methods the commoners were learning. Despite the fact the relic wielders were learning to build, they would still be the ones receiving the greatest rewards and roles from the King.

Chapter 14

It took Jasmine three weeks to reach New Evenwright. She could have made better time, but she decided to make a few stops at some of the construction projects already being completed by the new workforce being trained at the Institute. New Evenwright was to the northeast of Garrin in Kingdom lands that had been more favorable to Medrick's ascension. As a result of this favor, the Institute and new construction were all started and showcased along this route.

Jasmine did not hide her intentions to visit the Institute, but she wasn't sure if her arrival would be met with hospitality or hostility. The King could have told them she was coming if he thought it was warranted. Either way, she was prepared to make her case since she knew they would want to question her motives.

New Evenwright was new. The town had been built to function as proof of the King's progress. The layout was organized and ripe for future expansion. The distances between buildings, the quality of roads, and drainage were impressive and not clumsy like other places. The location of the town would not have been chosen in centuries past, but the unsettled land was being conquered and forced into order by relic wielders and new technology.

Jasmine saw controlled blasts with mixtures made by the workforce, machines made for pulverizing the stones, and workers using the stone to pack areas for foundations to build on. It was hard work, but every worker she talked to seemed eager to follow the King's vision. Her mother might be wrong. There was a revolution occurring. But it wasn't the people overthrowing the King, it was the King overthrowing the people and the old ways.

The distance north dropped the temperature and made the summer heat more manageable, but she knew it meant harsher winters. The Institute was three miles outside the town. It shared the same thoughtful placement and construction, but the buildings were considerably dull and impersonal.

It seemed that the construction she had seen up to this point followed the King's method, but those workers had added color and some design details to make it their own. No one but the King owned these buildings. They were gray, square, complete utility, and stable. Gravel paths connected each building in all possible directions. Trees and bushes had been intentionally planted between the routes to prevent travel on anything other than the paths. She imagined the whole area had been cleared and then laid out to his design.

People were coming and going along the routes. Everyone had a clear direction they were heading. Jasmine guessed which ones might be relic wielders. A few had red armbands. It might be another organizational method for leadership, but she would know more once inside. The lead building in front of the cluster had the signage in place. 'Institute of Vocation and Service : IVS, Admissions.'

A couple was talking to an administrator behind a desk. The inside of the room was just as dull as the outside. Only the desk had some color. It had been personalized by the administrator. He finished giving them directions and addressed Jasmine. "Good evening, I'm Gene. Welcome to IVS. How can I help you?"

Jasmine stepped up to meet him and bowed. He immediately looked cautious. "I'm Jasmine, a daughter of the Sister of Forn. I've come here because I've heard so much about this institute, and I wanted to see it for myself. And maybe learn a thing or two along the way." She wanted to be casual and refrain from loading up too much information at once. However, now Gene looked slightly scared.

He responded, nonetheless. "Of course." It was a confusing task to admit people from so many backgrounds. Nobles expected service, commoners wanted help, and relic wielders wanted respect. What did a witch want? "I'm just going to contact Master Anthen. He works with the relic wielders and the occasional noble. But you're my first witch." Gene smiled like he had been instructed.

Jasmine smiled back. It was horrible. It was a form of formality prescribed for commoners. His actions seemed like a breathing embodiment of the standardized buildings that formed the grounds of the Institute.

He pointed to one of the chairs to the side, "Please take a seat." Jasmine complied. He wasn't disagreeable, but Jasmine saw something unnatural and slightly sad. Gene moved to the side wall and pulled a red lever two times.

Nothing seemed to happen when the lever was pulled, but minutes later, a relic Master walked in, having entered through the rear door. He was wearing robes that were a deep red, unlike the normal clothes that most everyone else she had glanced at on the grounds wore. His eyes were a brilliant green, but his hair was too long and fell over them as he moved to meet her. "Jasmine," He replied quickly, giving a nod of his head, "I am Master Anthen. Please come with me; we can speak in our building".

Gene smiled as Jasmine stood. Master Anthen seemed prepared, so they must have received word about her from the King. Jasmine nodded to Gene as she left, "Thank you." She followed Anthen out the back door and across the grounds. People started to watch her now. They must assume she is another relic wielder. He led the way to another building almost identical to the Admissions building, but this one had a crest above the door. It was a red circle with three jagged lines running horizontally across the middle.

The interior of the building was the same as the first one. Master Anthen sat at the desk and pointed to the chair sitting across from him. "Please, take a seat." Jasmine sat and prepared for the inquisition. "The King informed us that you would be coming here. And while we are surprised your kind would ever care about the work we are doing, the King made it clear that we are to welcome you. We are to let you observe and learn about anything we do here."

Jasmine accepted his introduction. "I see." She wasn't ready for the backhanded comment about the witches not caring. Her planned arguments weren't needed, and the King's preemptive action had already undermined the opening opinion she wanted to convey. She pressed her confidence and stuck with her plan but changed the question. "I saw a few people with red armbands. Are those the relic wielders? And would you like me to wear a band of sorts to let people know who I am?"

Anthen scowled, then smiled, "Impressive for a girl your age. I know you're not a Sister yet, so they must teach you how to get on people's good sides." Witches are a manipulative bunch, but sometimes it's nice to be manipulated in such a sweet way. "Take this." He reached into his desk and pulled out a yellow armband. "No one wears these. Red is for relic wielders. Blue is for the King's engineers. Those without an armband are just common workers here for the King's construction training."

Jasmine accepted the armband and placed it on her lap. She didn't put it on immediately since she needed some courage to enter the King's fold. "Thank you. This is a large place, and I'm sure everything runs on a tight schedule. Is there someone that can show me around?"

Anthen nodded. "Once you get that armband on, head back to Gene in the admissions building. He'll give you everything you need. Map, schedule, a room, that sort of thing." Jasmine looked overwhelmed, and it made Anthen laugh. She was still young. "There is help available if you need it, but as you said, there are schedules and an organization of duties. Follow the instructions, and everything will be provided."

The Determined World

Jasmine nodded slowly. It was difficult to keep the wonder she had fostered coming to the Institute. The uncertainties and fears wanted the normalcy she had become familiar with at home. Now, Anthen offered her new certainty, the King's prescription, if she just did what he told her. The allure of being certain again was enough, and she stood up to head back to Gene. Her mother was right about the journey challenging who she was. She now had to decide who to listen to and if she was going to obey.

Gene gave her the map of the grounds. The parchment paper was new and thinner. It was being made with a new process Gene knew little about, but he did boast about the machine that made replicas of the map in moments. It all made the once cherished paper cheaper. He explained that reading and writing were available at the Institute and that most common folks needed it since it was a requirement of service in the King's new workforce. Jasmine agreed with his wonder but quickly took her room assignment and left.

Jasmine had been granted her own room while most people shared sleeping space. The yellow armband also drew attention, and she had to explain that she was a witch to three people who were brave enough to ask. She imagined that the rumor of her would spread quickly, and she wouldn't have to explain the armband many more times.

The dining hall bell rang for dinner. It was six chimes from a single bell. Jasmine arrived at the hall and found another example of the King's change. There were no servers or food on the individual tables. Instead, each person took a plate and moved along a line to get their food from a designated location. She realized at that moment just how prolific the labeling and naming were. Buildings before Medrick became King could have assigned names, but every building here had a sign with its name. There were also instructions by the doors, names over the food areas, and a place to return the used dishes. The system meant there were fewer servers, and reading was indeed required. It was everywhere, rules telling them how to act, and these people were conforming to the King's new vision for the future.

Jasmine followed along the line, and her puzzlement must have shown. A voice behind her said, "You must be new." She looked to see a beaming man, perhaps in his forties, with some gray hairs and wrinkles around his eyes. He wore a red armband and fine clothes. He was obviously noble and an example of the change in laws. Nobles couldn't be relic wielders unless they gave up their titles and land in the past. This man had kept whatever wealth he had and was being trained with a relic. Since the change in relic laws, most newly discovered relics were being bought from the finders. Possession of a relic granted training now.

Jasmine was pulled away from observing this new world. Her instincts for conversational opportunities took control. This man wasn't acting under instruction. "Indeed, my name is Jasmine." They continued to move through the line together.

He beamed and carried on with his introduction. "I am Sir Watson, and you, my dear, are wearing the yellow armband I heard about. You must be the witch." While Watson loved the chance to wield a relic he hated having to share the space with the simpletons. Jasmine was much more in his league. She needed to be welcomed in.

She smiled back, "Just a Daughter of Forn. I like to think I'll be a witch when I become a Sister."

Watson didn't know the process since the Sisters of Forn don't recruit into their ranks, nor do they share internal procedures. All he knew was that they passed the title from mother to daughter. This girl's mother must still be alive. "Does that happen at a particular age?"

Jasmine wasn't going to answer a question so close to the truth, so she deflected slightly. "When my mother decides." She thought about sharing more, and a little more wouldn't hurt. "She thought visiting here might be a good experience before I take up the duties of a Sister."

The Determined World

Watson suddenly had access to the oldest influential group of the Kingdom he knew of. He was eager for more. "Fascinating, wonderful. And I'm sure you could tell me all about what's happening in Garrin."

They got to filling their plates, and Jasmine was glad to have a dining friend. As much as she wanted to know what the common folk were learning, she knew she'd have an easier time breaking into the ranks of the relic wielders. Jasmine mentioned a few things about Garrin while Watson led them to seats at one of the rows of tables.

They all had red armbands. He introduced them as they sat down. "This is Pamela Tullian," he pointed to the motherly woman with full chestnut hair and wrinkle-free skin, "Clyde Avery," he pointed to the man with thick black eyebrows and a scar in the middle of his chin, "and John Jones," a man with a devilish smile, blue eyes, and wavy blond hair. "Who we're all sure gave a false name." They all laughed.

John smiled but replied as Jasmine and Watson finished sitting. "The King saw it in his wisdom to find loyal servants, regardless of their name or station."

Watson didn't believe that was true, but it was the King who gave him this chance to be a powerful relic wielder. A person's name still counted for something, in his opinion. "The lineage of names may be breaking, John; it's up to us to make our names memorable now. If you want to write John Jones in the history books, that's on you."

As they continued to talk and eat, Jasmine observed around fifty red armbands among the eight hundred or so people. The blue armbands of the King's engineers occupied two tables off in the corner of the hall. There were other tables of red armbands. The Masters had their own table set off from everyone else. The Masters' attire was more traditional to the Relic Order. They wore robes and cloaks instead of everyday clothes. All these people had been put into the system, and it looked as if everyone wasn't completely comfortable with it. Still, they all accepted the conditions with an understanding of what they were getting in return.

But the observation was so impersonal, and Jasmine asked, "I have to say, as unusual as these new practices are, the line for the prepared food and all, people from all backgrounds are sharing the same tables. It's almost hard to believe, but it warms my heart also."

John smiled and laughed while Watson felt his throat dry. Pamela and Clyde nodded. John spoke because Watson was short on words. "I feel the same thing. Even though Sir Watson here begrudgingly shares a table with us."

Watson replied quickly, "I have not insulted you, John. Please be considerate of what you say." It was true, but at least he wore a red armband and wasn't at one of the commoner tables.

John bowed his head and continued, "Of course. I just come from a past where we're not afraid to talk about thorny stuff. Don't worry, I'll explain this part to our new lady friend. Jasmine," he paused and looked right into her eyes, "You're astute. Most every practice and activity here strips away any ranks that the King doesn't want to remind us of, but it is a struggle for many."

Clyde added, "But new ones are being created. Not ranks, but groups, like the four, now five, of us." Clyde wanted to show that he could talk about the change, too.

John elbowed Clyde, "Oye, my speech. Get your own pretty girl." Clyde punched John's shoulder, but that's as far as it went. Both seemed in good humor about their exchange. They were also part of the red armband group.

Jasmine took the chance to speak. "Like a large pot of stew. Everyone is in the same mix, but not all parts are equal."

John smiled and locked eyes with her again. "You got it. All the same pot."

Watson couldn't help holding back his understanding, "People need that order of rank and command." He continued with an elevated voice before they could protest, "This is just a new one. There are still thousands of people who are not here. There are still Masters and those beneath them. And I, for one, am not opposed to earning a higher rank in the new system. I'm here after all."

They were all quiet. He had come a long way since they met him, but he was in the minority, and this was the only way he could keep his old beliefs while still having folks he could talk to. Jasmine replied, as she had stoked the tension, "I understand. As soon as I arrived, I started to feel the pressures of this place molding my expectations. Still, everyone stays." She smirked and leaned into a lower voice, "So what makes it worth it?"

Sir Watson replied, sitting up proudly, "Opportunity to be part of the new order."

Pamela shared, "A chance to be something other than a wife."

Clyde looked forward distantly and not at anyone else when he said, "Hope."

John whispered, "I'm training with a relic. This is an opportunity of a lifetime. Heck, look over there at all those tables without armbands. I'd be over there if it weren't for this relic. And that... would have been alright. But I'm over here." He laughed and drank. They all returned to finishing their meals.

The next day was a workday. It was the warmer months, so everyone was participating in construction. Relic wielders and commoners, everyone from the dining hall last night, were working to construct and build the Institute grounds and nearby town. The relic Masters were each taking a group of wielders with similar skill levels to focus on the many projects taking place.

Jasmine stayed with her new friends for the first weeks. Witches could demonstrate all the talents of a relic wielder but rarely did since their signature ability was scrying and not drawing the suspicion of their hidden Tokkin nature. She quickly realized these people were one of the least talented groups. She made up an excuse that her mother wanted her to see as much as possible, but she wasn't thrilled to be around unskilled relic wielders. It was the first time in her life that she got to choose to walk away from a situation, and it made her queasy and remorseful.

The headmaster of the Relic Order, Master Matthews, brought Jasmine into the group he was directing. They were working on splitting logs down by the nearby river. It wasn't a roaring river, but it had enough power to operate the building the commoners were using alongside the relic group. She had seen woodworking before, but it was done with whipsaws by skilled craftsmen. This sawmill was being loaded and operated by the workers as it made the cuts for them. It was just the sort of innovation that was so startling about Medrick's rule.

One of the workers called to her as she watched the operation. "Hey, darling. You like the look of a real man?" He lifted his arms and flexed his muscles. The constant work with his body, lifting and carrying of the wood, had endowed him with more mass. "Bigger than those wimpy relic wielders."

Jasmine turned away from the caller and brought her attention back to the relic group. There was some attraction to learning and seeing them work, but she knew her talents would be diminished around them. She could shine around the relic wielders. "Master Matthews, how efficient is that contraption?"

Matthews smirked, "I've never seen them more productive. But I've also never seen them more boastful. Thankfully, we could boast more than them if productivity were the measure. Also, we don't depend on water always flowing." He introduced her to the already working group of relic wielders. "Wielders, I'd like to introduce Jasmine, a Daughter of Forn. She will be joining us for a while. Please be courteous and open as someday you may be interacting with a Sister of Forn."

Everyone made their greeting gestures, and Jasmine cleared her throat but didn't speak. They all got back to their work as she remembered that she was wearing the yellow armband. She looked at the marking. She didn't want to be seen as an outsider, but she was one. Her group was the Mothers and Daughters of Forn. It made connecting with these people that much more important. She missed the close connection she had built with the other Mothers.

This group was more on pace with her skill. The sawdust from the mill could be seen in the air. The relic wielders were splitting the logs without dust and extremely smooth with consistent thickness. She had never done it herself, but she followed Matthew's side-by-side instructions.

They started small on a short piece. "Place your hand like so." He put it on the flat exposed end. She had already been part of cutting down trees with the other group, but this was more careful. "You could skip this step, but I've always liked to find the right angle as it'll prevent bowing later on."

He watched her hand meet the log. "Good. Now, I trust you've got enough sense. Press against it and feel down the length. You are looking for a curve, for density. Our eyes might deceive us, but there is strength in the wood. Years of light and wind have made it stronger in some places. When we make our split, we want the strength to be in each piece. Over time, without the strength through the cut, it'll bend or break at the weakness."

Jasmine followed his guidance and, after a few minutes, found what he meant. It required all her attention, and she had to build a relationship with what she was touching. She had never gotten this personal with wood. She respected the forest and all of nature as she had been taught by the Sisters, but this new understanding was almost embarrassing. It needed intimacy with the wood.

Matthews continued. "Turn the log so the strength will be equal down a vertical line." She followed his order and turned the log 30 degrees. "Now. The hard part. We split it. Some are skilled enough to press from here, and some can even make multiple splits at once, but right now, we'll go slow.

Come above the log and place your hand above the middle to feel the wood. And what I do is part my fingers to draw a mindful separation between the two halves I'm making."

She watched Matthews gather a steady breath, looking down intently at the log. He moved the hand along the wood while stepping along. The log cracked and popped along the length until he reached the end, and the two halves fell apart. It wasn't like a split with an axe. The exposed surface was smooth, and with a few more cuts, the halves could be planks.

Jasmine took her chance at the split, following the instructions. But Matthews had made it look easy. Her split was jagged and broken in places. Matthews examined it and patted her on the shoulder. It was the first time anyone had patted her, and she almost fell forward. "You did good, kid. The workers can plane that nice and smooth. With a little practice, your pieces won't even need that. Now, get to work on making some inch-thick planks. There's a measuring tool by the stack." He pointed over to the large pile being filled by the relic wielders.

Jasmine sputtered, "Thank you." It was the first time that she realized that the Relic Order truly had changed. They were formally a secretive enforcement group. Now, they were common workers with a special tool. They could still be enforced as is the case with the Ginru, but they had to work with other groups of the Kingdom.

Matthews started to walk away when he turned to add, "If you need help moving the log, ask your new fellows. I'm sure they'll help for the chance to meet you." He continued to the other side of the work area to speak with a man wearing a blue armband. Matthews was satisfied that Jasmine wouldn't be a problem now. This witch wasn't a disruption, just as the King had mentioned in the letter. She wouldn't be there forever, and she was just a fifteen-year-old girl in truth.

This group of relic wielders was all men, but they were all closer in age to her, with the oldest most likely in his twenties. She reached the log pile and picked up the measuring ruler. The logs were some twenty feet long and over a foot wide. Jasmine could move it herself, but she heard footsteps approaching and turned to meet the potential offer.

A handsome young man a foot taller than she had approached and placed his hand on the top log. "Where would you like me to place it?" He had long wavy brown hair that he brushed back from his eyes with his free hand. His broad nose drew her attention to his eyes. He might have been from a noble background as his clothes were of fine quality, but the clothes were of a simple design so as not to get in the way of the work. "My name is Carl Borman. I could bring it to where you were, or you can join me." Everyone had their work areas, though some had positioned themselves close to each other for conversation.

Jasmine followed his lead. "By you would be great." She knew the others were watching, but he had gotten there first. She let him do the lifting this time because she wasn't against his eager behavior. After this, she would get her own log.

He wrapped his arm around the log, controlled his breathing, and directed the relic's flow of energy through his muscles and bones by believing he was this strong. He lifted it, walked it over to his area, and placed it calmly on the ground. Jasmine bowed when he was done. "Thank you."

He was winded. "You're welcome." It required more attention than other times because he usually just throws it down, but he was distracted by trying to impress.

The two continued to chat as they barely worked on making planks. Together, they did only the work of one person. He was from the furthest northwest you could get in the Kingdom, and his father was a third cousin of Medrick, though that wasn't why he was there. His father watched over a fishing operation on the coast, and they happened to find a relic in one of the catches. In the past, it would have gone to the Relic Order, but it was given to him, and he was sent to the Institute two years ago.

"My father could see that his position wouldn't have the same value when I took over. Just a matter of time before they get a mayoral charter. So there you go." Carl wrapped up so much of his life in the last few hours that it felt small. He laughed at himself.

Jasmine hadn't had to talk much at all. Carl was eager to talk. As informative as it was, it was boring, and he had distracted her from improving the splitting technique. She decided she would move on, but she'd use her talkative friend for reconnaissance. "It's wonderful and maybe a little terrifying to hear of all this change in the order of things."

Carl was eager to reassure her. "Well, we're young. We have an easier time with it. I know it's been tough for my father to accept. Your mother's probably the same way." He made a clean cut on his log.

Jasmine replied, "Yes," but she was tired of his pattern. He had an opportunity to ask about her mother rather than assume for her. She could offer the insight, but would he listen? "What about the rest of this gang?" She loosened the terminology to relax him into replying about the other men. "Did they all leave behind anxious parents?"

Carl stopped his cut, stood up straight, and looked around as if to make sure none of the others were watching her for their chance. Still, he obliged her request. "They've all got parents who are trapped in the past. Rick's father is in the military, and not much is changing for them. Still taking orders and protecting the land."

Jasmine watched him nod in Rick's direction. He was probably younger than Carl but older than her. He had a dark skin tone that matched those from the southern coast. Rick kept his black hair short, displaying small ears pressed close to the side of his head. She'd have to get closer to know his face better. "Looks like he's a friend of the sun."

The Determined World

Carl chuckled, "Yes... I mean, you can tell that I'm not great with the sun." They were working in the shade, and he did get burned occasionally, but he laughed out, "though nothing like Talphi." He nodded in his direction, "he has his own shelter that he made."

She looked over at the boy, who was near her age. He had some red on the exposed skin, but he had made a shelter from the sun. It was large enough to provide shade while he worked, but he still had to leave it to get a new log. As Jasmine watched, Talphi stayed at one end of the log, touching the exposed surface. In one sound, the log broke in half the entire length.

Carl continued, "Though as parents go, Talphi's got no father we know of, and I think his mother lives in the first mayoral charter town, Saven. So, that's all there is to him."

Jasmine watched Talphi a moment more. He looked over in her direction. She smiled, and he quickly looked back to his work, embarrassed that she caught him looking.

Chapter 15

Jasmine's new group kept a brisk pace of work. Matthews described their work as important since they were part of several projects requiring the planks. Meeting minimums meant new arrivals to the Institute had housing while meeting the entire requisition provided comforts such as winter halls for relaxing in the cold months. Jasmine had been taught that her training at home was necessary as a Sister of Forn would protect the Kingdom, but being so close to the King's building efforts made her involvement profoundly more personal.

But it was also distracting. Jasmine realized after five months of work that she had only gotten to know this group of men. She had imagined bouncing from group to group, taking only a month or so to meet the people and breeze through the work. The work had become more consuming than she realized. They had met their entire requisition request and had two weeks before the changeover.

During the winter months, the workers would stop working at the Institute and travel out to projects in the warmer south. Some left for permanent positions, having learned all that was required of them, while others were continuing training at project sites and would return to the Institute in the spring to continue.

The relic wielders completely shifted gears. With the grounds mostly to themselves, they focused on the other disciplines of relics that would otherwise draw attention. The Masters would choose who and what training they would continue with as opposed to having everyone working on the construction projects. This training promised to match more of the forms she had expected of the Relic Order.

Jasmine relaxed on their day off from work with the young men she had been working with. Other relic groups were still working on their projects. They had tried to flirt with her over the months, but she always described her feelings in return as brotherly. She stood with Rick, Carl, Gregor, Portheus, and Russell outside the simple gray rectangular breakfast hall. It had a formal name, but it was jokingly called the Food Cube. They had nowhere to go. "This is so weird," she explained. "We've been working for months, and having no project feels wrong." She beamed her smile at each, hoping they'd have some cheerful insight. They had all been through this before.

Rick scoffed. "Well. You only have yourself to blame. Before you arrived in the crew, we had too much work." They laughed. "I guess it's a good thing you didn't want to be my girlfriend. We could have used all this free time during the summer." The laughter started to fade. Rick was two years older than Jasmine and the closest in age after Talphi. The other men had accepted her attitude. Rick still fought it. "We'll just have to use it now." He stepped closer to her.

Jasmine smiled. She knew how to fake a smile, but she was growing tired of coming up with gentle pushes against Rick's persistence. Thankfully, Portheus, the oldest of the group at twenty-five, took Rick into a one-armed shoulder hug, drawing him away from Jasmine. "Let's go for a hike. I know this amazing vista about ten miles to the east. We pack some bags, take our time, and we'll be there for sunset. Then we can stay the night and hike back in the morning." His large biceps hugged Rick close and made the decision mandatory. Rick looked up at Portheus' broad chin and narrowing eyes. "Men only, sorry, Jasmine," Portheus added.

Jasmine knew Portheus had gladly picked up the brotherly mantle. "I see.

Well, that will give me some time by myself. I could chat with some other wielders."

The men agreed and walked away to prepare themselves. Other people continued to leave the hall, and Jasmine watched for a moment, preparing herself to talk to them. They were almost all busy looking and heading to their project sites. Then Talphi walked out of the hall. He didn't have the canter of a work-free person like the rest of the group. For five months, he had been nearby working with them, but it was as if the other men were repellent to him. The more of them around her, the further he was. But now, she was free of them.

Jasmine got up and walked after him. She got to a few feet from him. "Talphi, where are you headed?"

He stopped as hearing his name ripped through the barriers he had up in his mind. Talphi turned to her but only looked at her eyes for a moment. He looked away and pointed with his head, "Out into the woods." The heat he felt on his cheeks made him entirely aware of his embarrassment.

She wondered if he had his own vista like Portheus. "What's in the woods?"

It was slightly confusing, and he answered the question, "Well, it's the forest. Trees and rocks. Some streams, I suppose. Nothing special."

Jasmine giggled and walked to be closer now that he was standing still. This wasn't like talking with the others. He had been around, but it was like meeting someone new. "I know that. I was just wondering if you had a spot that is yours. Or maybe a path you like to hike on."

He wasn't trying to be funny, so laughing wasn't necessary. Looking at her was insanely distracting. Talphi looked down, but her chest was there, so he looked up off into the corner of his view. After a moment that seemed like forever, he replied, "No one is out there. I can be alone." He didn't explain further.

Jasmine watched his eyes as he looked at her for a moment and then away.

The Determined World

She tried to understand what he was saying. Was he saying he wanted to be left alone and that he wanted her to stop talking to him or what? She couldn't think of anything else but that she was intruding. "I'm sorry I asked." It hurt that he would push her away like this. She walked away without another word.

No words came out of Talphi's mouth. All the fast, tiny moments and all of his long-drawn-out reactions crumbled into heartbreak. He turned away in the previous direction and took a step. His mind created an answer to her question now that he had space to think, "It's quiet and calm out there. It gives me a chance to sort out my thoughts," he said to himself.

He took another few steps and returned to his original pace into the forest. Talphi continued the conversation in his mind. "Would you like to come out with me?" His heart raced, and he imagined her happy answer. Jasmine would be close to him. She would have chosen him, and he would be so calm and collected. That was a lie. He wouldn't be calm and collected, but he wanted to daydream of her so badly.

He had to get further from the Institute, deeper into the forest. No matter how deep he would travel into the wilds, each time he always found his way back. And he always came back because as much as he wanted to be left alone, he didn't want to be lonely. He wanted to be around people.

Talphi continued the conversation in his mind with Jasmine. She was so perfect, and he loved to see her smile even though she shared her smile with so many others. They would talk about his mother and Saven. She would share her experiences in the Kingdom. She would share her secret, whatever real reason she was there for. Maybe it was to find him.

He slowed his pace and allowed the thoughts and feelings to fill in his fantasy. They would kiss. And touch. She would want him, and he would... he would. It happened again. Letting the feelings take over his imagination turned sour. Instead of wanting more of her, he imagined himself telling her to stop. She wouldn't. Talphi stopped walking and put himself against a tree.

He tried to force the imagination. To set it straight. He would like it because he wanted it. He knew he desired to touch her, but as his imagination pressed her body up against him, as she touched him deeply, he wanted her to stop. Talphi couldn't force his feelings. What he yearned for always turned into this pit. This feeling, this desire, this want always turned into some pathological panic. The source of the panic was buried somewhere deep in him, and he couldn't find it. He hated it. This hatred could burn the world. Talphi imagined rampaging through civilization after a woman's touch.

He hit the tree with his fist. Pain. Release. Talphi had let his want and feelings get out of control. He hit the tree again to share the pain. This had worked before. No one was there to get hurt or to see him. Letting go of control was the only way forward. He threw his relic to the side, still believing that it helped control his power as the mayor had suggested.

Talphi attacked the tree using all his rage. The hits no longer hurt his hand as he focused on making them indestructible. Hit after hit broke into the trunk, sending pieces flying. He had been angry before, and it subsided after a few hits, but today was different. The lingering thought of Jasmine made it so. He hit harder and broke the tree as it fell to the side. Talphi turned to the next tree and gave it everything he had.

The intensity ripped from his skin, creating cuts while producing blazing heat of whipping purple flames. Not only did the one hit break the second tree, but the impact location exploded into wooden shrapnel. The tree bits touched by his power burst into flame. Pure release. Talphi's thoughts snapped back into place and reacted to his actions.

As startled as he was by his display, it felt appropriate. He picked up the relic, a one-inch square with a hole through the middle, and began stomping out the flaming pieces. A forest fire wasn't needed. No one should get hurt because of him. Talphi needed to see to that. He needed to make sure that he took care of his wants and desires. People would get hurt if he allowed those wants to determine his actions. He must act through need, like needing to put out the flames he made. Feeding want only brought him pain. Wanting is just another form of pain.

His years at the Institute had been joined with these trips into the forest. Talphi had taken this time out here to explore the full range of power that lurked without using the relic. He could feel the difference between using the relic and letting go of it. The relic took critical analysis and thought to use while being without the relic was heavily impacted by his emotions. He had to learn to use his raw natural power as if it were a relic, but all the wild emotions made it a struggle.

Jasmine stayed hidden. She had decided to follow him after he walked away on the Institute grounds. The conversation with Talphi and all his previous isolation made her wonder if it was just a miscommunication. She had forgiven him quickly under this assumption and returned to wanting to know more about him.

Watching his outburst was terrifying. She didn't find herself fearing for her own life, but instead fearing for his. He was clearly frustrated and angry about something. She assumed it was her. Was he trying to avoid her? Did he have a secret he was hiding from her? The display of power was how she imagined relic wielders and Tokkin fought in combat. But did she see him drop the relic?

Jasmine decided she would scry for him to learn the answer. The daughters of Forn were taught some scrying, but once you become a Sister, you have the experience you need to make it straightforward. She had only successfully scryed three times for her hundreds of attempts. It takes a clear mind and a very direct purpose. Her mind wasn't exactly clear, but her target and purpose were very clear. She was going to see what troubled Talphi so much.

She moved away from her hiding spot and found a level patch of earth for her to take a seat on. This wasn't a requirement of scrying, but she found it helpful to sit and have stillness around her. Jasmine closed her eyes and began putting her feelings in agreement by focusing on the curiosity of the question. What was Talphi hiding?

She saw Nothing. Either she was doing the scrying wrong, which was totally possible, or he wasn't intentionally hiding anything. In either case, she decided to seek another question. One that would gauge her success. Who is his mother?

A woman's figure started to appear, and she was teaching children. She didn't know if his mother did teach children so it might be real or imagined the way she wanted. Jasmine shook herself out for a moment. This was the real problem with scrying. What you want or hope can force its way into what you perceive.

How about his father? It had been suggested by the other men that his father was no longer around, or alive for that matter. She focused on seeking out the fate of his father. She could make out a figure, but the size and shape of this man kept shifting. It was of normal size to a grand mountain of mass. Without pinpointing a moment in time, she was seeing a figure fluctuating at any moment. She stopped and tried to process the meaning.

Was this a successful scrying, or had she failed again? She hadn't been fully taught to interpret and gauge for herself in this matter. All the daughters dabbled with scrying, but the answer during training was always the same. "When you're a Sister, you will know."

She didn't want to waste any more time with this uncertainty. Thoughts of Talphi exacerbated uncertainty. This journey to the Institute was already stressful enough, even if she had found mastery of the place and its patterns. Thinking about it all didn't make her happy. Jasmine instead looked around this quiet spot, and there was no one out here. She was alone. Talphi had said as much.

She needed to head back and take charge of her education. There was still reason to follow the patterns of the Institute, but there was no reason to see success in going along with the flow. After all, it was designed to have everyone follow a predetermined path.

Jasmine made her way back to the campus, aware that Talphi was still out in this area and that she should avoid him lest she is found out for following him. When she got back, the quadrangle between the buildings was silent. She looked at each building and picked one she hadn't been in more than once or twice.

It was quiet as she entered. This building was two stories high, and its hallways and rooms appeared vacant as she looked up and around. There were tables and vats in them with multiple bottles and tugs filled with liquids or powders. Witches had a good sense of the chemistry of the world, given their journey into aiding people. Some things didn't need relic power to solve.

Suddenly, she heard a sound and stepped back, realizing it was below. There were people here, and her mind dabbled into the nefarious unknown. She found the only door that could be to a cellar near the back corner, far from the front door she had entered. The mystery was slightly deflated since it had a sign next to it with instructions. Anatomy Room: Please keep the door secure. Ideal conditions are required below.

Jasmine opened the unlocked door and felt the chill. It wasn't warm outside anymore, but she imagined this chill was more important in the summer months. She closed the door behind her and stepped down the well-lit passage. A musky and more rotten smell lingered. It was wider than she thought it needed to be, but as she descended, she was thankful for it. Dark and tight would have raised her anxiety. This was intentionally open, clear, and demystified.

They must have heard her coming because before she reached the bottom steps, one of the relic masters appeared at the base. It was Master Pearson. His short blond hair showed off his large ears, while his nose was so large it looked goofy. He looked ready to reprimand her but changed his expression when he saw it was Jasmine and laughed. "Come on down, Jasmine. I had no idea you'd be stopping by," he waved her down with his hand.

The area below was opened into one large area with many tables and storage cabinets. There was also another door on the other side with a ramp that must lead directly outside. There were seven other men around a table. All of them had blue armbands, meaning they weren't relic wielders, but they were no simple workers either. Pearson continued, "You might have some insight. But there are buckets if you aren't prepared for our methods."

Jasmine slowed. The other men parted enough, and she saw the body on the table. They had kept a corpse. She had seen the dead before, but they were meant to be buried. The smells were death. "What are you doing?"

All the men seemed to try and hold back an emotional response. They wanted to appear orderly and certain. Pearson wiggled a bucket near her, but she didn't take it. "No?"

Jasmine didn't need the bucket. This didn't make her sick, just concerned. "I have seen the dead before, Master Pearson." She got closer and saw that there were cuts and intentional openings in the body. Not as grotesque as wounds or death she had seen while training with the Sisters of Forn. Healing and aiding the dying was a typical request for them. "But what are you doing with that body?"

Pearson had no shame and nothing to hide. "Seeing is understanding, my dear. I see through the relic, you can see through your abilities, and others must see with their eyes. I'm guiding them." He approached the table. "We're looking at the veins in the arms right now. With some new techniques, they could save a man's life."

Jasmine wondered if she should have left this place alone. "How?" She knew how she would heal the wound, but what could they do?

One of them answered, "Stitches or cauterizing. But we're exploring more options all the time."

Jasmine accused, "Sowing them back together or burning them?"

Pearson replied sternly, "It's about the tools that are available, Jasmine. You cannot be everywhere, and neither can I. But this knowledge and understanding will give more people the chance to help themselves."

She pointed to the table, "But at what cost? This man should be buried."

Pearson agreed but continued. "And he will, but he has a few more lessons he'd like to share with the world. These are bold people doing what they need to do to make life better for everyone." Pearson defended his understanding of it. "I have taught many relic wielders to understand their bodies and heal their wounds, but you know what? We weren't allowed to heal others without permission until Medrick became King. Do you know what it's like to have your hands tied when you could be helping?"

There were no such restrictions on witches, but they did learn to limit their interactions and allow life and death to occur. Even when they healed, they would guarantee a scar existed to remind the wounded of their luck. It was impossible to save everyone. "No. I haven't been told I can't help someone. But then, sometimes, helping someone doesn't actually help them. Or they don't see it as helpful. It's complicated."

He thought she'd understand, but there must be some learned behavior holding her back. "Well, it's not complicated to me. For the first time, I can teach those without relics to help themselves. They will, in turn, teach more men, and soon everyone will have the same chance to help themselves. And they won't be your complicated problem anymore." Pearson was hoping for more understanding, but most people reacted poorly. That's why they kept this hall of learning out of sight.

Jasmine had enough miscommunication today after Talphi and pushed back, "I applaud your effort. I'm not here to assault your work, but I am here to learn. It just so happens that I have learned many things already. Very different approaches. So, I guess I am asking you to explain your approach. And I will judge it against what I know, but maybe you could still explain it to me?"

Pearson eyed her and tried to assess her sincerity. She was just a girl. He put his hand on her shoulder and led forward with the other arm, "Come on over, and we'll begin."

Chapter 16

Talphi swirled between dread and hope. He hoped Jasmine would break his emotional obstruction and confess a passion for him, but he dreaded the dark place his feelings always led him. He kept his thoughts as protected as possible and avoided her for the next few days before winter training began. He couldn't bring himself to walk the painful bridge of want and desire just to be rejected and hurt.

Master Mortimer was leading the relic wielders for their winter series. He specialized in human behavior. There were many terrifying ways non-relic wielders imagined they could be targeted. In fact, the Institute had to provide constant information to the other workers about the limits of relic wielders. The explanations made sure they could share the Institute grounds.

They answered questions like, Could I be mind-controlled by a relic wielder? Do they know my thoughts? How do I know if I am being manipulated by a relic wielder? The short answer is that they can't do anything to you without sustained physical contact and the willingness of the non-relic wielder. And that was the truth. Just like the logs they split needed time to be understood, each person at each moment was unique and had their unique nature to contend with.

Mortimer was a foot shorter than any of the other Masters. He always wore a bundle of cloth around his neck, even in the warm months, as he needed it to keep his head up straight. He was bald on top with a thick band of hair from ear to ear around the back of his head. Each time he looked at someone, he had to squint. He had kept everyone in the dining hall today before they broke off into groups with the other Masters as supervisors.

He talked over the few remaining voices as he stood between them and the entrance. "So much excitement and anticipation. So many possibilities and wonders. You can stop being excited because most of you are going to fail. A lot of you will fail. People are not rocks. They are not trees to cut down and make planks out of. The flesh may cut easier than a rock, but you will not find an easy way to split a person."

Everyone stopped talking and was keenly hoping there was a BUT. One didn't come, it just kept getting worse. Mortimer continued, "You are at the service of the King, and your abilities are still directed for the Kingdom's benefit. You will be heading into political situations and conflict areas. Cutting someone in half in those situations won't help anyone. You all agreed to this, but I would like to remind everyone since the mind wanders into possibilities come wintertime. Manipulating a person is only for the service of the King. You practice now, on each other, with that permission."

Mortimer split them into groups by some randomly chosen characteristic of each person. Hair, eyes, height. Each day, they would break up and go with one of the Masters to an empty room on the Institute grounds to practice. The practice was learning how to get some information, like a secret word of the day, from one of the people.

It was an interrogation. However, torture, pain, and pleasuring were not allowed. The word holder each day was allowed to keep their relic, but it wasn't needed. Keeping a secret was a matter of belief and obstructing thoughts. The relics could act as a fast way of connecting with a person's beliefs and thoughts, but they didn't overpower a person. The wielder's belief and understanding were matched against the target's traits. People who were easily manipulated with words would equally be susceptible to the relic.

Talphi placed a hand on the shoulder of the word holder and was instructed by Mortimer, "See if you can't get him to speak the word Talphi. Share friendship with him." Mortimer was testing the clash of beliefs today. While the struggle takes place in one person's mind, the connection allows each personality equal power. This is why the willingness of the subject is important. Still, people can be convinced, making it appear as some sort of mind control.

He was touching Gregor, and friendship was very far from reality. "How do I make him feel friendship if I know he feels quite the opposite?"

Mortimer gave the only advice he knew. "How would you go about convincing yourself? Know what it feels like to trust someone. The beat of your heart, the size of your eyes, and how you sit. That's the place you want to bring him. All minds respond to what pulses through the body." Mortimer had some hope for Talphi. When left to the request, Talphi was able to retrieve the word from the guarded person, but he couldn't get the person to flip their allegiance. It was the hardest thing and mostly meant Talphi wasn't adept at manipulating people, but he surely had insight into navigating the mind.

Talphi couldn't share what he didn't understand. The only friend he had was back in Saven, and their friendship was based on laughter. He tried to remind Gregor's body of the enjoyment that he associated with friendship, but all Gregor did was laugh.

Gregor did speak, "Talphi," he laughed, "Talphi, you can do this all day. I am having such a good time, but I'm never going to tell you the word."

Talphi didn't even trust himself. How could he make other people trust him? The word was mouse today. He had figured it out a few moments after he put a hand on Gregor. Finding a way through a person's defense and the organization of their thoughts was easy. He spent all his time navigating his own mind, testing thoughts and feelings. He stepped away.

Mortimer stepped up next to Gregor and excused Talphi. "Well, that's disappointing. But this failure costs you nothing. Jasmine," he turned his whole body to face her, "why don't you demonstrate."

Jasmine had not been included in Mortimer's lists, and she was free to observe any of the Masters. Today, she had chosen Talphi's group, having built up enough courage to face him again. This sort of activity was easy for her. The mindset of scrying applied to the exercise, and it followed in line with how witches chose a price for their service. They liked to figure out what a person would and wouldn't give up to teach life lessons.

Jasmine tried to pass on the option. "I know Gregor too well." She was also trying to keep herself a little more removed from the King's pattern. This place was indoctrinating followers, after all. Even if she agreed with much of it, she had her own duties waiting for her. "He might just give it to me."

Mortimer nodded, "Good point. But who's to say that we won't have to perform a service for the King with our friends being the target? Gregor, don't dare let her have that information. Your life depends on it. Believe it." Gregor nodded to Mortimer, who asked Jasmine again, "Alright, Jasmine, break his belief."

She breathed in deeply and took up the challenge. Jasmine stepped up next to him and put her hand on his shoulder. It was a burst of realization. Gregor was giving it his all. She could feel him reciting that she was an enemy, warning himself to push away the thought of giving her anything she wanted. She spoke to him, "Gregor." He heard her call his name, but his mind repeated the mantras.

Mortimer quietly spoke to the others. "The word, his name. It's an external stimulus that sends an echo through his body and mind. She maps him with it." He had taught this to the relic wielders, but already, her display was leaps ahead of their execution.

Jasmine made small movements and expressions. It wasn't necessary, but moving yourself in the moment can get the target to mirror your movements.

The Determined World

People keep the aspect of the young brain that likes to copy all through their lives. Gregor moved and shifted mostly in line with her movements, but sometimes in opposition. After a minute, he stopped resisting and looked up at her with a little sadness, and she looked down at him with understanding. "Mouse," he spoke.

Mortimer started clapping, and everyone followed suit, realizing it was the correct word. They were still clapping as Mortimer spoke again. "Remember, this is a battle of beliefs. While the stone only requires your belief, this requires both people to believe. Keep in mind that no relic is required. This is a contest of personalities."

Mortimer cheered, "Another." He took out a piece of paper and gave Jasmine the word.

Jasmine started to decline. "Oh, I shouldn't."

Mortimer brushed her concern aside. "Nonsense. It's just a word, and I'd like them to test themselves against the most talented woman at the Institute." He pointed to the chair that Gregor had vacated.

Jasmine accepted, curious about what it would feel like to be the subject of the manipulation. It was a safe environment to experiment. She sat down and asked, "Who's first?"

Mortimer stepped back and prepared for the real test. "Talphi, of course. We'll see if he can get the word, and then he'll try to get you to speak it. I doubt the second part, but he's got a talent for navigating defenses."

Jasmine tightened up for more than the test. She focused on hiding the word, amount, in a sentence with other boring words. Still, she had to create a belief that she wanted him to fail and that she didn't want them to know each other. It was a wall she didn't want to build, but she did it.

Talphi stepped closer but stopped before putting his hand on her. He could make a scene. He wouldn't refuse, but just touching her was a dangerous violation of the space he had built, and he knew that he wouldn't be able to do anything without risking his pent-up feelings for her. There would be no word searching. He would just fail willfully.

He touched her shoulder, and the timer began. He didn't say her name, but he tried to keep his lips from trembling. Talphi didn't look, press, or venture into her mind. Soon, he would release her and declare his defeat.

Jasmine waited, but he didn't challenge her defense, nor did he navigate to find the word. So, she pressed back into his mind. He was a concentrated ball of resolve. Pain, anger, desire, and fear all held to one point at the front of his thoughts. He was counting down the time till he would let go and accept defeat. Before he had touched her, she had won. Was that right?

Talphi took his hand away. "I can't. She's too good." He turned his back on the group and walked to a wall and faced it while he fought back tears. So weak.

Jasmine sighed, but Mortimer quickly picked up the pace, "Alright, then who's next? Tara, you can try next." He looked over to Jasmine. "If that's fine by you?"

Jasmine nodded, looked at Mortimer, and drew a breath in of resolve. She would think about this later. "Next."

While Tara followed her process to pull the information, Talphi's separation from contact helped him establish control over the emotion. He, too, began his process of organizing his thoughts and feelings and preparing to navigate those defenses. He still wanted to prove that he could do it even though the subject, Jasmine, broke his resolve. Talphi imagined making the connection with Jasmine without the contact and much to his surprise he was there.

He was witness to the same defense from Jasmine, though she was responding to Tara's contact. Talphi didn't think he could make the connection with another person without close proximity. They had been told as much, but there he was, connected to Jasmine a dozen feet away. It wasn't his imagination; it was happening at that very moment. He began the search for the word.

Jasmine felt more than Tara pressing her hand on her shoulder as snippets and thoughts started distracting her from the mantra of belief she was focusing on. Tara was met by the wall, but this person was picking at the grout between the bricks. She focused all her attention on it and recognized it as Talphi. He was back in her mind, and she had to stop him. How was he back? He was standing on the other side of the room. Witches could pick apart people without touching the person, but she didn't think relic wielders were skilled enough to do it.

Tara couldn't get past Jasmine's strengthening defense, and she could not see a way to convince her to speak. She let go and stepped back. "I can't." She laughed, knowing it would have been ridiculous for her to succeed.

Jasmine didn't respond, and Mortimer called for her, "Jasmine. Are you alright?"

She was in a heated race, and Talphi smoothly picked apart the holes in her defense, and her mind stepped on the word, amount. Jasmine suddenly stood up, releasing all the defense, and pushed back the chair, startling everyone. "I need to go."

Mortimer asked again, "Are you alright?"

The defense Jasmine had set by coming to the Institute had been stripped away from her. "Yes. I just need to go... to the lavatory." She excused herself the rest of the way.

Talphi stayed completely still without moving a thought. He had thought of it as a game. It was a challenge she had accepted. But the last thing he interpreted from Jasmine was, 'Get out of my head, creep'.

Mortimer called over to Talphi, "Come back over, Talphi." He could see Talphi's watery eyes as he turned. "It's alright. She's a daughter of Forn. I didn't expect anyone to beat her. But now you all know why it's important that we follow the King's guidelines in these matters. Because the Sister of Forn might be sent after you."

They all nervously laughed in agreement. Talphi kept the word, amount, to himself. As he returned to his room from dinner, he found Jasmine waiting for him. It was a tight corridor with nowhere to escape. He had hoped that maybe he was mistaken or maybe she was now waiting for someone else, but as soon as she saw him, she called him by name.

Jasmine looked daggers at him. "Talphi."

He imagined the melting feeling was something like Gregor had felt when she called him by name. "Yes."

Jasmine had agreed to allow the relic wielders to fish out the word, but Talphi's actions had to be addressed along with her confusion. She backed him up into another room set aside for holding brooms and buckets for cleaning. "You didn't even try to break through when you had a hand on me." She stopped. There was more, but she wanted to break it down piece by piece to understand.

He couldn't look her in the eye, but she deserved to know his regret. "I couldn't. I was afraid you'd retaliate."

Jasmine scoffed at the oddity. "Retaliate? I had agreed to let you all try. I was going to do that." She hadn't expected this answer.

Talphi explained the best he could. "Well, from before. When I told you about the woods. I knew you were angry, and I felt..." the words made him sad, and she seemed to be responding to him. His quick glances at her face mirrored some of the pain he was expressing. He changed to ease her reaction. "You don't want anyone invading your mind. No one does. He asked you to volunteer, and frankly, I don't like doing it."

Jasmine agreed with him, but that wasn't what he was saying at first. "Yes, but you did come back and invade my mind, didn't you?" She felt violated, and he just admitted it was wrong but had done it anyway. "You understand, don't you?" It looked like he was going to cry, but she wanted to make sure. "It's why we train under careful supervision. So that no one is panicking or fearful for their life."

Talphi wanted to explain. He needed to express his fear. "I don't. I don't really understand. I try to, but I don't understand why everyone else isn't afraid of this power." He clasped the relic he carried. He needed to protect people from his power. Shutting it away would just cause it to burst out. Understanding was the only thing that helped, and this place was the only thing that tempered the danger.

He had backed away from her and shrunk toward the door. Despite the trespass, she wanted to forgive him. Jasmine forgave him, believing he wouldn't do it again. "You have a funny way of showing fear of power. I'm not sure how you even made the connection to me without touching me." Jasmine reached out to put her hand on his arm.

Talphi pulled back from the touch on instinct and stumbled back onto the ground, knocking the door open. She could burn him with her touch. Not literally, but the heat he felt and the explosion of fear overwhelmed any calm reaction that could have occurred. His thoughts fought for control over the sudden reaction.

Jasmine grabbed the door frame and knelt to him. "Are you alright?"

Talphi hurried himself up and back. He didn't want to be touched by her less unsettled feelings, which would cause him to hurt her. Why? Why was the fear stronger than the acceptance of her touch? This was no place to understand. He needed to leave. "I'm fine. I have to go, bye." He turned and walked away.

Jasmine piped out one small word, "Bye?" Thoughts of the explosive display in the woods, the scrying, and the range of his abilities formed a mystery. But she still wanted to be closer to him. She wanted him to feel the same. That was the reason she yearned for. Maybe love could be so dangerous.

She wished she had the experiences of a witch's previous lives to know for sure.

Talphi ran outside. He was wearing thick pants and long shirts in layers, but he wasn't dressed to spend a long time outdoors. It was already dark out, but other relic wielders were making their way about the campus. The evenings were free for personal practice or socializing. Everyone seemed to be moving in a determined direction. He was standing still in the cold night air.

The ground was covered with a few inches of snow, but the paths they all walked in were cleared regularly. Talphi wanted the spring to be there so that he could walk into the woods for a while. His thick jacket was still in his room, and Jasmine was up there. She might be gone by now, or she might be exiting the building soon, and he'd have to face her.

Entering the woods would be like embracing death. He started trudging through the snow in the woods he had explored. It wasn't death he moved toward, but a self-imposed punishment. The cold pierced through the layers, and the wetness of his feet quickly made him regret his decision, but he had only gone a short distance. If he was to last longer, he needed to fight the cold.

The Institute did teach survival training, but it was saved for those who would actually need it. The Relic Order was always cared for in this matter, and only their most adventurous wielders needed the training. The tradition was carried into the Institute. Regardless of the reasoning, Talphi needed to protect himself with the relic power.

Talphi thought about creating heat. He didn't want to burn himself, but trying to believe that he was warm didn't seem to do anything. His warmth was relative to the outside temperature, and he couldn't change the seasons. Even if he made a fire, he could make something burn, it would struggle against the cold air. He needed to change just enough of the air. It would be a constant effort. That made sense.

They had done all their training through physical contact, but he had just connected to Jasmine from a distance. Talphi questioned the method of his teaching. It worked, but maybe he could do it a different way. He reached out with the same sense when splitting logs, but this time believing he already touched everything through some extension.

Every molecule bounced off another. It was everywhere. Everything overwhelmed his senses for a moment, and he got dizzy. He only focused on what was close, and the movement and interaction of the bits made sense. Talphi pushed them faster. They were already moving, but he excited them faster as they bounced off one another. Heat.

He felt it in the space around him. The air slowed at the edges, but he pushed it faster around him. This explained so much. It was like being able to hold fire. The mystery was gone. The friction of molecules was clear. He kept the orb of excitement around him. Focusing near his hands, Talphi opened his closed fist quickly and imagined the intense collision of air. A momentary burst of heat created a flame above each hand for a flash. It was a bit much and singed his skin.

He practiced for another hour, keeping the cold away. Maybe there was some way to make himself immune to the cold, but this was good for now. Altering oneself created a slew of dangers, but he imagined it was possible. The relief of the cold and the return of heat made him wonder about the sunburns he would get. There might be a way to prevent that too if the air could be changed like this.

Talphi accepted that his short exile from the Institute grounds was over and headed back to his room. He imagined Jasmine would be gone by now. As he reached the edge of the woods and the beginning of the grounds, a powerful sense of the two zones caused him to stop.

The woods felt different than the campus. The woods just accepted his actions, while the existence of other people clashed with his effort. His understanding and interaction with the air were being resisted by the completely unaware people. Their voices and jovial laughs poked holes at the silence around him.

Talphi wasn't cold from the air, but a chill ran down his spine, making his hair stand on end. He stood at the edge of existence. Each person's belief bends the world to how they feel it. The relics amplified those effects, but they still followed the way the world worked. He couldn't just be warm; he had to understand warmth.

The feeling was gratifying. Talphi Understood separately from everyone else, and he felt their unaware ignorance clash against his manipulation of the air. He pressed the radius of his interaction and saw the snow melt away from the heat he made. The frozen water wasn't so mysterious anymore, but it was wonderful to know.

Talphi released the effort and felt the rush of the cold air collide with his skin. Now there was another chill up his spine. He quickly ran to his room. The idea of sharing his discovery with everyone seemed foolish. Who would listen to him, and why should he share? Perhaps they all understood in some way without him sharing, or maybe they'll just discover it on their own. What worked for him might not work for anyone else.

Jasmine came to mind again. Could he connect to her through this discovery? The other questions could be passively ignored. But maybe he could share with Jasmine. It was a good way to gauge her. How she reacted would tell him quite a bit. Maybe she would understand. Talphi played out what he would say and how she might react for two weeks.

He continued to refine his own understanding and descriptive words. Jasmine kept her distance from him, it seemed. She hadn't gone to any of the group assignments he was in. She didn't sit near him at meals, but she was usually in his eyesight during those times. He wanted to follow her after dinner one evening.

Jasmine walked out into the bitter cold and was prepared to hurry back to her room when Talphi called her name, "Jasmine."

She stopped, hopeful that he had something nice to say, but regrettably, it was cold, and she didn't need a conversation outside. "What is it, Talphi?" she replied with a hurried voice.

Talphi stopped from getting too close. The cold air pushed away his blushing, but it was overly distracting, as usual. "I wanted to know." Already the planned words changed. He felt rushed. "Can you make yourself warm in this weather?"

She raised an eyebrow. Was he suggesting they could get close for heat? Jasmine replied with some haste, "Yes. Inside my room with a nice fire. You want to join me?"

Talphi was starting to get cold, too. "That's not what I mean." This location was a horrible idea, but it was also an excellent testing ground. Other people were walking by looking at them. He had to truncate this speech. "I mean, with your relic, well, with your abilities, can you make yourself warm without a fire or extra clothes? If you were just standing outside without any other protection?"

Jasmine wasn't warm enough to play hypothetical situations with him. "Yes, sure. If I needed to. I could make a fire or something. But my room is right there." She pointed. "I'm going to go there to stay warm."

It wasn't working, and he had his answer. She wasn't looking for what he wanted to share with her. He knew he was doing it wrong. Pushing harder would just cause more cold feelings. Talphi cut his losses, "Never mind. It's not important." He turned away.

Jasmine stood dumbfounded. He was completely unaware of her feelings. It was clear he was excited to tell her something, but did it have to be on this cold, neutral ground? Jasmine offered again. "It's warm in my room. Would you like to go there and talk?"

Talphi was already disconnecting, and that room was hers. The idea of being trapped alone with her repelled him even as he blushed to think about being there with her. It wasn't about that. He needed this neutral territory to keep himself on track. This was about their abilities. Why couldn't she meet him here? "You answered my question." She had.

Jasmine called out. "About keeping warm?" He was leaving speaking range. She thought about following him, but she still felt guilty about him falling back when she touched him. Waiting for him to talk to her again felt like the safe course. She would keep herself close as she had been and hoped that he would come back to her, even if it was cold.

Winter warmed to spring, but Talphi and Jasmine didn't speak for the next two months. Talphi devoted himself to understanding more objects in their relationship to heat and cold. The mental games that Mortimer was teaching convinced Talphi that he couldn't make people loyal to him. He didn't trust them and didn't need them to understand how broken he was.

Jasmine stayed close to Talphi during the meal hours. But he was never so bold again. She wanted him to like her, and pushing him seemed to repel him. She tried to be approachable, but in the meantime, she kept observing the workings of Mortimer's methods. She observed him grouping and categorizing the wielders. He was looking for the right sort of person for the manipulative games the King would use them for.

Those future interrogators ended their training at the Institute when spring came. To Jasmine's pleasure, Talphi was not one of those people. Even if he could get the information, his inability to connect with targets like Mortimer wanted had disqualified him. The return of spring meant the return of physical labor and the workers without relics.

Chapter 17

The road network connecting the Kingdom had improved travel and trade among the many cities and counties the King was nurturing. Some areas that had been resisting his changes were being left out of the network and were slowly starving into acceptance. The road network was now taking up a new stage for communication and control. There was going to be a series of towers spaced strategically along routes for transmitting messages visually.

The vast working crews that had developed over the last few years were going to be working to make the link between Garrin and the Institute active before next winter. The towers were going to be durable icons of the progress being made. Only the newest arrivals to the Institute remained on the grounds. All capable relic wielders were being given assignments off-campus.

Talphi was organized into a group with other relic wielders. They were being sent out with tents and arrangements to receive food and supplies on a schedule and at their building site. An architect would be traveling to many of the sights, spending a day or so at each to direct progress.

Talphi's group included Sara, Evin, and Angie. Sara was the oldest among them at thirty-two and had only been at the Institute a few months longer than Talphi. She had been designated the leader by Matthews. It was clear that she was the right choice. Her matter-of-fact manner and precise sentences made it easy to speak with her. She was rounder with a short physique, but that didn't burden her confidence.

Evin and Angie were in love. They were both just about twenty and had arrived at the Institute as a couple. It didn't affect their progress, so the Masters didn't try to separate them. They, too, had been at the Institute longer than Talphi. Evin was tall and lengthy, always standing around with his shoulders rolled forward in an attempt to personify ease. Angie accented Evin's ease by being perky and welcoming. Her green eyes sparkled, and thin eyebrows were always raised. Together they made, 'Come on over and take a load off'.

They were a fine group of people, but Talphi wondered about their work ethic. However, people don't have to be alone so they can focus on their work. It would have been nice to just be with this group of people who didn't know him. It would have given him a chance to start over, but Jasmine asked to follow his group. She would be with them for the entire build.

Jasmine had gotten to know quite a bit about the Institute and the King's plans over the last two months. The subject matters of the relic wielders weren't as fascinating as the collision of the King's vision and all the old institutions. So much of the building was in synergy with the social changes taking place.

The King's organization was frightening when studied. It wasn't a threat to life, but it was terrifying to see such a long-term goal so expeditiously followed. The only thing she wanted to learn about here was Talphi. She was sure there would be more things in the future, but for now, her vision of the world was taken up by resolving her feelings for him.

The five of them only had to travel two days to their construction site. The architect arrived the next day when their campsite had been set up nearby. They met him at the construction site. He wore the blue band of an engineer, and Talphi recognized him from the Institute. He kept a short, scruffy beard and wore a telescoping monocle for reading the layouts he brought. The nice clothes would have made a better impression if not for the traveling dirt that had started clinging to the articles of clothing.

Sara knew him by name and called to him as he dismounted his horse and opened the satchels. "Good day, Peter." She noted the rolls of paper. "I see you've brought us our plans."

Peter called back, "That I have." He smiled at her even though he was in a dreadful hurry to get all the crews he was watching over started. He looked around at the other four. "You will all call me Mr. Seyman. Only Sara can call me Peter." Peter handed off the rolls to Sara as she unrolled them at a table they had constructed. He drew the monocle down into position to begin explaining.

Sara had been through these sorts of documents before. She translated some things he said and asked a few questions that he would understand for their work. Talphi nodded and absorbed the interaction, hoping to understand the process from planning to finish. Maybe he could learn enough to build a tower all on his own.

Jasmine recognized Sara as the bridge the King had created. Under the old Relic Order, Sara would have never been given a relic. She wasn't imposing or dedicated to secrecy and social stratification. Her personality was informed and supportive. This constructive and extended attitude was perfect for relating to people from other backgrounds. She would build the King's bridge, or in this case, tower.

After Peter drew out the physical location for the tower in the ground, he prepared to depart. His last words were just extra notes. "You'll get food every four days. The chap's name is Darrell. I understand he doesn't have a wife, so Sara, you mind yourself." Peter sounded like a father when he spoke to Sara. He might be old enough for that to be the case, but he winked at her to show his affection.

Sara had a husband for a short time years ago, but her independence and work with the relic since had made her a dependable collaborator for the Kingdom. Her husband wasn't supportive of the change, and she left him to do something that mattered to her. Sara crafted a reply, "Love makes the ground feel like sinking sand. I'm making this building on a stable rock."

Peter replied, holding a hand over his heart. "A woman after my heart." He rode off enjoying his job a little more today. Every group he visited gave him some pause for concern. Sara's crew was smaller than the other ones, so while he was confident in their understanding, he wasn't entirely confident of their skills.

It had taken hours to move through all the details, and it was now early afternoon. Sara motioned everyone over to the layout of the tower. "We have our work cut out for us. I know that each of you hasn't been completely trained in all the building techniques. We'll all be doing a lot of first times. Today, we're moving dirt and rocks to build a foundation. So, follow the lines, dig five feet down and three feet wide. Remember that all matter can be understood and moved."

There were a few moments of everyone looking around before Sara added, "I'm going to be working myself, not just organizing. I can't supervise you all, so you're all going to have to motivate yourselves. Let's get to it." She turned away and went to a corner of the layout and lifted a foot-sized ball of dirt guided by the connection of her hand. She then threw the dirt a dozen feet off to the side. They were going to have to deal with what they dug out, but not today. Sara wanted them all to get dirty now.

The rest of them began in uncertainty. They tried lifting more than they could connect with, and many balls of dirt split in half, making a mess on the ground. Angie and Evin kept a conversation going as they worked, though it didn't seem to affect their speed. Jasmine stayed at an opposite corner from Talphi. She knew she couldn't talk and move dirt at the same time. She had to give all her attention to one thing at a time.

Talphi found that his eyes were bigger than his understanding. His experience with manipulating air let him feel deeper into the ground than he expected. Every attempt to lift from deeper was met with constrictions and forces keeping the ground together. He kept scaling back the depth of his understanding to achieve the same measured results everyone else was able to produce. Someday it might be different, but right now Sara was depending on a consistent result.

Sara kept them all focused each day, making sure they always had tasks available no matter how much time was left in the day. The tower was mostly stone, so they were given the location of a nearby deposit that would be suitable. They also needed some trees turned into logs and planks. Sara split Evin and Angie off to focus on the wood. Sara led Talphi and Jasmine to the quarry.

It had come to Jasmine's attention that Sara wasn't just organizing the tasks; she was organizing her crew. Jasmine was never alone with Talphi. They had talked, but it was always construction talk. He seemed more at ease because of the situation, but it occurred to Jasmine that Sara was setting the conditions.

Part of what made Jasmine upset at Sara was that after the second food delivery, Sara asked Darrell to deliver food late in the day, and he ended up spending the evenings and nights with them. Jasmine knew she was jealous of Sara's handling of the situation. Sara had so easily found herself some companionship, but she hadn't let Jasmine get closer to Talphi.

On their next trip to the stone deposit, Jasmine made sure to work near Sara. Talphi had found a wall of stone out of sight of the two of them. He had made some progress the prior days, getting nice big cuts out of the wall. Sara might have made a good witch if she had been born into the family because before Jasmine had gotten the courage, Sara asked her, "What's wrong, Jasmine? I get the sense you want to talk about something."

Jasmine realized she must be transparent. It wasn't a typical state, and she tried to recover her disciplined state. She shaped her words, "I just wanted to compliment you on the way you've kept this project moving. There's no reward or punishment, and you've kept us all motivated."

Sara appreciated the compliment. "Well, thank you. I had my doubts, but you've all impressed me." She stopped and gave her full attention to Jasmine since that wasn't the reason Jasmine was lurking. "I imagine there is an exception, though."

Jasmine smiled to cover the dissent for a moment. She thought about mentioning Darrell and some of her jealousy since saying she was being kept from Talphi suddenly seemed silly. Sara hadn't kept her from him. "It's about Talphi." She steered it toward Evin and Angie instead. "You send Evin and Angie off on their own, but you could send me and Talphi off together, too."

Sara didn't say anything immediately. She wasn't angry or upset but was instead deciding just how frank to be with Jasmine. "I think I know what you're feeling. When I've been around a boy I wanted, I could hardly stay focused on anything else. So, no, I don't think I can send the two of you off alone."

It confirmed that Jasmine was not mistaken. Sara was doing it on purpose. "You don't think I could handle it? You found yourself, Darrell, and that doesn't interfere with the tower."

Sara laughed, "Yes, it does. It interferes, and I try to keep it limited. Evin and Angie's relationship interferes with the tower's progress, too. There's a balance between keeping people happy and keeping them productive. Talphi is very productive. I've witnessed his immersion. It doesn't happen if you're close by."

Jasmine wanted to push Sara out of her way. She could do it. Sara was still shorter than her even though Sara was over a decade her senior. "And what about me? Is it productive to keep me where I am?"

Sara took a step back. Jasmine was the dominant force, but she was the one in charge. She tried to avoid confrontations like this. There was an empathetic path forward. "You're not here to be productive. Seeing you two happily together would fill me with joy. But I appreciate what we're trying to build. This exciting new chance for the world. I need Talphi's help doing it."

Jasmine's anger felt like poison, and she let it go. None of this was going as planned, all the way back to the day her Mother suggested she see the world. "I suppose you do need him. Maybe I can wait."

"Well," Sara was sympathetic, "Maybe if holding off falling in love was a thing. If he were comfortable around you, then I'm sure you could remain relatively productive alone with each other. He trusts me to focus on the work. Focus on the work and get him to see you as a collaborator. You'll have to prove you can work together."

Jasmine nodded. She had had Mothers, but this might be what it was like to have a sister. Or was this just a good boss? "I'll think about it."

Sara patted her on the shoulder, "I know you will." They got back to work. At the end of the day, both the ladies went over to Talphi's location and found his productivity. He had excavated as many squared stones as either of them, only they were approaching nearly twice the size as theirs. Only he was able to carry the ones this size.

Talphi had pressed his understanding of lifting. The more he knew, the less he had to pretend to believe. Lifting was a matter of knowing that he couldn't balance an object with his weight. He needed to have enough focus to apply a force equal to the weight he was carrying. It was a point of realizing that the weight of the mass is the force being applied to the mass.

It was gravity. The masses pulled themselves together. He mimicked the pull in the opposite direction. The limit was how much mass he could focus on at once. They each started carrying what they had cut, making several trips. The carrying was done in silence, and the trips back to the quarry could be talkative. Sara's voice usually filled that space, but today, she gave Jasmine a chance to try out what she suggested.

Jasmine racked her thoughts for a good open question. She put their past failures out of her mind and focused on the work they had done since coming to the tower site. "Want to switch? You can take my stone, and I'll take yours."

"Seriously?" Talphi knew he could carry hers, but "You can't lift my stones."

Jasmine retorted, "I'll just cut it in half. We can always just put them back together." She knew this wasn't exactly what Sara meant, but she wanted to get his attention.

Talphi protested, "No. I spent a lot of time making sure I got good cuts."

Jasmine glanced at him but didn't try to catch his eye. "Look, all I'm saying is that the pieces you make need to be a size we can all handle. Your big stones are impressive, but we're just going to seal them back up together. They don't need to be that big." She laughed and let him see she was joking with him.

Talphi looked at Jasmine and then at Sara. She was right there with them. Sara nodded and smiled, "They are a bit bigger than we need, Talphi. You've already seen the mortaring and shaping we do, so you know perfection from the quarry isn't needed."

Talphi wasn't angry exactly, but he did think they were missing an opportunity. "But imagine if the stones were so big and so well shaped that no mortar was needed?"

Sara smiled less, "That would be amazing, but this tower isn't designed like that. If you were to build a tower on your own, you could do it that way. I'd love to see it."

Talphi wanted to clarify, "So you're saying, stop making blocks so big?" He'd accept Sara's directions.

Sara nodded, "Yes." She didn't know about Jasmine's decision to bring up the stone size. It was work-related, but not too friendly.

Jasmine added, "Well, the ones we split, we could always pair them back together at the tower. Less mortar, maybe a unique split."

They all pondered the suggestion. The tower and methods had all been planned for them by builders working with limited tools. The sudden possibilities and danger of expending time on failure ran through their minds. Sara would do it if it saved time and improved the tower.

Talphi wondered if it could be taken further. The body repairs, trees grow, and matter can be separated, but could he fuse it back together? He'd have to see and practice that.

Jasmine asked, "Well?"

Sara spoke up, "We've got to stick to our timetable. Talphi, carry your own stones for today, but make them a more manageable size for the rest of us. I love the idea, Jasmine, and I'm totally going to bring up the possibility when we're done. Thank you."

Jasmine was satisfied enough with her prodding. It was just the sort of thing she imagined the King didn't plan on. There was uniform progress toward a copacetic future. Then there was pioneering toward that which isn't prescribed. She wasn't just along for the ride. She could have an influence.

That evening, when Darrell arrived with the food, he also brought a letter. The letter was for Jasmine from her mother. She read it alone as the others prepared dinner. She had never mentioned her mother's situation, so no one thought it was unusual or as foreboding as the feeling Jasmine had in receiving it. Darrell had been given the letter from a courier who knew all about his assignment.

She broke the seal and read it by torch near the tent. "Jasmine, it's time. I have pushed off nature as long as I can, and I will be dying soon. The other Sisters are shocked I have waited this long, and they scarcely understand my reasons. I scryed to make sure this letter would reach you in good time. Please come home with all haste. Your Mother, Tiffany."

Jasmine placed the letter on a stone and lit it on fire. The answer wasn't no. She would return home, but she couldn't let everyone else know. As much as she was trying to connect with everyone, she needed to keep the workings of the Sister of Forn to herself. Tonight, after everyone was asleep, she would go.

Jasmine returned to the group and made up a pleasant answer for the letter's content. Throughout the meal, she watched Sara and Darrell playing with each other. Evin and Angie were curled up together. These were the evenings that made her regret her distance from Talphi. Wasn't he there, too? She could see him distracting himself from watching the cuddling. This was it. She would talk to him before she left and explain it. There was no more waiting.

They finished eating, and Jasmine went over to Talphi. "Talphi, can I talk to you for a moment?" She pointed away from the group.

Sara caught her attention, "Jasmine, is everything all right? You seem distracted after the letter."

Jasmine understood why Sara was intervening. Again, it would be an action applauded by the Sisters of Forn. "It's work talk. Don't want to ruin the mood around here." The four of them pulled out of the cuddling, suddenly aware of the scene. "I wanted to talk with Talphi about his insight into carrying those stones he cuts. I mean, my training suggests a counterbalance of force, but it gives out at a certain point." She looked right into Sara's eyes.

Sara looked back coldly. "Don't go far."

Jasmine reassured her, "We won't." She looked down to Talphi, who got up, having received Sara's permission. Jasmine led them dozens of feet away, but they were still within view. When she stopped, she turned to Talphi and just said, "I'm going to be leaving tonight."

Talphi was fearful and hopeful about Jasmine wanting him. Weeks of being near her exasperated his desire and dreadful engagement. Her answer was immediate relief. The worry evaporated to trust. He was eager to be a confidant. "The letter? Is something wrong?"

Jasmine wanted to be completely open with him. "It's not wrong." She looked back at the campfire. "It's time." She looked back at him and smiled. "You're not like them, you know."

Obviously, but there were many ways to not be like someone. He asked, "How so?"

Jasmine now wondered if it wasn't love or lust but pure fascination. You have to know someone to love them. Talphi was different in the same way witches are different than Tokkin. "In the same way that I'm different from a relic wielder or Tokkin. Your skill with a relic is connected and tangible. It's a tool to them, but it's part of you. I've seen it."

Talphi blushed, but it was dark, and she probably didn't notice. "It's terrifying. Without the relic and the training... I don't know who I would hurt." It might be a compliment, but he was afraid of that raw anger still bubbling below his exterior.

Jasmine saw his sadness and was confused. "Who did you hurt?" She was close to knowing what she thought he might be hiding. But this time, she cared about how it was affecting him. Before this moment, she only wanted to know for her own satisfaction.

Talphi assessed the possible damage. She was leaving, and she might just understand when no one else would. Maybe he'd be stripped of his relic and kicked from the Institute. "At home, before coming here. I got in a fight, and I lashed out," he felt a surge of anger that came from his assault, "With all my anger I picked another kid up off the ground, pinned him to the wall, and squeezed his neck."

Jasmine absorbed his fear. "Did you kill him?"

Talphi pushed the memory back for now. "No, but I was so close. Training with the relic is the only thing keeping that in check."

Jasmine was a little confused. Relics could be found in the world. Did that mean he had found his? "You had a relic?"

Talphi suddenly felt caught. "No." He explained quickly, "Relics are means of focusing and channeling intent. I needed one to control my anger and give me focus. You said it yourself, that I use the relic like it's part of me. It's more natural."

Jasmine thought about it. What if you gave a witch or Tokkin a relic? The relic would be their tuning fork, except for the fact that they already have perfect pitch. The silence grew as Talphi waited for her to confirm. "Talphi." She looked into his eyes and became fearful. What had she just discovered? "I don't know if you need that relic." She pointed to the relic hanging around his neck.

Talphi needed her insight. "What do you mean?" His information was just based on what his mother and the mayor had told him. The Institute had taught him means and methods and didn't contradict what he knew.

Jasmines explained what she knew about relics. "Relics don't control our abilities. We do. The only thing that stopped you from killing that other boy was you. No relic controls. They are links. Tokkin are not being controlled by their abilities. Your good intent. Your diligent work. That's who you are."

Talphi took hold of the relic with his hand. "Witches don't use relics?"

Jasmine smiled, "No. They are Tokkin, but not in appearance. And I suppose the answer is obvious if anyone asked it, but my Mothers spent a long time defining who they are." She saw him pulling on the string holding the relic, ready to be torn off. "But there are expectations. And I don't think I would trust the Institute with understanding anything more than they expect."

Talphi looked into Jasmine's eyes and stayed there. She looked back, and they waited for him to grasp her meaning. Mark and his mother had lied to him, but the lie had protected him up to this moment. Jasmine was agreeing to keep his secret. He was some sort of Tokkin. "How did witches do it?" Talphi asked.

Jasmine sighed. "Only Mothers know. They don't tell their daughters." He had backed away from holding his relic. "Don't tell anyone, Talphi, or try to explain it to people, seriously. Just do what you need to do. Define yourself, or else other people are going to decide for you. That's why the Sisters of Forn exist." He didn't argue, and Jasmine could see Sara looking over constantly. "Let's go back over to the group.

Talphi looked up and down at Jasmine. He wished he could have known her sooner and felt like he did now. Her confidence was with him and not in opposition. There was trust now, but she was leaving soon. She needed to do what she needed to do. "Alright." He would let her go because, frankly, he was a disaster, and she needed to be as far from him as possible.

It wasn't a surprise to Talphi the next morning when Jasmine was missing. Her tent was still standing, but her pack was gone and a short note for Sara simply explained that it was time for her to leave and that she would not return. Evin and Angie worried about the letter Jasmine had received.

Sara questioned Talphi, guessing Jasmine had talked to him about leaving. Talphi confirmed, "She did tell me she was leaving, but she wasn't particularly worried. Like she knew the letter was coming before she even came to the Institute, you know?"

Sara nodded. Jasmine only telling Talphi felt practical. He was the only one whose work might be slowed by wondering and thinking about Jasmine's whereabouts. "Well, it's too bad. Thankfully, we were tasked with a project that could be done without Jasmine. Let's get back to work."

The group met their schedule and finished the tower in three months. The rapid pace left Talphi little time to experiment with fusing split stones back together, but he had a new confidence that extended past his relic. It matched what he always wanted to feel. He didn't need to be crippled or handicapped to be safe. He didn't even need to see the world as everyone else did. All he had to do was make sure the results of his actions helped and didn't hurt.

When the tower was nearly complete, the communications installation team arrived. Sara made sure her crew was present for the installation. This was just one step into the future of communication. Light signals had been used before, but this system was more complex and designed for rapid messaging across the entire network.

The large panels being installed had nine ports that could be opened and closed by a control box. The open ports would shine light out in the direction of another tower. That other tower would observe the combination through optics and relay the signal in the correct direction with their light panels. Some of the light combinations were full names or locations, while others were letters for spelling.

The towers would relay announcements for now, but there were rumors that this was just a step toward other systems. Perhaps the next system wouldn't need an operator in each tower. Or perhaps more panels, detailed messages, or even private correspondence could be sent rapidly. The possibilities were exciting, making the first installation so much of a pivotal moment that Sara wanted them all to see.

Sara beamed as the panel tested its opening and closing light ports. "This is the future we're building. I can't wait to see what happens tomorrow."

Talphi smiled too, but he wasn't looking at where the world was going. He was looking at his accomplishment. All of them had worked on the tower, but there was a personal pride in seeing the standing structure.

Their schedule wasn't complete, however. This was just the first tower their crew needed to complete. There were more months for building before fall and winter. Another tower and a larger group project back at the Institute all needed to be done before the temperature fell too low again.

Chapter 18

Jasmine thought about the problems leaving would cause for Sara and Talphi as they built the tower. Even though Sara had told her that they didn't need her to finish on time, she still felt guilty leaving a project half-complete. The restless night's sleep had produced one thought she hadn't fully considered. What if she didn't return to Garrin?

Not returning would mean that her mother would die. She was dying, and the ritual to transfer her memories and status as a Sister of Forn would end Tiffany's life, but letting her die like a normal person was heart-wrenching. She wasn't going to let it happen, but having spent all this time away from her mother gave it new relevance. It wasn't her birthright; it was a wonderful bond.

Jasmine awoke just before the morning light arrived. She took a look at Talphi's tent. Her mid-conversation decision about her feelings made this departure easier. She might have found love with this boy, but at that moment, he was a friend, and she trusted him. "Perhaps some other time," she said softly into the still air. Seeing him in the future would be likely, given the trajectory she saw in his life, but she might be quite different after the transfer.

The sun now cut through the lowest branches and leaves. They would discover her missing soon. She had left the tent and was only carrying what she had arrived with. Sadness crept into her sides as she walked through the forest to get closer to the road network. The Institute was the King's manipulative creation, but she was still sad to leave it.

She thought through the days between her mother's desire for her and this moment. All the changes and feelings were not what she expected. Still, those changes in how she thought and interacted with the King's other subjects felt natural. Tiffany was right. Back then, she was waiting for her mother's memories because she didn't believe she could interact properly with the world. Now, the memories she would receive wouldn't be needed to guide her interactions, they would only be additional knowledge.

Jasmine had met back up with the road after a cut through the woods. She wanted her mind to be as clear as this vacant road. Time was of the essence, so using her abilities was necessary. Before coming to the Institute, she had trained to glide. It was a matter of compressing and decompressing the air to encourage movement. It could be exhausting, but the compressions happen in bursts rather than through sustained interaction.

Being near the road would let her keep track of her direction. Some additional trees had been cleared from the sides of the road. It looked like they were expecting to expand. She climbed a tall tree a short distance from the road. It's a rare sight to see a witch travel in this manner. Anyone who might see her could consider themselves lucky. She took in one more moment of stillness, finding a sweet calm within.

She took a step, merged into the branches, and propelled herself. Jasmine grazed a branch, and her adrenaline jumped as she pulled at propelling herself forward. The air rushed past her. Her body was set free, and her stomach lurched smoothly with the rise and fall. Quick snaps around branches too close to glide past made her heart leap with excitement. She had not unleashed herself like this in months, and it was grand.

Jasmine reached the castle and her home, panting for breath. It only took her three days instead of three weeks of traveling on foot. She felt her hands and wrists against each other. They had worked their part well, and her heart purred with the freedom and the comforting thoughts of home.

The Determined World

Jasmine walked through the castle and noticed a few of the other Sisters of Forn. They said nothing to her and barely looked at her. All they said to her was that Tiffany was in their chamber and that she should go to her. Jasmine assumed that Tiffany's actions had gone beyond the approval of her Sisters. They weren't angry at Jasmine but couldn't condone the risk the two had taken.

"I'm home, mother," Jasmine called as she breached their chambers in a very unladylike fashion. She heard a rustle in the next room, and her mother came through the doorway leaning on a walking stick. It was the first time Jasmine had seen her mother putting weight on the stick to keep herself up. Her warmth was chilled with concern. Her mother was in pain.

Tiffany beamed at Jasmine. "You're back. I didn't expect you so soon." Seeing Jasmine revived her to the point of selfishness. Before calling Jasmine, she thought that she had weeks to live. Jasmine's flushed cheeks, youth, and smile made her feel months away from death. The frown of Jasmine's concern added to her guilt. Loneliness lets death creep in more quickly. Tiffany moved into her chair as Jasmine came close to guide her.

Jasmine finished entering the room quickly. "I..." The truth was that Jasmine hadn't truly considered the pain Tiffany might be in, but her mother's appearance and brave smile set her perspective, "wanted to make it here in time. Who knows how long that messenger actually took." She hadn't been so worried at the time, but she felt so worried now. The tugging guilt was debilitating.

Tiffany now read the guilt on Jasmine's face. "Oh." She knew her daughter well enough to not assume anything. She was a good daughter. "It's alright, Jasmine. I should have dated the letter. I would have waited longer." Tiffany nodded to let her daughter know she loved her no matter what.

Jasmine wasn't going to let these moments be misunderstood. "No, wait. I had no idea that you were in such pain." It was the perfect moment to tell her mother how she felt. Tiffany had wanted her to experience some of the world before she passed, and this was the moment to share and not be quietly understood. "I can see that you were hiding it from me even before I left. Why would you wait?"

Tiffany smiled now. "Youth has the privilege of experiencing pain for short intervals. As we get older, pain becomes a daily reminder of the choices we made. Doesn't matter if they are good or bad decisions. Old bodies experience more pain. Unfortunately, we all learn that in time. But that pain isn't important. Being without the ones you love is a real pain." She sighed and corrected, "I sent you away, and having you come home is an overwhelming relief."

Jasmine had never experienced such concern, even after the letter arrived. She was distracted by the Institute. It wasn't so much of a relief to know her mother accepted the pain. "Do you regret sending me away?" Even though it was done, Jasmine was concerned that her leaving left resentment.

Tiffany considered, "No. I knew what had to happen for you. I should have had you when I was younger, and all this wouldn't be a problem. If anything, I regret not seeing you grow into a full woman. But here we are. How was the Institute?" She wanted to meet the mature daughter before she expired through the coming ritual.

Jasmine screwed up her face unable to capture the past in the face of current emotions. The sadness she felt before leaving was different now. It was still relevant, but it felt smaller. "It wasn't what I expected." There was so much to share, but discussing it all would hurt her mother, who called her back with so little time left to live. "It's not important. But I'm here for you now."

Tiffany sat back in her chair. "Oh, come now, we have some time to talk." They were going to talk more. She had wanted to hear a fantastic tale, but an honest story would be worth more. "Tell me about your trip." Tiffany wanted to make sure horrible things didn't happen first. It would have meant she made a huge mistake and that there is a very good cause for sheltering daughters so much.

Jasmine only stared at the ground, and Tiffany stared at her. She grappled with her desire to talk and just get on with the ritual to save her mother before she died. A vague description might help gauge her mother's actual desire to listen. "I don't know if I would ever feel like I do now if I hadn't gone. I knew how I felt all the time and each day before going there. I can't be certain now. I felt happy and sad and just confused sometimes. Is that good?"

Tiffany sighed with some relief. It didn't sound like anything horrible. It sounded like she had lived. "Yes. It is good. You're more grown up than when other mothers share their memories. You may be confused, but it just means you're more aware. It will mean a lot."

Jasmine asked, "So rattling my confidence is good?" She wasn't being mean or angry, but she wanted to make sure that it would help. "And this will help when I take on your memories?"

Tiffany wasn't sure. "Well." She didn't have a certain answer. "I'm not sure which memories are mine, Jasmine. I'm confused by them all now. Before you went to the Institute, your life could have been mine before I was given my mother's memories. The memories you have of there have given you a life of your own. I like to believe that difference will make you the greatest witch since the Grand Mother herself."

"Oh?" Jasmine hadn't seen her time as so definitive, and the grand suggestion seemed silly. She hadn't accomplished any great works or mighty feats. It was just some time at the King's worker training.

Tiffany wanted there to be more time. "Tell me," She asked only the important questions, "Are you glad that you went? Did you learn as much as you could from the people you met?" Every little insight Jasmine experienced and understood wouldn't help Tiffany. She just needed to know Jasmine had those insights.

Jasmine nodded automatically and guessed that her thoughts and feelings weren't really in agreement since she didn't feel glad at the moment. "I met many people and watched them learn and explore. They are making such progress without knowing exactly where it will lead them. They're just solving problems the King is asking of them. He's got a plan, and it's working."

It wasn't a description of happiness, so Tiffany prodded. "I know we talked about the King's plan, but I hope that's not all you learned while you were there." Her eyes started to fall closed from exhaustion. "The excitement from seeing you again is taking more of a toll than I thought. Tell me about the other stuff. Not the King. I'm just going to rest my eyes."

Jasmine knew she'd need to share more. "Alright. I'll tell you about the Institute." The plots of the King could be an entertaining conjecture, but she understood that Tiffany had wanted her to grow.

Tiffany rested her eyelids and listened. "Good."

Jasmine launched into the blue armbands and the alterations of the Relic Order. She covered the people she met and the fantastic machines that were being used by all the workers. As she listened to herself, Jasmine found that she had pride in being part of such a brave endeavor. She worked around to speak about everyone except for Talphi. He was a secret. Seeing her mother made her realize that Talphi would be a Tokkin of profound interest to the Sisters of Forn. She trusted Talphi and imagined that he should trust her. Jasmine finished her story with the feelings of the return glide.

Jasmine waited for her mother's response, but several moments of silence passed. She didn't know if Tiffany was asleep or waiting for more, but Jasmine spoke up, "Mother, are you awake?"

Tiffany roused her eyes and gave a small smile, "Yes. It sounds like you learned quite a bit." She couldn't be asked to recount what her daughter told her, but she is sure she listened. If there had been a problem, she would have discussed it with Jasmine.

Jasmine smiled with some pain. "Thank you for letting me go and explore."

Tiffany coughed and began to sit up. "Of course, I'm glad you had a good time. Are you ready to begin?" The ritual for transferring her memories was all she had left to do. It was her final and most important duty.

A single tear of Jasmine's gave way. She had missed their time together and even if she would still be with her in memory, it wouldn't be the same as being with her like she was now. "Yes. I love you, Mom."

Tiffany replied warmly as she held out her hand so Jasmine could help her out of her chair. "I love you too, Jasmine." Jasmine guided her into the adjacent room where Tiffany had set up for the ritual days ago. As soon as Tiffany had sent the letter, she and the other Sisters prepared the ritual.

The room was warm and dimly lit. It was as comforting as a womb. There was a circle traced onto the floor with a symbol representing each of the mothers. The circle was relevant in meaning but wasn't needed for the transfer. Truthfully, very little was needed, but there is comfort in performing a ritual. "Please, help me down." Tiffany lay on the floor with Jasmine's help.

Jasmine knelt beside her sitting on her feet. Tiffany took one of Jasmine's hands and placed it over her heart. She took the other hand and placed it on the side of her head. Tiffany then placed her hand on Jasmine's heart and the other on the side of Jasmine's head. They looked into each other's content faces. "I am so proud of you, Jasmine. You are more wonderful than I could have ever wished, and from this moment on, I'm certain you will become the greatest Sister of Forn." At the end of the last word, Tiffany's warm hands parted from Jasmine's body and fell limp. Tiffany was dead, but the warmth from her touch was below the skin, and Jasmine had her mother's memories.

The process transferred some of the body mass of Tiffany to Jasmine. It connected and shared its experience as it brought her to full maturity. Jasmine laid backward from her kneeling position onto her back. What was at first a warm inclusion of her Mother's life was suddenly a violent crash between her own memories and the memories relayed to her by Tiffany. The new feelings and experiences struggled to find a place.

If she had been more like the mothers before her, this might have been a smooth transfer, but this was a struggle for supremacy. The voices that rippled through her were her own voice, but they were foreign. The dozens of voices all had a shared memory of independence and worldly understanding. Jasmine had formed her own unscripted version of the world because of her time away from the Sisters of Forn.

The relic training under Mortimer kicked in, and she started to push them in line. They needed to be distinguishable from her own thoughts. It was like the evasive probing Talphi had done, but this time she knew how to react. She had to retain herself, so she started to sort the flood as it attempted to mix with her own memories and overlap into desired positions. Each mother would have a place, and she'd put them in there.

But Jasmine had received more than just memories, there were thoughts and feelings of her mothers. The sorting made each mother's voice distinct and less potent as they became individual personalities. But they all shared the same brain, and they all witnessed her personal memories as she protected herself from indoctrination.

A voice scolded. "Who was this Talphi?"

Many memories and dreams of Talphi kept coming up, and she knew meeting him was her own memory. She couldn't help but leave the memories exposed as she protected them. "He is my memory. This is my mind." The memories of the Institute were so distinct, and the ones of her time before leaving Garrin were barely distinguishable from the mothers'. She focused on protecting those memories as it was her journey into adulthood.

The voices became a chorus. "Don't keep this from us. We are a Sister of Forn." They wanted to be part of her like every daughter before her. It was clear now. They all saw this as immortality.

Jasmine pressed back. "I am Jasmine." She cried. "You are dead." She could feel it. Saying the words made the personalities thrash and struggle. They made their mark by invading the memories and attempting to transplant themselves into the scenes. But some of the personalities were weaker and gave into Jasmine's sorting and chronology of their lives.

"Jasmine," It wasn't the voice of her mother, it was the oldest voice, "Our life is for the Sisters of Forn. The protection of the Kingdom we built. We heard what you told of the Institute, and you left out this boy. Tell us about him."

This is what her mother meant. Through all the layers and lives, their original mother was still there, calling the shots. The vision was as striking as literally standing in front of her with each silent daughter behind her. Jasmine was face to face with the truth of this process.

Jasmine stood up to meet the challenge. "Talphi, is what you care about? What about all that the King is doing?"

The Mother replied, "It's known, maybe not through the eyes of a young girl, but we know. But you seem to know that Talphi is an exception."

They were no longer trying to overtake her through force. Jasmine felt the danger of letting them try to overtake her through conversation. They would have insight and history on their side. She would have to be stubborn. Jasmine saw all the mothers in front of her but then realized that Tiffany wasn't over there; she was by her side. She looked back at their first Mother, "That's right. He's exceptional. He's Tokkin, and he looks normal, just like us."

All of the memories of Talphi came into view, and the Mother picked the most concerning piece. "You cannot scry for him. You did it right, Jasmine, but he is just like Tal'Abrac. That was the name of the Tokkin who led the army that would have destroyed our Kingdom. He is a threat to us all. You know it, and now we need to do something about it. Fortunately, you met him, but unfortunately, you resist our traditions."

Jasmine continued to resist. "This is my life, my body. My mother, Tiffany, was right to doubt you. For all the complaining the Sister of Forn do about Medrick taking over the Kingdom, you would do it again just to stay immortal." They were silent. "That's it, isn't it? Because you can't see the future, you think there is none."

The Mother tried to see a way around Jasmine's divergent thoughts. "If we cannot see our future, then we can't be certain there is one for us. We have a future if we steer the course." She wanted Jasmine to give over control. The Mother radiated fear of the unknown.

Jasmine was frightened by the Mother, but she equated it to the fear she had heading to the Institute. She could handle the unknown moments. "I'm steering now." Jasmine stopped the Mother. "Talphi will not be interfered with."

The Mother watched her as those behind her faded into accepting Jasmine's decision. When the Mother stood alone, she gave her last rebuttal. "Love is built over time. And you will never have time with Talphi. Of course, you tell yourself this action has meaning, but he will never know what you sacrificed to protect him." She faded from Jasmine's view.

Jasmine could see the room in view. It was still warm and welcoming, but she couldn't help but feel hostile toward what had just happened. Her mother's duties were now hers. She was a Sister of Forn. Tiffany's body was next to her, and she would need to see to the burial. It felt like she had just aged years. Some of that tired pain Tiffany described was pulsing through her joints.

Jasmine's body had actually aged. She surveyed the growth. She was inches taller, and her body was fuller. The clothes she wore were too tight, and she removed them in favor of the spare clothing the Sisters kept at this location. She could recount memories from different times and lives, with each personality of previous mothers keeping track of her. The only memories she couldn't recall were of the first Mother in their line. She might remain resentful.

Jasmine opened the chamber to find her Sisters waiting for her. They could all see the change in her body, but the silence led to the question from Surbozza, "Is it done?"

Jasmine nodded. "Tiffany passed on her memories to me." She stood back and let all the others come into the chamber for a discussion. When she closed the door, she remembered the heated conversations between Tiffany and them about the risks of her leaving and coming back. Most were afraid of Jasmine dying and losing a sister. Clair was the only one who was curious if the transfer would go smoothly. Jasmine picked up on the conversation now. "It's not what I expected. It took a bit of effort."

None of Clair's past transfers took effort, which reinforced Clair's concerns. She spoke up, "Are you alright, Jasmine? We heard all the talking and didn't realize Tiffany was gone till you opened the door."

Surbozza reassured Jasmine, "It's because you were gone for so long. Did something happen at the Institute?" She stepped in to speak for the other Sisters. Clair wouldn't be able to stay on what's relevant to all of them and would be too concerned about Jasmine.

It was at Jasmine's fingers. She reviewed conversations and old memories between Sisters lifetimes ago. Jasmine had a distance that the Sisters immediately picked up on. "Yes. I grew into my own person." They all remained silent, remembering Tiffany telling them that's what she wanted. "I remember, but I am Jasmine. I am not Lanora." Lanora was the first Mother of her line, one of the original seven Sisters of Forn. They all knew their lineage, but they didn't acknowledge it daily.

Surbozza stated, "None of us are our Mothers, Jasmine." She had some tremble in her voice. It was their family secret. None of them completely understood what had happened to them as young girls, and they couldn't do anything about it now.

Jasmine stepped between them all. They formed a circle around her. "They were wrong. We, the Sisters of Forn, must save the Kingdom from that pride. Our mothers didn't have all the answers, and we have to question those impulses they put in us. We have to do better."

Charity asked, "What can we do?"

Celest answered before Jasmine could respond. "We have a lifetime of experience, Jasmine." Francesca continued, "And that gives us insight that no one else could ever understand."

Autumn cracked in, "This is the wrong conversation to have. You wanted to talk about the Kingdom and where it goes, Jasmine. Fine, but we are not going to question our Mothers. They did nothing wrong. What Tiffany did to you is your problem."

Jasmine protested, "This isn't about any one small problem, because it's all the same problem. We need to stop thinking of this as our Kingdom and our legacy and start by realizing that we're trapped in an old vision that hasn't been revised for centuries. Our daughters should live their own lives so they can build something unimaginable by us."

Surbozza took the lead again. "Jasmine, I can see the transfer was difficult, and I'm sorry Tiffany did this to you. Clearly, the Institute got you seeing things the King's way. But we have duties, and I'm not going to forsake the future of the Kingdom for your bimbo idea."

Jasmine kicked Surbozza's toe, who jumped back. This wasn't the first time Surbozza had used bimbo when talking at Tiffany. But it was the first time Jasmine heard it. "Stop that. Stop repeating your old insults." Jasmine was overwhelmed by more than her sisters. Her lifetime of memories recounted the ridicule. "I have so many memories of you, but maybe it's time to let our daughters grow into women. Just that will change the Sisters of Forn and

Kingdom for the better."

Srubozza again stepped forward for her sisters. "No, Jasmine. I know you think you know better now, but consider the struggle you faced. None of us struggle against ourselves, and confidence is what's needed to safeguard the Kingdom." She was done. It was regretful, but she would have to let Jasmine struggle till she understood. The other sisters followed her to leave.

Clair lingered, "You're going to have to prove it, Jasmine." Jasmine looked her in the eyes, and Clair explained. "We've all got our doubts, but if you have something different or better, you got to prove it to them. You can't just say it. If you have a chance to do it differently, you know, differently than Lanora, do it and prove them wrong."

Jasmine thought about Talphi. Keeping him a secret was the opposite of what Lanora had wanted. "I'll keep that in mind." Keeping a secret from the Sisters was against their promise to each other. She recalled the memories of trying to prove someone wrong. Only if the person wanted to be proven wrong could it work. What did her Sisters want? Were they just the result of their Mothers' influence, and would they ever be ready for change?

Chapter 19

Talphi was disappointed Jasmine had left. Their final conversation had been the best one they ever had. It was authentic. Neither of them was following a script or chasing a goal. She had trusted him, and he was only required to be himself. He wished he could go back and plant the feeling in all their other conversations, but such wishes usually devolved into fantasies that turned rotten on him.

It was poetic that her goodbye was the best moment they ever shared. He would cherish the memory. After all, it was a moment of revelation as well. Talphi didn't need his relic. He was actually a Tokkin. It didn't destroy how he felt about himself, but rather, it was permission to be different from other relic wielders. Of course, he needed to keep up the pretense and use the relic. Thankfully, the urge to share the secret fell flat because he hadn't formed other trusting relationships.

After the second tower was complete, his crew returned to the Institute to complete another campus building. There were more than enough relic wielders and workers returning from other projects to complete the building in time for the winter switch. These returning crews had completed their spring and summer projects on schedule, so part of the reward was that they earned an additional personal day each week.

Talphi was reunited with his old crew before the tower building. His placement with Sara for the tower building was about making functional teams for the smaller projects. His placement back with Rick and Gregor was about cultivating a specific skill set. That skill set was finally revealed to them.

Master Remus gathered them a short distance from the site of the new building on a crisp October morning. The building would be done in a few weeks, and it was being built with their new training in mind. It was speculated that the building would be another hall, like the dining hall or some other meeting chamber. While it would function as a meeting hall in the warm months, it would serve as a combat training facility in the winter.

Talphi arrived at the meeting location before Portheus and Russell had arrived. Master Remus was waiting quietly as Rick, Carl, and Gregor chatted. They nodded at Talphi's arrival, having now expected the gathering of the old crew. Remus wasn't a familiar face at the Institute. The few relic Masters that weren't at the battle weren't all instructors. His specialty must only now be required at the Institute.

Remus held his jet-black hair back into a bun with a string. Not one strand was out of place or in danger of coming in front of his face. His narrow eyes kept a watch on them without looking directly at them. It was as if he was squinting but without any effort. His broad chin and cheeks dominated his unwavering face.

He spoke with a raspy, almost quiet voice as the last two arrived. "You're all here. I'll begin. The time has come for the Relic Order to restart our combat training. You all have the privilege of being the first of your generation. Not every relic wielder will be trained in combat, so make sure you don't mess up. You get one chance."

There were several forms of combat a person could be trained in. The use of a relic could be applied to any of them, but relic combat, according to the Relic Order, meant no weapons and a prescribed movement set developed over centuries for their role as enforcers.

Gregor asked, "This is what we're building?" He pointed to the building a dozen feet away.

Remus knew the Institute had its methods, but he had his own standards. "We are in session right now. When we are in session, you will ask questions by raising your left hand to the height of your head, and when I have answered, you will reply, Thank you, Master. I know you've all had a relaxed standard here, but you are learning from me now. I have an elevated standard. Bow your head when you understand."

They all bowed their heads in response. It wasn't a tough standard to meet, but it did contrast with the camaraderie they usually felt around each other. Talphi didn't like the formality, but he tried to reason it out as not a hard standard to meet. It felt more important now to remain unnoticed because he was Tokkin.

Remus answered, "Yes. This will be our building in the winter."

Gregor replied, "Thank you, Master."

Remus droned on. "You will not need your relics until the last month of training. So, when you arrive on your first day, I will start collecting them each morning. Until then, go use them to finish my building." Remus waved them away. Rick raised his hand. Remus pointed at him, "Speak."

Rick asked, "Is this the last thing we will be taught before our assignments?" He had been at the Institute for over two years, and there had been a few there longer and some there for a shorter period. While Rick was happy to get the training, he was eager to visit home and become a full member of the Relic Order.

Remus's lips widened as if he wanted to smile. "Looks that way. Before this place," he gestured around, "it could take four or eight years before we'd let relic wielders partake in Order duties. Obviously, we had to lower our standards and follow the King's leadership. Duties have changed, times have changed, and sadly, you will be the closest thing to a traditionally trained Order member." Rick was silent after Remus was done speaking. Remus prodded, "Say, thank you, Master."

Rick replied, "Thank you, Master." He spoke partly in defiance and partly in resignation.

Talphi played with his relic, spinning it between his fingers. Since his conversation with Jasmine, he had explored the feeling of not using a relic. He had learned that he was using it, channeling his intent through its limited size. Talphi also discovered that he had been using his inherent capacity without realizing it. The training without the relic would present a challenge of sorts. He would have to make sure not to use his ability when they turned over their relics for training.

Talphi took the time to learn about the relic. It hadn't been possible to use his relic to examine itself like he had used it to understand any tree or rock. The relic had always reverberated back and physically hurt him when he had tried to gauge the nature of the relic.

Now that he knew the relic wasn't required or that he needed it, analyzing it was possible. The relic wasn't a stone or a tree. It wasn't a piece like other objects. Sure, it could be touched, broken, and treated like any other matter, but its difference was in reaction. Rocks didn't react differently if you were angry or happy when you placed a hand on them. The rocks only reacted to the physical world, but the relic did react to feelings.

The space around the relic moved with thoughts and feelings. Belief made the most movement since it was a collision of thoughts and feelings. The movement was intangible. But it was a real connection. The relic was a literal path between the physical and a belief. It was fascinating but also terrifying since Talphi realized a belief was open to interpretation.

Knowing what to look for, Talphi found another relic while he was on one of his forest walks. It was like looking for any object, like a gem or insect. Once you know how to look, it wasn't too difficult. He would place his hand on the ground and make the connection outward as he had with so many blocks cut for building towers. Bits of relic reflected, unlike all the other matter. There were many tiny bits as small as a grain of sand, so finding one the size of his thumb just took time.

He played with the extra relic, seeing if the physical composition changed its bandwidth for manipulating the world. Removing bits from it did change it, lowering its potency, but changing color and shape and adding inert material didn't change it. Talphi kept the second relic with him and would play with it from time to time, molding it into a new shape as if it were clay and not solid. It was only because of his realization about the nature of relics that he now played with one like a toy.

On their first day of training, each of the boys handed their relics over to Remus as they entered the main hall. Talphi left his second relic in his room, so there was no confusion. He felt he was ready to throw a punch without using his Tokkin ability. The mayor's lie to him about needing a relic to control himself took on a new meaning. Was the belief that he needed the relic enough to limit his behavior and prevent outbursts? Regardless of the relic, he now needed to be under his own control. His own gatekeeper.

The open room had four large columns supporting the slanted roof. The pitch of the roof was low like all the other buildings, so it needed to have the snow pushed off in the winter if it got too heavy. There were a few rooms surrounding the exterior of the main area, which was 60 feet square and thirty feet tall. The walls, floor, and columns were all padded. There were also padded shields and person-sized figures with the same padding.

When Remus finished taking and setting the relics at the front, he addressed them as they gathered in the center. "Welcome to our sanctuary. Sanctuary can mean many things. In this case, I think of sanctuary as a place where we don't have to hide our truth from those without the red armbands. Our orders are to play nicely with everyone here, but we all know how important our role is. We are the enforcers; they are the ones we have to enforce upon."

No Master before Remus had promoted such an elitist view to them, at least openly. Other Relic Order Masters had suggested more responsibility in their position. None of them questioned it, though. Who would they be defending by questioning Remus' opinion?

Remus went on to explain. "You are first training without your relics because you are training in partners. When you strike, it'll be your partner's pad that you're hitting. We are not looking to injure each other. Perhaps you already fight, or you're comfortable hitting another person, but we are going to do it in an organized manner so that everyone learns and no one dies. Understood?"

They all bowed, "Yes, Master."

The six of them followed Remus' instructions, pairing off and beginning their training. Jab, jab, cross. They practiced the hits and the movement of their torso. There was power in the length. Talphi found not using his abilities wasn't a challenge as they were focused on their actions. It wasn't emotional, and they were all in control of their reactions. They practiced for hours using padding and strapping as the skin got raw and torn.

Remus was the only one with a relic throughout the day, so when one of them got blisters or bloody, he would heal the skin. His healing was intentionally rough, and it started to leave the skin callous. That would mean less healing in the long run. "Our bodies heal on their own," he explained, "so when we heal, we can either work with that natural and wise process or force it into the state it used to be in. I say, take the scars. You'll be stronger for it."

Remus kept them going at a higher pace using his healing and energizing techniques. Without his relic manipulation, they might only be able to practice a few hours a day with more resting required. He was able to push them to train six days a week for six hours a day.

Remus got them kneeing, kicking, pushing, throwing, and twisting into their opponents. This wasn't the distant bombardment they had imagined relic fighting might be. This fighting was close and aggressive. It intentionally got that close to make blocking improbable and to unbalance the opponent. There was one intent, to eliminate the threat as quickly as possible. Showy displays or long fights were a waste of talent, according to Remus.

The future possibility of distance fighting still existed, but the close and aggressive model put them into the intended mindset of the old Relic Order. Be effective and ruthless. They were there to enforce the King's law, not to make a spectacle of fear. Talphi approved of the discretion. Still, he wasn't looking to instill fear, but being an enforcer wasn't what he wanted from the Institute either.

Talphi had never matched well with the personalities of the crew, but they all had a working respect, and they didn't try to change it or make Talphi a friend. He imagined they had no problem being enforcers, but he wasn't sure. Talphi asked the question after a month of training and not learning an answer through observation. The group was finished for the day and heading to dinner when Talphi caught their attention, "Are we being trained to be enforcers, or is this just another skill set we're being taught?" Remus wasn't around, so he felt safe to ask.

Rick asked snidely, "Don't want to be an enforcer, Talphi?"

Talphi had expected this in planning out his words, "I hadn't planned on it. We've been here for years, and construction had been the only option. I wasn't sure if we got a choice."

Portheus spoke before Rick could speak again, "I've wondered the same thing myself. I don't mind being an enforcer, but he never talked about choosing tasks."

Carl added, "The Relic Order was devastated. Part of rebuilding might be assignments we are not comfortable with because they need to get done. No one says I have to punch someone to do it, though, at least, well maybe we don't choose assignments, but we choose how to get them done."

The Determined World

It was a better possibility, but it confirmed only one thing. They hadn't been told how it works, and they needed to know more. Portheus nodded at Talphi, "We'll have to ask Master Remus how that gets decided." He patted Talphi on the shoulder, "And you're just the man to do that tomorrow, Talphi." They all laughed except for Talphi and kept walking to the dining hall.

Talphi hung back in the cold air and diminished daylight. It wasn't mockery to suggest he is the one that has to ask, but assigning him as the point man kept them from looking foolish for not knowing. Talphi could 'not know' for the lot of them, and they would give him respect for keeping them from looking like fools. At least, that's how Talphi understood the relationship.

Talphi did it the next day, first thing. They had handed in their relics, and Remus began like every day, "Any questions about yesterday?" In the first days, he had made it clear that they didn't need to know where they were going, so questions about the coming day's training were not important.

Talphi had tried to word it without sounding like he needed to know about their future training. He raised his left hand, and Remus pointed to him, "The Institute has given us the chance to use our relics in many ways. How is it determined what we will be doing once we leave?"

Remus' narrow eyes pierced into Talphi and punctuated after several silent seconds. "You don't think you should be here, Talphi?"

Talphi had guessed this might come up, but the scenarios along this line of question weren't favorable. He just wanted a clear answer. "I believe I need all the training I can get. I would like to know where I might be going after the Institute." It broached the future, but he would risk the reprimand.

Remus never smiled, but the corners of his lips might go up or down the slightest amount before speaking. They went up this time, but still, his eyes were narrow and intimidating. "I don't know. The King gives the orders, and he doesn't tell me. I have to operate very much like you all. Maybe, years ago, the Relic Order had more choice, but we act only at the King's bequest. Don't worry, he has a plan, and from what I've seen, he always knows where your strength lies."

The silence fell back on them, and Talphi knew he was still being stared down. "Thank you, Master," he replied, and immediately Remus began his instruction for the day.

That evening, Talphi walked off into the woods. He walked through the foot of snow but kept warm with his technique for heating the air. His relic revelation, the communication towers, and the explanation that the King was the source of decisions for their training all aligned. It was a series of cogs and moving parts like the water mill and the devices the Institute used. He knew he could fit the shape and work with the King's plan, but he didn't want to. Was the feeling youthful rebellion or something else?

Talphi muttered a few words out loud. "No, thank you, I'll decide my purpose on my own." The words were right. He didn't need to belong. He didn't need to be part of the King's vision. He only needed to know he was good enough to be accepted. He just wanted to be treated fairly.

The hierarchy wasn't fair. Titles and claims of rank seemed futile. That was their world, and he didn't need it. What he told Remus was true. He needed all the training he could get. But could he do it without playing the game? He rolled the second relic into a new shape between his fingers. He needed to continue his training.

The next day, much to everyone's surprise, Remus only collected relics from three of them. No one had a question regarding yesterday, so he began, "You will not be using pads for blocking today. You will be using your relic to block. Relic wielders pad their bodies against impact by directing the force back. You've already learned how to direct force with your relic, now, you must quickly direct precise force back against an attack. This method will be required in a month when you use the relics in attacks."

They began. The human punching bags started to hurt as countering the rapid points of contact was difficult. It was a line between getting hit and knowing where you were going to get hit. You can't exactly prepare since the contact location might be off by inches. It was more of a reflex of the entire body. They needed to have the counter force available in their body, and it would flood to the contact.

Remus explained in the following days, "Besides your concentration, each relic has a limit. You may never find or test the limit of your relic, but you need to draw as much counterforce as you can. Push the limits of your focus. Believe that you can draw in so much force that each point on your body could take a punch, and you won't have to direct the entirety of your defense each time."

Talphi understood the limits of relics. He didn't understand the limits of Tokkin, though. He hoped he might be able to measure it like a relic, but when he measured himself, it fluctuated. The relic was a known quantity with a human's belief applied. Tokkins were mixed too deeply to separate the quantity from the belief. How he believed and what he chose to believe would have profound impacts on the scope of force and energy drawn to his intent.

Believing he was not part of the King's vision for the future seemed to have the greatest impact on the force he could generate. But it was more than just the King. It was an infectious idea around him that the future was determined and known. So many around him thought there was a reason to exist beyond their lives. Whatever strength they pull from that belief, he did not.

He was responsible for his own reason to exist. When he thought that, while performing as the punching bag, the attackers started hurting their hands. It caused Remus to give Talphi one extra private instruction, "Just enough force so you and the attacker aren't hurt for now."

Talphi was aware that he could generate more force than the relic he carried. The trick was whether others could discover that. Being safe meant holding back, but he didn't want to hold back anymore. He needed to know his limits. Remus stopped paying close attention to Talphi's defense. The instruction stopped, but Talphi had the urge to keep progressing.

With at least two weeks left in the punching bag games, Talphi started traveling out at night to test the limits of impact he could take. He started by testing himself for a fall. The weight of his own body hit the ground from a three-foot drop. A ten-foot drop. A twenty-foot drop. Each drop didn't exceed the force he could accumulate. But at twenty feet, the surface he hit did have a noticeable impact. He gained speed on the fall, but how much speed could he gain?

He found a cliff fifty feet tall and leaped. The ground burst away from his landing, and he felt the wane in his force. It sprung back with a moment of focus, but he shook out his legs because some of the impact did hit the bone. All their training with relics in combat so far had been about taking a hit they didn't have time to react to. But what if, as in the case of the ground, he saw it coming far in advance?

Talphi took the chance to test the theory. The cold air he heated was all around him. It wasn't the ground he would land on that needed the force. It was the air. He stepped off the cliff again, and it worked. He put the force into the air and landed as if he had jumped from three feet.

But that wasn't all. Of course, they were applying force to the bits that made up their body. This is where people would break themselves. Applying force to yourself could be disastrous. It was not just application but resistance to the force. Talphi looked up at the cliff and tried to force his way up.

He didn't move at first because he was defending too well against being moved. When he released his defense, he lifted, but it wasn't pleasant. It was like being pulled by a string attached to one point on the body. Talphi dropped to the ground and felt the edges of pain. His trials and mistakes were piling up, and he stopped for the evening.

It took two weeks of trials before Talphi figured it out. It was quite by accident that he caught an idea. He was a punching bag that day, and he was practicing with Gregor. Gregor knew Talphi could be like punching stone, so he challenged Talphi to a game since Remus wasn't paying too much attention. "Talphi, how about you pick a pose, and I try to move you? You don't need any more practice, and I'd rather not break my hand."

Talphi saw no harm in the game. "You mean," He took a stable fighting stance and held the position, "like, I'm a statue, and you have to re-position me like a marionette?"

Gregor nodded, "Yes. Just like that." He moved around Talphi and tried to lower his hand. Talphi moved the slightest amount, but the more force Gregor applied, the more hardened Talphi's position became. He stepped back and moved to a different location. Remus looked over but didn't stop them. Talphi didn't need more training from small hits anyway.

Talphi replied, "That's different. I've got to be a lot more aware of what you're doing than reacting." He had felt Gregor like any other object. The bits and the connection to the relic all came into view. He could react to Gregor's intended action rather than the impact of his actions.

On the next re-position attempt, Talphi became much more aware of Gregor. As Gregor pulled on his leg, Talphi became aware of the series of contracting muscles along Gregor's body. It happened as fast as he thought. Gregor wanted to use his arms to pull, and his abdomen tightened instinctively, giving his whole body the support it needed.

Talphi realized the same about himself. His body had learned how to respond to his desired movement, creating a chain of whole-body reactions to support it along the way. It was unaware and involuntary. His attempts to apply force in moving himself didn't have all that full-body support. Could he learn to apply a force that would naturally go along with his desire?

The beginning of relic use in attacking confirmed that he had to answer that question on his own. As Remus explained, "You know where the force of your strike is going, so when you make contact, push with your force in that direction. This is important. If you try to push your hand faster with force, you will break your hand or arm. Your relic power is there to add the extra bit. It just so happens that bit can be several times more than the force you are defending your own body with."

Talphi would come to modify and contradict the method. So much so that he started applying force in odd directions. With a straight punch, he sent the force down, making the opponent's guard drop low when they were expecting to be pushed back. He expected the same from the others when he was in defense, but they couldn't express the angles he could.

For the next two weeks, Talphi coasted through the sessions with Remus so he would have spare energy to practice familiarizing himself with all his body's reactions. Instead of pinpoint awareness, he had to encompass every cell of his body with awareness. Then, when he moved with the force of a Tokkin, his entire body would respond. It required presence in the moment, not hopes for the future. It reinforced his belief in the reason for his existence. He was here to be present, to be himself. Fulfilling some future vision was not the goal.

Talphi's diminished effort in the training didn't go unnoticed, and Remus took offense. With only three weeks left in the session, Remus had been given orders from the King that each of his trainees would be going to the Relic Order's full service. What their assignments would be after that, he didn't know, but Talphi's lack of enthusiasm for combat made him challenge Talphi's worth.

Remus announced the King's order to the crew. "I have received directions that you will all be given Relic Order membership at the end of our session here. You will be the most well-trained relic wielders in years, and I hope you are all ready."

The crew jostled a bit as they looked around at each other in appreciation. Remus continued, "I thought we'd take the day in celebration with a little one-on-one challenge. I know you've all practiced and sparred outside this building," Remus had seen the five minus Talphi practicing, "but perhaps it's time to bring it inside. You'll each have a chance to face me so that you know what it's like to fight a real relic wielder or maybe even a Tokkin someday."

Remus waved them all closer, "I won't hurt you that badly. If I break something, I'll heal it, and it's on to the next challenge. Any takers to go first?" Russell raised his hand. Remus approved. "Russell, I saw you spar with your comrades; it'll let them know what to expect."

The rest of them backed away as Remus and Russell set themselves in the center of the room. Each took up a stance, and they began to fight. It appeared Remus gave Russell a chance to warm up, allowing him to get in the first attacks because when Remus attacked, the third hit caused Russell to fall and roll backward. Remus spoke as he got back up, "Now you know. You're going to have to give it everything you have. Don't hold back."

Russell's intensity became absolute, and he attacked with enough force to destabilize Remus, who stepped back and away. It was just a moment, then Remus countered, striking Russell side to side with cross hits and causing him to fall to the side with a push. Russell rolled backward and up to a stand and came right into Remus. It was valiant, but Remus had skill and power. Russell took a hard hit to the chin and fell back, dazed. Remus walked over and put a foot on his chest to keep him down.

Remus said calmly, "You're out, Russell."

Russell nodded, and Remus let him stand up and walk out of the center. Each of the others wondered if this was just a way for Remus to express his dominance now that it was confirmed they would be leaving soon. But that's what fighting is, a struggle for dominance.

Gregor went next to much of the same effect, giving it his all, but getting soundly beat. Remus didn't wait for a volunteer since he was now warmed up enough for Talphi and didn't want to be tired when fighting him. "Talphi, you're next." He waved Talphi into the center. Each of the crew looked at Talphi, realizing this was very much about dominance. All of them had wanted to be able to break Talphi's defense, though they didn't go out of their way to do it because Talphi never bragged and had always been a competent worker.

Remus stepped into his stance and prepared for Talphi. "You may strike first. I know you've been holding back."

Talphi made a quick three-hit strike, not adding all the force Remus had suggested. Instead, he added an odd directional force, causing Remus to tilt, turn, and step back to regain his balance.

Remus repositioned and led with his foot and a smile. Talphi's lack of force was disappointing, but he enjoyed the directional force that had taken him by surprise. It was a nice trick that he hadn't taught them. He didn't put his full force into it because he wanted Talphi at his best, and the boy deserved a warm-up, too. "Don't be afraid to hurt me, boy." His voice was confident.

Talphi stopped the kick and pressed Remus with a series of very fast punches compliments of his full body awareness. The hits were a blur of motion, and Remus only had time to throw up his arms to block.

Remus stepped back and away. He thought he understood what Talphi had just done. "Be careful there. You might get away with using force instead of your own body for a few strikes, but you surely will break yourself." He came at Talphi without holding back. He got in his punches, elbows, and kicks.

Talphi responded with the right blocks but couldn't counter fast enough. Remus had years of experience, and the hits were perfectly distracting against any response. But it was like hitting a stone for Remus. He stepped out before

Talphi could counter. Remus took a moment to rub his hand. Even he needed to follow his own advice and care for his body's resistance, but the force he generated with the relic wasn't enough to break Talphi. Fighting weaker opponents had made him soft.

Talphi stepped up again and took his swings at Remus. Again, when Remus blocked, his defense was broken by the directional force that Talphi applied. Remus moved back, and Talphi sweep kicked for his legs. Remus jumped back further, but Talphi wasn't ready to let him get away. Talphi sent his reaching leg up and forward at Remus as he was in mid-air.

Talphi had no leverage and was lifting the leg with Tokkin force, but his body went along as if it was meant to without any pain. The kick connected with Remus' blocking arms, but Talphi added more force, pushing Remus five feet higher and a dozen feet away.

Remus came crashing down onto the padded floor. Again, Talphi had done what Remus warned about but hadn't suffered the right consequences. "Talphi," he stood back up because Talphi gave him the chance, "If you keep that up, a guarantee you'll kill yourself."

Talphi didn't respond. He let Remus take another shot because each moment of the fight was just reaffirming his confidence. Remus breathed back into focus and took Talphi's silence to mean he was ready again. He rushed forward, kicking into Talphi straight and then on landing swung the other leg up to kick Talphi's side. Talphi hadn't felt that much force before and stepped back in distraction. Remus's next few hits actually hurt, challenging the standard defense he applied.

Talphi needed to be more active in his defense. He needed to block the intent of Remus's attack. One, two, three more hits, and there it was. It was like a second stopped for a moment. It might have been mind work Mortimer had taught them, the time he spent applying force to all manner of objects, or the understanding of the body's reactions, but he knew where Remus was going in the moment. He responded with his inclination.

Each strike Remus committed had the perfect responding force from Talphi. Talphi took even more advantage and matched strike for a strike like Remus had choreographed it with him earlier. Remus stopped his pattern and did a roundhouse kick directed at the side of Talphi's head. Talphi dropped low and stepped into Remus. He caught Remus while his kick should have been connecting with Talphi's head. Talphi lifted and threw Remus up and away.

Remus came down with a thud but rolled back and up to stand as if he was afraid of being stepped on. "Talphi, you have been holding back quite a bit. And to think you were questioning the reason for combat training months ago." He stepped in closer, within arm's reach of Talphi. He wasn't done. "Still feel like you don't need it?"

Talphi replied, "I wasn't sure I wanted." Remus grabbed Talphi in mid-sentence under his armpit and threw him over as he stepped into and under Talphi. Remus pulled down to make Talphi generate the next thud. Talphi stopped his body from hitting the floor by applying the right force. There was no thud and no touching of the floor. Talphi was floating a few inches off the ground. Remus stepped back to set up a downward kick to Talphi's head.

Talphi, still floating above the floor, put a hand above his head and grabbed Remus's foot as he kicked down. With a hold on Remus, Talphi pivoted on that point at Remus's foot and pulled his whole body around, so his foot came and hit Remus square in his chin. Talphi continued the pivot, pulling his body upright and drawing Remus's head to the floor. Talphi's foot led Remus's head into the ground with a thud.

Talphi was upright, floating above the floor. He released Remus's foot and let him fall unconscious. He moved back and stepped to the ground, looking down on Remus as his heart sank. That sort of hit could have killed Remus. He remembered Chris and his promise to come and learn to control his power. This was a fair fight, but he had still reacted with fury when Remus attacked him in mid-sentence. The regret was the same as he talked himself away from the anger.

Rick squawked, "You killed him."

Gregor chirped as he fumbled for the door, "I... I'm going to get another Master."

Chapter 20

Talphi couldn't shake the chance that he killed Remus, and he needed to know for sure. He had to see if Remus was still breathing, so he knelt to the body.

Portheus stepped up on the other side of Remus's body, "You need to stay back now, Talphi." He was quickly flanked by the others. They were united in this. They had all seen what had happened. It was a condoned fight. "I'll check." He reached down as Talphi stepped back.

Talphi looked at the others as Portheus checked. He recognized the fear in Russell's eyes. Rick was putting on a determined face, but his eyes conveyed worry. Carl had narrowed his attention to Talphi as he watched him coolly. There was a chance that he had earned Carl's respect. Talphi looked back down at Remus. He was that monster he feared in his youth, but Talphi tried to justify his actions rationally. He started by standing still and waiting for the conclusions of others.

It was steadily different than when he attacked Chris in Saven. The longer he looked down at Remus and remembered their fight, the more liberated he felt. It started to push the terror aside. Remus and he had engaged knowing full well the possibilities, and that mattered with this outcome. He hadn't lost complete control but had pushed back against an authentic threat. This time, the rage he had reacted with could be accepted.

The movement of Remus's breath couldn't be easily seen, so Portheus was checking with his hand near the nose. "He's breathing," Portheus spoke with relief. All the others released their breaths and breathed in the next stage of emotion. He stood back up and looked at Talphi. While Portheus wasn't their assigned leader, everyone took their leads from him. "I'm not confident enough to heal him, so we're going to wait for Gregor to get back. Everyone take a seat."

Talphi complied and sat facing each other around Remus. Rick still looked at Talphi like he was ready to attack him at any moment, but he followed Portheus's lead. They waited a few minutes before Gregor returned with Master Matthews and Master Mortimer. As soon as they entered, Rick yelled, "Talphi attacked Master Remus and nearly killed him." Their pace to Remus was hurried as Rick called out.

Portheus responded as they reached the center, "He's alive. I checked his breath, but I didn't want to try and wake him. He was knocked out while sparring with Talphi." He had decided to guard Talphi for what it was worth. There might be punishment for Talphi, and this might be the best chance to mitigate some of the punishment.

The two Masters slowed slightly on Portheus' words. Matthews checked for himself. Mortimer stood a bit back and kept an eye on Talphi. After a moment, he spoke to them, "Remus and Talphi were sparring?"

"That's how it started," Carl replied. He smiled at Talphi. "Then it escalated."

Matthews had his hand on Remus' chest. He had taken full account of the damage, and it was a bad concussion. He was able to reverse some of the damage but decided some of the fractures should heal on their own to remind Remus he was injured.

Remus opened his eyes and, with some pain in his voice, spoke up. "Matthews," he said, blinking the blinding light away.

Matthews watched Remus's eyes respond to gauge if more healing was necessary. "Remus. Your student came for me. Are you alright?"

Mortimer watched Remus closely and added, "He said you were killed by Talphi. I can see the death part isn't true." He started really looking at each person. This situation would have many viewpoints and jaded perspectives. Finding the truth may take some time.

Remus looked back for a moment and prepared himself for Mortimer's interrogation. "Help me up first. You five, go practice in the courtyard." He addressed his other students. They didn't immediately respond, so Remus narrowed the order, "Portheus, take your crew outside. Talphi stays here with us."

Remus wished he had more of the Relic Order here. Their membership was scattered throughout the Kingdom. He supposed he should be happy to at least have Matthews and Mortimer. Only three other Masters were on the Institute grounds, but they shouldn't be necessary.

Talphi wasn't going to run from this. He had built a good defense and wouldn't accept a punishment. There was nothing to be sorry for. He fiddled with the second relic in his pocket as the others left slowly. They wanted to witness this.

Once they were gone, Remus began, "Talphi is unacceptable for the Relic Order. I know we must expand our ranks, but he has flagrantly ignored my instruction and used his relic in dangerous ways. Whatever means we have Matthews, we need to remove his relic from him and give it to someone more deserving." Remus went from looking right at Talphi to talking about him like he wasn't even there.

Talphi didn't cry out against the rant and knew it was geared to sway the other Masters by reminding them of their old bond. At the very least, he needed to explain his position even if he was set to lose. He explained, "Master Remus was taking turns beating each of us to prove he's better. I did some risky things, but I had to if I wanted to win."

Mortimer smiled. "That sounds about right," he chuckled. Each of them was telling the truth. Remus had mentioned a week earlier that he was suspicious that Talphi might be augmenting his strength in dangerous ways and that testing him in a fight would teach Talphi a lesson.

Matthews sighed. "Mortimer, this is serious. We have a duty to see that every new Order member is prepared. Talphi is out of line." He was going to protect Remus's interests. But Matthews had a limited staff and clear orders, so Remus needed to continue to teach Talphi. He needed to find a way forward.

Remus cheered up as Matthews sounded ready to defend his position. "Oh, good. It sounds like you're finally going to stand up for a higher standard, Matthews. He doesn't deserve his relic. It's about time we started thinning these ranks."

Mortimer looked incredulously at Matthews. "You don't intend to ignore the King, do you, Matthews? Remus can't see past the old ways. Seriously Remus, if you just took the time to follow the King's directions, you'd realize the strength and loyalty of the new Relic Order he's building. They don't all need to be your assassins."

Matthews looked at the two Masters and Talphi. "I know that Talphi has been competent. Your words aren't enough to have his relic taken. No one is supposed to have their relics taken and be kicked from the Institute, Remus. The King gave clear instructions on how to deal with relic wielders. We have our laws."

Remus frowned. "We used to have laws that worked for us. Now, they force us to work for them. It's like we're the pupils, and they get to be the masters of us. We shouldn't have to cater to them."

Matthews tried to calm Remus. This had been a long-running problem. Remus had the most trouble adapting to the new system of the Relic Order. It's why Remus had only arrived at the Institute years after its establishment and with a very narrow set of responsibilities. "It's only a short while longer,

Remus. I imagine Talphi will earn his Relic Order status after this."

Remus didn't like that answer and replied, "I'm not going to let this pass unchallenged, Matthews. Oh, sure he's good enough to meet those standards and yes he may have bested me in a fight, but we are the Masters, damn it! What have all the years been for if they don't even know how much suffering we've endured? You won't let me really push them. They are not prepared."

Mortimer voiced his opinion, "That's what you don't get, Remus. They don't need to suffer to prepare. This isn't about making new relic wielders suffer. It's about making them loyal to building a new Relic Order."

Matthews stamped down with his authority. "No. It's not about any of your beliefs," he addressed both Masters. "We follow the King's orders." He looked back at Talphi. This wasn't the place to have another one of these debates. "Remus, you will continue to train Talphi for the remainder of the winter."

Mortimer snorted. He didn't believe Remus could do such a thing. Even if Talphi would just stand at the edge of the room without participating, Remus would protest. "Forget that, Matthews. Let me train Talphi for the rest of the winter. He had some potential last year that we could tap into."

Master Remus stepped away from the two and faced Talphi. "No, he's mine then. Don't worry, Matthews, I'm sure there's more for him to learn." He would find a new way to explore suffering for Talphi. Something inside the guidelines.

Matthews knew that Remus was broken. He would always yearn for the glory days. "Remus. Don't make me supervise you. That's an option that I don't want to do."

Remus knew he couldn't hide his intent from them. He stepped closer to Talphi. There were other options. People die. However, it wasn't Talphi's fault that he didn't belong in the Relic Order. Relics need to be guarded. "Talphi," Remus' words were thick with false kindness, "how did you get your relic?"

Talphi didn't know if he should reply. The question was benign enough. He had to answer it during his entry into the Institute. "The mayor of the town I came from acquired it, and I was chosen to learn with it."

Remus nodded and asked, "You came from one of those towns. No noble lord, just a charter from the King." He should have figured. It fits the narrative of this boy's exploration into dangerous relic use. "Does it have any unusual markings?"

"What are you getting at, Remus?" Mortimer defended Talphi against the meaningless questions.

Talphi reached and took the necklace, holding that relic up to his view. He wondered if there was something more to it now. There might be some insight into the relics that he's missed during his appraisal. Remus was only a few feet away from Talphi when suddenly Matthews realized what was about to happen. He had seen Remus do it once, decades ago. "Remus, no."

It was too late. Remus grabbed the exposed relic and pulled the string off Talphi's neck. He then smashed it between his hands with enough force to shatter it into dozens of pieces. Talphi stumbled back, barely keeping his footing. His excuse for having relic-like power was gone. If Remus attacked him now, he would have to make a fatal choice of defending himself without a relic as an excuse for his power.

But Remus didn't attack. He smiled and laughed, "All done." He turned to Matthews and a slack-jawed Mortimer. "I found a solution. Since relics aren't handed out by the Order anymore, there's no replacing one that has been accidentally destroyed."

Mortimer knew it was true but couldn't handle Remus' selfishness. "You are not the judge for a relic wielder's worth Remus."

Remus cackled and sighed, "Say whatever you want Mortimer. It's done, and he has no place here." He kept his back to Talphi. There was no reason to give him any more attention. Talphi was beneath him.

Matthews kept looking at Talphi, gauging his reaction. Fury, sadness, confusion, or worry. Anything and everything could be possible, but he hadn't expected Talphi would regroup to defiance so quickly. That's how Talphi stood as Remus wrote him off. Talphi was right to stand defiant. It wasn't so easily done as Remus suggested. "You're right Remus, but I'm going to have to take this up with the King. Talphi learned to build with a relic, and at this point, he's useless as a builder without one."

Remus coughed. "Just send him packing."

Mortimer wanted to compensate Talphi for his loss and defended him, "It's still winter Remus. He can stay here at least till the roads are better for travel." He wanted to strike Remus, but it wouldn't solve anything.

Matthews spoke simply to all of them. "He'll stay here while I inform the King. He enlisted as a relic wielder, but whether he's allowed to continue or re-enlist without a relic is up to the King." He addressed Talphi. He had other words for Remus, but Talphi didn't need to be here. "Talphi, you can go back to your room. You are welcome to meals and all the Institute services until otherwise. You won't need to come back here anymore."

Talphi nodded. "I understand." He felt more of an urgency to leave now that no one expected him to have relic-associated abilities. Every second near their observation was a chance for him to make a mistake. He left the space and returned to his room. The others were outside and watched him leave. They didn't approach him since he moved in a hurry.

The walk and space he was given gave him time to think about the possibilities. He had one purpose in coming to the Institute: to learn how to control himself. He had accomplished that in a way. Talphi didn't see himself as learning much more here anyway. It had created a safe environment for him. The mention of the King and the Institute's purpose by the Masters finally made the path after leaving the Institute clear to him.

The Determined World

Talphi was supposed to become a tool of the King's vision. He didn't come here to borrow or adopt someone else's vision. The quiet way each person treated him after the destruction of his relic told Talphi he needed to act sad. It's what was expected of him, even though he embraced it as a way out of the future obligation.

Talphi kept his spare relic hidden. The chance to say he found a second one in the woods was rare but possible. He could continue and join the Relic Order, but this was a chance to escape. Did he owe the King for his education? Yes, but he knew he wasn't a relic wielder. According to Jasmine and his own observations, he was Tokkin, and that was the truth he needed to follow.

It took weeks, thanks to poor weather, for Matthews to get a reply from the King. In the meantime, Talphi was free to leave the grounds each day. Everyone thought he was crazy for continuing to go into the woods without a relic during winter, but they knew it was his habit. They all imagined him building a little hermit house in the woods and retreating from the world but staying close to the Institute in a miserable fashion.

It gave Talphi the chance to expand his understanding. He could safely move using the infused intent and belief. He pushed the levitation he had been working on into flight. It was mentally exhausting but thrilling. Also, this year's interaction with Mortimer made him realize there was more for him to learn from the persuasive forms of relic use.

Just like feeling the air and bits of matter around him, he started to feel the attitude of others. He was the focal point of people trying to ignore him. It was as if there was a taste in the air. It wasn't an obvious use of Tokkin or relic-like power. No one had ever suggested that he could change the air and touch everyone around him to encourage this feeling of ignorance. By the time the letter arrived, Talphi could encourage an entire room of people to ignore him. It helped if they already wanted to ignore him, but he could see those who stared looking away when he pushed back with this aura.

Matthews came to Talphi in his room late in the evening of mid-March. It was well timed with the switch over back to the Institute's warm month schedule. He read the King's decision to Talphi. "Given the scarcity of relics at this time, it is our decision that replacement relics will only be granted to full members of the Relic Order. Any wielder that loses a relic in training will have the chance to reapply with another relic at a later time or may reapply as a non-relic wielder." Matthews finished in his own words, "A very open and generous opportunity. If you wish to come back with a relic, you may pick up where you left off, or you can now go through the tool builder instructions."

Talphi tried to cover his happiness with a nod and a turn away as if in difficult thought. "What do you think I should do?"

Matthews smiled, liking Talphi's adult handling of this situation. "You're not a member of the Relic Order yet, so you can't have a relic from our vaults. And I think you're far too good with a relic to enlist as a traditional builder. We'll keep you in our books. Maybe things will change one day, and we can provide a relic, or you will earn another. For now, head back to Saven. From what I've heard, even without a relic, that town will find work for you."

Talphi feigned sadness. "Alright." Matthews left, and Talphi began to pick up his possessions and pack them for his trip home. It had been months since he had written to his mother. Since he had learned about his Tokkin nature, he hadn't thought about sharing much of his experience with her. She wouldn't be expecting him in the slightest.

Remus must have heard about the letter because he was there as Talphi left the Institute grounds. He didn't say anything, just smiled and waved goodbye. Talphi had gotten good at acting how people expected him to react over the last month. He hung his head low and hid his face to hide his relief from their expectations.

Chapter 21

Talphi felt a new expectation creeping up on him as he returned home. He imagined his mother would expect him to act like a grown man. His imagination ran rampant with everything his mother might say to him. She had mentioned in her letters that many others his age were becoming stable members of the town. The anger he felt remembering his past was old, tired, and not who he wanted to be. He wouldn't stay there for long, even if his mother wanted him to.

The weather turned warmer than expected as he traveled south. He couldn't use his Tokkin ability to travel, so he walked the five-week journey. The return trip to Saven was extremely informative. The new communication towers had many different sizes. Some were at more strategic locations and appeared to have housing for contingencies of guards or enforcers. Previously hazardous sections of roads by swamp lands or through passes had been repaired and expanded. The King's work was designed to make defense and security in the Kingdom of Garrin an easier task for his army.

The bottlenecks of the wilderness had been eliminated through all the land claimed by Garrin. Besides defense, it meant merchants and underclass people could move faster and safer. The focus of securing the King's hold on the Kingdom of Garrin was doubling as a way to secure his popularity among the masses. It had taken him over fifteen years to get to this point since becoming King. The leaps in progress were admirable and flawlessly executed. It was clear to see the vision at this moment, but Talphi couldn't be sure what was next.

Talphi arrived in Saven in April. The road led by the place where the town hall used to be, but the large new tower had replaced the location on the hill of the town. It raised the question of whether the mayor's office had been relocated and if Mark was still mayor. His mother hadn't mentioned Mark in her letters.

People had loved that town hall, and it would have been a shame to tear it down. Being so close to the former location reminded him of his mother and Mark together, talking him into going to the Institute. The crisp memory made him wonder about their relationship. He had put the two of them together in his mind as they intertwined at that moment in his life. After all the conversations about relics at the school, he knew acquiring a relic was expensive. Was his mother that close to Mark that he would have paid the price for her? Were they still that close if so?

Talphi stopped examining the tower and shook himself back to action. He started toward his mother's house. It was approaching evening, and there was a better chance that she would be at home rather than teaching. She continued to talk about her teaching in the letters, and he could only assume she was doing it more without a son to care for.

There were new houses along the path. The population along the way had doubled. He worried that the house might have been encroached on and changed to an uncomfortable proximity to the other homes. Happily, the house looked unchanged, and there were still enough trees around to block any view from other homes. He walked to the front door and knocked. There was a rushed silence, indicating someone was inside but was startled by the untimely knocking. There were some footsteps, and then he heard her slight voice.

"Hello? Who is it?" Rachael wasn't expecting anyone yet, and it was too late for a visit from a neighbor.

The Determined World

"It's Talphi," Talphi smirked, imagining her surprise. He hadn't sent her a letter to let her know he was coming home. If he had sent it, there was no guarantee it would have arrived before him, but that was the excuse for his inconsideration.

"Talphi? Talphi! Oh my, Talphi?" Rachael's voice cracked and pinched. There was fumbling and shifting of the lock and handle. The door pulled open, and Rachael screamed with delight to see her manly becoming son.

Talphi had a few moments to look over his mother before she pulled him into a hug. She had not just come from work. Rachael's hair was styled with flowers with a bun, and there were well-placed locks of hair framing her face. Her face was glowing with delight but also with fresh makeup. She was in a fitted evening dress much like something he had always associated with Madame Scully, who occupied his foggiest first memories.

It was very arousing, and as she squeezed him, the flowery perfume overpowered his status as his mother as it emphasized her gender. Talphi pushed away from the arousal. "Please, Mom." He continued to force her away so that her chest wasn't so firmly pressed against his. "I'm a grown man." It was an excuse that he didn't necessarily believe, but at the moment, it may get her to release. He kept his eyes averted from her and worked to desensitize himself.

Rachael had been happily preparing before Talphi arrived, and this surprise was enough to elevate her to blissful happiness. It wiped away any worry or thought and left her completely unaware of any awkward action. She beamed as she allowed him to pull back. His embarrassment at being hugged was as cute as a nine-year-old boy and girl kissing for the first time. She quickly looked him over. "My boy is a handsome man," she agreed with a twinkle of pride.

This flattery didn't help his flushed pulse. Talphi forced a smile at the compliment against his feelings. Only his thoughts said it was a compliment, while his feelings called it a trap, incest, and a hasty observation. "Thanks." He looked her over again out of reflex. It was hard not to, and his unintentional lingering felt completely wrong. He looked past her into the house. The way the light entered the room from the windows made it look softer than he remembered.

Rachael looked around outside. She was trying to quickly learn the meaning of his visit before asking. She saw his satchel of clothes and asked, "Have you finished your training at the school?"

He had prepared for that question. "Yes, though I'll need to talk to Mark about the particulars. Is he still the mayor? I saw the town hall has been replaced by the tower."

Rachael felt suddenly trapped. "Mark," she snapped from the blissful wash, and her thoughts returned. The foremost thought was the thought she had just after the door knock. She had wondered if Mark was early. "Oh, yes, he is still the mayor. The tower was regrettable, but Mark made sure we could continue to operate the town our way. We were all worried that the King would take direct control, I struggled not to mention those worries in the letters."

Talphi still stood on the steps, and he knew he was a stranger to this house now.

Rachael realized the same feeling as she was blocking the doorway. It made things worse that she was hesitating to let him in. It was a shame she hadn't needed to acknowledge. She moved quickly, "Come in. Why are we out here? I'm so shocked from surprise that I completely forgot to step to the side." She stepped back and to the side to let her son into her home.

It was lit softly inside on purpose. The shutters had been improved to shelter more weather, and they were closed just enough to let in the fading light. There were candles lit in a few spots to round out the effect. They would have been unnecessary if the shutters were opened all the way at this time of day.

The door closed, and Talphi tentatively moved to a familiar chair. Rachael quickly moved to open the shutter to let in the full light. "That's better," Rachael called to Talphi, who had sat with his back to her. She stayed at the fully viewed window a moment and cowered her chest down as far as the dress would allow. She imagined Talphi suddenly turning and yelling at her as he recited all the things she was ashamed of since he had been away.

Talphi sat looking at a wall as the falling light turned shadows to darkness. There wasn't much mystery as to what was going on. His mother was a woman, and women did prepare like this when they were going to have male visitors. The school's close living quarters had confirmed this many times. He asked a mundane question, planning the second, guessing the answer, and predicting her reaction. "How has your teaching been?" He watched her shadow rustle as she moved to a chair near him. His time at the school had also taught him that women didn't like to be ogled by men they hadn't prepared themselves for.

"Not much has changed. Though..." She thought about telling him all the changes between her and Mark, but it wasn't a spoken truth. Rachael changed her direction to avert judgment, "I've had to hire out some of the work around here to some younger students. Their parents offer their children's time for chores here. It's good for the students to work beyond their own homes."

He turned the chair to see her since she had stopped moving and hadn't sat down yet. "They seem to do a nice job. I'm glad to be home." He smiled. It was a foreign place now, but it was the best he had.

Rachael shifted her posture since he could see her again. "It's good to have you home." She meant it but didn't move closer to him. Rachael remembered the joy of hugging him moments earlier and stayed away as the inevitable approached. "It's been quite a while. I didn't expect it." She shook her head. All words seemed rude and un-motherly. "It's good that you're home."

She had stalled, and for a moment, he thought about the training with Mortimer and encouraging her words, but he knew that he wanted her to say it through her own influence. He asked his second question. "I'll need to talk with Mark. I didn't really graduate, and he'll want to know how things ended. Can you tell me where his new office has been moved to?" He put his hand to his chin. This would let him know if Mark was the man.

Rachael was struck dumb by the mention of Mark again. She could say anything but couldn't say a thing. Mark did have a new office, but the directions to his home escaped her. All she knew was that Mark would be there soon. She looked at the ground away from Talphi and tried to restart her thoughts.

Talphi was guessing he was right. His question had hit the anticipated point. He wanted to share his feelings about Mark since the mention of him had washed her of concern for his not graduating status. "I may not remember everything from years back, but Mark was always a good mayor. Even when he did things the people didn't like, everyone still seemed to respect him. For me, that day he helped me test my strength was the day he earned my respect. Something a father would have done." The lie felt dirty, but he was practiced at half-truths and managing expectations. They had lied to him about his Tokkin nature, and while he did appreciate Mark's effort, he didn't have his full respect.

Rachael felt some relief. "Really? I always wanted you to have your father." She felt comfortable saying it because it had always been on her mind. She thought about how long she had known Tal'Abrac compared to Mark. Her affair with Mark had grown slowly and become so strong. She felt the difference in how much she had wanted a relationship with each. How close she wanted to be with Mark was dwarfed by how much she had wanted to be with Tal'Abrac. "I wish I could have known your father for longer."

Talphi pulled at the threads around the truth to show he could handle the truth. "Well. We do what we can. I don't think Mark can compare to my father, but that doesn't mean he didn't fill the role. I don't know. I'm sure you know Mark better than you knew my father."

Rachael seized up, wondering if Talphi actually did know everything. "What?" Her ridiculous imagination can't come true.

Talphi sighed. "I don't care if you love Mark. He's a fine man." She wasn't acting that motherly, but she wasn't acting like one of the women from the school either. The two of them were having a conversation, and it wasn't difficult for him to talk to her. This might not be a mother-and-son conversation, but that didn't change the importance.

"Talphi. It's not that." Rachael wanted to deny it, but Mark would be arriving soon, and it would be an impossible lie. No lie could cover up this guilt that was surfacing.

Talphi was done nurturing answers and revealed what he knew. "I'm just guessing that Mark is coming over soon. You are dressed up for someone, and you react every time I mention him."

She folded her arms tight to guard herself against the indicators he mentioned. "I'm sorry, Talphi. It's not... I won't lie about it, but you're my son, and this shouldn't be your concern." He had discovered her so easily. Was it that obvious? Was it that obvious to everyone else, too, or was her son the only thing that disarmed her? The weight of the situation just made her want to embrace Mark more. She covered her eyes and tried to hold back the well building up behind them.

Talphi breathed in deep and cut into the moment. "Please don't cry. I don't need you to consider me." This was not what he wanted or expected on returning home. Yes, Mark was married, but he wasn't into shaming a person. He had enough of his own shame.

Rachael released her arms. "No, no. You don't understand." She moved forward, desperate for him to understand. "I'm horrible. All the things I've done. He's married, and I still did it. I still do it. It's taken my son catching me for me to admit it. I've been ignoring the guilt for so long." She came up to him within a few feet. "Look at this," she presented herself, "This is not the sort of woman I told you to find."

He glanced at her eyes and saw desperation. "Stop. I don't care what you've done. You don't have to apologize to me. You're my mother, but yes, yes, you are a woman, and you have a beautiful dress on. You've put on makeup, and you're waiting for a man to arrive. I can deal with that. If he makes you happy, then I accept it." He wasn't just talking about his mother. This is how he had to accept all women. They had other men they cared more about than him.

"No. I'm not happy; I've made a mistake." Rachael collapsed, kneeling on the floor. The affair had been her secret for years while Talphi was gone. This needed to be the moment of reckoning that she should have had long ago. "You have to be mad. Do you see what your mother has become?"

Madame Scully's dress came to mind, and he quickly asked to break the rhythm. "You have sex with other men besides Mark?" Talphi blushed, but he had to push her away from asking him to judge her.

Rachael was glad it sounded like he could be mad, but the truth was that it was only Mark. She sniffed and looked for him to cast his judgment, "No, just Mark."

"You're no Madame Scully then," Talphi retorted.

After a moment of confusion, Rachael remembered. She almost smiled, "You remember her?!"

He recited without looking at her. "You must always respect women. That's what you said. I respect you." He did respect his mother. There was no doubt about her love for him.

She waited for him to look back down, but he didn't. He had to be ashamed of her. "I don't deserve that respect." Again, she waited for him, but he continued to look away. She realized he wasn't yelling or attacking her. He wasn't making this difficult, so she tried to make it difficult for herself, but he was her son, her good son. "Thank you for not yelling at me. You're a good man."

He didn't feel like a good man. Would a good man reassure a woman, or would he shun her for finding love in a taboo place? He didn't even feel like a man. Looking at his mother's eyes had made it impossible to think, so he didn't look back down and didn't reply to her appraisal. "So, Mark will be here this evening. I suppose I could talk to him then, or I'll leave and wait till tomorrow." He didn't want Mark to arrive with his mother slumped on the floor.

Rachael imagined continuing the evening as planned with Mark, and it felt horrible. It would just deepen the hole she had dug for herself. She couldn't blame Mark for her actions, but he needed to know that what they had done was wrong. Talphi could confront both of them. "You can talk to him when he gets here." She looked at her son to give him her full confidence, but he didn't respond. She got off the floor and moved to a chair to wait for Mark. In silence, she realized he had mentioned not graduating. "I also want to hear what happened at the school."

Talphi still thought he should leave, but he wanted to finish this awkward event. "Once Mark gets here." He looked to his side and at his mother, who was far enough not to look into her eyes. "Could you tell me about the tower while we wait? You said it was regrettable."

Rachael began. "Let's see. I think it could have been worse. Many people loved that building. It had been built by the town in the earliest days of the charter to prove that they could survive without a noble. They ran the King's tower planners out of town when we were told that the tower was being built there. Mark wasn't happy about it either, but the town's actions didn't give him a chance to work out a compromise."

Talking about the history eased her grief, so Rachael continued, "The King must have figured something would happen because it was only three days later that the Ginru showed up. I was ready to run Talphi, just grab whatever I could and run, knowing what they are. I was so scared. This town never had to deal with them, and they had no idea. Thank goodness Mark was here. He met them outside of the town the day before they arrived. He went out to offer additional resources to make the tower bigger and more secure. I hate to think what they would have done if they had refused Mark's offer. All of the labor came from the town, and we drained our quarry for that thing."

Talphi was surprised that the town was able to suck up its pride. They had treasured that town hall, but taking it down and building the tower themselves may have helped transfer the pride. He shared, "The tower builders are trained up at the Institute. I've built a few, but they were all in remote areas. The ones in populated areas are the biggest, and they have guards. So where did they move the mayor's office?" Talphi added the question to steer it away from him mentioning the Institute.

Rachael replied. "The new office is on the other side of town. Though instead of a town hall, it was made into a stately manor for the mayor and his family." She had relaxed considerably and realized she didn't remember Talphi being so attentive during past conversations. "Did you make friends at school? You didn't mention much in your letters."

He smiled quietly. This world, this home, felt so far from his time at the Institute.

She dared to imagine that he had a hidden love interest that brought a smile to his face. "What are you smiling about?"

Talphi corrected her imagination of the Institute. "They call it the Institute of Vocation and Service, or IVS for short, or sometimes just the Institute. School is for children, and it was a place of skills and training for service for the King. At least, that's how they talked about it." He laughed about his mother's belittlement of the place.

Rachael took the chance to pry. "Oh, sounds like a school," She laughed, "Though I thought that the reason you said so little was that you were keeping all your lady friends from me. So, no lady friends?" She smiled and hoped to crack the truth. It wasn't worth imagining that he had been so lonely since leaving.

Talphi had a powerful mix of emotions bouncing from laughing and crying to yelling. He just looked confused, not knowing what the right thing to say was. Ignoring it may be the best solution. "I'm sorry I didn't write more. I'm a horrible son in that way."

She smirked since writing little was such a small trespass. "You're a great son, and I forgive you. Life can make you forget to keep your mother informed. So, no lady friends?" She smirked at her question being dodged.

Talphi breathed in deeply, wishing for Mark to appear and eliminate the question. He struggled to decide between truth, lie, or declining to talk about his time at the Institute. It was important not to be a complete failure, and discussing it would only help to solidify that conclusion.

Rachael watched the pause and became anxious for the answer. Her smirk was pleasantly nurturing now. She was ready to be happy or consoling of her son no matter how he answered.

He felt like she wanted the truth and for it to be happy, but he couldn't meet that expectation. Talphi let her down. "I admired many of them, but none of them felt the same." Maybe it was a lie since he had felt a connection to Jasmine in the end, but she left. It was the best way he could softly code his misery with girls and women.

She was ready for such an answer. "They don't know what they are missing. Maybe they weren't in touch with their feelings for you. The King's school must have had some strict rules, so I wouldn't be surprised if those girls had trouble being themselves. It probably wasn't easy."

"I suppose," he answered honestly, "It was easy for me, though it may have been harder for the women." Talphi didn't include his interactions with Master Remus as easy since he hadn't gotten along with Remus' rules. His strength and power weren't the struggles. The struggle was his interactions with the people around him.

Rachael consoled him. "Well. Now that you're out of there, I'm sure you can find a woman that will be able to express themselves freely." She had a few in mind.

Something told Talphi that while he would like to believe his mom, it wasn't true for him. Single women would always guard themselves against him. He felt like they should since he had too much anger, which was always undesirable. He spent too much time hating himself, so he thought of something else. "Do you know what happened to Aaron? I didn't keep in contact with him."

Rachael was happy to share. "Oh, yes." She took a moment to connect what she had just said to what she was about to say. "He was just married, and he and his wife are still waiting for a house. He did some building of roads for the King. They've needed people familiar with the area to help build the roads. There was a chance he'd go to the Institute too, but I don't think he wants to leave Saven." She marveled at the involvement of the King's actions in their lives now. "It's incredible how involved the Kingdom of Garrin is."

Talphi nearly regretted asking. "Good for him." He felt like the marriage comment about Aaron was an attack on him, even if it was spoken with a soft voice. It was the wrong question to ask, given their conversation. Hearing about Aaron made him less interested in what he was doing. He wasn't surprised by the marriage, but he wondered whether Aaron could work on projects with his wife. Most women at the Institute were relic wielders, but there were a few learning with the normal builders, maybe two that he remembered. "Does the King's coordination demand other things of the town?"

Rachael watched Talphi's unenthusiastic expression. "Yes, but most of it is a labor requirement. It's given many of the boys a chance to do something other than apprenticeships. They don't have to wait years before they can start supporting a family. There's more than enough of the King's work to go around, though the distances and time away can be trying."

Talphi asked, "So, they are paid the same as the King's trained workforce?" He hadn't asked how the non-relic wielders were dealt with, but he imagined it was good enough to draw so many to the Institute.

Rachael considered the arrangement. "Well, I'm not sure, though I think he's paying them with the wealth he's taken from some of the noble families like the Fullers and anyone else who crosses him." She was distressed by the prosperity at the expense of the good people she had known.

Talphi enjoyed the chance to talk about broader matters far away from his feelings. "The Fullers. That was a long time ago?" This was a good line of questioning.

Rachael had some deep opinions about this. She hadn't expressed them to Talphi in an adult conversation, though. "Not that long ago. It's still happening to other families. They may have had more than they needed, but to have it taken from them like it was, it's not right."

He proposed an idea she may have missed. "Would it be right if the King had taken just as much from every other noble?"

She closed her eyes and imagined. "Yes. I think I wouldn't mind as much."

He teased her mind and sense of right and wrong. "So, you don't like the singling out, and you think taking from gluttons isn't wrong?"

Rachael sighed. "What? Oh, Talphi." She remembered similar questioning from before he left. This was more refined and not as hostile, but it was her son. "I don't know. I like to see more people with full bellies and some work to keep them honest."

Talphi smiled. "Good answer." It relinquished her from the means and set her desired ends. The ends were sweet, and the ideal was counter to reality. He didn't need to pursue her cruel means. She had none.

The rest of what she had to say filled the moment till a knock came on the rear door. She stopped and looked at Talphi with the same renewed panic he had helped alleviate with their conversation.

Talphi asked in the pause, "Would you like me to get it?"

She didn't know if he was the man of the household now or if there was an appropriate course of action. Rachael looked away from him to the door but didn't get up. She asked herself if she had imagined the knock even if Talphi seemed to have heard it too.

He ordered his mother, "Get up and get the door." Talphi decided he was just a guest and that he would leave after talking to Mark. His mother may always say he is welcome, but she is a woman, and he is a man in age. It was basic courtesy, he told himself.

Rachael got up without arguing. She was glad he had made the decision, but she couldn't think as fear raced through her. She opened the door for Mark, who entered from the darkness.

Mark asked as he saw her face when she opened the door, "Are you alright? Your shutters aren't closed, and I thought I heard you talking to someone," he added as he quickly stepped in. Mark stopped as his eyes caught Talphi. He was far enough in for Rachael to close the door. Mark asked, "Who's this?" to Rachael as Talphi stood.

Talphi realized the light was low, so he stood up. "It's Talphi, Mayor," Talphi introduced himself.

Mark looked at Talphi and saw the boy he helped send away after a moment's silence. "Talphi," Mark said, "You must wonder what I'm doing here as much as I am wondering what you are doing here." He raced to assemble an argument and reasons. He had practice at these sorts of sudden engagements in his dealings as mayor.

Talphi smiled facing Mark. "No. I don't wonder why you are here. And I'm sure you could guess why I'm here as easily as I figured out why you are here." He delivered the quickly assembled riddle for his amusement.

Mark had been caught in infidelity and was not ready for a blackmailer's riddle. He threw out a defensive answer, "You made her tell you? So, you found out what was happening, and you've come to defend her honor or squeeze some *mints* out of me and this town?"

Talphi frowned and looked at his mother's shrinking form. Her nightmare was coming true, and everything was unraveling.

Mark continued, "You are not in a position to negotiate, given all that I have done for you. Choose your words carefully."

Talphi spoke, "I'm not here to blackmail." It was foolish not to realize Mark would be so defensive. His reply to Talphi was inciting, and it took a great deal of composure not to reply rashly. He scratched his forehead and thought for a moment in the silence he generated. Apologies always got people's attention. "I'm sorry, I was kicked out of the Institute," he humbled himself putting his mother's action aside, "I didn't think of everything you risked for me. I'm sorry I let you down."

Mark didn't speak as he thought about what Talphi had just said and reconsidered Talphi's unexpected arrival.

Talphi moved further off to the side so that his mother wasn't in between him and Mark. "I didn't come here about my mother." Rachael moved to a chair to sit. Talphi continued, "It's not my place to come between anyone. I respect my mother." Maybe hearing him say it to Mark would encourage her.

"I respect her too," Mark said definitively to show Rachael that she was not on trial. He quickly looked around the room and then to Talphi. "Well," he pushed his thought as they stalled again. "Well. I understand why you are back, but I think I'd rather discuss things in the morning at my office, Talphi."

Before he could excuse himself further, Talphi spoke, "Would you like to spend some time with Rachael? I'm headed to the Inn now."

Rachael paid attention to this as she watched Talphi and Mark's faces. It was as if Talphi had just sanctioned their actions.

Mark felt the urge to retreat. "You should stay here tonight. This is your home, Talphi. I'll leave," he explained and started to turn to the door.

Talphi moved closer to the front door. "Mark. I don't want to argue, but I want you to stay with my mother as I leave. I want you to talk to her because she's upset. Stay, I'm going."

Rachael looked longingly at Mark. She would go along with Talphi's judgment even if she thought she should be punished. Being near Mark made her want the comfort he could give her. Mark knew her so well.

Mark looked the best he could at Talphi's face in the candlelight. He wasn't surprised by Talphi's presence anymore and was reassured by his candid reply. "We'll do this your way then, Talphi. I'll have to trust you don't plan to use this against me."

Talphi reassured him, "There's no way I could do that. I won't hurt my mother, and I owe you too much." He nodded, left the house, and quietly headed into the dark town. There were a few oil lamps at the intersection to guide his way. He walked quickly and tried not to think about his mother and Mark. He could see their bond. It made him feel lonely.

Chapter 22

The Inn at the center of town next to the main road was inviting and bigger than expected. It wasn't there before he left for the Institute. The building was three stories tall and made of stone. There were foot-thick center beams inside to support the height. He wasn't given any suspicious looks as he approached the counter. Guests and travelers had become very common in Saven.

"How can I help you, son?" The clerk asked in a coarse, smoky voice. Talphi wondered if this man was old enough to be his grandfather, given his silver hair and wrinkles.

Talphi replied, "I'd like a room just for tonight." He imagined himself sleeping alone and feeling lonely within a few minutes. The prospect of retreating to privacy was comfortable even if he thought it made him look weak. The mints he paid with were old, from the days he first went to the Institute. There had been nothing to spend them on at the Institute.

The bed was very comfortable. That was his first thought as he started to wake up the next morning. It was the soundest he had slept since leaving the Institute. The prior day had been exhausting, but he had fallen asleep knowing there was nothing more he needed to do that night. Talphi wondered if he would have slept better at home, but he had become used to a different nature of bed while away. This was just another place to sleep.

Talphi gathered up his satchel and automatically straightened the bed. He went downstairs to the entryway. There was a side door with a food and spirits sign hanging over it. He decided to take his time before heading to Mayor Hilbin's office and went in for breakfast. After breakfast, he returned to the Inn counter. The clerk was a younger man today. He was slightly younger than Talphi. "Good morning, sir. How can I help you?"

He must be one of the new residents of Saven since Talphi didn't recognize him. Over the night, Talphi had moved from being called son to sir, it seemed. "I need exact directions to the mayor's office. I haven't been here in some time, and the tower seems to have replaced it." He laughed inside as he thought of himself as an old man reminiscing over the olden days.

The clerk replied, "Oh yes. His office is now on the west side. It's five streets over. Just follow our side street." He pointed off to the north side of the building.

Talphi strolled out and followed the directions. Five cobble streets over, he arrived at the office. The two-story manor had been painted bright white and was surrounded by a lawn and a stone wall with metal fencing on top to guard the borders. The other houses around it did not have the same open space around them. The lawn was a luxury in the condensing town. Before now, Talphi thought only nobles kept large, mostly useless open spaces like this.

The guard at the simple metal gate asked Talphi before he was too close, "You here to see the mayor? Have an appointment?" The guard carried a spear but wore clothes closely resembling an everyday outfit. Only his dropped-back red hood stood out. It was obvious that the town didn't have any standard guard uniform.

Talphi shrugged, "I am here to see the mayor, and he knows me. I just don't know if he set an appointment for me."

The guard replied lazily, "Then you can't see him."

Talphi wondered if Mark was expecting him this early. "Oh, then how do I know if I have an appointment?"

The guard explained the logic. "Cause he would have given it to you. So, you don't have one if you don't know. Simply put. You're not allowed to pass."

Talphi wasn't offended that he was having it explained to him like he was simple. He was actually amused. He thought about plays he had seen and begged himself to come up with a clever reply, but he came up empty. "He told me to meet him this morning but didn't write it down. Can I go in then?"

The guard continued to defend his post. "I don't believe you. A moment ago, you said you didn't have one." This was a rare occasion that someone he didn't know came without an appointment, and he wasn't going to make a mistake.

Talphi hadn't clarified the process with Mark, so he tried to talk his way around the situation. "How do you know I don't? Do you have a list of appointments? Maybe I can point myself out."

The guard didn't know all the ways people got appointments, but he knew he was told who to expect in advance. "I'm not expecting you."

Talphi sighed. It was like trying to navigate the admissions office at the Institute. A procedure or code was blocking personal interaction. "I'm Talphi, and the mayor is expecting me. I wouldn't think that you would be expecting me since I got my appointment so recently."

The guard was angry that Talphi was trying to ignore the importance of his job. "Now you listen, Joker. You're not getting in because I say you don't. I'm in charge of protecting the mayor and his family, well, he's in there, but his family decided not to live in the house," his thoughts were sidetracked by the technicalities, "but they could if they wanted and I'd be protecting them too if that was the case."

Talphi smirked over his waste of time. "You're right. Could you check with the mayor while I wait here?"

The guard didn't argue or agree. He just watched Talphi for a minute. Talphi wasn't leaving, and it was his job to know who should and shouldn't enter. If Talphi should enter, he needed to know. "Stay here."

Talphi nodded to show his obedience. "Yes, sir."

The guard couldn't be sure if he was being mocked, but he started to plan his choice of words if Talphi didn't have an appointment. He walked up to the house. A few moments later, he came out and waited till he reached the gate to speak. "He said you can come in. He had forgotten to let me know you were coming," he justified his duty and let his planned retort go to waste.

Talphi replied in an understanding tone, "Of course." The inside was just like a house. The office door had a sign hanging from the ceiling pointing out the door into the office space.

Mark sat at a desk and wasn't busy. "Good morning, Talphi." He seemed to be waiting. Off the office space was a larger conference room that could be closed off with a double door. There was a large table with several chairs.

Talphi asked while listening for the sounds of a normal home. "Good morning. Your family doesn't live here?" It was quiet, like the old town hall could be at times.

Mark took some time before answering. "I already owned a house when this was built. This can be a family home, too, but I chose to make it a place of order and governance while I'm mayor. That, and my wife didn't want to move the children."

It may have been by convenience that Mark's personal and workspace were separate, but Talphi thought it would be a good idea in practice. "Am I free to speak?"

Mark informed Talphi that he could discuss the Institute or Rachael without fear of being overheard. "As free as within manners, but no topic's off limits." There was still the possibility that Talphi was angry about Rachael and him and was merely protecting his mother.

Talphi wondered if Mark was going to keep his calculated mayor mask up the whole time. Others may find the formal structure honorable and proper, but to Talphi, it was just a guarded posture. In some way, the informal conversation from the previous night was preferable even though it was uncomfortable. "Officially, I was released from the Institute because my relic was broken in an accident. They have a policy of not handing out new relics to people who aren't a member of the Relic Order." Talphi still had his second relic in his pocket, but that wasn't relevant. "Unofficially, my relic was broken in retaliation by a Master after I beat him in a fight."

Mark replied, "That relic wasn't cheap, Talphi. I imagined you'd be able to pay us, Saven, back someday." He watched Talphi for his reaction. Talphi had gone through years of training and had lost the relic after assuming he needed it. The lie, the need for a relic, must be on Talphi's mind.

Talphi had expected this but wanted to clarify one thing first. "I can still pay you back without it, but I think you knew that the day we had our tug of war." He sat across from Mark, imagining what he might be assuming of Talphi's position. Was it revenge, fear, or maybe gratitude?

Talphi didn't confirm anything Mark wanted to hear yet, so Mark asked, "And when they broke your relic and made you leave, did they ever assume you didn't need a relic?"

Talphi was relaxed with his answer and glad Mark wasn't feigning ignorance. "Not that I could tell." He wanted Mark to be candid. Talphi understood some of the risks, but he needed closure on this. "You knew I was Tokkin or something, right? I'm assuming my mother understood too." He watched Mark grit his teeth, so Talphi added, "I appreciate the training you arranged. I would have never been able to get where I am now, but you knew, right?"

Mark had planned for a lot worse to happen. He had prepared a lie when Talphi was caught and figured out. He would have placed the blame on Talphi and his ignorance of Tokkin and relics. He would have gone as far as to blame Rachael, but he didn't have to. He didn't answer Talphi's question.

"The whole reason for sending you to the Institute was so that you could learn to control yourself. Did you accomplish that?"

Talphi nodded. "Yes. I think I surpassed that expectation. But Mark, I don't really have a place in the Kingdom. If I'm Tokkin, it doesn't matter if I can control myself. I can't do anything about it. I mean," Talphi thought about the towers, the Fullers, his dismissal from IVS, and the direction of things, "I'm not part of the King's plan." It made him sound toxic, and they should just want to get rid of him, but that's what he felt about himself as well. The only real way to deal with that was with some pride in his division from normalcy. He was uniquely foreign.

Mark put himself in Talphi's position. He thought he would be very angry, but thankfully, Talphi was hard on himself rather than him. At first, it was a relief that Talphi hadn't been found out. Now it was a threat again. He suddenly had the urge to distance himself from Talphi. "I think you need a relic, and if you have to go through the Institute all over again, then so be it. I don't see a Tokkin sitting in front of me. So, you have that going in your favor."

It may have been a nice thing to say, but Talphi liked thinking he was a Tokkin now. A relic would just be another lie that he could do without, so he didn't reveal the second relic. "I doubt you have another relic in your drawer," Talphi smiled falsely. Even though Mark had helped him, Talphi still found it hard to respect Mark. There was something incredibly self-serving about his actions. He could tell Mark would take advantage of how hard this was for Talphi.

Mark snorted. "I most certainly don't have another relic. You're going to have to earn it on your own. The most I'll do this time is to be a contact." He talked through to the obvious conclusion. Mark wanted to get Talphi out of Saven and gone for good. The relic problem just added another layer. Thankfully, Talphi seemed willing to work for it.

Talphi imagined several disastrous things he could cause by not going along with Mark's plan. "Fair enough." But this time, he would make sure the deal was in his favor and not forced on him by Mark and Rachael.

Mark explained. "I'll have to check some requests that I've gotten. Mayors and nobles from all over send out letters all the time asking for some type of support. I just have to find one that you can do and hopefully get you a relic to continue your training. You don't have to wait here; just stay out of trouble till then." Mark moved to some drawers that had already been opened before Talphi arrived.

Talphi asked now that Mark was looking away from him, "Is my mother all right?" He hoped Mark had done his part, whatever was required to settle things.

Mark snapped his head to Talphi and stared, "You were right about me staying. We talked for a long while. She's confused but not as desperate as I thought she might be. She won't do anything drastic like confessing our love to the town, but she needs to speak with you again."

Talphi accepted the conclusion. "All right. I'll see her while you're searching."

Talphi turned to leave, but Mark continued, "She sees your father in you, Talphi. She'll listen to you more than anyone else." Mark added the final insight into Rachael's confusion. It was the key to negotiating a favorable outcome. From what Mark had seen in Talphi, he might not lose Rachael's affection to a public confession as he first thought.

Talphi didn't consider that, but Mark should have let him leave without mentioning his father. It made him want to call attention to the truth. "At the Institute, people had relationships, and I watched them cheat. They thought no one saw them, but I did, and I have to imagine other people saw it too." Mark glared at him, but Talphi didn't look away from his eyes. "Might not really be a secret."

Mark waited as Talphi didn't back down from the gaze. He concluded, "Some things are better treated as secrets." He turned away from Talphi and continued the search.

Talphi exited without further reply. It made horrible sense. It was the exact reason why relics work. Mark and probably countless others wanted to believe something that wasn't true. As if believing it hard enough made it true. Was his thought, his reaction to the world, Tokkin nature? Could someone who subscribes so completely to their belief ever want to see beyond their narrow scope?

The relic Talphi found twisted in his hand as he thought and walked. Mark didn't need to know the range of Talphi's abilities. Sure, it might help find him a job to earn a relic, but that wasn't what he wanted. Mark was not the father figure his mother had hoped for. He wondered if his father would have treated him the same as Mark.

Talphi tried to plan out his interaction with his mother as he walked. That was the important thing, and preparing would give him the insight he needed to control the conversation. He finally needed to know about his father. There had always been mentions of his character, but not anything that suggested he was Tokkin. Tokkin parentage was not required to explain his nature, but real physical descriptions of his father were lacking from what his mother had told him years ago.

The daylight helped him see how much things had changed in the rest of Saven as he walked back to the house. A lot had happened in the years since he first demonstrated his power. It may have felt smaller for how much he had grown, but the town had doubled in size.

The other successes must have added to the population boom. The town had responded to the population explosion by making alleys tighter and bringing buildings closer. It smelled like everyone was living too close.

The once-quiet path to his mother's house was populated now with newer homes. Whether it was the King or Mark, Saven seemed to be profiting. He missed the quiet, peaceful path. It was a rutted road now. Talphi reached the home in less than an hour, but it was late enough in the morning to guarantee she would be awake. He politely knocked and waited.

Rachael opened the door and immediately said, "I don't care what you said about being a guest. You are my son, and you don't need to wait for me to open the door after knocking."

Talphi drew up one of the reasons. "I'm not being lazy," he smirked, "I'm being polite."

Rachael was glad to hear his style of unique truth. "I know," she hadn't considered that he was just being lazy, "but you are welcome here."

Talphi opened his posture to make himself huggable if she chose to. She took the bait and hugged him quickly. She was dressed in work clothes today and didn't produce the same arousal problems as the other day.

Rachael released him after a few moments. "Come out back with me. I'm just about to start gardening, and it would be great to have another hand. You do remember how to work, right, lazy bones?" She thought his clothes were worn enough to qualify him for gardening labor.

Talphi would have been fine just talking, but the work would be a nice distraction if the conversation were to stumble. Rachael's garden was three times as large as when Talphi was at home. "Wow," he scoffed, "it's huge. I thought it was too big before. How can you find the time?"

"Well," Rachael smiled, "you find a little more time when you don't have to guard a child against falling out of trees or searching for them when they miss their curfew."

It was a simple reason that could have been guessed, but it was nice to see her smile. Talphi asked, "What would you like me to do?" He decided that he would talk after they started working. After an hour, he prompted, "Those beds at the Inn were nice. I slept better there than I ever did at the Institute. I hope my visit didn't keep you from getting your sleep."

Rachael answered shortly, "I worried too much to sleep," and didn't add any more. She focused on the weed she was pulling.

Talphi let it stay silent for a few moments and refined it to a question. "Mark told me you had a good conversation after I left. Did you work things out?"

Rachael ignored many of her reactions before answering. Digging her hands into the soil helped relieve the emotions. "If by good you mean cried my eyes out, yes." Things were not even close to having been worked out, though. She coughed, "Did you really sleep so soundly after all that?" It seemed inconceivable that he couldn't have been troubled by everything he had learned.

Talphi thought a moment as he picked up a pile of stakes. "It took a little while to sleep, but I slept through the night." He had more jealousy of Mark and Rachael than anger. Maybe the jealousy made him angry because he wanted to experience the intensity they shared, but that wasn't the same. He shook the feeling off, knowing that his mother was the one with the real feelings. "Strange room, new sounds," he concluded.

Rachael dug into the ground. "Amazing. You're lucky." She continued to dig and wished she could have slept soundly. The thought that she could sleep with a clear conscience at this point was inconceivable.

"Well." Talphi came back simply, "I want you to sleep better. What can I do to help?" He thought that sleeping well meant being happy and at peace for his mom, not disconnected and distant like it felt sometimes for him.

Rachael stopped digging and started crying. She put her dirty hands on her face and made two smears down her face. "I don't know, Talphi. There are so many things I want, but when I think about it, I can't have them. If you're wise, you won't make the same mistake I've made." This growing man was her child, and it was wrong to burden a child with the troubles of a parent.

He had stopped and moved closer to her but stayed a few feet away. "There may be things you can't have, but there may be things I can help you get. I want to help." Understanding the mistake could help him avoid making it. "I want to understand the mistake." This turn in the conversation could also help him learn about his father.

Rachael brushed his offer to the side. "I shouldn't depend on you to solve my problems, Talphi. You're my son, and you don't need to worry about me." She turned to him, "You know, there are still a few ladies that aren't married that you went to school with here in Saven."

He breathed in deeply and looked down at her. "I'm happy when I see you happy. Seeing you distressed makes me the same. So, if I could solve your problem by courting one of these women, I would." He had no intention of courting one and merely used the suggestion to draw attention to the problem.

Rachael put the hope back on Talphi. "I want to see you happy too."

Talphi expressed his nature. "And if not courting one made me happy?"

Rachael was stumped. She didn't know how love wouldn't make him happy. "You don't want a wife?"

"I do," he said uncertainly. Talphi was confused about what he wanted after years of repressing himself, but that wasn't the problem right now. "I wouldn't be happy courting a woman just to make you happy. I need to do it because I want to."

She didn't reply. It's the sort of insight she'd imagine Tal'Abrac would have. Rachael longed for the meaningful relationship she had had with him. It was so short that she could rationally say it might not have lasted, but it didn't feel as small as the lustful embrace with Mark. She had distracted herself, and that was a problem, too.

Talphi had to come at her aggressively to get her to move. "All right. You were happy before I got back, and you weren't worrying about what I thought. I want you to be happy, so I will remove myself, and you can return to being happy with Mark." He knew that wouldn't work, but it was dramatic enough to stir up a response.

"You can't," Rachael protested the move.

Talphi cut in to draw her out, "Why not?"

"Because..." Rachael had to think of how to explain her feelings. She felt so trapped. "I'm having an affair, and I started doing it because I was lonely for so long. It feels so good to be touched by someone I trust, and I had been missing that." She couldn't look Talphi in the eye and stopped. She didn't want to talk about her regret anymore. Rachael hadn't wanted more from Mark at any point. She knew he couldn't be with her.

He didn't mince words, "So it was just about sex then."

"Yes," Rachael whispered, but it wasn't the full truth. She was happy to let Mark be in control. He fulfilled her in small intervals, but there was always a voice in her letting her know she wasn't fulfilled. "It's wrong."

Talphi didn't expect her to say that. He wanted her to confess her love for Mark, but it could just be about sex. This conversation was beyond his own experience, but he needed to stick with the basics. "I don't care if it's sex or love. If it makes you happy, keep doing it."

Rachael didn't expect such a ruthless answer from Talphi. "I'm not sure it can make me happy anymore. I can't simply go back."

Talphi used Mark's comment. "Well, I think my father would say the same thing. You don't have to be faithful to his memory."

Rachael's jaw dropped. She could almost imagine Tal'Abrac in the place of Talphi saying it at that very moment. She scrambled to find a different problem with her infidelity. "I've wronged Karen, there's that." In truth, it was the first time she had placed Mark's wife as a reason. She just didn't want to talk about her time in Grubein and Tal'Abrac.

Talphi thought she didn't sound convinced, but that was the real problem in this. Mark's wife was the only one with a complaint that could be levied. Playing as his father's proxy produced no complaint. "That's the one other person you should worry about."

Despite the reference to Tal'Abrac, she was going to dodge talking about him. Rachael closed the topic. "You are my son Talphi, and this isn't a matter that you should have to concern yourself with. I worry about you and your happiness."

He couldn't believe that she deflected by bringing it back to demonstrate her commitment to his happiness. Talphi replied pointedly, "That's fine. But I'll be leaving again once Mark determines how I can repay my debt to Saven, so you can stop worrying about me again."

Rachael felt a mother was not supposed to be as selfish as Talphi was suggesting. Not worrying or caring about him was a dismal prospect. She loved her son and cared about what happened to him. Doing the opposite would make her unhappy. "You don't have to go. I want you here in Saven."

Talphi was ready for her protest, "I have other places I need to be, but thank you for the invitation. The deed is sure to take me to some other town, and I'm not sure when I'd come back."

She opened her hospitality, "You should stay here. Not at the Inn."

He plowed onward to express the fleeting time they had, "That depends on how long I'm here for. It shouldn't take Mark more than a day to find what he needs."

Rachael denied it. "Then where will you go once you pay off the debt? You could come back here and be a teacher." She liked her suggestion. It was time to set things right. "I don't want you to leave, and I don't want you going back to the Institute." She remembered that she hadn't heard the whole story. "What happened? Why were you released?"

Now was the moment. Talphi had been waiting for this. There was time to talk and relevant questions that needed to be answered. "My relic was broken.

Plain and simple. But I never really needed the relic, did I?" He sat in front of her and made sure he had her attention.

Rachael was worried now. Tal'Abrac may be unavoidable. "That's awful." She addressed the incident first, not engaging in his real question. "You didn't write much, but it sounded like you were getting along well and that you were almost done with your training. Wasn't there anything they could have done?" She didn't answer his question. It was more of a secret than her affair with Mark. It had been incredibly wishful to hope this would never come up.

"Well," Talphi wouldn't let her get away without addressing the topic, but he replied first, "They have their limits, and they can't just hand out new relics." He brought it back to the real question. "But I don't belong with relic wielders. I'm more akin to Tokkin, right?" It felt starkly different to be himself at the moment. Usually, he would look away from people as he talked to gather his words, but at this moment, he had no urge to look away. Talphi watched every moment of her reaction, waiting for the words to finally follow.

Rachael stopped what she was doing to address Talphi. "Your father. Mark mentioned your father. You've now mentioned your father, and I know I've talked about him. His qualities and features could be any man, but he wasn't any man." Rachael paused and watched Talphi's expression. He wasn't looking away. He wasn't angry. It's like he already knew. "He was a Tokkin."

It was a relief and confirmation for Talphi. Either or both, he had to pull it from his mother, and now that he was through the barrier, he was going to get the full truth. "Was his name Talphi like you had stated?"

Rachael had been holding this back for so long, but the return of her son home was a reckoning. She had to finally come clean. "It was Tal'Abrac." She didn't need to hide it from her well-receiving son. "And how we met was the truth. Out on the border region, when I was all alone, I found him hurt and wounded. And the soldiers came and killed him. But he was no deserter, he was their enemy."

Talphi's voice sank, "You and Mark lied to me. I get it," He added quickly. "Didn't he know Tal'Abrac?" He needed to learn the depth of the lie.

Rachael answered what he asked. "Mark didn't know Tal'Abrac, and while he might guess your father was Tokkin, I told him he was just an ordinary man." She smiled because Talphi was smiling for some reason. "You're smiling. I thought you might be angry."

He was an enigma, even to himself. "I don't know." Saying he didn't know worked in so many ways. So much of what he didn't know possessed him to learn, but the discovery wasn't made in anger. He brought it back to one reinforced conclusion. "I don't belong in the Relic Order. I'm better off outside of the Institute."

Rachael knew he had a strong point. The lie enabled him to go to the Institute, but removing the ignorance of his Tokkin parentage jeopardized his safety there. "You could still stay here. Maybe become a teacher and find a wife."

Talphi didn't reply and just started gardening again. Rachael would have explained more to him. She would have told Talphi anything about Tal'Abrac. She would have explained how her relationship with Mark was dwarfed by the time with Tal'Abrac for her. Rachael could have explained how Mark served as a distraction and a way to relinquish control. And that her guilt was linked to a self-promise to raise Talphi with the mindfulness Tal'Abrac had taught her.

They continued the gardening till noon. Rachael had a bucket set aside for cleaning. While washing his hands, Talphi asked, "Do you want to be with Mark anymore?"

Rachael didn't know. She thought of many things to say as she washed. Fulfilling her promise to Tal'Abrac would mean that she should be mindful and aware as an example for him. "Mark makes me happy when he's with me, but he has a wife, and I wasn't considering that."

Talphi dried his hands on his pants. Some of the dirt was transferred back onto his hands. "So, seeing her never took away your happiness?" He found it fascinating that his mother had blocked out consideration of Karen. Knowing that made Rachael much more human.

She hadn't said exactly that, but that is what it meant. "She was never a reason to stop. I've tried to be the best version of myself since you were born. But I lost some of that effort when you left. I see her again. I see what I'm doing."

Talphi nodded. He could understand losing his way. It was normal, and he saw the person she was more clearly after returning home. "I always knew you were human besides being my mother." He shrugged. "You know, she probably knows."

That didn't seem possible to Rachael. She had always assumed that if their affair were known, she would have been accused of it at the time. "If she knew, then..." all the times they saw each other meant something else, "that would mean she accepts it."

Talphi replied, "I accept it, but maybe it doesn't matter what other people accept." He had no idea where to go with his comment. He thought about whether people would accept him now. Maybe it shouldn't matter, and he should act regardless of other people. Was that something to be learned from his mother's situation?

Rachael put herself in Karen's place quickly. "That's not right." She could imagine her holding back the knowledge to protect her position in the community. "I have been taking something from her. Mark may give it to me willingly, but keeping it a secret from her is wrong. I don't know," She sighed. Rachael considered that not knowing was a good place to be by Tal'Abrac's definition. "I'm glad you came home when you did. I need to be my better self. You reminded me."

Talphi was glad she welcomed him home. "I missed gardening with you."

Rachael considered him with a long look and volunteered information. "Mark has never spent the day working with me. The day after I met Tal'Abrac, he joined me as we gathered food and prepared a meal. It wasn't much time, but it mattered. What we build with other people matters. I believed we could build a better future with the Tokkin. I wanted more than hostility. And while my life has improved in the Kingdom, I realize I still want to end the hostilities between the Kingdom and Tokkin. I'm glad my son is Tokkin. You are a better future." She smiled sweetly.

Talphi didn't know what to say. There was an impression that if he had had the outer appearance of a Tokkin, she would have loved him just as much. He was too hard on himself to think he was better than those who preceded him. "I don't know about that."

She understood his disbelief and saw a bit more of Tal'Abrac in him. Rachael reached out and pulled Talphi close. She squeezed and tried to let him know he was loved. He stood still and let her squeeze. When she finally held him back, she looked at him and stated, "You are so courageous."

Talphi was just being himself. There was nothing courageous about what he was doing. "How?"

Rachael explained, "Talking with me like you have is courageous." She beamed at him, truly expressing the joy of his growth into a man. "You are my son. And you have spoken with such consideration. I have seen people run their entire lives from difficult conversations, make harsh judgments, and seek revenge." She brought it back to an earlier point. "Any woman would be lucky to have you take an interest in them."

It was a joyful compliment, but it hurt. There was a deeper pain he had pushed to the back of his mind. The courage his mother described was a reaction to the repressed anger of his arousal toward women. Conscious control was the only thing he could do to keep him from reacting with anger. "Maybe."

Rachael recovered her strength and started to feel the midday hunger. "You'll see."

Talphi didn't believe her. She continued to advise in the hopes he would want to stay close. He couldn't see himself following her suggestions. Not because they were bad, but because he always imagined some hidden hostility or exploitation. This town was tied to his worst experience, but at this point, it was a repressed memory that continued to harm him without fear of consideration. He let her advise him through lunch. She relented with the suggestions when they finally got back to work.

Mark arrived in the afternoon. He found them out behind the house mending the stone wall. Rachael took the opportunity to use Talphi's strength to move the largest boulders. Talphi used his Tokkin ability sparingly in case someone was to see. He only moved impossible stones when they were sure no one was looking.

Mark approached them like the mayor. He didn't know how Talphi fared in conversation with Rachael, but it appeared that they hadn't fought from their genial expression toward each other. They would need to move inside to have their conversation. He couldn't trust the outdoors. "Hello, Rachael and Talphi. I've come by to finish our conversation from earlier."

Talphi nodded and made sure the stones were all in stable positions. "Of course." He looked at his mother but decided that he wasn't going to wait for her reaction, so he started to go to the house.

Rachael watched Mark. She felt disappointed by his formality, unsure of what she wanted from him, sad that they had come to this point, and angry that she found herself in this position. It was too much for her to reply at this point, so she followed Talphi and Mark back to the house in silence.

Talphi didn't waste time once they were safely inside. "So, what have you got for me?"

Mark took his time sitting down. He didn't want a standing conversation.

Rachael sat too, but she made sure she was on Talphi's side of the conversation area. "I found a few options, but most of them consist of extended service in different towns that have access to a relic." Rachael didn't look happy, but Mark continued. "I imagine you want to put your talent into one repayment and move on."

Talphi smiled. "Yes. Something with a clear time frame would be nice."

Rachael thought about Talphi's treatment at the Institute. He hadn't had someone to join him in the protest of his broken relic and advocate its replacement. "Are you saying he can't repay his debt here? Why does he have to leave?" She needed to defend him now.

Mark fell back to some diplomatic thought since Rachael's tone was angry. "The relic costed favors to other towns. I haven't repaid all those debts completely, so Talphi's repayment could best be made with those same towns. No one will give me another relic without making sure they benefit. With the changes in law, Talphi can use another relic and not graduate from the Institute as long as he is using that relic for chartered towns."

Talphi looked to the side at Rachael with a sigh. He didn't want to tell her to stop defending him, but he didn't see it as defending his interests; she was defending her vision for Talphi's future. "I agree with Mark. I'd like to repay my debt quickly, and Saven doesn't need my help," Talphi told the both of them.

She reiterated her point. "You shouldn't have to leave. So, what are these tasks then?"

Mark continued with Talphi's approval. "There are a few tasks here and there, but it would take years of arrangements. I have one task in the high-value category. Lord Taylor in Coventree has a problem that, if solved, provides a relic. A month ago, he sent out messages to several towns and various nobles. He was put in charge of building the King's tower down there, and he had a setback. Apparently, he was tasked with building the tower without the Institute's assistance, so he hired who he could afford. They happened to be smugglers between there and the Tokkin lands, and the Ginru quickly came in and killed them all. However, the King has demanded the tower's completion on schedule. The letters were a request for labor. As far as I know, no one has sent any laborers since nearly every other town is occupied by their own schedules."

Talphi smirked over the experience he had with the towers. "So, you want to send me?"

Mark smiled back and replied, "Yes." He wanted Talphi to take on this task. It would do more than cancel out Talphi's debt. It would in-debt Lord Taylor to him and conclude his involvement with Talphi.

Talphi clarified, "So, I'll get a new relic, and we can go on pretending that I need one." By mentioning the lie, he wanted them each to know they could talk about the issue freely. They still seemed ready for an outburst from him. He didn't appreciate the lie, but he couldn't imagine what would have been a better path.

"Mark," Rachael spoke for Talphi, "That's unreasonable. Talphi couldn't build a whole tower on his own. Why would you ask that?"

Talphi replied before Mark could, and he addressed his mother's concern, "I built a tower up at the Institute. I can do it."

Mark beamed and chuckled. He knew the Institute was the center for training the workforce, but he didn't think the relic wielders would be assigned such mundane work. "You've built one of the towers? Why, then, it shouldn't be anything you can't handle. Could you build it by October?" He was excited because this reduced the chance of failure dramatically. Neither Rachael nor Talphi seemed to share his inappropriate enthusiasm. He embellished the information. "The tower's completion is the only requirement. Once you have it built, his relic will be yours, and you can do what you please. There are additional payments we will receive that will pay off the debt of your first relic." That was the real incentive for Talphi to take this contract. He wouldn't have to come back for a second task.

Talphi appreciated Mark's candor about the value of the task. That alleviated some of his concerns about being indebted for too long. "Oh, right." He paused but decided it was a task within his ability. The tower still needed to be made by himself in six months, but his debt and the use of his abilities would be guarded. "That sounds fair," and sufficiently clever of Mark.

Rachael didn't think that anything Mark requested was fair right now. "Aren't there any other ways? Coventree is even further away than the Institute was." It was like Mark was purposely trying to send Talphi away. Even though she had spent so much time with Mark since Talphi went to the Institute, she couldn't help doubting Mark's fairness.

Mark tilted his head to favor his first suggestion. "This is the best way, especially since Talphi has had experience with tower building. He'll be able to build it without help, though Lord Taylor may have found others to help by now."

Rachael looked to convince Talphi instead of Mark. "You could stay here, Talphi." She wanted her trusted son closer now more than ever. It wasn't fair to her.

Talphi loved his mom, but not Saven. He wanted to kick it like a loose stone on the road. "I want to do this. I don't think I could live in Saven. I didn't have that many friends here."

It was depressing to think that her son didn't think of Saven as his home. She couldn't help but feel responsible. "I'm sorry."

Talphi saw her set in stone. She might be in limbo over her relationship with Mark, but she held fast to her expectations of him. There was nothing Talphi thought of that would change that. He hoped never to worry so much if he had children. "Don't apologize for the people of Saven," he explained. It wasn't her responsibility to make him like a place.

Mark closed his eyes over the exchange. It was obvious that Talphi had tried his best, but he knew Rachael was critical of fairness. Life hadn't been fair to her, but she still talked like it should exist. He needed to be fair to her if he hoped to hold on to their relationship. "I can make a letter for you to bring to Lord Taylor; it will explain that you are capable of building the tower and how we shall handle the other terms."

Talphi was curious how profitable his debt would be. "What are the additional terms?"

Mark explained what was at stake. "Your service guarantees his continued position as a noble. We could name heavy terms, but honestly, that part is very cheap for him, and I'm sure he won't object with his back to the wall." Mark didn't dictate the contents of the letter since he didn't want to share the bonuses.

Talphi saw Mark dodge his question. He asked a different question. "Where is Coventree?"

Mark was glad Talphi didn't pry further. He brought a map, too, with the hope of Talphi accepting, and he pulled it out. He pointed out the route to them. "Southwest of here maybe some eight hundred miles. It's over two weeks by carriage in ideal conditions."

Rachael sighed and spoke solemnly before Talphi answered, "I can help you put together enough mints and food for the trip since there aren't many towns along that path." She wanted to help her son and touched his shoulder while conveying, "You could still stay if you want."

Talphi didn't want to argue anymore with his mother but didn't want to look too eager to leave. "I think this is the best thing, Mom. With such a short time frame, I need to get going as soon as possible." Talphi confirmed with Mark and nodded to his mother.

Mark stood up and said with satisfaction, "I'll go back to my office and seal the letter for you. Come by when you are ready." Rachael and Talphi stood, too.

Talphi did a short nod. "I will. I hope I can be ready by tomorrow."

Mark nodded to them both and moved to the door. As he passed Rachael, she grabbed his hand. They looked into each other's eyes for a few seconds. Rachael whispered in Mark's ear. "I don't know how we'll move forward, but I know you've helped my son." She let go of him since touching him was more upsetting than thrilling now.

Mark nodded. "I understand." He didn't need to be told that she was confused, but he did need to be told that she hadn't completely turned against him.

Mark left, and she closed the door behind him. Rachael looked at Talphi, "Let me help you get ready. I won't take no for an answer." Rachael wanted to demand this request to solidify her position. She was his mother, and he was the most important person to her.

Talphi nodded, and as she helped him, he realized it was good she had insisted. He had impulses to send her away as she chatted about life in an attempt to make up for the time he was away. It clashed with the walls he had put up and broke them down. Her words made him feel more relevant than just useful. He had always wanted to feel useful, but being relevant to his mother was contrary to the barriers he put between himself and others. She cared about him and wasn't using him.

The children of Saven and the time at the Institute had put him on the defense for how other people might take advantage of his desire to be appreciated. She reminded him of what it was like to truly have his guard down. He wanted to lower his guard. But what was the way to lower his guard and not be exploited?

He wanted a deeper connection with other people, but wanting had led to so much pain and frustration. It had always felt like a fraught relationship with wanting from other people. They guarded themselves against his fumbling attempts to relate. He couldn't make anyone give in, much like his failures with Mortimer's training. Trying to pretend he was worthwhile so that they were inspired to open up always made him question his worth.

No, as they prepared for his departure, Talphi was sure that staying observant and doing what was needed was his only solution. His mother had chosen to care for him despite his lack of charm. She was proof that compassion was given, not earned. Still, her vision of what was best for him proved that the beliefs of other people were beyond him. He needed to go his own way. This solitary trip and mission to build a tower was the right thing for him.